the
'idiot spy'
(the series)
book two of ten

conjured and distorted truths

c. benjamin lattimore

conjured and distorted truths
Published: May 2020
Printed in the United States of America
ISBN: 978-1-7334945-1-9

This book was published with the assistance of Writer's Relief.

Cover design by Writer's Relief

To my bride, Marisa,
thanks for helping me bring book #2
of the 'idiot spy' series to life.
Your constant reviews and questioning were invaluable.

ACKNOWLEDGEMENTS

To my wonderful and smart children, Christopher, Monica and Courtney, as well as, my grandchildren, Isaiah and Desmond for just being special. A unique and heartfelt expression of love to my sister Mary E. and my brother Darryl A. Esteem regards to Maurice C. and Reggie W.

A special shout out to Marisa, Dawn Marie and Nikki; their contributions were priceless. A very special thank you to Writers Relief—Jill.

Lots of love ethereally, to my mother, Mary Alice, my father Walthro M., my little sister, Barbara Ann, and my brother, Walter Eugene.

CHAPTER ONE

How do you train a 900-pound voracious beast? The answer is astutely simple, you don't, if you're smart. You don't get near it and you let it do whatever the hell it wants. Walter E. Lassiter, being the spy that he was, thought he could completely control the likes of the Fab 10 + 2, along with Asiram a former spy/extractor, who was engaged to the 'idiot spy'. Exactly forty-two days after being targeted by "some of the best" wet work people in the business, Zanthius made the choice to ask Asiram to be his partner in crime for life. Zanthius realized the significance of that statement in his proposal. The course that the Beckmire clan had agreed upon, would involve them in dastardly deeds for decades. Their group was perfect for many of the assignments that they concurred to do. They were such an innocuous looking and acting bunch that no one in their right mind would have considered them, wet work specialists.

After swallowing a capsule that was slipped into his mouth by a kiss, Zanthius was still in control of the Carbon Factor formula and Scottie's sole purpose in life was to see the members of the Beckmire clan annihilated. Scottie was the head honcho in the after-market spy world and was known to be treacherous.

Scottie told her people that she wanted the Beckmire clan so dead that their deaths would give new meaning to the state of being deceased. At each aspect of the negotiations, it appeared that Scottie was working for Scottie and not the United States Government.

Exactly fifty-five days later, Larry, Rashida and Marisa began to ask questions about their safety. The Sarge told them that he was not 100% certain that any of them were safe at this point in time. He got Courtney, their mom, involved in the discussion who reinforced the notion of staying the course as a collective. She told them that individually, they were more at risk in being used as a bargaining chip against the group. She informed Larry that she realized that their employers had probably terminated them from their jobs and acknowledged that the group had enough funds to support them way beyond their paychecks. She advised her family that if anyone decided to leave, they would place everyone in the compound at risk. Courtney told them that she loved them and would understand their decision if, they decided to depart.

Additionally, Ava approached Beckmire and asked him how long she was expected to remain on the farm. He gave her the same spiel that Courtney gave to Larry, Marisa and Rashida.

Although the farm was situated on over 120 acres, there was a total lack of privacy and personal space. The need for mental relief from the shootings, killings, and assaults, began to take its toll on everyone, especially the children.

Beckmire summoned Mallory and asked him to walk with him. The two men began to discuss the inconvenient nature of their current conditions. Mallory said, "Sarge, I prefer this arrangement to the one we had in Vietnam. Shit, this is paradise. We have a full food supply, security, space to wander around and strategic options for defensive purposes. What more can we ask for? I think what we all need is time to be humans without the threat of an assault."

Beckmire looked at him and declared, "Screw it! We are all going to town for seafood tonight. I'm placing you in charge of maintaining the compound and securing the house. Is that a problem for you?"

"Absolutely not. Just keep in mind that those who stay behind will have to have the same opportunity at taking liberty, Sergeant."

"Duly noted, my friend," the Sarge stated.

Beckmire requested Zanthius and Asiram to huddle with him for a minute. Asiram asked, "What's up, Pops? Can I call you Pops since your son has asked me to consider this ring as a sign of his intent and desire to live out his life with me?"

"Asiram, you can call me anything you like. If not for you, all of the people that I love would be in a terrible state of nonexistence. So, call me what you want, but I must admit, I like the idea of Pops. Can I call you in the interim, my future daughter-in-law?" Asiram walked up to Beckmire and gave him a magnificent hug and kiss on the cheek.

She turned to Zanthius and exclaimed, "You're my hero and I am glad I wasn't pitted against your father and his friends. They are formidable!"

After blowing smoke up each other's asses, Beckmire said, "I propose that the entire group leave the compound and go into town to have a normal dinner, save a few to monitor and manage the farm. What say you?" Eyes lit up and expressions of joy were obvious on the faces of Zanthius and Asiram. They knew the farm was shrinking in on them and everyone else, and this suggestion was paramount to being absolved of their sins.

At every juncture of her discussions with Zanthius and the group, Asiram disagreed in principle on the transfer of the capsule to her.

CHAPTER TWO

At the restaurant Ava began to act a little giddy towards Carlos. She discreetly whispered, "I hope I didn't offend you by kissing you on your cheeks a while back."

Carlos responded by saying, "Ms. De Lombardo, you could never offend me. I am here because I promised your father that I would always protect you. No, you could never offend me." Ava reached over and touched his hand and noticed that he had a wound that was becoming infected.

She said to Carlos, "How long have you had this injury? It's becoming infected." She asked Courtney, "Can you look at his hand to see if Carlos needs immediate attention."

Courtney rose from her chair and walked over to where Carlos and Ava were sitting and said, "Carlos, let me have a look at that."

As he turned his hand over, Courtney said, "Oh my, we need to put some peroxide on that ASAP, soak and rinse it with alcohol, and then place a bandage on it. This is becoming extremely infected." She then asked the waitress if they had a first aid kit.

The first aid kit had all of the things that Courtney needed. Ava said, "Come, Carlos, I want to play doctor on your hand."

In the ladies restroom, Ava made Carlos wash his hands. She first poured the peroxide on the wound and then alcohol. There was a tube of Neosporin in the box that she squeezed on the wound as well. She asked Carlos, "Why have you never said a single word to me other than to respond to me when I ask you a question or direct you to do some menial task? You knew I was lonely and my soul was in turmoil because of the decision I made about Ben. Why didn't you console me?"

"Ms. De Lombardo, that is not the mission your father had in mind when he appointed me your protector. My role was to do as you asked and to make sure that no one harmed you."

"My father has been dead for a long time and rules and roles are made to be changed and even broken. Perhaps you find me unattractive, fat and old or something else. Why is it, Carlos, that you have never approached me as a man? The one time that you walked in on me while I was in the bathtub, you turned and ran like a schoolboy!"

"Ms. De Lombardo, may I speak freely without any recourse or embarrassment?"

"First of all, you will no longer address me as Ms. De Lombardo. You will call me Ava. Is that understood?"

"Ms. De Lombardo—I mean Ava, I have been in love with you since you were nineteen years of age and I was twenty-four and working as your father's chauffeur. On one of our trips, he said to me, "never compromise my daughter". Your father was a man of few words but the words he spoke to me were as cold as could be. I respected his wishes and never attempted to compromise you, in any manner. Therefore, I still have a job. Do you think we should leave the ladies' room? I don't want to give anyone any wrong ideas, plus I would feel more comfortable discussing this elsewhere and at another time."

"Carlos, I am going to hold you to your word. Let's get out of here." When they walked out of the restroom, everyone began to make strange noises indicating that they suspected that a sexual coup had just been successfully orchestrated.

Courtney asked, "Dr. De Lombardo, how is our patient?"

Ava responded, "Oh, I think he's going to live but he will require some serious monitoring by me, Dr. Beckmire. I will keep you apprised of his status. I'm sure he's going to be in great shape once we completely desensitize him of things from the past such as the wishes of an old man who died extremely lonely. Now, that is something I certainly prescribe for him," Laughter filled the air.

CHAPTER THREE

When they returned to the farm everything was in place and the outing was just what everyone needed. Beckmire called the guys together and announced, "We have to talk. It has been almost four months and some of you guys have got to get away from here and get back to your normal lives until Walter decides what is going to happen next. Zanthius, Asiram, and I are going to retrieve that damn package and get it into Walter's hands in the next day or so. I might need a little backup, but I don't expect any real issues with the transfer. Is that correct Asiram? What's your take on that?"

Asiram in her own inimical way answered, "Even though he has given us invaluable information, Walter is still known as the finisher and I don't trust that guy. But it looks like he's the best source that we have to conclude this issue. I would make the play at a dummy site, say ah, Zanthius's place, and see what the outcome is and whether or not we are being followed or set-up. That way we will always be in control until the transfer is made. I just don't trust any of those guys. As a matter of fact, I think we should ask for 'get out of jail' cards from Walter for every living soul here, including the children. I strongly suggest that we do a straw deal first and if there are no problems, we go and get the real package and be done with all of this mess."

Beckmire uttered, "I agree with all that you say. I want to plan a trip to Australia. By the way, can any of the jets that we have make that kind of run?"

Mallory replied, "They all have that capability."

"My purpose for asking for this huddle is to find out who has to go and who can stay. By a show of hands, please indicate to me who has to leave and when?"

As anticipated, no hands were raised.

Bernstein inquired, "Why do you keep asking us these kinds of questions? We aren't going anywhere until this mess is buried deep in those woods out there where John Lee and his lover Jilkes like to frolic around."

#

Around 0830 hours, or so, headlights were seen on the road. Jilkes called ahead and told Beckmire that a black suburban had just entered the access road. Beckmire told his people to scatter but not too far and to keep a watchful eye on the environment. Minutes later, the vehicle appeared in front of the farmhouse. Walter exited the vehicle, greeted the greeters and asked if he could have a cold one.

Beckmire asked, "What brings you out here this time of night?"

Walter repeated, "I sure could use a cold one, right about now." Zanthius walked into the house and came back out with a single Coors Light and handed it to him. Walter took a huge swig and let out a loud burp indicating that he was satisfied, and responded, "I may have to talk to my favorite horse to make you understand what we are up against. However, I'm going to try to have this conversation without him.

In our discussions, I mentioned Scottie, didn't I? Well, anyway, I think she too has her fingers in someone else's pocket. An old buddy of mine found out that she advertised for a group of highly motivated individuals, that's defined as cold-blooded assassins, who are capable of working together under a team leader with experience, who is Scottie, to obtain information and research areas where a significant treasure might be unearthed, from the 'idiot spy'."

Beckmire yelled, "Are you kidding me? You told me that this thing was over."

"For me and the good people of our agency, this thing is over. As a matter of fact, as you are aware, we were going to make the transfer in a day or so. Well, obviously, that can't happen now. Zanthius, as long as you are in control of the package, the greater the odds you will survive this shit. Not so sure about the rest of you, but Zanthius's stock is high at the moment. So, the transfer is off. I think Scottie has someone following me and my boss. This thing gets bigger and bigger.

Walter tossed the empty beer can into the trash and turned his back to Zanthius and said, "Some good news is that I brought you guys some of my personal equipment that fell off a government truck one day and I just happened to be there to pick it up. I have enough earpieces to support each person here. Also, I brought you a shit load of ammunition and a few sniper rifles, all with suppression devices. I have two of my most loyal men camping out at the post office. I convinced Asiram's neighbor on the other side of the road leading here to take a vacation and I have placed three of my men in their home for advance warning. Money is a powerful motivator and it will make the best and most loyal people turn tricks to enhance their retirement packages.

"I am convinced Scottie is a crook. Thanks to my buddy, we may have avoided a catastrophe by not proceeding to retrieve the package. Listen, I know you guys don't know me or trust me, and most of our people that you have encountered turned out to be working for themselves. However, I am still your best weapon on the outside and I will stay true to my word. Consider my cleaning up this issue as a down payment on your obligation to the United States of America."

John Lee from out of left field said, "That sounds like a bunch of pig shit to me. Is the whole government, except for you, crooked? Why is it that your ass ain't on the take like my pigs back home are?"

Walter responded, "I come from a different fabric than they do. I worked my ass off to get where I am and took my responsibilities as my highest priority. I fought in Vietnam and that is why I know so much about you guys. I flew a gunship and sprayed the enemy with bullets when I was called upon to do so. I know you people are regular Americans and I also know that my agency is composed of a lot of people looking to make long term deals with the devil.

"I ain't crooked, because I come from a family of means and honor. Those 'means' mean a lot to me because we earned it the old fashion way—we not only worked for our fortunes, but as said, we have strong family values. These guys today are all about me-me-me, and if they aren't the center of the me—then they collect funds by selling information.

"Scottie is a powerful person in the agency and has a shit load of senators and congressmen suckling her tits. In other words, she screws them and while in the act, she records them and their dastardly proclivities--if you know what I mean. After that, she has them by the balls and everything else."

Mallory, facetiously asked, "So you made your deal with the devil early in your career and now you're seeking righteousness?"

Walter shot back, "I have never made a deal with the devil and I can look in the mirror each morning and say to myself, 'I have not been corrupted'."

After unloading the hardware and ammunition from his truck, Walter said to Mallory, "Your statement really pushed me to look inwards. I must admit, I shot my partner who was a thief and gave vital intel to paying customers on you people. Now, if that is what you consider being crooked, then I guess I fit the bill. He sold you guys out to those other groups and worked directly for Scottie. She assigned me to him knowing that I would discover his weaknesses and then they would have me disappear. I am not safe in this adventure at all. I'm at risk by deploying guys and having them advise you of impending threats. It might appear that I work both sides of the street, but I implore you to believe this spy--my family made theirs the old fashion way and are honorable."

Meanwhile on the other side of the farm, Carlos was in the pool swimming when Ava came upon him in her two-piece bathing suit. As he reached the end where she was standing, she started to walk away but he called out to her. "Ava, the water is for all of us. Please join me. I would like to finish our conversation."

Ava dropped her towel and announced, "Remember, right now you still work for me, and therefore, no funny business." Carlos smiled and so did Ava. She dove into the pool and swam to the end where Carlos was hanging out.

He said, "You are a powerful woman with a lot of means. I am your protector and anything else that you may require. That is all I have to say and that is all that I will discuss."

Ava swam closer to him and asked, "Does that mean if I request a nontraditional professional act by you that you are compelled to carry it out?"

"I am yours to command."

Ava swam even closer and whispered, "For the next ten minutes, I don't want you to do or say anything unless I request you to do so. Is that clear?"

"Absolutely!"

Ava swam several laps in the pool, and finally swam back, to where Carlos was treading water and said, "I recently realized that you are the only person that I can trust other than the people on the farm. For years, you have yielded to my commands and requests and you were near when I met the formidable Ben Beckmire. I want to let you in on a major secret and I don't want you to judge or respond to my statement."

Ava swam to the other end of the pool, then back, then to the other end again and finally back to where Carlos was. She came up for air and pressed her body against his and advised, "Don't say a word until I have finished." She kissed him on his lips and began to fondle his mouth with her tongue. After a few minutes of bewildering and passionate kissing, she confessed, "I have wanted to do that since I was nineteen years old. I have loved you since then, but I knew that if we were ever seen in a compromising position my father would have you hung from the rafters in the meat salting room. I have one other request before I release you from your commitment to me. After you finish swimming, I want you to meet me in the barn and that is where I want you to make passionate love to me on the hay. Say nothing or I will keep you in my employ in your current role until you complete my father's mission.

"I realized a few days ago that I was hiding something from myself, and it was you. Yes, it was always you, but I never wanted to acknowledge it. I need you as an employee, but more importantly, I need you to consider making me your lover. Your choice, but the choice has to be real and not for any gain in money or stature. Am I making myself clear?"

"Ms. De Lombardo, I am in shock. More importantly, I want to quit my job and be the person who makes and keeps you happy. I have loved you since you were nineteen years of age and that is why I am so diligent when it comes to gigolos coming and looking for a payday. Now, I must admit, my heart sunk when you met the charming Mr. Beckmire. From what I could see and hear, you two had an amazing love affair, consummating in Zanthius, the love child. I was certain that Sergeant Beckmire would be the one to take you away from me. I never could fathom why you ran away from him after realizing you were carrying his child. I liked him above all of the rest that have attempted to court you. My problem is that I do not want to tussle in the hay with you. I prefer to draw your bath, wash your back, and relish the thought of legitimately making love to you. I am not sure we're out of the water with your son's situation. I need to remain focused and sharp."

"Walk with me a minute." As Carlos exited the pool, she handed him a towel and asked, "If you're not going to make love to me when I most need to be held and loved, what should I think of that kind of rejection from you?" Carlos extended his hand and drew her close to him and began to kiss the nape of her neck and stroke her wet hair.

"My love for you is and has been real for many years. I don't want to begin our relationship by hiding in a barn or sneaking a kiss by the pool. However, I am so lightheaded and excited that I will make love to you standing right here in front of prying eyes. You know that there are guys all over this place looking at every move we're making and have made."

Ava smiled, kissed him on his ear lobe and whispered, "The barn is where our people are watching at the moment. Why don't you go in, send them back for something to eat and tell them that you will call them when they're needed, and that they should stay at the house and relax for a while?"

"Excellent thinking Ava, give me fifteen minutes. I want to at least get something else to throw on and look like I'm there to genuinely relieve them." They both smiled, kissed and went their separate ways.

CHAPTER FOUR

Walter was about to realize how difficult it was to tame a 900-pound voracious beast. Beckmire and his boys were meeting to discuss nullifying the agreement they had made with him. Everyone concurred that it was not about the money. They drew analogies of situations in Vietnam when they had considered assassinating a captain who was insensitive and a megalomaniac who endangered their very existence. Walter, to them, became the captain they wanted to kill.

The group was becoming battle fatigued and weary. It was obvious that this situation could go on for some time. The introduction of Scottie into the equation was a bit over the top, especially since Walter had told them that this thing was pretty much over. No one realized that at the top of the agency, people were still people: greedy, ambitious, and ruthless. Scottie was no different. She rose from the ranks to become one of the top analysts in the agency, as well as, an excellent field agent and spy.

Scottie's promotions were at hypersonic speed, one after the other after the other. She slept with all of her bosses and secured information to destroy them in the process. She was ruthless enough to send her favorite newspaper contacts exclusives of her conquests who weren't team players. Scottie was the master vixen.

Scottie had been known to go to her conquests' homes and show the wives pictures of their husbands doing the nasty in bed with her or other people. She had developed a reputation for being a necromantic in the field. She would often torture her subjects and used chicken bones and rooster feet to determine the type of torture she would dish out. She was extremely nefarious and once murdered two children in front of their father because he would not cooperate with her.

When rumors of her deeds began to swirl around in high places, she was called in from the field and placed in charge of the "Information Analysis Division" (IAD). That is where Asiram learned to implement her trade under the watchful eye of, none other than Scottie, who at the time, went by the pseudonym of Jaci Benoit. If Asiram had other demons in her life besides her family; Jaci Benoit, or Scottie, was the sole source of them.

Back in the farmhouse, Asiram was also thinking about Scottie. Zanthius noticed that Asiram was in the midst of some kind of internal mental turmoil and decided to give her space.

Later in the day he asked her, "Honey, did I do something to offend you? If I did, I am terribly sorry and if you let me know what it was, I guarantee you it won't happen again."

Asiram looked at him and responded, "My dear sweet man, you could never offend me. I feel that you respect me and you are getting to know me well enough to know what I like. Who I like is, Zanthius De Lombardo. If I have been a little distracted, it's because of that evil person, Scottie. Honey, that woman was spawned by Satan himself. I swear to you that she is his living daughter. I assure you that she will be a formidable foe and won't stop her crusade until we are all dead, including the children. She hates children for some odd reason. She worries me and I am considering taking her on by myself without the knowledge of the rest of the group."

Zanthius adamantly said, "You will do no such thing! If anyone takes her on in a one-on-one contest, it will be me. I have everything that she wants and needs to make her untold illicit millions of dollars. No, my love, you will do no such thing. We are in this thing together, right?"

"I guess so," Asiram replied.

"Don't guess. We have been through a lot lately. So, don't guess. We are in this thing together along with my father, my mother, his wife, and a few good friends. We can do this if we all stick together. We have come too far to yield to the daughter of Diablo. We will kick her ass as well, if she wants to show up here on earth and try to engage a bunch of people who do good by other people and are a strong family with unequivocal friends. She can't win this battle even with her demonic associates, no way. We can handle this."

"Scottie is a force to reckon with. She is the evilest person that I have ever encountered. Her dastardly deeds even supersede those of my family. She is pure evil with no compassion or heart."

"Her problem is that she has never met a De Lombardo or Beckmire. She sure as hell should have looked up the sleeper and his friends in Hell's Ledger. Now, if those guys aren't from a deeper part of Hades, then I sure want to know who is."

# # #

Elsewhere, after discussing and thinking about their predicament, Beckmire huddled with Mallory and advised, "Let's call that stinking agent and tell him all bets are off and see what he says."

Mallory agreed, "I think we should call all bets off because we are operating with a group of people who have no reliable rules of engagement. It's worse than fighting in Vietnam, think about it. In Vietnam, if you were not one of ours and had a gun then you were shot on sight. Here, we don't know who the enemy is, and they all have guns, but we can't just randomly shoot these assholes."

Beckmire uttered, "Perhaps you're right, but from all that we have learned and besides the fact that I don't fully trust him, Walter is still our best option. I think we have to push him to his limits and see what he comes up with."

Beckmire made the call. He told Walter that all bets were off and that they had decided to risk their fates within the framework of family and friends and no longer deal with outsiders.

Walter said, "Listen, I'm coming back out there so that we can have a face-to-face talk. Is that okay?"

"We have concluded that we are best served when we listen to ourselves and not get compromised by a man who talks to a horse. Your mental stability is of concern to us and we need 'get out of jail' documents and guarantees that, apparently, you can't provide. It is obvious that in your agency everyone is out for themselves and to hell with the American people. Perhaps you guys should think of renaming your organization to something like 'SFM'—Steal for Me!"

Walter raised his voice and yelled, "Everyone is not a crook. I am not a crook!"

Beckmire retorted, "That's what you say. Everyone in your upper echelon that we have had to deal with, has bartered their soul for the almighty dollar. And you want us to believe that you are not enriching your pockets from a myriad of sordid deals and opportunities by exploiting people, such as us?"

Walter reiterated, "Please, may I come and discuss this matter with you in person? Please recall, I shot my greedy partner because he was willing to sell that devastating device to the highest bidder. I killed the man in front of you, with my own weapon. I am your friend in this matter and your only legitimate option on the table at this moment. You'll have some bad people visiting the farm with the sole notion of terminating your lives, including those children. I will stand in arms with you and against them, but you must trust me. I am no crook."

Beckmire stated, "I don't believe your associates thought they were crooks either, but they seized the opportunity to make untold millions of dollars by sacrificing my friends and family and the entire world for this capsule that is alleged to provide information about a killing device that can fit in a milk carton. How sick is that? You people are not trustworthy and don't share the same commitment to humankind as my friends and family do. We want to destroy this thing and not let any side obtain it.

"Neutralizing effects are apparently not very useful in this day and age. Everybody needs a bomb, no matter the size of their little country. Everyone needs a damn bomb to kill not only one another but everyone in the entire world. When will it stop? We think that we can stop this insanity by destroying the capsule and letting the chips fall where they may. We want to go at this alone without any additional suggestions from the very same people who created this mess and botched it. They tried to kill me and my family. I don't trust you people on any level."

Walter proclaimed, "Sarge, I will fight with you and your family until this thing is over! I am your family. Just trust me. Don't try to do this as a novice, alone. You will eventually run out of bullets and body bags. I can help, but you must trust me. I am not a crook."

"Pay me a visit tomorrow. Enjoy your family today and I look forward to seeing you then. Call first so that I can make sure I have your favorite horse in the stall."

Walter responded, "Thanks for being so considerate. That horse is as smart as most people I know. Have a good day and the horse and I will talk to you and your people in person. Thanks for listening and call me anytime you have a question or an issue. I will fight with you and your guys against the evil that just wants to get paid or control the world."

CHAPTER FIVE

In another mind set and body, Ava and Carlos were enjoying their newfound intimacy. Prior to consummating their relationship, Carlos said, "Ava, this is the greatest moment in my life. I finally have you, body, mind and soul."

Ava, whose words were slurred said, "I am so sorry I waited so long to acknowledge my true feelings for you. I am sorry I made it seem like a do-or-die situation, but I have dreamed about this moment for many years. Carlos, I absolutely love you. Please be kind and gentle with me and we will love for an eternity."

As they both reached the zenith of their lovemaking at the same time, a stirring could be heard that cut short their moments of pleasure. Neither had bothered to bring a weapon to their lovemaking venue. Carlos placed his hand over Ava's mouth and placed a single finger to his lips indicating that she should be quiet. As he realized he didn't have a weapon, he scanned the barn for anything that could provide protection for him and his love. Nothing stood out. As he began to panic in the midst of completing his love making, he looked at Ava with tears in his eyes because he recognized that he could not protect her, or himself.

His fears and apprehension were cut short when that damn horse walked into the stall and neighed. Carlos let out a big sigh and whispered, "Now, that was an unconventional and inconvenient moment that should lead to that damn horse being shot. In the midst of a magnificent explosion, I was almost frightened to death by the entrance of that damn horse into its stall."

Ava laughed and said, "How the hell do you think I felt? I too was in the middle of an earthshattering finale and you grabbed my mouth and placed a finger over yours. How do you think I felt?" They both laughed and began a new round of arousal and intimacy.

Elsewhere, Asiram was in the kitchen when Zanthius walked in and asked, "What are you fixing and is there enough for two?"

She answered, "There is enough for four, but I must warn you that your mother has entered a new domain."

"What on earth are you talking about?"

"Your mother has finally realized that she is in love with another."

"Honey, I hope so. She needs companionship, but how would you know that she is in love?"

Asiram smiled and answered, "That damn horse knows and sees everything."

"You're not talking to the horse, as well, are you? If so, I think we need to reevaluate our relationship. I thought Walter was well over the top when he was talking to that horse. I hope you're okay."

# # #

Without a clear invitation and a couple of hours later, Walter returned to the farm and was greeted by a team member who called ahead and received an okay from Beckmire. When he reached the farmhouse and exited the SUV, Beckmire said, "I thought we were meeting tomorrow."

Walter responded, "I didn't like the tone of your voice. Therefore, I felt that I needed to be here with you tonight and work through our differences. I need you and your people to trust me, regardless of what some of my associates have attempted to do to you. I am also here because I have to convince you that I am not a crook, and that I am the only viable option available to you and your people. Listen, I explained the situation when I talked to the horse.

"No one is going to believe that you people just stumbled upon this world changing product. I hate to repeat myself, but who in their right mind would believe that the 'idiot spy' came upon this world changing product accidentally in his new role as the Director of Human Resources for a nonexisting group called the HCBL Company? Who is going to believe that story? This is called conjured and distorted truths.

The Carbon Factor is as great of an accomplishment as man's first steps on the moon or anything earth shattering that has occurred in the last century. Oh, and by the way, the 'idiot spy' just happened to kiss a woman who 'made him swallow'. It's usually the other way around, isn't it? Who would believe that story? And let's not forget a spy on the run, Asiram, a Vietnam vet and his eleven buddies, who just happen to show up to provide security. Oh, and by the way, as a group, you have taken control of untold millions and stashed them in offshore accounts. Oh, and don't forget about the mother of the 'idiot spy'. Wasn't her family a part of the mob in Spain? Who in their right mind would believe that story? The entire event is about, 'conjured and distorted truths'! Who in their right mind is going to believe that? It just ain't going to happen that way. Everyone here will be annihilated unless you trust my judgment on certain issues."

Beckmire was about to respond when his cell phone rang. It was Allen, another trusting agent on the lam. Beckmire excused himself for a minute and walked out of Walter's hearing range. Allen told Beckmire there was a recruiting campaign in effect for obtaining mercs, and that it emanated from someone who was above his bosses, McPherson and Amster. He indicated that a woman by the name of Scottie had placed a coded advertisement in a magazine looking for people who were efficient and ruthless.

Beckmire said to him, "Yeah, I heard about her yesterday and I am about to have more dialogue about her with one of your comrades."

Allen paused and asked, "Is Walter there?"

Beckmire responded, "In the flesh. Would you like to speak to him?"

Allen in a soft voice replied, "No, I don't think I need to talk to Walter, and I suggest that you entertain and respect his suggestions. He's a good man, and I am embarrassed to speak with him. Listen to him and if I get any additional intel, I will hit you back. Good luck."

Beckmire walked to where Walter was standing and said, "You seemingly have a loose opinion of me and my family. I mean, you forced our hand into entering an arrangement with you to do a limited amount of wet work. Let it be heard from me and directly by you, we have put a contract out on you and your family. If you think that you can pull the wool over our eyes and retrieve the product, you are absolutely mistaken and that will cost you a family member. I find myself in a desperate situation here and there is nothing on this earth that I wouldn't do to protect mine, including killing you and yours."

Walter was about to respond when Beckmire admonished, "Please, don't interrupt me. Listen, Walter, if you want to play us in some future situation, then we decide the morality of the situation, not you. We determine if we want to take out some bad guy. Since you are into horses, don't bring us any horseshit to clean up. The situation has to be presented in a way that is clear to us that this person or persons need to be eliminated. Am I making myself clear to you? We don't just kill people indiscriminately. We will set boundaries and conditions. Are we clear, Walter?"

Walter looked at Beckmire and replied, "So, these are the feelings of your clan, eh?"

"You got it brother and that thing about a contract on you and yours, is as real as horseshit."

"Ben, sometimes I don't have full information on the people we need to make disappear."

Beckmire rapidly emphasized, "Then you need an alternative team. We determine who we will engage once we know what their personal threat is. Those are our terms and conditions, Walter. You have to make a choice, but the contract will remain in effect as long as one of us lives. Oh, and by the way, we paid some seasoned people from our days in Vietnam, who work alone, to carry out our last wishes."

Walter said, "Let's take a walk."

Beckmire and Walter walked approximately a quarter of a mile from the farmhouse.

Walter said to Beckmire, "Ben, I take it very seriously when people threaten my family. I don't like it and I won't tolerate it." He turned to Ben with his pistol in his hand and declared, "I can blow your head off right here and now and have my people swoop down on this place like the plague and there is nothing you could do about it! Those red dots on your chest are from my men at a place that you didn't think was accessible."

Beckmire with a sense of bravado asked, "Are you sure that those dots are from your men? I want you to calm down 'finisher' and watch the flow of the dots. Your men are tied up like sheep. I'm going to raise my right hand and if you shoot me, your family will be tortured and murdered tonight. I'm going to raise my hand. Don't shoot me damn it! Don't you shoot me."

Beckmire raised his right hand and the flow of the dots moved from Beckmire to Walter who immediately, acknowledged defeat and said, "Nicely played, but I wasn't going to shoot you. I don't even have a bullet in the chamber or a clip in the gun." He handed the weapon to Beckmire.

After inspecting the weapon, Ben said, "You have got to go and ask the horse for a better strategy. I could have had you blown away. Are you really that crazy?"

Walter asked, "Are my people okay? Did your people kill them?"

Beckmire answered, "Naw, they're not dead but my boys are going to give them a helluva ass whupping for pointing a weapon at me. I am perplexed, Walter. You point an unloaded weapon at me, send three neophytes to laser their weapons at me and I am supposed to feel what, Walter? Are you really that crazy, man?"

Walter retorted, "If you check my peoples' weapons, you will find that they're dry as well. I guess I was trying to one-up you on the détente shit."

Beckmire called his people and asked them to check the weapons and was told that Walter's peoples' weapons were empty.

As Walter and his neophytes were led to the barn, Walter passed Asiram and she exclaimed, "Oh no, do I have to do work on you tonight?"

Walter responded, "I hope not. It was just a matter of poor judgment on my part. I'm hoping Mr. Beckmire will recognize what I was attempting to do and forgive my poor presentation."

Beckmire said, "Asiram, hang around. I may need you to demonstrate to Walter and his people the way we do things when people double and triple cross us. Hang close, please."

Ironically, as the group entered the barn, Rjah waltzed into a stall and began to eat treats from the bucket. Beckmire exclaimed, "Well, I'll be damned! That crazy ass horse is here to vouch for Walter."

Zanthius muttered, "Wait, people, this horse shit is going too far. First, Walter talks to the beast. Second, Asiram says the horse told her that my mother is in love with someone new. Third, my father is saying that the horse came in to vouch for Walter. People, in the real world even Mr. Ed, when put on the spot, couldn't talk, so can we please dispense with the horse shit?" Everyone broke out into laughter and Asiram replied, "If you don't believe me, then ask your mother if she is in love with someone new."

Beckmire said to Walter, "Seems like we're trying to establish who is in control here. Under the format that you have mandated and the new rules that I say we must play by, there is a Mexican standoff or there is no deal. The fact is you pointed an unloaded gun at me, and your people with their scopes, placed dots on me until they were compromised. I believe that I am in charge here. I also think that my people will follow me to the grave and for damn sure will not follow you. Let's call a truce and stop the one-upmanship horseshit and attempt to develop a real relationship that is based upon honesty, trust and full disclosure. What say you?"

Walter answered, "I'm happy you didn't hurt my recruits and for that show of mercy, I am willing to negotiate a new relationship with you where there is mutual respect and agreement about the here, the now and the tomorrow. What say you?"

Beckmire responded, "I have to huddle with my people and get back to you. While we are gone, please don't have any conversations with the horse or place a weapon to its head since we are trying to work on our relationship skills. You and your people remain here until we return, and we will attempt to reach a happy medium. I must admit, your prank that took place during our walk has transformed our relationship to the extreme negative side of the equation, but to your benefit, the weapons were dry. We will decide by vote.

My team has really been suspicious of you and your kind, and they have felt all along that we should not trust you or make any deals with you. They want to eliminate all of your agents. Your show of stupidity tonight proved them right and me wrong. We do have a problem. I'm not sure that my people buy the rationale that it was okay to point guns at me even though your people spotted me with dry weapons, and you placed one to my head. Not a good way to start a relationship that is based upon people killing people without a reason. You tried to take advantage of me, but the table was turned, and you got taken advantage of instead. My question is simple. Are you that damn dumb on the battlefield?"

## CHAPTER SIX

In the barn and alone with his team, Walter told them that he liked Beckmire's guys and had concluded that they were the best potential wet work team in the world. He spoke highly of their loyalty to one another and their code of conduct. He told them that with the addition of the extractionist, they were a formidable foe and were capable of doing dastardly deeds, if in fact, there was an attempt to harm one of them. He also told them that he was praying that they understood the nature of their acts and he believed since no one was harmed, no fouls were committed.

Beckmire, Mallory, Asiram, Jilkes and John Lee entered the barn and found Walter stroking Rajz's head. He said to Rajz, "I will bring you organic treats the next time I come here, and you can take that to the bank. It is so difficult to explain to your owners what conjured and distorted truths mean. Try to work with them on that one, would you?"

Zanthius walked in and exclaimed, "Really, Walter. We are not buying that mess this time. Your ruse in the field remains astounding to all of us. Why would you put your people and yourself in harm's way by conducting an act like that one? What on earth were you thinking and what did you think our response would be? I mean, you placed a weapon to my father's head, and you had him targeted by your associates, albeit, with weapons that were not hot. Did you consider the consequences of attempting to hurt one of us? What the hell were you thinking?"

Walter looked at the new faces in the barn and stated, "You must be John Lee and you are Jilkes, nice to meet you both. To answer the question at hand, I have many reasons and answers for my actions, but you have to believe me when I tell you I was simply making a point. My point is that you guys are good, and as I was telling my associates here, you have the potential of making the best wet work team in the world because of your concern for each other. Let me introduce you to my team. Of course, the names I use are not their real names, but for conversation's sake, we are just going to call them Harry, Larry and Moe.

"Now, Moe, has some unique qualifications in that he can hit an apple at an incredible distance, and in the dark of night. Harry and Larry can do the same thing, but they need wind and moisture and all of that shit calibrated, but Moe here, naw, he is just that good. We put our lives on the line tonight to prove to you that you are vulnerable and exposed. You remember that helicopter that flew over here a week or so ago? Well, that asshole has sold copies of his aerial photos to some very unscrupulous individuals.

"Now, what bothers me is that they can't be Scottie's people because she hasn't completely assembled her task force yet, according to my sources. As a matter of fact, one of her recruits is a distant relative of mine who is providing me with intel on her movements. I say all of that to say this, you need to go on high alert now.

"Whoever this new group is, they have the entire complex layout, in terms of exposure points, access and retreat positions and the ultimate fire power that kills all the people here except the 'idiot spy'. The vantage points that we targeted you from are examples of your poor planning, Sergeant. My people waved those damn lasers around so that your people could pinpoint them. Listen, this is over a hundred acres of land and you have only twenty-four people to cover every aspect of it. That just ain't gonna work."

Beckmire said, "You're a great horse whisperer, so why don't we let the horse decide your fate."

Walter responded, "The horse has already decided our fate and, fortunately for all of us, we are in this thing together until the bitter end. We, noticed that I said we, must figure out a way to cover every part of this farm. By the way, you can thank me later for suggesting to the people who have the house across from the access road to take a vacation, and for assuring them that when they returned home, all of their tax problems will have disappeared. Not now, but you guys can thank me later. As I mentioned, or maybe I didn't, I have people with eyes open 24/7 to catch those coming on the open road. Our problem is the area north of the barn, the owner of that property is a real Nazi and a US Senator, so I'm led to believe."

John Lee screamed at the top of his lungs, "You sound like my pigs when they be hungry! We's not be interested in weak spots. We be trying to get all of us out of here alive. You sound like you be talking pigshit instead of horseshit. Get us all the hell up out of here. That's what we be wanting."

As Walter was about to say something, Jilkes said, "Be careful how you respond. He understands everything and will just blow your head off if it's bullshit."

Walter said, "John Lee, I work with some very crooked people. Seemingly, a lot of people have been seduced by the Carbon Factor. Everyone wants that package. I am not a crook. I showed you guys some weak spots based upon aerial photos. And finally, me and my boys are here to fight. If I live to make a phone call, a truck will pull onto the access road and will be loaded with all kinds of new toys that will cover the weak spots that I tried to show Sergeant Beckmire when we pulled our little stunt. Listen, I am not going anywhere. Oh, by the way, that truck has enough bulletproof vests for everyone here. Now, tell me, do I sound or act like a friend or foe?"

Jilkes looked at the Sarge and announced, "I have a question for slippery tongue." The Sarge nodded affirmatively and Jilkes asked, "Why are you doing this? What is your interest? And what do you gain from this adventure?"

Walter replied, "I am doing this because your fearless leader has placed a perpetual contract on me and my family. My interest is to live beyond tonight. The payoff is that I rid the agency, that I represent and love, of a lot of sordid and despicable people. I have no further interests or desires. However, I do want to see the product in the right hands so that whenever we deal with the other side, there is at least the notion of détente in the conversations. I am a true American, born and raised in this country. I do not want to see the likes of an Assad being able to hold us for ransom. I have no personal goals of wealth because I have already achieved that status through marriage and financial planning and investing."

Beckmire asked the group to join him outside the barn where they discussed the merits of their conversation with Walter. John Lee said, "I don't trust him because there is a dark side to this guy. The horse trust him, maybe that is because he gave him snacks. However, a horse don't trust people with bad karma."

Jilkes jumped in next and said, "I always go with Old Country because he has kept us alive and well."

Asiram interjected, "If you consider the definition of a spy, you certainly wouldn't consider Walter to be the shining example of one. He is in too many conversations. Although he is called the finisher, because of some past history, he seemingly has been up front with us. Okay, just think, if he wanted to shoot you, Mr. Beckmire, he could have easily pulled that off. If his people wanted to place a bullet in you, they could have easily pulled that off, as well. If you recall, when we talked about money, his interest was dedicated to benefiting charities that helped people. I'm with Jilkes and John Lee, if Rjah trusts him, then I trust him, but with one eye always on his ass."

Zanthius looked at Asiram and then at his father and said, "I haven't quite learned this horse talking shit, but my lady makes sense and so does Jilkes and John Lee. I'm in for sparing their lives."

Mallory looked at the Sarge and said, "I would like to kill him, but I feel that we need him, so I am with the group."

Beckmire looked at Mallory and asked, "Are you leaving me hanging out here all by myself on this one?"

Mallory answered, "That doesn't mean you're still not in charge. We may have taken a democratic vote here, but your decision will lead me and the guys. That is the way it was and that is the way it will always be."

Beckmire looked at the men with tears in his eyes and declared, "I agree with you guys, but I would kill the Virgin Mary if she hurt one of you. I love you all."

Asiram inquired, "Well, what about me?"

Beckmire cleared his eyes and answered, "I'm working on that one."

Later, Walter asked, "So, are we now a part of your family?"

Beckmire replied, "It's not that easy. In this family, you have to earn your slots. This isn't an open tryout for a football team. This is the stuff that lasts for an eternity—family!"

CHAPTER SEVEN

After a wonderful chicken dinner prepared by Courtney, Marisa, and Ava, Beckmire asked Walter and Mallory to walk with him. Walter looked at Beckmire and announced, "From this point forward, my weapon will always be hot and so will my guys. Do you have a problem with that?"

Beckmire responded, "Absolutely not, as long as you and your guys aren't pointing them at me and my guys."

By the fence that kept the horses in check, Beckmire said, "I think we should deploy a small contingency of people for security tonight."

Walter said, "Oh my, I forgot. I have some new listening devices that we can plant all around the place that distinguishes animals from humans by the pressure of their footsteps on the ground. And this stuff is remote, so that we can gauge from a command center whether it is an animal or human trying to break through our defenses. Each one covers up to fifty yards effectively. All we need is a place to monitor the devices. I was thinking we can set that thing up in that saddle room in the barn and place the antennae on top of the barn and we should be good to go."

Mallory asked, "How full proof is this system?"

Walter replied, "Nothing is totally full proof, but it will at least give us a heads up about an impending group of uninvited guests and allow us time to deploy. I don't know how you guys handled it before, but I suggest that we keep the fight away from the house and as much in the fields and woods as possible."

Beckmire said, "That has been our method of operation so far. Our weakest point, as you so well noted, is the northern area of the barn. It's fenced-in but remains a constant concern of ours. Perhaps that would be the best place to deploy your devices. I like the fact that my boys do their best work in wooded areas."

"Well, let's place some of the devices in that area prior to dark and see if the damn things works," Walter stated.

Walter had his guys strategically place the listening devices in the wooded area north and east of the barn at a distance approximately 200 yards from the barn. Walter, himself, climbed on top of the barn and planted the antennae. After running the cable from the antennae to the console, he plugged it in and received a message that the system was recharging. Thirty minutes later, a message appeared on the screen that indicated the charged system was good for ten plus hours.

As he clicked on the scan button, the system picked up eight devices that were fifty yards apart. The system engaged each device and they all came online, the final message on the monitor was an all-clear sign. To test the system, he had his guys run east and west. They were picked up by each device. As they began to run south towards the barn, the system indicated how close they were to the command center.

Everyone agreed that this could be a life saver and thanked Walter for supplying them with the technology.

#

Asiram walked into the barn to attend to one of her horses and saw Walter feeding Rjah treats. She advised Walter, "I have eleven other horses that could use treats."

Walter said, "I'll have my guys feed them. This guy and I have bonded, and he gives me some great suggestions."

Asiram exclaimed, "Wow, I wish they had turned you over to me! I think there is a lot to learn by exposing your brain and examining it. After all, not many people can have intelligent conversations with a horse and give details of the horse's response. Now, that's special!"

Walter responded, "I'm happy we didn't have to get that close to one another. I'll just hang with your most astute horse." Asiram looked at him, shook her head and went further into the barn.

Twenty minutes later, Walter received a call from his guys who were occupying the house near the entrance to the farm. They reported that three men were examining the road that lead to the house and that they had, what appeared to be, an aerial drawing of the property. Walter told them to keep a sharp eye on the strangers and report any attempts to breach the property. He also told them under no circumstances were they to leave their post.

Walter saw Beckmire and asked him to walk with him. He told Beckmire that it was just reported that three men were checking out the access road to the property, and that they may have had an aerial map of the property and those that surrounded it.   Beckmire asked Walter if he thought they should deploy their men. Walter told him, that in his opinion, they were just a scouting team. Walter then asked Beckmire if he had people near the entrance to the road. Beckmire confirmed that he did. He radioed Jilkes and reported, "There seems to be people interested in our access road."

Jilkes responded, "Roger that. We have our eyes on them. They are a mixture of types: brown, yellow and white."

Beckmire acknowledged, "Roger that and keep me posted."

"10-4," Jilkes replied.

Beckmire and Walter walked towards the pool. Larry saw them coming.   Beckmire nodded and Larry hustled the children out of the pool. Marisa asked Larry, "Are we in danger?"

Larry retorted, "I'm not sure, but the Sarge seemed concerned enough to give me an old 'not so clear sign'." The children knew the drill, went straight to the basement and cleared the entrance way to their hideout.   Larry was impressed and told Rashida to keep an eye on them while he ascertained what the problem was from the Sarge.

One of Walters's men called him and told him that there was movement in the northern quadrant. He told Walter that they wanted to test the capability of the system and had placed another unit approximately 150 yards north of the seven devices and that they were already receiving information from it. He indicated that according to that device, there could be upwards of thirty people or more moving erratically through the woods.

Walter told Beckmire that he thought the roadside gang was a ruse, but trouble was mounting in the northern quadrant of the farm. Beckmire knew that his guys were always watching him when he was in the field. He pointed towards the area where Chakes and Montomie were and raised both hands in the air and pointed north. Beckmire then looked south and raised both hands in the air and pointed north.

Walter said, "I don't know if we have time to pray."

Beckmire retorted, "Prayer is a constant thing, especially when you always have eyes on you."

Walter asked, "What do you mean?"

Beckmire looked at him and replied, "I am surprised you don't recall the incident when you put a dry weapon to my head and suddenly found circles all over your body. My boys don't need to hear my voice to know what I need done. I just sent two of my guys north and two others to cover their position. I also drew my tailgate in by 200 yards and I am now sending neophytes to assume their position. Where have you been all of this time? Haven't you learned anything?"

Walter looked at him and answered, "Let's head towards the barn. We need to see what's happening on the horizon. Just between you and me, you were praying out there, weren't you?"

"No, I told you what I was doing," Beckmire responded.

"I didn't see anybody move or hear anything," Walter stated.

"Hell, if you see and hear them, then we're all dead. My guys work like ghosts," Beckmire announced.

In the saddle room in the barn, one of Walter's guys was monitoring the movement in the northern quadrant of the farm. As Walter and Beckmire entered, his guy said, "The threat is real unless this thing is picking up and multiplying sounds from animals. I mean, we did take it to its limit to test its capability but look at this screen. In the righthand corner individual footsteps are being calculated while in the center, there seems to be no movement at all. If I had to guess, they're planning their attack and listening to instructions. I suggest we go to Code Red."

Beckmire inquired, "What is Code Red?"

Walter interjected, "He means we need to be prepared because the threat is imminent."

Beckmire answered, "I have a group of eight and a group of four close by. I have a house full of people who are good up close. I have Mallory and me to do the field work. I have you and yours to handle the top of the roof and cover both north and south sides of the barn. Now, more importantly, we have identified the potential direction the threat will come from, but I need you to make sure that your people never shoot east or west. If they fire in that direction, return fire will be forthcoming. Are we clear on the rules of engagement?"

Walter looked at his people and emphasized, "Don't muck this up!"

Walter told the kid who was the best shot to get on the roof and he would join him once the enemy began to move. He told him to take plenty of ammo for the both of them. Beckmire muttered, "According to this device, no one is moving at all."

Walter walked over to the monitor and said, "You're correct. Perhaps it's a false alarm."

Mike, the guy monitoring it, advised, "Not likely. Look at the movement status over the last ten minutes. Unless this thing is wrong, those people have slowly moved forty yards in the last ten minutes."

Beckmire and Walter looked at the screen and Walter exclaimed, "Shit! He's correct. They are moving like turtles to minimize the breaking of twigs and making noise but whatever that blimp is, it is moving directly towards us. When and if it hits the 200-yard mark, we go to full kill status."

Beckmire called Jilkes and reported, "This may be a long gun fight, possibly up to 300-yards."

Jilkes looked at John Lee and asked, "Really, Sarge? If they flash and stay, me and Old Country will have a field day. We got this. Check with the others and make sure they understand to flash and move, flash and move."

Mike said to Walter, "Whatever is coming this way, it is about 75-yards away from the 200-yard markers that we set up."

Walter looked at the screen and then said to Beckmire, "This group is quite cunning, if in fact, this thing is correct. Mike, is there any way to tell if these are animals?"

Mike responded, "Sir, I have not heard of any animals traveling at night in a herd of 25 to 35 in the woods in the state of Virginia. I will bet you $50 that this is an assault team. Mike began calling out numbers: 25 to the 200; 15 to the 200; 5 to the 200; minus 10 under the 200. Mike continued, "It looks as though they are in a holding pattern."

Walter commanded, "Mike, when they get to the 100-yard mark, I want you to grab your gear and position yourself on the north side of the barn. On that side you will have the long-range protection of two of Beckmire's best. Stay covered by the trees and the tractor. Keep your earpiece in at all times and tell me if you feel that you have been breached. Your retreat is back into the barn with covering fire from me and Beckmire's people. Stay focused and move if you feel you are compromised. Don't pull out your pistol and start playing like Custer—I want you to retreat."

At the 150-mark, Mike began to communicate with Walter, who was now in full gear and on top of the roof. Mike radioed, "150 and the targets are in a huddle. The targets are being extremely careful and cautious. In my estimation, they know that this is too easy, but yet they continue to come forward. I am positive that this is no group of animals. The footstep counter is off the charts. There may be as many as fifty people and/or deer coming this way." Mike gave everyone tuned to his channel a blow-by-blow commentary of the developments and movements of the unknown foes or animals as though it was an old-time radio show featuring *The Shadow Knows*. How apropos, given the notion, "Who knows what evil lurks in the hearts of men?"

Beckmire called Larry and asked, "Are we locked, loaded and secured?"

Larry responded, "The kids are in their place and the adults are hanging around with shotguns and pistols. I think we are ready, if they get this far. Sarge, be careful. A lot of people are depending upon you and your judgment. Stay safe and remember we love you."

Mike called Walter and reported, "The targets have breached the 125-mark and are rapidly on the move. The targets have paused at the 110-mark. Definitely not a herd of animals, the footsteps are accurately displayed and definite. This is, without a doubt, a group of humans following someone's lead. As I discern their patterns, they start and stop on a dime. Humanoids are what we are about to receive. Once they breach the 100-mark, I will assume my defensive position."

Mallory whispered to Beckmire, "That kid is extremely anal, isn't he?" Beckmire responded, "Yeah, you're right, but damn, he sounds like those old radio shows--extremely descriptive."

Mike announced, "Okay people, this is real. There are at least 35 to 50 people in the woods on their way towards the barn. I am abandoning my post and I am relocating. They are 50-yards from the barn. Alert—Alert—Alert!"

CHAPTER EIGHT

John Lee whispered to Jilkes, "Can you see them there fellas at 12 o'clock?"

Jilkes answered, "Let's first take out the front men giving the signals. Sarge, what's your call?"

Beckmire said, "I see them, but there are more of them than I can see. Let's wait until we know their numbers, then draw their fire towards Chakes and Montomie. McArthur and Gladstone cover them in a hurry because they're going to have the first shots. Bernstein and Brown, are you guys ready?"

Brown responded, "After the first shot, we can slap ten of them before they know where the fire is coming from. Confirm that Chakes has the first shot."

Beckmire came back on and said, "Affirmative."

John Lee had the uncanny ability to spot things that normal human beings cannot. As he scoped the field by 180 degrees, his focus became laser-like when he saw movement approximately 150 yards behind Chakes and Montomie.

He yelled, "Abort, abort. There is movement behind Chakes and Montomie."

Beckmire exclaimed, "Shit! Jilkes, you and John Lee have the first shots. Everyone else, hold fast. McArthur, you and Gladstone focus your attention on the west to cover Chakes and Montomie."

Gladstone whispered, "Sarge, we have six predators on our doorstep."

Jilkes announced, "There is movement behind us as well."

Beckmire shouted, "John Lee, I need the men in front taken out now! Jilkes cover Montomie and Chakes and take out whoever is in front. Drop your long guns and spray behind you with the machine pistols."

Like clockwork, the distracting shots were fired, the assault team was disoriented and entered a killing zone. After almost stepping on top of Chakes and Montomie, the remaining four people in that area were slaughtered by pistol fire. Chakes hit two and Montomie hit two—all head shots. After securing their rear, Chakes and Montomie, as well as Brown and Bernstein, went to work. They were joined by Mallory, Beckmire, McArthur, and Gladstone on the major forces approaching from the north. Jong and Whitmore were targeting people from the rooftop while Walter and his people, targeted individuals near the barn area. It was a killing field.

Chakes yelled out, "We have two or more on the run. They are heading towards McArthur and Gladstone."

Beckmire announced, "I need someone alive. If you can manage that without compromising yourselves, it would be greatly appreciated." Pow-Pow-Pow-Pow! Two members of the assault team were wounded in the arms and captured by McArthur and Gladstone.

As Chakes and Montomie came out of hiding, two shots rang out. Chakes fell to his knees and Montomie was knocked backwards. A weakened Chakes wailed, "I've been hit! Montomie is down as well. Help!"

Beckmire yelled, "We have men down and we are taking fire from their position. Can anyone see the shooters?"

John Lee responded, "I saw the flashes and they are flashing and moving. Damn, they be good, but not that good." John Lee tuned the scope on his weapon and fired a shot. Two seconds later, he fired a second and third shot and hit the people who had shot Montomie and Chakes.

Beckmire advised, "Guys, keep eyes on the field. Mallory and I are getting the mule to retrieve our guys."

A few minutes later, the two men got into a mule and drove at maximum speed across the farm into the adjoining woods. When they arrived at the place where Chakes and Montomie were lying, Beckmire exclaimed, "Oh My God!"

Mallory attended to Montomie who was unconscious and Beckmire assisted Chakes.

Mallory said, "Montomie isn't bleeding from what I can tell. We got to get him back to the farmhouse. How is Chakes?" No sooner had he asked the question, they heard footsteps coming up behind them.

John Lee radioed them and reported, "That noise be Bernstein and Brown--friendlies."

Beckmire said, "Roger that." As Mallory and Beckmire lifted the listless bodies of both men into the mule, Bernstein and Brown began a close encounter sweep of the area to make sure it was safe and that there were no more snipers. Jilkes and John Lee had their weapons locked and loaded, and they too were scanning to make sure there were no more active shooters.

Bernstein signaled to Mallory to take off and leave them, and that they would assume their fallen comrades' positions. Beckmire drove the two injured men back to the house. Walter left his post and headed for the farmhouse but left his three men on alert. As the mule pulled up, Walter assisted Beckmire and Mallory with the bodies of Chakes and Montomie. They carried the two men into a bedroom on the first floor where Courtney and Ava were waiting to assist them.

As Courtney tore open Chake's shirt, she yelled, "Thank God, he's wearing a vest! His wound is superficial. Thanks to the Teflon, the bleeding is coming from its impact with his body. He's going to be in a lot of pain, but he's going to live."

Ava searched Montomie's body and discovered that he too was wearing a bulletproof vest. When Courtney came over to him, she felt for his pulse, opened his eyelids and decided that he was just unconscious. There was no blood and he had a strong pulse. Her prognosis was that he was knocked out by the impact of the bullet. She opened the first aid kit and found a breakable pack of smelling salts. After a few whiffs of that stuff, Montomie began to choke and reach for his weapon at the same time.

The group was lucky once again because without the advent of Walter and the bulletproof vests, two of their comrades would be in serious condition with large caliber bullets lodged in vital areas of their bodies. Beckmire thanked God and asked the ladies to watch over the two injured comrades while they patrolled the area to make sure it was clean. When Beckmire left the bedroom, Zanthius and Asiram were waiting outside of the room for the status of Montomie and Chakes. Beckmire told them that the two team members would be alright. Beckmire indicated that he had a special assignment for them and they should join him in the barn.

As Asiram, Beckmire, Mallory and Zanthius were heading towards the barn, the sound of a single shot from a muffled weapon could be heard. The group scattered and approached the barn with caution. Mike, one of Walter's men, who was on the east side of the barn had yet to fire his weapon until that moment because from his vantage point, he didn't have a target to shoot. He raised himself from a prone position and onto his knees when he saw an image coming his way. Mike aimed his weapon at the advancing and disoriented person and shot him in the leg. Unbeknownst to any of the team, it was the leader of the pack.

When Beckmire arrived at the barn, he looked at Mike and said, "Thanks."

Mike tied a wire-tie around the man's leg to slow the bleeding. Other team members brought in three other wounded intruders. They were evaluated to discern which one was going to be the immediate sacrificial headshot victim, which would be based upon the extent of their injury. Beckmire thought about how and when Zanthius, without hesitation, shot the guy in the head, the other prisoners quickly loosened up their tongues.

In the barn Beckmire announced, "Listen, I am going to leave this matter to you and Asiram. Walter will be here to ask a few questions, but this is your show. Son, what we are doing is trying to save lives. I have two injured men, fortunately not with life-threatening wounds and I need you and your bride-to-be, to do what you people do best, and that is extract information. Asiram, I know you are trying to illustrate the softer side of you, but I need to know as much as possible as soon as possible. From now on, I want to take the fight to them, even if it means on Pennsylvania Avenue."

Zanthius looked at Asiram and whispered, "I love you. If this is too much for you, let me know and I will take the lead and do what's necessary. What we do to stay alive has nothing to do with what we do once we are not looking over our shoulders. This is survival, my love!"

Asiram whispered back, "I will do whatever you ask of me, because I know at any moment, that could be one of us laid out on a bed, struggling for survival. Let's get this over with."

The messy stall still had small brain parts splattered all over the place. Zanthius walked in and announced, "Hi, my name is Zanthius De Lombardo and I am also known as the 'idiot spy'. I wouldn't recommend that you call me that because my fiancée takes offense to that title and it inspires her to do dastardly deeds. By the way, her name is, Ms. Extractioner."

Walter walked into the barn and asked, "Did I miss anything?"

Asiram replied, "No, we are about to start." She stood directly in front of an intruder with several serious wounds and inquired, "Who sent you here?" He looked at her and said, "Screw yourself, dike."

Asiram said, "Apparently, you believe this world is just made for macho men like you and there is no room for people who enjoy a different persuasion. Isn't that thinking small in a world so big?"

Despite the obvious pain the intruder was in, he screamed, "Bitch, are you crazy?" Hearing that comment, Zanthius walked over to the man and shot him in the head. The remaining prisoners' eyes opened wide, illustrating their immediate surprise and fear.

Zanthius declared, "I will not tolerate any disrespect or name calling directed at my fiancée. Am I clear?"

Asiram began to question the second man in the queue and asked, "Who is your leader?" The guy who had a gut wound, and would probably be dead in five minutes, yet remained arrogant and defiant, answered, "Your theatrics by shooting my associate doesn't bother me. We know the risks when we sign on for this kind of work."

Asiram unsheathed her serrated knife and dug it slowly into the intruder's side and asked, "How does this feel?" She began to twist the blade, ever so slowly, as Zanthius placed duct tape over his mouth to quell the sounds of his anguish. Walter stepped outside of the barn with Mike and they began to vomit. Asiram removed the tape and asked him once again, "Who is your leader?"

"I don't know and if I did, I wouldn't tell your sick ass." POW! Zanthius terminated his life with a shot to the head.

Asiram wiped the blood off the knife and asked the third guy, "Who sent you here?"

He replied, "He's in charge."

Asiram asked, "Who is 'he'?"

The man answered, "He's in charge. It's his operation and he's the banker."

Asiram inquired, "How did you get here?" With two dead men in front of him and Asiram holding her knife, the intruder was cooperative and talkative.

He replied, "We came in a van that dropped us off at your neighbor's house."

"You mean the righteous Senator from Virginia?"

The guy responded, "I don't know much about that, but the Senator met that guy and they had a drink together. The Senator immediately, left for Washington, DC, after finishing his drink."

The man in the fourth chair kept grunting and finally yelled, "He's lying. He's the one who brought us here and hired us all. He is lying to save his ass."

Asiram asked Zanthius to tape his mouth while she tried to figure out who was who in the scenario.

Walter walked back into the room and once again began to observe the inquisition. As he walked behind the injured men, his attention was directed at the ring on the guy's finger that Mike had shot in the leg. Walter asked, "Asiram, can I have a moment with you and Zanthius?"

As they walked out of the stall area, Walter asked, "Did either of you happen to notice the ring that guy is wearing?" They shrugged their shoulders and couldn't figure out the relevance of the question.

Walter said, "There are only 100 of those rings in existence and they belong to a secret society, much like the 'Illuminati'. Asiram have you ever met your neighbor?"

Asiram responded, "I met him last summer at our annual wine and music festival."

Walter asked, "Was he wearing a curious looking ring that had diamonds shaped in the form of the pyramids?"

Asiram replied, "I don't really recall. I do remember that he was weird. Speaking of weird, I need to call the dry cleaning man ASAP. We don't want anyone walking in the woods to stumble across our dirty laundry. However, we will finish with these two men and figure out the connection. I can't believe that senator would be a part of this kind of treachery. Would you like to finish the inquiries Walter, since you think there may be a connection between the ring, the senator and what's happening here?"

Walter answered, "I am not sure that I can follow your act. However, I will try."

The three walked back in and Walter said, to the remaining intruders, "I am new at this game, but let me tell you this, if you lie to me, I will cut your manhood off and stuff it in your mouth. Now, that we have agreed upon the terms of engagement, one of you is telling the truth and one of you is telling a fabulous tale. This is what I am going to do. I'm going to stab each man in the leg until one of you tells me who is telling the truth. Okay? Who wants to go first? Oh, Zanthius, can you assist by taping their mouths with duct tape?" Asiram pulled a bale of hay near the action and sat on it to watch this novice attempt to extract information.

Walter asked Asiram if he could borrow her knife and she flatly rejected his request. Asiram said, "To be a good extractionist, you should bring your own tools to work. Check out that box near the window and perhaps you might find some useful instruments."

Walter opened the box and exclaimed, "Eureka! Wow, you have scalpels and other funny looking tools. What is the hook for?"

Asiram answered unemotionally, "I use that when I want to hang a man by his testicles."

The second guy who was bleeding profusely from his wounds and probably wouldn't last the night but was still squirming, said, "Listen, I have a wife and kids and this smirking jerk next to me is the man who called the shots. I just want to go home to my family and let this be a bad dream." Zanthius looked at him and Walter knew that the guy had just signed his death warrant.

Zanthius said, "You have a wife and children, but you came here for a few dollars to kill my mother, father, fiancée and good friends, and yet you want us to let you go?"

Asiram, having witnessed Zanthius's antics in similar venues, began yelling, "No! No! No!" It was too late. Zanthius executed the guy and then pointed the weapon at the remaining intruder. Asiram walked in front of him and said, "I need you to calm down. I need you to put that weapon away. Don't go down this path, it's hard to return. I am fighting this thing every day. Please, love, let's at least find out what he knows and who he is. Listen, Walter is doing an excellent job. Why don't you and I go have a drink. Please!"

With tears in his eyes, Zanthius looked at the final intruder and declared, "I'm not going to have a drink as long as he's alive! So, I am going to sit here until Walter finishes his work, and if I don't think he gave him accurate information, I am going to blow his dick off." Zanthius turned to the man and said, "Don't try to act as though you are not the leader of this event. Your ring has significance and meaning. A secret society designed to lead this government and eliminate the poor and disadvantaged people. Is that correct?"

Mike and another one of Walter's men entered the barn and began to remove the bodies from view. In the meantime, Asiram called the dry cleaners and told them that they had a lot of dirty laundry lying around.

Walter asked the man who was in total shock from watching Zanthius blow three guys' heads off, "So, is it true? Was this your OP?"

The man lowered his head and replied, "Yes. This is my OP."

Walter said, "Good at least we are talking a lot of good can come from talking. As a matter of fact, it wasn't that long ago that I witnessed exactly what you just saw, two men get their heads blown completely off. It was only through my honest dialogue that I was allowed to live another day and recognize that these people were set up from the very beginning. Now, if this was your OP, who made the funds available to hire your men?"

The guy looked at Zanthius and then at Walter and responded, "I can't divulge that information." Zanthius leapt from his sitting position and chambered a round in his weapon.

Asiram screamed, "Zanthius! Please don't. Please leave the room! Walter has this under control."

Zanthius yelled, "He's not telling the truth. Let me just shoot him in his dick. When he sees the mess that makes, he will sing the Star Spangle Banner, backwards."

Asiram pleaded, "Please, let me and Walter handle this."

Zanthius turned to walk out of the room but snapped around and pointed the weapon at the intruder's private parts and then left the area. The intruder said, "He is off the reservation and is crazy as hell. Are you sure he is the guy called the 'idiot spy'?"

Walter replied, "That is the one and only 'idiot spy'. What is your name, if I may ask?"

"My name is Sam Snead."

Walter said, "I would like to call you Sam, if that's okay with you. Now, Sam, there are a lot of people who just want to kill you in the worse possible way. I'm looking for something of value that you can give me that may just save your life and your private parts. Would you like some water or something, while I give you a few minutes to think over your responses?"

"Water would be fine." Mike opened a bottle of water and began to pour it slowly down Sam's throat. Sam thanked Mike and turned his attention to Walter, who was waiting for something earth shattering to come out of Sam's mouth.

Sam said, "I don't have many bargaining chips and I am sworn to secrecy. I can say this, however, your sanctified neighbor and US Senator is in cahoots with some very powerful people who want to obtain the product the 'idiot spy' received from some woman in Switzerland. Although my ring associates me with an unidentified secret society, I have grown to detest what it stands for.

"Your associate is correct, while in college, I met a group of guys and the next thing I knew, we were talking about how to rid the world of people who, as a result of poverty, failure to take advantage of a free education and due to their mental inferiority are a drain on our economy and planet. Needless to say, after writing about this from each of our perspectives, we were asked to attend a meeting at the Dean's house where the discussion centered on the 'proletariat'; in essence, people of color and poor white trash."

Walter said, "Hold that thought for a minute, I need to get my people back in here to hear what you are saying." Walter nodded to Mike and he called Beckmire to come to the barn.

Zanthius turned the corner and asked Walter, "Do you believe that shit he's talking?"

Walter looked at Zanthius and replied, "As a matter of fact, I do. That ring on his finger tells a story that is so much bigger than what is going on here. I asked Mike to get your dad up here to listen to this. If, just if, what he says is true, our problem has multiplied itself by light-years."

Walter looked at Sam and said, "I am going to ask the Sarge if he will allow someone to look at your wound. The blood is getting darker and that is not a good sign."

# # #

Beckmire asked Courtney if she would give assistance to one of the people who tried to kill them. She looked at him as if he were crazy. Nevertheless, Courtney walked with Beckmire to the barn and looked at Sam's leg and announced, "He needs to be in the hospital. His wound is more serious than it looks. Whoever put those plastic ties on his leg, probably saved his life."

Sam looked at Mike and said, "Thanks, man."

Courtney washed the wound and placed two other ties on his leg and said, "If he does not get attention in the next hour or so, oh well." She turned and walked out of the barn. Courtney informed the Sarge at the entrance to the barn, "It's not bad at all. I just wanted to give his ass something to think about."

The Sarge grabbed her and whispered, "I just love you all the way to heaven. You are my heartbeat." They kissed and he walked her back to the house.

When Beckmire returned, he looked at Sam and said, "My wife, the doctor, told me to kill you or take you to the hospital. My son wants to blow you away. Walter, is he cooperating with you?"

Walter turned to Beckmire and replied, "He is giving me some mind blowing information that literally takes us to a place beyond the stars. Sam, give him the short and skinny of our conversation."

Sam took about three minutes to bring Beckmire up to speed and when he was finished, Beckmire uttered the word, "Damn!"

Sam continued his presentation and midstream asked, "What are the chances of me getting out of here alive?"

Beckmire looked at Walter and then Zanthius and responded, "Depends on how much additional, useful information you can provide us with. I mean, your indictment of the senator is truly huge, but is that enough to save your life or to keep our extractionist from performing her art on you? I'm not sure. I'll tell you what, I'm going to huddle with my people and ask them to take a vote on your situation. I can tell you now, my son just wants you dead and ready for the dry cleaners. If you can provide him with additional information that he deems useful then we can discuss your departure. Remember, the time frame my wife put on your life with relationship to your wound. Don't waste any time. If you got something to tell us, it's now or never."

Sam reported, "I probably have more information than your brains can digest. This entire scenario is larger than the few dead people in the field. If the Senator and his people get their hands on the 'idiot spy' and the product, anarchy will be the order of business in this country for a long time.

The proletariat will completely disappear, and people of color will be shipped back to Africa, India, Mexico or wherever else they come from. They no longer need people to pick cotton or build testaments to their greatness. You see, they have already made each other rich by instituting legislation that enriches their friends and placing the ominous burden for paying for their chicanery on the, soon to be obsolete, proletariat.

"Listen, these guys have conducted DNA tests on every child whose parents have signed up for vaccinations and/or free lunches. For example, if your parent signed you up for free lunches, then you were assigned a number and that number went into a database that would eventually conclude your existence in this country, systematically. You can thank the senator for that one because that was his idea. People, this product in the wrong hands has the potential of not only shifting the balance of power, but also providing a new form of genocide of the poor and disadvantaged."

Zanthius said, "This sounds like some story out of the Nazi playbook."

Sam asked, "And who the hell do you think lives directly behind this farm? He may not proclaim allegiance, but his movements mirrors that of the Nazis, which is why I am disgusted with their new notions. Listen, there was a consensus among members to use the product, on an experimental basis, to eliminate a major city in this country that housed a significant number of the disadvantaged, poor and people of color. These guys have left the reservation and mirror the worst dictators that the world has ever known.

"I am not making this shit up as I go along. This information is factual. Now, you know what would be cool and significant is if you caught one of their members and placed him in front of the extractor. That would not only be informative but would corroborate my information. I am willing to help you obtain one if you will get me to a hospital. I will also remain a captive until you are positive that my story is on the up-and-up."

Asiram asked, "So, how do we find a member of your 'secret society' who would not be missed? We just can't kidnap a sitting US Senator. The entire planet would be looking for us."

Sam replied, "That is where I come in. I know a few of them who have dared to unmask themselves before our sessions were totally over."

Beckmire said, "So Sam, it looks as if you are prepared to jump ship to save your ass."

"I wouldn't call it that. I would proclaim this an enlightening experience." Sam continued and said, "Perhaps even an epiphany. What I wouldn't call it is a request to have the 'idiot spy' put a bullet in my head."

CHAPTER NINE

Sir William "Billy" Montague had been knighted by the Queen of England and held several auspicious titles in her Majesty's government. Seemingly, a prudish individual but also considered cunning, and in some quarters even conniving. He had many friends in America including a brother who sported the same ring as he did and shared his vision of a society free of the proletariat. Sir Montague was often seen as a champion of the poor and disadvantaged. His usual holiday dinners at the local charities were heralded as a sign that he cared about the plight of the poor. In reality, it was a front and a ruse to gain greater notoriety and solicit like-minded individuals who shared his vision of the poor being a drain on the system.

Sir Montague had a two-hour meeting scheduled in New York with none other than Asiram's neighbor, the US Senator from Virginia. When they met, Sir Montague, first, congratulated him on succeeding in getting the product back in the United States. Sir Montague said, "Seems like I owe you ten dollars. My people weren't able to accomplish that simple task. However, the carrier got out of Switzerland and landed safely in America. Will you accept the payment in Euros?"

The senator laughed and replied, "I have always told you that we don't have a lot of protocol when it comes to stuff like that. We make it happen. Your people were at the wrong place at the wrong time. I will take my ten dollars in any currency you want to pay in."

The two men had a drink and then began to discuss the status of the product. The senator asked, "If I told you that the package is in my backyard, would you believe me?"

Sir Montague responded, "Probably not, but humor me. Where might this backyard be, and do you have access to it?"

The senator replied, "I'm telling you the truth. It's literally in my backyard. Now, this is an incredible story. There was a piece of property that didn't appear on the books and was sold without my having an opportunity to bid on it. I mean, hell, it was only 120 acres or so, but it would have given me two additional exit routes from my farm. So, when I had my people investigate the identity of my neighbor, the report came back that it was not a new neighbor, but it was an in-family transaction. I mean they built a beautiful house, complete with a bunch of horses, cattle, swimming pool, tractors--the whole nine yards. I never saw a single person other than the caretaker, ever. I didn't pay much attention to it and I would occasionally ride my mule over on their property and just scan the place.

"Well, I'll be damned. The person that got the carrier out of Europe is the owner of that property. She is also called the 'Extractionist'. Well, at least, she was until now. I sent one of our brothers along with a crackpot team and I am sure that they have her and her companion, the 'idiot spy' and know the whereabouts of the product by now."

Sir Montague reported, "I came all the way from London and heard, while in flight, that your team was obliterated and one of our brothers slain."

The senator yelled, "Don't fuck around with me on this one, Billy!"

"I am not, as you say, fucking around with you on this. I have solid intel that your people were slaughtered by a bunch of Vietnam veteran types. I mean they would have to be old as shit today, correct?"

The Senator dialed a number and there was no answer. He then tried another number and when the person answered the phone, he inquired, "Did my local team lose last night?"

The voice on the other end answered, "They lost forty to nothing."

The Senator hung up and exclaimed, "Shit, I thought we had beaten those people down. I am going to have to send in tanks and make this appear to be one of those rural Midwest torture themes where the old men are having carnal relations with children and pigs or something."

Sir Montague said, "I thought for sure you had heard the news. I guess my spies can do something right, eh chap."

After deliberating about the outcomes of several assaults on that farm, the senator said, "I hate to suggest this, but I only have one other option and that one involves that crazy bitch, Scottie."

Sir Montague stated adamantly, "We can't use her. My people are investigating her, and we think that she is tied to a radical billionaire person of Arab descent."

"No way in hell." the senator countered. "She is one of our most reliable operatives and besides, she hates anyone from the Middle East," the senator replied.

"Money can make a good looking woman fall for a ninety-year-old man who will allow her to live a lavish lifestyle," Sir Montague stated.

"Regardless of that, I mean we all have our hands in someone's pocket," the Senator announced.

Sir Montague replied, "Yes, but he is tied to an extremely anti-American group and is said to be the source of their funding. Our intel tells us that he wants the product so that he can make the world equal. We believe that your most reliable operative is on his payroll. As a matter of fact, a significant amount of money has been transferred to an offshore account that bears some tracking information that leads us to her. We think that she intends to pull this off by gaining access to the product, and then faking her death and disappearing into the night.

"With the kind of money that's in that account, she could go anywhere in the world and get a new identification. Not a bad play for a Yank, but rather obvious in her case. Too many telltale signs of disenfranchisement on her part. If you guys were really serious about this thing in the beginning, why didn't you bring her on at first light?"

The senator answered, "We heard some rumblings, but they were from a biased higher level. A high-ranking senator, who slept with her and her friend, hinted that she would be more useful if she were no longer alive. It appears the woman recorded her session with him and threatened to use the information if she wasn't elevated to a secure position."

Sir Montague said, "Sounds familiar, doesn't it? Word on the street has it that you were one of her playthings and you thought that it was all about you until you got that cream colored envelope with a secure link to her website."

The senator answered, "So, you heard that rumor as well? I hear it often, but it doesn't annoy me since there was never any evidence that connected me to her."

"Yes, you're correct, old chap. Sir Montague laughed. "Strange that she got that new job a week after you received that envelope. I guess it was just a coincidence, so be it. I don't think she is reliable and remember, we have three constituents here that want resolution: your government, my government and our Brotherhood. The Brotherhood of course supersedes any established governments. Don't you agree, Senator?"

"Absolutely, and it is up to us to make sure that we can move our agenda to the forefront and save the world from itself. I will personally get involved with how this thing is resolved in the next two days and we will raid that place with tanks and shit. There will only be one survivor, the guy they call the 'idiot spy' and he will be in critical condition. Thanks for coming by and I will see you soon at our convocation with good news. I promise you that. Thanks again and tell your people to stop following me. Goodbye now."

The senator looked in his briefcase, pulled a flip-phone out and searched the room for his glasses. After securing his glasses, he autodialed a number. The person on the other end asked, "You got me, so what do you want?"

The senator replied, "We have a real problem with securing that product. I need advice, when can we meet?" The person on the other end answered, "Tomorrow at noon in room 339. You know the place. Bye."

CHAPTER TEN

Back at the farm, the interrogation of Sam continued. Sam stated, "The lady that looked at my leg gave you guys a timetable relative to my developing a serious medical problem. I mean, I have given you guys the kitchen sink including that ignoble sonofabitch that lives behind here. I need help guys. I really don't want to die like this and I sure as hell am not going to give some lame shit excuse such as my wife and children as a reason to live. I know the response to that plea."

Beckmire said, "Give us more and we will huddle to decide your fate."

"That doesn't sound all that appealing to me. However, I trust that you are gentlemen first and, therefore, at least have a code of honor. This group has Senators, Congressmen and Englishmen with titles, such as, 'Sir'. They're all rich, privileged, highly educated, and more importantly for this project, they have people at the highest levels of government masquerading as secretaries of government departments."

Zanthius yelled, "Whoa, Whoa, Whoa. What do you mean by masquerading as secretaries of departments?"

Sam answered, "I mean just that. Guys, this issue that you have assumed is larger than life. No pun intended. If you recognize the massive number of people who have lost their lives on this property, then that alone should tell you that people want this product and at any costs. I mean, The Society has placed people at every level of our government and we want it."

Zanthius declared, "We captured a spy that said we should turn the product over to the Secretary of Defense or Secretary of State. Are you saying that would be a mistake?"

Sam smiled and replied, "Whoever suggested that must have been low on the food chain. If you agree to not slaughter or maim me, and let me go, I will tell you all that I know."

Zanthius spoke first, "Agreed."

His response caught Sam off-guard, and Sam stated, "Now, I know I am in trouble when the first person to agree to free me is the 'idiot spy'. I don't believe you."

Zanthius said "Your problem is that if you call me the 'idiot spy' once again, I will terminate your life."

"You should feel exulted. The people who want you dead all refer to you as the—ah, that name. If I were you, I would embrace it and use it to your advantage. They thought you were an—that name but have now come to realize that you are much smarter than they are. I would embrace it and use it."

Barely hiding his anger, Zanthius replied, "I will take that under advisement. However, I meant what I said, I agree to free you if you can provide more details of substance."

"Okay. However, I need something to eat. I have that sugar problem and I am about to go under. There is a box of pills in my pocket. Just let me have one and something to eat."

Later after Sam had a sandwich and took his medicine, he began his free flow of information by expressing his concern about turning the product over to one of the heads of the aforementioned departments. He indicated that two of the men who held those positions were ring wearers and were not to be trusted. He told them that there were levels of security, as they well knew, and that the persons being recommended were key decision makers and were also off the reservation. He suggested that they locate images of the two heads of those departments and try to zoom in on their left hand and wedding ring finger.

Beckmire summoned Jong and asked him to get him photos of the heads of the two departments. Jong inquired if there was anything specific, he was looking for and Beckmire told him.

After viewing almost 150 photos of one of the men, there it was, a glaring and close photo of a department head wearing the societal ring. Jong went through approximately twenty-five pictures of the other man before he stumbled across him wearing the same ring. Beckmire thanked him and told him to get some rest.

Beckmire walked into the barn, pulled a knife out and went behind Sam who yelled, "I told you the truth."

Beckmire responded, "I know, I'm just cutting you free. The first step in your journey to total freedom."

He looked at Walter and mumbled, "What a freaking government we have. Is there anyone who can be trusted?"

Walter shook his head and replied, "Now, I'm really afraid. I think we are going to need a few tanks and battalions of men to surround this place because I know their next move. They need to align us and possibly are going to label us as cult members who are holding children in sexual bondage. That will create a lot of news coverage and before you know it, this place will be on fire and the only survivor will be the 'idiot spy'."

"Perfect scenario," Sam agreed. "You have a hot commodity and they will use any nefarious scheme to burn this place down with everyone in it. Trust me and him. That will be their ruse unless they decide to use a drone to drop a bomb on this place, much like that imbecile in Philadelphia did to that group called, 'MOVE'. I think it might be a good time to consider a new location, but you can't move this many people without someone taking notice."

Asiram, who was standing nearby, asked Beckmire and Zanthius if they could huddle with her. She said, "I have another place and I know how to get us all out of here. What is the capacity of those jets you rented?"

Beckmire answered, "They're not rented. Our private foundation owns those planes, clear title on each one. I don't know their capacity but let me ask Jong."

Beckmire once again summoned Jong who, upon his arrival, said, "Sarge, I think I'll hang out here for a while."

Beckmire asked, "What is the capacity of our jets?"

Jong responded, "The one that Brown and Bernstein use can handle ten. I think the plane that Chakes has is an eight-passenger plane and the one that I use can be turned into a ten-passenger plane. Why, are we going somewhere?"

Beckmire answered, "Maybe. I needed the particulars first to see if it is feasible. Okay, don't go anywhere. Asiram, my love, I will walk you down the aisle and give you away, to my son if you get us out of here. He will marry you, if I have anything to do with it. What were you thinking and what did you have in mind when you made that suggestion of getting us out of here?"

"Oh, Zanthius, I forgot to tell you about my ranch in middle America. I own three thousand or is it five thousand acres of land in Wyoming. I have a huge house there that I bought with part of the money I received from the sale of my family home when my family died tragically in a fire. I haven't been there in two years. I have a faithful family that works for me there and they take care of everything. The best thing is, I told them that I am a private person and that they may never meet me, but I want my place kept in immaculate condition. Any repairs are to be handled by real professionals and not neighborhood handymen. If we can get there, we can hold off an army, unless they use planes."

Beckmire asked, "Did you call the dry cleaning people yet?"

"I got you, Ben Beckmire. I got you. You are as cunning as a fox. I got you. I am going to tell the dry cleaner to delay his arrival time by two hours. That will give us time to get some of the dead people out of the barn and into the house and just torch that bitch. I got you, Daddy-in-Law. I got you."

Zanthius inquired, "Am I missing something?"

Beckmire said, "Yeah, your ass is getting married in a few days, so write your vows."

"Pops, what are you talking about?"

"You have impregnated this woman and you will marry her."

Zanthius looked at Asiram and inquired, "Why didn't you tell me first since I am the father?"

"Because I was afraid that you would run out on me, like someone else did."

Zanthius walked over to her and said, "You are my three 'H's'. You make and keep me 'Healthy, Happy and Horny'.

Did you forsake me overseas? No, you took me under your wing and got me out of imminent danger. You have provided for my family and friends here, but now that you are pregnant you tell my father first?

"Anyway, I love you and you make me proud. I would have married you the first night I met you. I felt weak and lost all control of my senses when I saw you. I knew that I could love you. I am happy to be the father of our child and I will be here for you. Oh, and by the way, tell my father I make the decision about who I am going to marry. It doesn't hurt that he loves you, too. So, there we are. Let's have a wedding."

Asiram went back to the house and asked Ava, Courtney, Rashida, Marisa, Larry and Carlos if they could huddle with her for a minute. Ava asked, "What's going on?"

Asiram declared, "I'm going to make this short and sweet! That land behind me is owned by a US Senator, who happens to be involved in a secret society that prefers us dead and your son alive, until his utility is exhausted. I want you guys to trust me and do as I ask. We are all in great danger. I need you to gather all of the things that are useful to you and needed in the wilderness. I need to find a way to ship guns on private planes. If you have any ideas, I am open to suggestions."

# # #

The die was cast. Walter asked, "Are we going to honor Sam's request?"

Zanthius responded, "Absolutely."

Sam said, "Listen, I am as good as dead if I'm found anywhere near here. I need additional protection. I can be useful. Consider taking me with you."

Zanthius reported, "According to the manifest, we are overbooked on these flights."

Sam said, "I have a final request. I want the 'idiot spy' to shoot me in the head. I am as good as dead if caught, anyway."

Zanthius looked at Beckmire and then at Sam and asked, "Are you sure you want me to shoot you?"

"I am positive. Do it."

Zanthius whispered "Okay, if that's what you want." He pointed the gun at Sam's head and said, "You know this isn't personal. I like you, so, therefore, I am not going to shoot you. I guess that means we're taking you with us. Is that right, Pops?"

Beckmire looked at his son and mumbled, "Your decision makes me proud of you, Son. Give me one of those man-sized hugs."

# # #

The dry cleaning people arrived and Asiram said to the lead guy, "I think you blew it on a couple of occasions but that didn't erode my confidence in you. I need a special favor, but if you are not the one controlling the action, then say so."

The dry cleaning expert, replied, "I say this with admiration, but sorrowfully. This place is burned! Lessons have been learned from each attempt to compromise it. The opposition seems to have eyes on this place and can figure out strategically, a better invasion plan, based upon body placements and firing patterns. It is rumored that satellite footage of every incursion on this farm is available to the highest bidder. I recommend that you abandon this place, or the next call may, unfortunately, be for your own bodies."

Asiram said, "That is exactly why I am asking you for a favor. Every time your vehicle leaves this place, it is with dead or near dead bodies. I need you to take live bodies to the airport without asking any questions. Can you do that?"

"And what shall I do with the cleaning job?" he asked.

"You will collect them all and bring them to the farmhouse. What will happen next, you don't need to know. I just need your vans to load, discreetly, a bunch of live bodies. Can you do that for me, for a quarter of a million dollars?"

The cleaner answered, "That is against protocol, but I can make that happen for $125 thousand. We feel we owe you for that indiscretion that was committed by one who was not family. Do we have an accord?"

Asiram replied, "We do. This must happen under the cover of darkness. After you and your trained no barking dogs find the bodies, I will cut all power and then we move the dead bodies in the house and load the live bodies in your vehicles. Agreed?"

# # #

Asiram told Beckmire, Ava, Carlos, Larry and Marisa, "Unfortunately, I am going to put a device under that half full tank of propane that was just serviced today and blow this place sky high. It's insured and besides, if they deny me, I will kidnap them and torture their asses. Just joking, my keeper will take care of my livestock."

Beckmire and Zanthius entered the house and saw a beehive of activity taking place. Beckmire asked Asiram, "Is everyone on board with the plan?"

"Absolutely. What I need is a way to smuggle these weapons onto the planes. Any ideas?"

Jong walked in behind them and said, "My guys can make that happen."

Asiram asked, "Your guys, as in whom?"

"The pilots of all three planes. No one knows who were on those planes that came from separate points of arrival, but all three pilots who work for us are ex-military and eager to get in on some of our action. I can put them in charge of that smuggling operation. I am sure they're bored as hell and would welcome a little action."

Walter said, "I don't want to know where all of this money is coming from, but I am happy that you have it."

Asiram stated, "Speaking of money, I need $125k. Courtney would you and Ava go down to the basement and count out that amount. After you finish, please secure large suitcases from of my room and stuff as much money in them as possible. If it is okay with you two, that will be your additional responsibility to manage the money and get it out of here safely. After that, please close the door to the safe and the rest of the money will be protected from any sudden explosions. The place is wired against people trying to do stupid."

Beckmire looked at Zanthius and announced, "I love my new son and his soon to be wife. I must tell you one thing. Asiram is not pregnant, but I hope she gets that way soon."

Zanthius declared, "I know she isn't pregnant and besides, if she were, she would have told me first. Had I shunned her; she probably would have cut my friend down there off."

Beckmire then turned to Courtney and whispered, "Oh, Courtney, when you finish with that chore, I need you to sterilize Sam's leg and stitch it up. He's coming with us as an ally. We need him but I feel he will eventually turn into a Judas."

Courtney said, "Okay dear." She looked at Sam and said, "My stitching is going to hurt a helluva lot more than that flesh wound did."

# # #

The plan was in motion when Asiram said to Zanthius, "I hate blowing up the barn; the horses won't have a shelter. Plus, I need to have the cleaners pay particular attention to it and make sure that there is no DNA in there."

Zanthius said, "Suddenly, I feel useless. I mean you have your shit together and you are thinking of everything. All I am doing is admiring you and wanting to be in your pants."

Asiram grabbed his hand and whispered, "So, useless, how about taking me into the barn like your mom did her new man but do me better and make me talk to horses." They laughed and walked towards the barn. Their game plan was derailed by Walter's men who were hanging around the barn.

Walter said, "Sarge, you know I can't come with you, but I will make all of my resources here available to you. I'm going to give you an alternate phone number for me. Call when you need to. In a week or so, after people realize what has happened here, me and a few of my boys will locate you and help keep things orderly. Right now, it would be suicide for us to disappear at the same time as you do. What we will do is make sure that the woods are free of prying eyes until you have boarded the vehicles. Tell Ms. Asiram that there will be friendlies around for six minutes after notification from you that you guys are at the top of the road."

The Sarge said, "It has been a pleasure. When I am on the ground, wherever it is we land, I will give you coordinates and a few phone numbers. Listen, do you guys need any cash to get home?"

"Naw. We be good. We be good."

As the sun began to set, the dry cleaner and his dogs were actively marking places for pick up. Brown, Bernstein, Jilkes and John Lee had loaded the mule with weapons and drove to the top of the road and then into the woods. From the house across the road, they were given the all clear sign and began to load the weapons into an old pickup truck that belonged to a neighbor.

The dry cleaning people collected spent cartridges and any other indications of a fire fight. They were meticulous and thorough. Bodies were loaded onto electric carts that made very little noise and were shuffled towards the three pickup trucks scattered around the farm. The process was methodical and pickup points were indicated by glow sticks that children play with.

Jong had made the call to the pilots who were on the lookout for the advance team: Jilkes, John Lee, Brown and Bernstein. It was a long ride from the place in Virginia to the airport in College Park, Maryland, where the planes were parked. The pilots knew there wouldn't be a problem because they had filed all of the necessary paperwork and a fictitious manifest. They also knew that they would be the last planes leaving the airport. Therefore, they checked to make sure that Air Traffic Control would be operative for the take-off.

All systems seemed to be in the go stage. The dry cleaners had loaded a total of thirty-three bodies onto the carts and into the vans. When the three vans converged on the house, the lead cleaner asked for the number of garments. It was reported that thirty-three had been collected. He astutely asked, "How many glow sticks did we put out?" The answer came back as thirty-six. He abruptly said, "Get the dogs and canvas this entire place again until you have collected all of the garments. No short cuts--full scan. We can't make another mistake, this is a high value client, the kind that makes or breaks your business. They will fire us and get someone else to do this very productive and financially lucrative work."

The members of the household were assembled in the basement because it was the nearest to the woods. All bags were gathered, and all heads were counted. Courtney told Larry and Carlos, "I am delegating this task to you guys. Watch these damn bags and do not let them out of your sights—not even for a minute."

Ava said, "Nicely done, Courtney. I didn't know money could be so heavy."

The dry cleaners' lead person summoned Asiram and told her that they had placed thirty-six glow sticks but had only collected thirty-three garments. He suggested that they remain vigilant until all glow sticks were accounted for. As he turned to walk away, the sound of gunfire could be heard.

He turned to her and said, "It's just a matter of minutes before we discover the other garments and dispose of them."

Asiram thanked him and said, "It is imperative that you wrap this up shortly. We have buses to catch." Everyone knew not to stand in front of a window or door, but Larry made the mistake of crossing the threshold to attend to one of the twins. As he looked out the door, he could see a person slithering through the grassy knoll. Larry turned and yelled, "Alert!" Everyone hit the floor. Larry and Carlos ran upstairs and out the back door. Carlos and Larry alternated in providing cover for each other. Simultaneously, three shots rang out. Carlos, Larry and Mike hit the slithering person. All shots were to the head. Larry said to Carlos, "I heard three shots. I only fired one. How many did you fire?"

Carlos responded, "I fired one as well."

Mike yelled, "Stand-down—friendly out here."

Suddenly, the horses began to run as if they were spooked by a predator or something. The sound of shots rang out again and all of the glow sticks were accounted for.

Bernstein, Jilkes, Brown and John Lee decided to hang around a bit to make sure there were no follow-up issues.

Jilkes called the Sarge and said, "You gave us orders, but we're going to hang around to make sure that there are no additional problems. Walter's guys are posted at the top of the road, and two more of his men are doing drive by observations. Bernstein and Brown are in the cemetery and me and John Lee are at the post office. We figure that with our talent missing, you guys would be vulnerable to the smallest attack, that is why we are disobeying orders. It was John Lee's idea."

John Lee screamed, "That boy be lying to you, Sarge. You know I can't come up with any solutions, let alone strategies. He be lying—with his red ass nose."

Beckmire said, "With all of these tenderfoots here, I'm glad that you guys are giving us additional support. Thanks to you all."

## CHAPTER ELEVEN

Walter and his people saw the dry cleaning vehicles successfully leave by the main road. He calculated that they had approximately twenty minutes to clear the area. Beckmire called him and said, "Walter, we are on the road. I will not let her detonate until I am sure my friends are safely out of range. As a matter of fact, call your people in the house across the road and have them clear out as well. Let's make this a total evacuation. How long will it take them to exit?"

Walter replied, "Let me hit you back. Tell Ms. Asiram that friendlies are still on the circuit."

Walter's people were out of the house ready to be evacuated and standing in the cover of darkness. Walter along with Mike and two other members of his team entered his SUV and headed towards the entrance to the farm.

The car that was providing drive by surveillance picked up the two individuals, and their equipment from the house at the top of the hill. Jeremy, one of Walter's men, called and said, "We are going home for dinner. Catch you soon." Walter took a good look around and saw that his favorite horse was rearing its front hoofs in the air.

Walter called the Sarge and said, "Abort that timetable. I have something personal I have to do." Without any further explanation, Walter told Mike to drive to the barn. In the meantime, the caravan of dry cleaning trucks was idling on the access road waiting for the sign to retreat. Walter went into the barn, got a bag of treats for the horses, threw it over his shoulder and walked back to the SUV.

Mike said, "Really Boss? I can't believe you're doing this."

Walter replied "Someday, you may understand the intense emotions between a horse and a horse lover. I can't explain it, but hopefully, one day you will have an epiphany like the one that I had about this horse."

Beckmire called Walter and asked, "Is there a problem? Do you need us to be backup?"

"No, Sarge, I got this." Mike then drove Walter to the field behind the house and that damn horse Rjah, was there kicking his feet in the air. Walter got out of the SUV and said to the horse, "Have a treat, but keep away from the house." He slit the bag of treats open and threw it onto the field. When he got into the SUV, Mike asked, "Can you explain any of your actions?"

Walter replied, "Drive, Mike. I'm still senior here. Drive."

As Mike approached the bend on the access road that lead to the main thoroughfare, Walter called Beckmire and said, "Tell Ms. Asiram, it's now or never. I talked to that horse and he told me that they would be okay. I told him to stay the hell away from the house. He reared up and took off into the field. The rest of the herd followed him. Tell her to blow it. I want to watch the sky light up."

Beckmire said, "Walter, you are not only special, but perhaps, reliable and trustworthy. We will see you soon. Love brother, and peace as well."

Prior to blowing the place up, the heads were counted once more and all were accounted for. The dead bodies had been deposited in the house and a final check of all systems was completed. The Improvised Explosive Device had been placed carefully under the propane tank.

The dry cleaner had started a huge fire in the massive fireplace as well as opened the valves on the propane stove. As he walked out, he said to Asiram on the phone, "It has been a pleasure doing business with you and we apologize for any missteps. Just in case your attempt to demolish this perfect house doesn't work because of the wind direction, I have started a massive fire in the fireplace and have opened the valves on the stove. I also placed a small amount of cleaning products in your microwave. Everything is scheduled to explode in twenty minutes. Again, it has been our pleasure doing business with you. If you are anywhere in the contiguous states, we can come and clean your garments. Thank you."

BOOOOOOOOOM! That was the next sound heard and the Beckmire clan was off to another part of the country with an even more formidable foe in search of the totally destructive, but financially enhancing, Carbon Factor formula. As the caravan proceeded towards Route 211, Asiram began to cry hysterically.

Zanthius whispered, "When this is over, I promise to build you a bigger and better place where our children will be able to play without anyone trying to hurt them. I promise you this on my life. I love you so much."

CHAPTER TWELVE

At the airport, the three jets were in a circle, so the pilots could take turns watching to make sure that no one got near any of the aircrafts. When the group arrived in Maryland, Zanthius asked, "Honey, do you have any other places that I don't know about?" The van he was riding in erupted into laughter.

She looked at him and answered, "That place we just demolished was my sanctuary. I loved that farm and would often drive down that access road into the middle of the field and just cry about the status of my life. I now have a new perspective on life, since I met you. However, I hated to destroy my home. I just want to sleep for about a week without anyone speaking to me. Just hold me and let me cry."

Zanthius whispered, "It will be even better when we fill it with children and more horses and cattle. I had never been in the country before, other than in Spain. There was never a connection to the meaningful experiences you can have in the open space. Here, however, I love the fact that we can just enjoy the clean air, the bright sky and each other. I promise you I will make our place your most favorite place on earth. Wait, do you own other places?"

"Yes and no, silly boy. I do have a timeshare in Bora Bora and a small condo in St. Thomas. Do they count?"

Zanthius looked at her and responded, "Does it matter as long as we're together? Does it matter?"

The group disembarked from the dry cleaners' vans. Ava said to Courtney, "Wow, not bad. Not bad at all." As she looked at the three planes.

Courtney said, "I have been on one of them a couple of times, but I really don't like to fly. My husband is planning a trip to Australia with Zanthius once this is over and I know he is going to want me to tag along."

Ava said, "I hope I get an invitation, as well. I would love to travel there and understand all of this hocus pocus that your husband talks about."

Beckmire stepped out of his van and declared, "People, this is not a convention. Get those planes loaded and let's get the hell out of here! I so desperately want to hold my wife and tell her how proud I am of her. I can't do it here, so let's get this show on the road.

"Jong, tell us who is getting on which plane?"

Jong made the distribution and said, "We are one too many."

The Sarge looked at Sam and mumbled, "Listen, don't let him see you, hobble over to the biggest jet and sneak on. You might have to enjoy the ride on the floor, but that's okay as long as we all travel safely. Don't talk, just go and get on that plane."

The Sarge went to Jong and said, "Nicely done. I believe he will work for us as long as we need him but he will turn out to be a Judas. By the way, there really isn't a safety problem, is there?"

Jong responded, "Naw. I just like to keep a little drama going."

The Sarge emphasized, "You're the best. I really don't know what I would have done without you and the guys backing me up. I thank the Lord every day that he hooked us up to be together for life."

Three beautiful private jets took to the sky in five-minute intervals. The planes were registered to a small discreet organization that provided opportunities for small nonprofits. It was virtually impossible to find the owners of the corporation since there was a long list of shell companies that had an interest in it.

As the jets reached the prescribed altitude, Zanthius looked at Asiram and whispered, "So far, so good. You know what is simply mind-boggling is that I saw you in that airport and couldn't think of a single thing to say to you. I was so spellbound by your beauty that my learned moves escaped me. I couldn't even make a complete sentence. I was bewitched by you and I'm happy that you had the audacity to turn around and look at me as I left. That was the closer."

"No, it wasn't. The closer was when I first looked at you and was captivated by your boyish mannerisms. You were easy to seduce, but unfortunately, it wasn't me who did the seducing, was it, Romeo?"

"Okay, let's not go back there again. It was a mistake and had I known that you were truly interested in me, it never would have happened. Just think about who I'm absolutely, madly in love with! Well, now, I can only think of one person and she is on this plane with me, my Mom."

Asiram punched him and said, "I think she is warming up to me. What do you think?"

"You know I have got to say something to her. I think she believes that I don't love her and that I am still mad about the fantastic fable she told me about my father. Hold on, I'll be right back."

Zanthius unbuckled his seatbelt and headed towards the seats where Carlos and Ava were sitting. He asked, "Carlos, may I have a moment alone with my mother?" Carlos got out of his seat and went back and sat with Asiram.

Zanthius said to Ava, "You know, Mom, we have been through a lot lately and I have not had much of an opportunity to talk with you. Listen, I'm over that Ben Beckmire story. It's so old, plus I have met him, bonded with him, and killed with him. It is old, so let it go. What I really want to say to you is that, I love you so very much."

Ava was about to say something when Zanthius interjected, "Wait, Mom, let me finish. I admire the manner in which you and Carlos have finally gotten it together. I like him and I trust him. More importantly, I love you, Mom, and will always be there for you no matter what. This has been an adventure that I wouldn't trade all the tea in China for."

Ava said, "That means so much to me to hear you say that you love me. I began to age by the minute when we stopped communicating because I thought I had lost my only reason for living. You have made me very happy, Son, and by the way, I like Asiram. I realize that if she didn't have the strength to do what she does, we would be in a very bad place. Besides, she is intriguing, beautiful, sexy and more importantly, she loves you. Don't mess this up, Son. I would hate to have to kill that little girl. Ava touched his hand and said, "Thanks, for coming to my rescue. Who on earth told you that Carlos and I are an item?"

Zanthius unbuckled his seat belt and said, "Mom, that damn horse told everyone." Zanthius reached over and planted a huge kiss on Ava's cheek.

Ava asked as Zanthius was walking away, "What damn horse?"

"Ask Carlos. I think he met that damn horse."

# # #

The captains came over the intercom systems simultaneously on all three planes and gave their usual announcements about time, speed, altitude and the lack of personalized service on the jets. All three Captains indicated that it was the flight attendants' night off, and therefore, cocktails would be served by anyone who was interested in providing that service. In the rear of each plane was a significant amount of various spirits. Beckmire turned to Courtney, "Honey, I think I would like a slightly dirty martini with two olives and hold the vermouth."

Courtney responded, "I will have the same thing, Ben Beckmire. I only like them when you make them. Thanks, Babe!"

Most of the group had a drink or two but in John Lee and Jilkes case, they each had three Jack Daniels straight up. Two hours out from Idaho Falls, the occupants of all three planes, save the pilots, were fast asleep and snoring. The flights were uneventful, the way most people like their flights to be. Jilkes kept trying to wake John Lee up because his snoring was creating havoc among the rest of the passengers. It was loud, throaty and obnoxious.

Jilkes finally grabbed John Lee's nose believing that was the only way to wake him up. John Lee asked, "What you go and do that for. You be snoring all this time and you wake me up?"

Jilkes mumbled, "Go back to sleep, man. I don't think anyone else is going to sleep while you are sleeping. You really snore louder than I remember. Go back to sleep."

## CHAPTER THIRTEEN

Asiram pulled out her cell phone and placed a call. It was to her caretaker, Clyde. She told him that she was flying in and needed vehicles to pick up about thirty people. The caretaker asked her when she would be landing, and Asiram told him in about two hours. He assured her that all would be taken care of.

Later, as the planes began to descend, Beckmire asked Asiram and Zanthius to meet him in the back of the plane. As the three huddled, Beckmire asked, "Do we need to be on alert here?"

Asiram responded, "I doubt it, but once the planes are in the hangars, we all shouldn't be without a sidearm."

As the planes touched down in ten-minute intervals, Asiram looked around to see where their rides were. As each plane pulled into the massive hangar, Asiram suggested to Beckmire that they should retrieve weapons prior to their rides arriving. Beckmire looked at Mallory and held up two fingers. Mallory in turn, held up two fingers and they each walked over to the bay of the plane carrying the cargo. Each man took a pistol and an extra clip and walked away, as if everything was cool. Mallory picked up an additional pistol and clip and handed it to the Sarge. When the Sarge saw Larry, he told him to grab a clip and weapon.

A school bus entered through the gate. It was Clyde and one of his sons. Asiram walked over to him and declared, "Clyde, it has been a long time! Is everything okay at the ranch?"

"Oh yes, Ma'am. The Missus is there getting things ready for you and fixing a bite to eat, for you and your guests."

"Clyde, you know how I like my privacy. Is that going to be a problem?"

"No, Ma'am. As a matter of fact, people won't even know you're in town. We always keep a large supply of fresh food there just in case you decide to drop in. The main house and guest house are warm and can accommodate all of your friends. My other children are making sure that everything is ready for you. Shall I get the bags?"

"That's okay, Asiram replied. We have enough strong men to handle that chore."

One hour and ten minutes later, Clyde turned the school bus onto a road. It took another thirty minutes before the house was in view. Asiram looked at Beckmire and said, "No more exploding homes. Promise me this." Beckmire made the sign of the Cross and acknowledged her request.

As the bus continued down the road, Clyde said, "Ah, Miss Asiram, we had some weather a few weeks ago and there are a few potholes. I will attend to them in the morning but other than that everything is working perfectly."

She thanked him and then lowered her voice and whispered, "You have taken care of my place for a long time. Is it a bother for you and your family?"

"Oh no, Ms. Asiram. Your place is a Godsend for us. Your payment each month allows me to send two of mine to college and helps us through hard times out here. I hope you are not going to sell it, and if so, please recommend us to the new buyer."

"I am never going to sell it, Clyde. I just don't want you and your family to be burdened with the responsibility of making sure that the place doesn't fall to the ground."

"Ms. Asiram, right now, this is all we have. Farming has been difficult this year with the drought and then freezing temperatures. The whole town is suffering, and a lot of people are having to give up their properties to some New York type crooks who offered low interest loans. When you don't pay on time, they put you out of your house and they take over. We have two such families living with us right now."

"Really? I have just the people with me who can take care of that problem and get those people back into their homes. I have some very important and rich friends with me, and they hate carpetbaggers. Tell your son, he is not to discuss my being in town with anyone. Once we get some rest and a chance to unwind, I will call you. Then you can bring those people to my house, let us talk to them and we will figure out how to help them get their farms back."

"My son is a smart man and ex-military. He never talks out of turn, if you know what I mean. We are so proud of him. He wants to take on those people, but they would just slaughter him."

"Clyde, this is your lucky day. I have the smartest people on earth with me and if you piss them off, they can be very, very bad for the appetite. Okay, we are going to take this problem on. Just don't say anything to anyone until we have had time to get some much needed rest and regain our wits about us. Can I count on you to keep people away from my property?"

"I guess you didn't see the signs I put up on all four corners of your property—Enter this property and you will be shot and never heard from again. No second chances. First view—first shot!"

"Wow. That seems a little draconian, doesn't it?"

"You pay me to watch and take care of your place. Anyone entering your perimeter is fair game. Suppose you were here by yourself and some nutcase came a-calling and he, God forbid, tried to hurt you? What good am I to you if I can't protect you? I give warnings first and then I shoot. That is the way it is out here. We protect our own and our neighbors, even if they don't come home but once every two years."

Asiram kissed her fingers and placed them on Clyde's cheek. She said, "We will make this right for your friends. You just can't get their hopes up until we have an opportunity to examine what they signed and how legal it is. Remember, there are two kinds of law—the written law, and the law of the land. I am inclined to uphold the law of the land when it is fair and straightforward. That legal mumbo-jumbo never sat too well with me and my kind. We fight for a different kind of people and those people are the everyday people. We will work on this. I will talk to my fiancée tonight and tell him about it. He is going to want to help them. I can assure you that, or he is not the man I should consider marrying. Thanks, Clyde. Remember tell your son, mums the word."

Zanthius asked, "Is everything okay?"

Asiram responded, "With us, yes, but with the people who live here, no. Carpetbaggers are preying on them and taking their farms. This has been a rough season for them and when they don't pay their mortgages on time, they are evicted."

"That's terrible."

"It is worse than terrible. Clyde has two families living with him and his wife, who have lost their property. I am going to do something about this. Will you help me? I need you to support me on this one."

Zanthius looked at her and saw the hurt in her eyes and responded, "When we all get some rest, I will ask my father and Mallory to give us their opinions in this matter. Even if they disagree, which I highly doubt, I will work through this with you. We are family and we have to do what is necessary to help our own and the world at large. I don't want to give my dad another chore on my behalf until he has at least had a full night's rest. I am with you, if it's that important to you. I am not doing this because you have saved my ass 123 times. I am doing this because I love you." As Asiram began to cry, Zanthius kissed away her tears.

Zanthius said, "I'm going to talk to my father now."

"No, let him enjoy his wife and rest for a while. Tomorrow is fine. I just feel so bad that we are all living so well and those people from New York come out here and take advantage of struggling people. It's not fair. Those bastards are going to make me come out of retirement."

"Now, sweetheart. It may not get to that, so let's not start planning mutilations until we know all of the facts."

She laughed and said, "You are truly the smartest 'idiot spy' that the world has ever known. I love you, Zanthius De Lombardo."

Clyde pulled into the turnaround in front of the massive ranch house. He stood up and said, "Welcome home, Ms. Asiram and guests." The weary travelers disembarked from the bus and when they entered the house, the smell of delicious food was in the air. Clyde's wife, Gilda, and her daughters prepared a boatload of food for the travelers. Everyone went in, made small talk and introductions and then went straight for the table that was laden with food. Beckmire and Mallory asked Asiram if they could have a look around and she replied, "I will accompany you."

Zanthius said, "You two old lechers aren't going anywhere with my wife to be without me." They walked outside and it was pitch dark. Asiram said, "In the guest house, there are six bedrooms upstairs with double and triple accommodations, and each one has its own bath. Downstairs are two more bedrooms and in the basement two additional bedrooms. In this house, there are four bedrooms upstairs on the east side and four on the west side. In the center, there is one massive bedroom and that is off limits to everyone except my fiancée. Is that clear?" Everyone laughed.

"In the basement there is a tunnel that leads from the main house to the guest house. I think no one knows about this, not even Clyde. There is an intricate set of codes to access the panels and I will have to look in the safe to see what those codes are and give them to you guys."

Beckmire inquired, "Speaking of safes, who is in control of the money?"

Asiram answered, "I delegated that task to Courtney and Ava."

Beckmire asked Mallory, "So, what do you think? Do we need coverage tonight?"

Mallory looked around and replied, "If we need coverage for the next five days, I would be surprised."

Asiram said, "Clyde has posted some extremely ominous signs around the property and he and the neighbors are always watching this place. As a matter of fact, Clyde installed surveillance equipment all over the place that alerts him when anything is approaching the property, including big bears."

Beckmire walked back into the house and asked Courtney and Ava if he could have a word with them. As they stepped into a well-stocked library, he asked, "Ladies, where is the money that you were put in charge of?"

Courtney answered, "Ava spent it."

They all laughed, and Ava said, "We delegated it to Carlos. By the way, where is Carlos?"

Beckmire responded, "I haven't seen him and don't remember him getting on the bus."

Suddenly everyone panicked and went into the anteroom. They asked if anyone had seen Carlos. At that moment, Carlos came in from outside and replied, "I have been watching the bags that I was given, plus, I don't do so well on airplanes, especially small ones. Sorry, Ms. Asiram, I left a huge puddle out there, but I didn't let the bags out of my sight."

Ava went to him, kissed him on his lips and in front of everyone said, "Don't be surprised that I did that. That damn horse told everyone that we are lovers." The place went into stitches.

Zanthius walked up to Clyde and said, "My name is Zanthius De Lombardo and I need a preacher to marry me and Asiram."

"Well, hell boy, I'm the local preacher as well as the school bus driver. When do you want to do this?"

"Don't move. Let me find Asiram and see if she will have me."

In the meantime, Asiram had ventured upstairs to draw her bath. When Zanthius walked in, she was crying. He asked her, "Did I do or say something wrong, again?"

Asiram just cried harder and louder. She said, "I have the world by the balls and these people who have nothing, wait on us hand and foot. They forfeited their properties to a bunch of carpetbaggers from back east. I am sick of people treating people poorly. I think of how my own family treated me like I was a piece of dirt." Zanthius started to approach her and she mumbled, "I don't need any fancy words Zanthius. You know I'm not pregnant and, therefore, I don't think we should continue this ruse about you loving me and me loving you."

"Wait one damn minute." Zanthius said before he went to the landing that oversees the first floor and yelled, "Clyde! Clyde, I need you up here right now."

Clyde walked to the base of the spiral steps and Zanthius shouted down to him, "Come up here, now!" Beckmire started up the steps. Zanthius exclaimed, "Pops, give me a private moment, please!"

Ava yelled, "What's going on?"

Zanthius answered, "Mom, give me a moment, please." Clyde reached the top landing and Zanthius said, "Come in here for a minute." The two walked into the massive bedroom and saw Asiram crying her eyes out.

Zanthius demanded, "Clyde, tell her what I asked you downstairs."

Asiram inquired, "What does that have to do with anything?"

Zanthius replied, "Sweetheart, calm down. You are speaking to the school bus driver and the local minister. I asked him if he could find a preacher to marry us and he told me that he was the local minister."

Between sniffles, Asiram asked Clyde, "Is that true?"

"I work for you and if he be a charlatan, I wouldn't have told him that I was the local minister. What the young fella says is accurate. He asked me to find a preacher to marry him. I have never married a man to himself, so I kind of thought that it was you he wanted to marry. Do you want to marry him? Now, that's my question."

Asiram exclaimed, "Oh, yes. Oh my God, yes. I want to be his wife."

Zanthius said, "As my wife, the only thing that I want you to do is trust me! Not obey me, worship me, or be an indentured slave. I just want you to trust me and any decision that I might make. That is all I ask."

Asiram declared, "I love you and I will do whatever you ask me to do."

From the landing, Zanthius yelled, "People, there is going to be a wedding in this very house in a few days. Asiram has agreed to marry me and Clyde the local preacher and school bus driver has agreed to perform the ceremony."

Cheers, claps and laughter were all about the house. Jong walked in from assigning rooms and doing his due diligence and asked, "Did I miss something? Did that damn horse plan a wedding or something?" The house really erupted after hearing his comments.

Beckmire yelled, "Is there any whiskey in this place or are we in Mormon territory?"

Asiram asked, "Gilda, will you show our guest to the bar?"

#

The night was full of romance. Those who were in love, made love. There were a few days of peace, reflection, and love in the air. Mallory called Monica and said, "We are now in Wyoming and I would love for you to come here and be with me."

She replied, "Where in Wyoming and what on earth are you doing there?"

"We had to abandon the other location. It was compromised and unsafe."

Monica asked, "Is it dangerous there? I mean are you safe and will I be safe?"

Mallory inquired, "How safe are you anywhere today, honey? There is danger on every corner of this earth. Think about it and let me know. I will send a plane for you, if you like. Love you and hope to see you soon."

#

In the guest house, John Lee asked Jilkes, "Are you going to have that wife of yours come out here?"

"Naw. I got you to keep me warm and safe," Jilkes replied, laughing.

"I always knew you liked men and boys. Freak, that's what I be calling your ass from now forth."

## CHAPTER FOURTEEN

Two days later and a day prior to the wedding, everyone was well rested. The guys were out in the field doing a slow two-mile run.

Later, Beckmire and Mallory asked Clyde if he would give them a ride around the property. Clyde responded, "I will have to get permission from Ms. Asiram."

Clyde went into the house and whispered to Asiram that two of her guests wanted him to ride them around the property. "I just want to know if it's okay with you?"

Asiram asked Clyde to accompany her. They walked out where Beckmire and Mallory were standing. She stated so that all could hear, "This guy, our leader, is going to be my father-in-law in a matter of a day. This is his best friend, Mr. Mallory. If any of my guests request a favor from you, please attend to it immediately. I would appreciate it if everyone treated my guests as family. Okay?"

Clyde responded, "Yes Ma'am. You know me, I don't like to assume anything."

Asiram exclaimed, "Oh, Clyde, this may be a good opportunity for you to tell Mr. Beckmire and Mr. Mallory about the problem that some of the farmers are having in this area."

"Excellent idea," Clyde replied.

As the trio headed out into what seemed like a never ending field, Beckmire said, "Clyde, Asiram isn't sure how much land she owns out here. She said three to four thousand acres."

Clyde said, "She really never concerned herself with the size of the place. She has exactly 6,500 acres of prime land. She sells some of the crops that pay for the upkeep of the house and the farm. She usually gives a ton of goods to the local charity. People don't know her and wouldn't recognize her from anybody else, but they sure are happy that she lends a helping hand.

"Speaking of a helping hand, I mentioned to her that I have two families living in my house who have lost their farms to unscrupulous carpetbaggers from New York. She said that you guys are good at making things right and that she would talk to you after you had a chance to rest up and all. I guess I'm doing the talking for her. If it's okay with you, once we get to the access road, we'll just jump across it. Then you can hear it from the horse's mouth what happened."

Beckmire asked, "Are you telling me that damn horse has a cousin out here?"

"Not sure what you mean by that."

"It's an inside joke." Beckmire answered. "We would be glad to talk to the people about what's going on here."

Two hours later, Clyde took Beckmire and Mallory back to Asiram's place where they called for a huddle with their guys, Asiram and Zanthius. Beckmire explained what was going on in middle America and that he didn't like it one damn bit. Sarge gave them a blow-by-blow description of how people were being duped out of their homes and wrenched of their savings by a bunch of New York crooks, who used a damn law book to cheat people. Beckmire told them he believed that they had an obligation to help people where and when they could, based upon the tenets of the charter of their nonprofit.

Surprisingly, John Lee asked, "How many fronts can we do battle? I mean, these here guys ain't gonna give back the money or the property. To me that means, we have to whup their asses and buy them out. I ain't saying I be scared, or nothing likes that, I just want to get home one day to my pigs, sheep and that woman of mine." Brown and Bernstein seconded the motion, as did Montomie and Chakes.

Jilkes said, "Seems like we are all a little bit tired. I suggest we investigate, and then decide. I'm with the Sarge and Mallory. Should we just walk away from this controversy, especially when people lives are so severely impacted?"

Brown said, "Since we're here, I recommend we give it our attention, but we must stay focused on the matter at hand. We need a lawyer first of all, who understands this shit."

Mallory said, "I think Monica is coming out tomorrow. That will be a good job for her. If anyone can smell a rat, it is definitely her."

Jong joked, "I guess she missed the smell of a big rat."

Everyone broke into laughter. Once he regained order, Beckmire asked, "Okay, by a show of hands, who wants to abort this mission and focus on getting the hell out of here?" No hands were raised. Beckmire said, "I think we will be doing a good thing if we handle this, as well as, make permanent changes to the actions of those carpetbaggers."

John Lee asked, "Who would call themselves a carpetbagger? Is that a new name for stealing or something?"

Back in the house, Gilda and the other women who lost their ranches, were decorating the house for the impending wedding of Zanthius and Asiram. Courtney asked one of the women, "Where do you live?" The woman looked at her and began to cry. "Did I say something wrong?"

Gilda replied, "She and her family are currently living with me and Clyde. They lost their ranch to those New York types, not only her, but the other lady as well. We have two families living with us who were swindled out of their properties and savings."

Courtney stressed to Ava, "We have got to find a way to help these people."

Ava said, "Let's have a talk with Asiram."

# # #

Asiram gave them the skinny on the situation and the ladies were angry about what they heard. Ava inquired, "Does Zanthius know about this?"

Asiram replied, "I told him about it."

"And he didn't ask how we could help?"

"No, he was supposed to talk with his father about it."

Courtney said, "We need to have a talk with those two. Where are they?"

Asiram answered, "I'm sure they are trying to figure out the other thing that has us all living like vagrants."

Courtney said, "Speaking of which, Gilda, where can we go shopping for staples and clothes around here?"

There's a Walmart thirty-five minutes away."

Ava said to Courtney, "Let's get the kids and go into town for the balance of the day. Carlos and my guys, along with Larry, can provide the 'you know what'."

Courtney whispered to Asiram, "We are going to need some cash."

"I don't know where they put it, but I have some in my safe. Come with me."

In her bedroom, behind a huge dresser, was a six foot stand up safe. Asiram opened it and Courtney uttered, "I wish I had that kind of petty cash hanging around. How much do you have in there?"

Asiram replied, "That's probably close to two."

Ava asked, "Two what, hundred thousand?"

Asiram replied, "No, silly, that's probably $2 million, if I'm not mistaken."

Courtney inquired, "Is that the money from the other place?"

"No, we have to find that and secure it in the basement safe. We can't have that kind of money hanging out in suitcases. Take what you want." Each woman picked a wrapped stack that was noted as $10 thousand.

As they went downstairs, Gilda was comforting one of the women who had lost her home. Asiram whispered to Courtney, "Get another stack of money and take them with you and buy them everything they don't need or want." When Beckmire walked into the house with Mallory and Clyde. Courtney said with a voice of consternation, "We have to talk, and I mean now!"

Mallory inquired, "Oh shit, what the hell did you do?"

Beckmire responded, "I walked into the damn house. I don't know."

Courtney and Ava jumped him and Courtney asked, "Do you know what is happening to these poor people out here with those New York land thieves?"

"Honey just hold on. Clyde just told me and Mallory all about it and the guys are ready to jump into action as soon as Monica arrives."

"Oh, when is she going to be here and why didn't you tell me she was coming?"

"I couldn't tell you because her husband just informed me."

Courtney commanded, "Come here big guy and give me a kiss. I should have known that you wouldn't let people just get walked on without having a word or two with those doing the walking. You are one of a kind, Ben Beckmire, and I love you so much."

Ava said, "Since that damn horse told everyone what we are up to, I want to announce that Carlos and I are an item."

Courtney said, "That's old news, Ava. We saw things developing in that restaurant in Virginia. Anything else?"

Beckmire said, "Since you guys are going into town, I think Mallory and I will accompany you along with the other people you have drafted. Clyde, can you come as well, and show me where the people of interest operate?"

"I absolutely can, Mr. Beckmire."

"Clyde, call me Ben or Sarge, okay?"

In town, the women had a field day buying pretty things and things that made no sense to anyone. At first, Gilda's two friends wouldn't take or accept anything. Ava walked over to the two women and said, "Listen, the rest of the team are working on that problem you have, and when they work on a problem, they usually find a solution. Now, we are here to shop, and shopping is what I expect you to do. Buy whatever the hell you want, or we will pick out things for you. You don't have a choice. This is not charity, this is friendship. You ladies prepared food for us, helped decorate the house for the wedding and we all came here to relieve some stress. What better way to do that than to shop? Now, get a cart and start picking things up for your menfolk, your children, the house, and mostly for yourselves. Remember, we are working on an open budget so take advantage of this moment. When our men meet your men, you can rest assure, this is what they are going to be doing—shopping a little but drinking more."

While the women continued making the merchants across town happy, Clyde introduced Mallory and Beckmire to his neighbors and friends. They stopped in an old store that still sold the original sarsaparilla soda. It was a fun day without any problems until they went to the local barbershop. There they saw a confrontation of sorts. The local police officer stood by watching as a big guy told a farmer his timetable for payment was up and forfeiture would be implemented. Clyde motioned to Beckmire and Mallory and said, "Looks like another one of our neighbors got caught up with these bandits. When they first came here, they had town meetings and offered food and drink and showed us how to get loans and how to structure payback. Most of the people here are simple farmers--not real smart about interest, principle, accumulated late payments costs or any of the new-fangled ways to steal people's property."

Mallory asked Clyde, "Have you personally done business with them?"

Clyde replied, "Thanks to Ms. Asiram and her farm, I haven't had a need to do business with them."

Beckmire interrupted and asked, "What is your property worth, if I may be so bold to ask?"

Clyde replied, "It depends on the weather forecast, the production and the selling price of our goods. I have 1500 acres, and if I went to the bank, they would probably offer to lend me up to $150,000 depending on my credit. Now, those New York bandits offered a rate of 2.5%, which was 2.5% lower than the average loan of 5% from the banks."

Mallory said, "So, the local bank rate is 5% if you have good credit which no one has, and the New York types rate was 2.5%. And 2.5% over a period of time is a substantial savings. Smart, but not too smart, based upon the properties placed in receivership to date. We have to figure out their scheme."

Mallory looked at Clyde and asked, "If we asked you to borrow some money against your land so that we can figure these guys out, would you help us? Now, I know exactly what you're thinking, but before you answer that question, we would place the amount borrowed in a bank in your name. Say I ask you to borrow $100,000 from them, we would put, say, $125,000 in your bank account to make sure you feel safe and to demonstrate we aren't thieves, as well. Would you at least ask Ms. Asiram about it and discuss it with your wife? You will always have access to the amount you borrow plus some cushion money. Just think about it. My wife, the lawyer, will be here later. She can help work through the details. Just think about it and speak to your wife. If you like, we will give you the money in cash, but we prefer to place it in a bank account in your name in the adjoining town. Think about it."

Mallory looked at Beckmire and asked, "Do you agree, Sarge?"

Beckmire answered, "It's a great idea, but I hate to ask Clyde, who just met us two days ago, to play along with us. Clyde, do you trust Ms. Asiram?"

"With my life," Clyde answered immediately.

Beckmire responded, "Okay, when we get back. We will ask her for an opinion. We want to do this in a hurry because we have other really pressing business that we have to attend to. We may ask you to help us with it, from afar, of course. Do you know that fella that they were manhandling?"

Clyde replied, "I do."

Mallory inquired, "Will you follow him and ask him to come out to your place and have a talk with some friends of yours. Advise him to bring his loan papers as well. Tell him we can help him, and if necessary, make the payment for him. We just need to know how he got hooked and what happened to make them react so violently to the situation."

Beckmire asked Clyde, "Where is their office located?" Clyde pointed up the road and said, "That used to be a church, believe it or not."

Beckmire said, "You two go on and talk to that fella. I'm just going to go and make eye contact with those guys and check out their digs."

Mallory muttered, "Sarge, we don't operate alone."

The Sarge remarked, "I am never alone and besides, you didn't notice Larry wandering around over there, did you?"

Mallory looked and answered, "He's good. I never saw him. Anyway, I won't be far away. Clyde, you go and discreetly talk to your friend. We'll meet back at the Walmart in ten minutes or so. Just try to calm him down and ask him to come and see us."

Beckmire strolled by the barbershop and as he had thought, the big guy was the buffer for the two men sitting in chairs. He walked over to their building, examined it from the outside, and then walked back towards the barbershop. The same police officer said, "I don't think I know you, sir. Are you new to these parts?"

Beckmire looked at him, and then at the men inside of the barbershop and replied, "I guess you're right, because I don't know you either. Have a great day." He then stared hard at the men in the chairs until the policeman asked, "Do you have ID?"

Beckmire responded, "I thought I was in the United States of America and that I could walk anywhere in public and not be approached for identification. This isn't a part of the old South Africa, is it?"

The officer answered sarcastically, "I have reason to suspect that you are a vagrant. Therefore, I can ask you for ID."

Beckmire warned, "Please be careful about your next move. I am represented by a great law firm, and we make a lot of money off public officials who violate my civil liberties. Have a nice day." As he turned to walk away, he gave a final look at the people in the barbershop.

The guy in the chair, who apparently was calling the shots, asked, "Who the hell is that?"

The officer replied, "I don't know but I'm going to find out. He might have come in on one of those three private jets that landed at the airport the other night. I think two of them developed some kind of mechanical problems but one of them left early this morning."

The guy who appeared to be the boss, advised, "Watch him, and let us know if he's a troublemaker. We only need to bankrupt two other farmers, and then we can proceed with our plan."

The cop said, "Gotcha, I'm on it."

As the group gathered at the Walmart and started loading bag after bag onto the school bus, the cop rode up and yelled, "Hey, Clyde, who are your newfound friends?"

Clyde replied, "I don't have any newfound friends. I just have friends. The new people in town are from that farm with that mysterious woman who never shows up."

"Is she here?" The cop asked.

"If she were, I wouldn't be in a position to tell you because I have never met her."

"Okay, Clyde, but that guy in the black jacket looks like he has a problem. Tell him that we don't have problems around here."

"The cop's implied threat annoyed Clyde who said, "You want to tell him yourself? He's on the bus."

"By the way, are you using the bus for other than school business?"

"Well, yes. These people donated $2,000 per day to the school to use the bus for transportation. Perhaps we should thank them for coming into our town rather than acting hostile about them being here."

"One more question, Clyde. Did these folks happen to come into town on those fancy planes at the airport?"

"I'm not sure, but I believe they have bigger planes than the ones that landed the other day."

As the bus pulled off, Beckmire made his way to the front and said to Clyde, "Nicely done. However, my intent was to get arrested and let them flash my photo over their network to see if I am a wanted man or not. I have my reasons, but you handled that extremely well, and I thank you. Those guys are crooks. Is your friend going to come over later?"

"He went home to get his paperwork and is probably heading for my place right about now."

Beckmire said, "Okay, drop us off at Asiram's place and then bring your friend over for a powwow with me and the boys. After we have a talk with him, I am going to show you some photos so that you will know exactly who we are. Say no more, just wait until you see. Once you see the photos, your decision will definitely be made about the question I asked you earlier. Just wait."

## CHAPTER FIFTEEN

Back at the house, Beckmire acknowledged, "I haven't seen my son all day. Where is he?"

Asiram yelled, "I have him locked in the safe. He has a tank of air so; he should be alright."

"Yeah, right. Beckmire laughed, "Where is he?"

"He went for a run."

Beckmire asked, "Who went with him?"

Asiram exclaimed, "Oh shit. I'm not sure if anyone went with him." She ran down the steps with a pistol in her hand and said, "Come on, Sarge. We have to make it to the shed and get those ATVs that I have."

Beckmire grabbed his weapon and followed Asiram. She ran faster than he could, but he managed to keep a respectful distance behind her. As they ran towards the shed, they could see what appeared to be Zanthius running down the road at full speed. Asiram, with her young eyes, could see that he was being chased by wolves. She hopped in an ATV, sped out of the shed and started firing in the direction of Zanthius. Beckmire finally got his ATV started and raced behind her. He too, began to shoot towards the converging herd of wolves.

The wolves had circled Zanthius and placed him in a capture and kill regimen. He was running his ass off trying to get away from them. As Asiram got closer, she stopped her ATV, fell onto one knee and began to pick the wolves off, one by one. Beckmire while still driving his ATV, began to shoot. He hit near them but didn't actually hit any. He finally realized that timing was everything and began to hit the wolves as well. Beckmire continued towards his son as the few still remaining wolves started backing down and turning away. When Beckmire reached Zanthius, he grabbed him and yelled, "Don't take a shit, without someone knowing where the hell you are and what you're doing! Is that clear?"

Zanthius hugged him and shouted, "Pops, I outran those suckers!"

Everyone near the ranch heard the gunfire. Clyde realized that someone was in danger. He grabbed his long gun and a clip, entered his truck, turned it on and headed towards the farm. When he arrived at the ranch, he saw people at a distance and drove towards them with the pedal to the medal. When he arrived at the scene, he exclaimed, "Oh my! I forgot to tell the city types that we have bears and wolves out here. I'm so sorry." Clyde saw that two of the animals were not quite dead yet but were in agony. He scoped them and finished them off.

Zanthius asked, "What about their bodies?"

Clyde answered, "Mother Nature takes care of her own. They will be food for other animals."

Asiram quietly waited for her moment and when it arrived, she asked, "Zanthius, or shall I call you the 'idiot spy'? I beg of you, please let me know what you are doing so that I don't have to worry about you. We can afford you the protection you need. We are supposed to get married tomorrow. Can you imagine the pain I would have caused those animals had they hurt you? Every animal rights group would be out here picketing my place."

As he walked into the house, Ava said, "I know I taught you better than that. You know better than to go jogging in a strange place without knowing who or what is out there. Love you, Son, but be smarter. Next time at least carry a weapon with you."

As everyone settled down, Clyde told Mallory that he had his friend at the house and would like to bring him over and have that discussion. Mallory asked him to hold fast until his wife got there so he wouldn't have to repeat himself. Clyde agreed and told Mallory that he would see him later. Clyde also asked Mallory if he wanted him to fetch her at the airport. Mallory told him no because he wanted to have the pleasure of personally picking her up.

As if Clyde and Mallory had talked her up, Monica called and said the plane would land in about an hour. Mallory told her that he would be there waiting with open arms. Mallory then asked Asiram if he could borrow one of her trucks so that he could pick up his wife. She told him that the keys to all of the vehicles were in the ignitions. Mallory informed Beckmire, "Monica is landing in an hour or so and I am going to pick her up."

Beckmire uttered, "Cool, but take one of the guys with you and always carry a piece."

Mallory quipped, "This is like old times, but a little less stressful. This time the enemy is telegraphing their moves. Not that I have a problem with that, but there has to be some smarter mercs out there somewhere."

Beckmire responded, "I prefer them dumb. That way our survival isn't compromised too easily."

#

Later when Monica and Mallory arrived at the ranch, everyone was introduced to her. She knew the guys, Larry and the rest of the crew but wondered about Asiram, Zanthius, Ava and Carlos. Beckmire hugged and kissed Monica and told her that it had been a long time. He then directed her attention to Asiram, Zanthius, Ava and Carlos.

After carefully considering what words to use to describe Ava, he said, "This is Ava, the mother of my son that I didn't know I had. Monica, meet Ava De Lombardo and this good-looking guy is my son, Zanthius De Lombardo and the stunning lady to his left is his fiancée, Asiram Lenovax and that guy is Carlos, an associate of Ms. De Lombardo. As a matter of fact, we're going to have a wedding here tomorrow."

Monica spoke briefly to each person and then said, "Courtney, girl, get your butt over here and give me some loving."

The two women hugged and kissed for the better part of a minute, concluding with Courtney saying, "Girl, they have really gotten us into some crazy stuff this time."

Beckmire interjected, "Honey, let Mallory bring her up to date. It might be in his best interest, if you know what I mean."

Mallory then said, "Sweetheart, I want you to meet Clyde and his wife Gilda. They are Asiram's neighbors and they keep an eye on her place when she is off extracting information."

Monica said, "I am impressed. This is some spread you have here. How many acres is this?"

Asiram looked at Clyde and he answered, "Precisely 6,500 acres."

Monica said, "Boy, I can't wait to see the whole place. Fabulous house as well. What do you do for a living, Asiram?"

Beckmire stepped in and said, "She is what some call an extractor. Like an up in your face judge who forces you to give the facts and nothing but the facts—Ma'am."

Mallory told Monica that he needed her to help sort out some property matters concerning ranch owners who may have been swindled out of their property. She indicated that she knew he needed her for more than her beauty, and he agreed.

Monica and Mallory went to Clyde's place with Jong tagging along. At Clyde's, she was told the story of certain people losing their ranches to a firm from New York. Mallory requested Gus, the person they had witnessed having a heated discussion in town, show his wife the agreement that he had signed. Monica asked Gus, "Will you trust me with this document until the morning? I want to have time to thoroughly examine it and figure out who has the right-of-way in this situation. Most of the time, unscrupulous people draw up documents for their sole benefit, leaving the signer little or no discretion to deviate from the agreement. If you signed a bad deal, then in a court of law that deal stands, and you have no recourse. However, my husband and his friends have a way of using the law of the land against unscrupulous people and they usually win. I hope that will not be necessary because they are spread very thin as it is, and I need him at home with me. Just give me until the morning and we will figure out a complete strategy, subject to your approval. By the way, do the rest of you have a copy of the documents that you signed?"

Jason and Walthro, two of the swindled towns' people, replied that they did not. Monica asked, "What happened to your copies?"

Jason responded, "I had a small suspicious fire in the house after I took them home. All of my papers were lost."

Walthro said, "My copy was burned when my truck was torched after leaving the loan office."

Monica said, "How convenient. Okay, let me use the copy that Gus is entrusting me with as a prototype. I will attend to it after I attend to my husband and he attends to me."

As they were walking out of the door, Gus said, "I didn't understand a damn word she said, but I trust her and him. I also trust them other foreigners that are staying over there. They seem like people who care about people and are not about stealing anything from us."

Clyde said, "They are friends of Ms. Asiram and she doesn't like double-dealing people."

Back at Asiram's guest house, Monica said, "I really need to know what has happened and why you guys are hiding out in the middle of nowhere? Have a lot of people died? What is this all about?"

Mallory spent ten minutes telling her how things began. How Beckmire was once in love with Ava and how she abandoned him once she knew she was pregnant. He told her people tried to kill them in a restaurant in Philly, and how since that time, they had probably killed over 150 people who were trying to kill them. He explained the source of the problem— The Carbon Factor and its impact on the balance of power and how many mercenaries had attempted to find the product but only Zanthius knows where it is.

Monica began to cry and asked, "Is this like that Mob thing all over again?"

Mallory hugged her and replied, "My love, no, this is worse. We have people from foreign governments, local governments, billionaires, unsanctioned warlords, and others trying to obtain the information that was passed to Zanthius by way of a simple kiss. We have the heads of the most important governmental agencies, who are part of a secret society, trying to gain access to it so that they can be enriched with unfathomable amounts of money. The product allegedly has the capacity to make what was dropped on Japan look like a firecracker explosion. More importantly, it has been said that it can be packaged in a half gallon milk carton."

Monica said, "I know you love the Sarge and so do I. I want you to help end this thing and come home to me. I have missed you terribly and I cry myself to sleep each night thinking that this is a ruse so that you can spend time with someone younger and more attractive than I am."

Mallory grabbed her and said, "I only love you and these guys. I married you after a sizeable amount of turmoil in your life and I am as in love with you today as I was when I first laid eyes on you. Don't you ever think that you can be replaced! If something happened to you, I would probably shoot myself in the head because I would not be able to exist without you and the love that you give me. I love you more than life." The two kissed and kissed and then the lovemaking began. It was thunderous and fulfilling.

After enjoying a long overdue monumental experience, Monica sat up in the bed and began to study the documents that Gus, the local who had the altercation with the lenders, had given her. At first glance, she concluded that the documents were authentic but wondered why the others had lost theirs under such mysterious circumstances.

She woke Mallory up and said, "Honey, the increase in the interest rate after missing a payment is beyond comprehension. Say that I missed or was late a single day on making a payment, the lender has the right to increase the rate from the agreed upon and stated amount, to that of prevailing rates of local banks. That means that the rate increases from 2.5% to 5% if you are late in making a payment for a single day.

"They claim that this is necessary because they are competing with local establishments, but the introductory rate lasts the length of the loan only if all payments are made on time. After a single day of being late, in addition to forfeiting the rate of 2.5%, you also must pay a $150 late fee for each day that the loan is not current. It also says that if the payment date falls on a Friday and payment has not been received, the late fee is in force because it applies to all holidays and weekends. They justify this by stating that, although the borrower has the right to not borrow money, the lenders have a right to protect themselves and their investment at all costs."

A groggy Mallory asked, "Honey, can you say that in English? I never took Spanish in school."

Monica explained, "These guys have the law on their side, but it is obvious that only a desperate person would enter into this kind of arrangement. The other thing that they know they have on their side is that, if you borrow from them, that means you don't have the resources to counter them in a court of law. You need a lawyer, have to pay court costs, and they can drag out a case for so long that it could bankrupt you totally. This is smartly done, but not impenetrable. If we agree to take this on from a legal perspective, we can show them they just screwed with the wrong local people who have friends in high and low places. I mean, I do what I do best, things within the framework of the legal system. You and your friends do what you do best and operate with your own law books."

Mallory asked, "Why can't we join forces on this one?"

Monica answered, "Oh, honey, I want to join forces with you, but it ain't about no damn stolen ranches, it's about me missing my man and needing to feel all of his brute strength upon and within me." And the clouds once again broke loose with thunderous clapping and sparks flying.

When Mallory and Monica finally walked into the main house, they were greeted by a meal that was prepared by Clyde and Gilda, assisted by Jason, Sarah, Walthro and Mary, the families that were staying in Clyde's house. Beckmire said, "Thanks to you two, everyone else wants to have their wives, girlfriends and lovers picked up. Thanks, Corporal, I knew I could count on you to start some stuff."

Mallory laughed and said, "I need to speak to you." He and Beckmire walked towards the fireplace and Beckmire said, "Listen, I know what you are about to say. Monica wants you to go home and I understand that. I really understand that."

Mallory looked at him and retorted, "No disrespect intended, Abo, you don't know shit. She wants to take on those land grabbers and I want to buy back their farms for them."

Beckmire grabbed him and said, "I love you. Do you want to kiss me?"

Mallory replied, "I just want to tell these people that I want to get their ranches back, and if you guys want to back me, then I will feel like I'm truly an angel."

Beckmire called the guys over and announced, "Listen up, Mallory has a new charge and I support him 1000%. We want to buy back the ranchers' farms or take them back. Show of hands of those who need more information." No hands were raised.

Mallory beckoned Monica over and said, "Look at those people, waiting on us hand and foot. Let's give them an early Christmas present."

Monica remarked, "I know you will do what is right. You are the man and the man of my dreams. Let's call them over and you do your thing."

Mallory yelled, "May I have your attention, please? People, may I have your attention, please?" After the room quieted down, Mallory said, "By now, I hope most of you have met the love of my life, Monica. As you are aware, she just arrived here and true to form, she dove right into a problem that is happening out here with the ranchers. I just want to say, my love for this woman is beyond words.

"Gus, our entire group has decided to support you on this issue. That means that in the next twenty-four to forty-eight hours, we will have you in a situation that you will never have to worry about borrowing from scumbags ever again. Jason, Sarah, Walthro and Mary, we have agreed to also get your ranches back to you within the next twenty-four to forty-eight hours.

Mallory continued over the excited applause of Clyde and his friends, "Now, people, you don't know us, and we don't know you. When we do this thing for you, you will only have to agree to make sure that you extend a helping hand to other people that need help. In other words, pay it forward. We will help you, but you must be the kind of people who also want to help people help themselves. It can simply mean giving them refuge, like Clyde and Gilda gave to you guys. We want to create a society of people that help each other and not try to take, steal or swindle people out of their hard earned property."

From the back of the room, Jilkes yelled, "Here, here!"

John Lee exclaimed, "Yes and yes!"

Mallory said, "In conclusion, we are with you and we will take these people to the cleaners, have them rethink their business model, leave town and never practice again in these United States of America."

Later Mallory asked Clyde, "If I need you to do that thing we talked about, is there going to be a problem with you following through?"

Clyde retorted, "Hell, no! I'm ready to go there now and ask for a loan."

Mallory advised, "Now, that we have a copy of what Gus signed, you won't have to do that. I just needed to know if you were sincere about helping your people. In a few days we will be gone and like a ghost, appear to be, a figment of your imagination. But if we are ever needed again, you will know how to reach us."

Clyde said, "After the ranchers meet back at my place, I can assure you that we will work on a plan to secure and help our friends, their families, and any newcomers for that matter."

Mallory declared, "Then as long as we live, you will have our support. Now, this is critical to our success, I don't want your people anywhere around when we go to do business with that New York group. If it gets ugly, we know how to handle ugly. We work best alone and with our own. What I will need you to do, subject to the Beckmire's approval, is to monitor any newcomers in this area. Your people may have to keep a gun or two on them, and we may have some really bad people coming after us in a few days and we might need all of the support that we can get."

Clyde said, "Ah shit, when all you people got off of those fancy ass jets, I said to myself, they are either really bad people or good people being chased by bad people."

Mallory asked, "What's your conclusion?"

"Hell, I'm still here, ain't I?"

Mallory grabbed him and said, "Then you and yours are our eyes and ears on the local front. Now, Clyde, I'm talking about some really nasty people. The kind of people that if they want to shoot you without a reason, then they will. Not your everyday soccer mom type. I mean real bad mercenary types."

Clyde remarked, "I think the term back East is, 'we got your back'. Listen, you are taking on our problem. If someone comes within the confines of our world and attempts stupid, then it will take a long time to find out which animal ate the remains. I mean, if you fall down and can't get back up out there in the hinder land, then your ass be grass because Mother Nature will find some vermin to feed on you. Think about it. Between Ms. Asiram's place, my place, my brothers' and sisters-in-laws' place, there are about 12,000 acres of land to trespass on. My people are shooters first, and then they ask questions. We may be remote, but we are not backwards. We got your back without any questions, just help us eliminate that New York scum and get those families their land back."

Mallory called out to Sarge and announced, "I have given our word. Will you sanction it as our leader?"

Beckmire walked over and said, "Whatever he promised, we will deliver on and I sanction this event as a member and director of our founding board. Are we now an extended family?"

Clyde replied, "We got your back from here to there."

## CHAPTER SIXTEEN

Walter called Beckmire early in the morning and informed him that it was determined that the bodies in the farmhouse, from the earlier attack were those of men and women. The DNA samples taken and evaluated, matched known miscreants and others who had served time in prison. Walter further informed him, "Scottie, in the flesh, was there and was so annoyed, she shot one of the horses."

Beckmire asked, "Which one?"

Walter responded, "I never got the chance to meet that horse, but it wasn't the one called Rjah."

Beckmire said, "I will pass the word on to Asiram. I am sure she will want to avenge her horse's death when we meet up with Scottie. We will take care to make her suffer extremely long and painful."

Walter explained, "The other reason I'm calling, is that the wife of one of your guys was hanged by the neck. She was found dangling over the foyer in his house."

Beckmire asked, "What the hell are you talking about?"

"John Lee's woman was found with a rope around her neck and a note pinned on her saying, 'we will get all of you and yours--real soon'. I suggest that you people get out of dodge, asap. I have sent people to watch some of your

conjured and distorted truths 125

families, but a few of your people are hard to find. I will find
the mercs responsible and provide a dastardly end to their
miserable existence."

Beckmire quietly said, "Thanks, Walter. I'll get back to
you soon. Talk to you later."

#

After locating John Lee, Beckmire asked him to take a
walk with him.

John Lee said, "Not without my colored boyfriend."

"I guess he should be here, seeing how you two are so
close."

The three men began to walk when Beckmire announced,
"I have some bad news for you, John Lee."

"Sarge, what you be talking about?" he responded.

"Your woman was found in your house hanging by her
neck. There was a note stating, 'we will get all of you and
yours--real soon'."

John Lee paused for a few seconds, looked at the Sarge
and said, "Request for a short leave from duty, Sir?"

Jilkes quickly asked, "Request for a short leave from duty,
Sir?"

Beckmire responded, "Leave denied unless half of our
people go with you, including me. I will leave Mallory in
charge here. Get your shit and let's get prepared to leave. One
more thing, soldiers, we have a wedding in twenty minutes. I
would like to attend to that before we leave. Is that an
appropriate request?"

John Lee said, "Absolutely, Sir."

"Okay then, I have a bride to give away. You guys do what you need to do to prepare for an immediate departure. Have Mallory assign who will accompany us. Is that a roger?" Beckmire asked.

"Absolutely, Sir." His two best men said in unison.

# # #

Later, at the main ranch house, Asiram was decked out in her makeshift wedding gown. Beckmire ran upstairs to escort her down the stairs to be joined in holy matrimony with his son. At the bottom of the steps, Ava stood and watched her son move to a new phase of his life—marriage, once again.

Clyde's performance was spectacular. He began the ceremony by offering a prayer—for peace, hope, humanity, love, and the termination of those who would take advantage of others in the name of money.

Zanthius and Asiram gave their vows from their hearts, therefore, there was no need to write them down. Everyone was crying and wishing them a wonderful life together as husband and wife. It was a good day, albeit, caught between a lot of mayhem and murder, but totally a time for the other side of life—love!

After the ceremony, everyone participated in a toast to the newlyweds. Beckmire asked Courtney if he could speak with her. As he led her to the door, she said, "No, Sarge. No."

Beckmire looked at her and said, "What are you referring to?"

Courtney replied, "I know that look and I know when something is up. Don't lie to me. Where are we going?"

Beckmire responded, "John Lee's lady was murdered and found hanging in his house with a note pinned to her. I must do this for John Lee. These guys came from all over to protect us and it appears this is related. We're not going alone. We are going to take half of our men. Clyde and the community have taken us in and will provide peripheral scouting for us. We will be in and out, when we take care of this business. Walter will meet me there and we can discuss how to end this new threat. You know I have a commitment to these guys who have suffered because of their pledge to protect us. Don't worry, I'll be alright. Don't tell Asiram or Zanthius until we have left the area."

Mallory made the deployment and decided to send Brown, Bernstein, Chakes, and Montomie with John Lee, and of course, Jilkes, as well as, the Sarge. The Sarge asked Chakes if he would mind if he asked Montomie to stay to even up the numbers. Chakes looked at him and responded, "We follow your command, Sarge. We can survive being apart for a few days."

Chakes then looked at Montomie and said, "Keep a sharp eye out and watch, not only our brothers backs, but your own. See you soon." The Sarge told Mallory that the person named Scottie, shot one of Asiram's horses. He asked him not to tell her and that he would give her the news when he returned.

Exactly one hour later, they were on their way to the airport. The Sarge asked Jong to find cars far away from where the plane landed so that they would not be tracked. Jong gave Beckmire a fake ID and credit cards and told him not to use it like it was free money but to give it to the person that meets the plane. Jong explained, "The man who meets you at the plane, is a relative of mine and he will take care of you and yours needs, insofar as hardware is concerned."

At the airport, they boarded the largest jet and watched as John Lee tried to check his emotions by keeping his eyes fixed on the sky. Jilkes said, "I don't know what to say to you at a time like this other than, I know you know that everyone on this plane and back at the ranch loves you. I love you more than anyone because you are, and have been, a real brother to me ever since I kicked your ass in that fight."

John Lee looked at him stoically and muttered, "Your wet dreams be still prevailing, I see. Ask the guys who won that fight."

Jilkes looked at Bernstein and said, "When you got to bootcamp, you were scared as shit. Who won that fight between John Lee and me?"

Bernstein looked at both of them and replied, "I didn't see a loser and I didn't see a winner. What I saw was two guys coming together, after a misunderstanding, to save the lives of complete strangers."

John Lee declared, "Now, that's a bunch of horseshit, stated diplomatically, I must admit. Thanks, Bernstein. Now, that is what I remember also, us two coming together to find a way to stay alive. The rest is pure pigshit."

Hours later, the plane landed in Birmingham, Alabama, and the group was met by a distant relative of Jong's who asked Beckmire for a credit card. Beckmire gave him the card. The guy said, "Nice to meet you and your people. I have everything that you will need. I took the liberty to have a few of mine stake out John Lee's place from afar to see if anyone was hanging about."

Beckmire thanked him. He looked at the pilots and told them to get some rest because he didn't know when they would have to leave or how fast.

When the group drove onto John Lee's property, Bernstein asked, "Is all this land that I can't see, yours?"

John Lee responded, "I guess I own about three thousand acres of land out here. I used to rent it out until I found out what it means to help people, so now I give them three bedroom houses and let them plant and sell what they want, and they take care of the property. I don't do nothing but ride around in my tractor or truck and ask them if they be needing anything. I have about ten families running this place and they take good care of me. I am surprised that someone got onto the property without them knowing it."

From afar, a house could be seen. Brown exclaimed, "Holy shit! Is that your house up the road?"

John Lee replied, "Yeah. It looks small doesn't it?"

Brown answered, "Hell no, Old Country. This is like one of those plantations. Way to go my brother. Nice digs."

Beckmire asked the driver, "Do you have some hardware for us?"

The driver replied, "I do." He stopped the vehicle and each man got out and retrieved a weapon. He apologized for having only .40 caliber pistols but told them that he got what he could on short notice.

As they got near the house, lights illuminated the area from all directions. Directly in front of the vehicle, two men stood on both sides of the SUV holding large shotguns. John

Lee rolled down the window and declared, "I sure hope you people ain't going to shoot the owner of this here joint!"

"John Lee. John Lee, if that's you, get your big Old Country ass out of that there vehicle," Jasper said.

John Lee slowly exited the truck with his hands in the air and Jasper yelled, "Stand down, it's John Lee."

The lights went out and the guys walked up to him and said, "We be sorry about what happened here. We had no idea that people had slipped up in here and did what they did. You know we don't live like them others do. Hell, you know we don't even lock our damn doors. But from now on, any living soul that comes on this here property is going to be fed a lot of buckshot. It won't happen here again. We be so sorry. She was a good and kind woman and we all loved her and it was just damn dirty to cut her inners out and put them in your ice box."

The preacher knew what she wanted done with her body and that's exactly what we did. Yes Sir, we cremated her according to her wishes. We did get a picture of the woman who was leading the intruders. My son took it with that there iPhone you gave him last year."

John Lee asked, "Do you know how to forward it to me?"

The guy answered, "Hell no! I still got this here flipper phone."

John Lee announced, "We are probably not going to stay here tonight. Can you fetch him so that we can see who did this?" Jasper whistled and his son came out of the woods toting a pump action shotgun.

John Lee said, "Well, I'll be damned boy, you been eaten that McReynolds shit? Look how big you be. How old you be now?"

Carl, Jasper's son, replied, "I'm 16, as of yesterday."

John Lee said, "Well, I be damned. I have to send you a birthday gift. Wait, as a matter of fact, if your daddy allows it, I'll give you my old truck, the one you helped me fix after I crashed into that tree around the bend."

Jasper exclaimed, "That truck is one year old!"

John Lee retorted, "I already told you it was old." On the sidelines, Bernstein, Beckmire, Chakes, Jilkes and Brown were in stitches laughing at the exchange.

John Lee said, "I'm being rude here. These here are my best buddies in the entire world. This here guy is our boss, Sergeant Beckmire. That there guy is Bernstein, next to him is Brown and that guy is Chakes. The next guy is my brother from another mama, Mr. Jilkes, my best friend. Some of you have met him before. He's been here more than he be at home."

Beckmire was on point, and after giving Carl his phone number, he asked him to forward the picture of the female assassin, to him. As Carl was forwarding the picture to Beckmire, Jasper muttered, "Oh, and John Lee, I have more bad news. That there picture of that woman who Carl is forwarding to your friend, well, ah, well, she done shot your favorite pig." John Lee looked at Jasper and walked away.

He yelled back in a broken voice, "I hope you didn't eat my favorite pig."

Jasper said, "No, Sir. We didn't even consider it. We built him a box and we wrapped him in one of those silk sheets you have and that there heating blanket that he liked. We buried him in the front yard. Yes, Sir. That be where his ass be buried."

John Lee said, "Jasper, you be a real friend to me and mine. If you don't be seeing me for a while, you know how to reach me. No unnecessary calls, just the shit that matters. We be going through some crazy shit and we need to be careful. You people need to be careful, too."

Jasper reported, "That there redhead man, well, he is walking around town looking for that there woman who done hung your woman. He told me if he found her, he was going to shoot her in her box. I tried to pick him up earlier and you know what he said to me? He said, "That there John Lee been good to all of us out here. We have ten houses and families working together and we can't just let them there people come down here and hurt us. I'm not going to rest until I find that harlot and blow it from down there to the top of her head'."

John Lee commanded, "Fetch him and tell him that I got this. Me and my boys got this one but keep a sharp eye out and protect each other."

Once in the house, John Lee began to look around, went upstairs and saw where his woman was apparently pushed over the banister. He fell to one knee and began to cry. Beckmire started to approach him but Jilkes waved him off. John Lee mumbled, "No need to hurt her. She was a peaceful woman who just loved doing good by folks. No need to hurt her." He went into his bedroom and saw that it had been ransacked. He went directly to the bed, pulled on the right post and a safe appeared from behind a picture of his favorite pig. Jilkes said, "Well, I'll be damned, is that where you hide all of your money?"

John Lee replied, "I don't keep no money in the house. This here is where I keep some weapons of choice."

John Lee pulled out two bows and said, "Now, these are the real deal. I brought them back from the Nam and when I feels bad, I just shoot them into the next room. I want to take these backs, along with my knife that I am going to gut and clean that there woman with, and everyone else that I think helped kill my woman and violated my home."

Beckmire whispered, "Let's get some rest. Where are we going to sleep?"

John Lee responded, "You can sleep wherever youse wants to. I'm going to the airport and going back to that there Asiram's ranch. No need for me to stay here. Memories are bad right about now. I just want to go. Jasper, can you have some of the women folk clean up this here mess and keep an eye open for me?"

Jasper answered, "Not to worry. We'll take care of everything and you take your time getting on back here. We'll be just fine."

Jilkes said, "Listen, brother, there is no rush to get back."

John Lee said, "I think we need to get back because this here be just a message. I feel it."

Jilkes looked at the Sarge and said, "Call the captain. We need to leave now."

# # #

Three hours later, on the plane, everyone silently thought about all of the times that John Lee had that strange and uncanny feeling that something was wrong, and how each time, he was correct. As they settled into their seats, John Lee announced, "I want to have a drink or two. Will you guys have a drink with me?"

They toasted their friendship and that was the end of the conversation. Though no one discussed it, the guys were unsettled by his sentiments relative to getting back to Asiram's ranch. John Lee was special, and they knew it.

As the plane touched down in Idaho Falls, John Lee said, "Now, that is a big ass private jet over there. Look at the size of that thing. Maybe we should buy something like that so we all can pile in like little pigs."

"Why like little pigs?" Jilkes asked.

"Because big pigs, make a big mess," John Lee replied. The captain, after pulling the plane into the hangar, came back to the cabin and reported, "I asked the ground crew whose big jet that was and the guy replied, "don't know, but a shitload of people got off it". He said they were mostly men and one woman who seemed to be in charge. Just giving you a heads up. If you like, we can give that big plane a stomachache which will delay any takeoff."

Beckmire asked, "Do you guys have weapons?"

The captain replied, "Are you serious? Sergeant, we're ex-military." He raised the armrest on one chair and then raised the armrest of a chair on the other side of the aisle and a panel opened exposing two assault rifles, four pistols, and four knives.

Beckmire said, "Jong said that you guys were the best and that you would always act on our behalf. Is that a true sentiment or just some cowboy talk?"

"Mr. Jong has arranged employment for a variety of former military personnel, and it is all through the largess of your foundation. Now, if you think we are going to let someone waltz in here and hurt our jobs and/or our benefactors, you must be drunk. If Mr. Jong tells me that someone is trying to hurt him, oh well, that person won't be paying taxes anytime soon or perhaps ever. We are loyal and reliable," the Captain said.

Beckmire asked, "John Lee, what would your favorite pig say to all that stuff he just said?"

"My newly departed pig would say that these here boys can be trusted. We can bet on them to keep our side right."

Beckmire inquired, "Jilkes, what's your take?"

"I'm with Old Country."

Brown looked at Chakes who shrugged his shoulders and then looked at Bernstein who asked, "The bigger question is, can you swear to silence even if it means getting your dick cut off?"

The captain replied, "Now, you are asking for a bit more than loyalty. If someone plans on cutting my dick off, then I am going to squeal like a pig in the slaughterhouse."

John Lee retorted, "Now, I know I like him."

Beckmire said, "Once we clear this place, give that plane a headache but nothing that will hurt it in flight." The captain assured, "Oh, it won't fly until a certain kind of technician checks it out."

As they disembarked from the plane, Clyde was there waiting. He said, "I guess you see that big plane over there, lots of bad looking people got off it, I hear. They have taken over the hotel downtown and are scaring the heck out of the locals. I think they might be interested in having some sort of encounter with you guys. So, what me and my kin have done is set up our boundaries. We have our people on the far corners of the properties. I mean we got people east, west, down south and up north. We got the best damn dogs in the world. They don't do a lot of barking and howling, and when they hear a noise, well they just jump to attention."

Beckmire thanked him and said, "We appreciate your help, but we can't get you people caught up in this situation. We just want to help you guys, not get you hurt or tortured by these sick types."

Clyde announced, "Hell, man, my people are feeling revolutionary. They are going to run the carpetbaggers out of town and make sure these people don't stay long. You know you don't always have to kill a thing to get rid of it. People got to eat, and my cousins run and own the four restaurants in town so, perhaps a little man made 'E. coli', and some other bowel blowing stuff, can lend a hand to the cause. If they come from the far north, low south, sun rising east, or sun setting west, you will have advance warning. See, this here is our home. We know the good from the bad and we are always going to help the good and damn the bad and the ugly. You don't have a choice, Sarge. We are already deployed."

## CHAPTER SEVENTEEN

At the ranch, everyone was solemn when John Lee walked in and announced, "I came back here tonight because I need happy meals, oh, I mean happy faces."

Beckmire looked at Mallory and motioned him towards the door. He asked an inebriated Zanthius if he could focus for a minute. Without fail, Asiram followed them out of the house. Beckmire said, "When we arrived, we noticed a big private jet at the airport. We were told that a large contingency of men and one woman were on the plane and the woman seemingly is in charge. Now, I don't know exactly what that means, but we need to be on alert. How they found us is a mystery. The only person of suspect to me is Sam. Where is he?"

Asiram replied, "I think he is in his room nurturing his wound. Let's go and check."

When they got to the room that Sam shared with one of Carlos's men, they found his man was bound and gagged. As they released him from bondage, he said, "That asshole hit me and took my weapon. He can't be far because he is limping and can only stand on one leg."

As they were searching the property for Sam, Clyde came in and asked, "Did one of your people borrow one of the trucks?"

Beckmire responded, "It's more like he stole the truck and turned us in. Mallory, get the guys, and everyone in the house together, we need to get into a defensive position."

Clyde informed them, "My wife's brother's sister's daughter works at the hotel. I already told her to call me if they decide to take a walk. Also, my nephews, and their mother's aunt work there. I think we can have a party without fear of a surprise."

Beckmire said, "That's a lot of people we don't know who we have to depend on."

Clyde retorted, "You are a lot of people that we don't know, and we are depending on you—quid pro quo, I believe is the sentiment that I am sharing."

Beckmire stated, "I will rest better if I know the best place to put two of my best people."

Clyde said, "That would be the roof, it offers a 360-degree view of the ranch and has gun ports. I can signal my people with a ping, to find out where they are. A small flash in the night out here goes a long way."

Beckmire asked, "Do you want to run this OP?"

Clyde replied, "Naw, I did enough of that in Korea."

Clyde's phone rang. It was someone on that long list of relatives working in town. The voice on the other end announced, "A man just showed up here who is bleeding from the leg. Don't know much more than that. Talk to you later."

Clyde turned to Beckmire and reported, "It appears that your man Sam has shown up at the hotel where the rest of the newcomers are staying, including the leader."

Beckmire announced, "I didn't realize you were a veteran. Let me tell you something, we're not church boys. The people who are staying in town are not church boys. They are here to kill us and anyone else that gets in their way. We can handle this. We don't want your people getting caught up in an international spy mystery. We appreciate all that you have done, but I must insist that your people stand down. We don't like to involve civilians in our affairs."

Clyde responded, "Mr. Sarge, you gave us hope when we didn't have a lot of it when those people were swindling our land from us. We will stay safe and distant. If any of them get lost in the fields out here, well they will be food for our animal friends. We will not stand by and watch anyone related to Ms. Asiram take a licking without our help.

"As I said before, we know the good, we know the ugly and we are currently experiencing the bad. You won't see us or hear us, but you will know where we are. We are ranchers and we know our land. Them there folks don't know shit about existing out here. This here be a test of your faith in God. This land is unforgiving."

Beckmire looked at Mallory. Mallory shrugged his shoulders and said, "We need some code words so that we know who is who? He told Clyde, "Anything near the ranch house we've got covered. Anything in the outlying areas is yours. You and your people will not come to assist unless we call out a certain word, and that word is, 'family'. If we can agree on those rules of engagement, then we can use your help."

Clyde declared, "Now, we're talking."

When they went back into the house, Beckmire said, "I would like to have a word with all of the menfolk here for a minute. Will you join me in the library?"

Once in the library, Beckmire said, "Sometimes, as humans, we make a mistake when it comes to determining whether to end a person's life or to allow that person to live. We allowed Sam to live and he has decided to take refuge with the enemy. There is a large private jet that landed tonight, full of a potential threat to all of us. Clyde has people monitoring their movements, but I think that we should deploy our safety nets and try to get some rest. I am asking John Lee and Jilkes to provide us cover from the roof of the main house, and McArthur and Gladstone to provide cover from the roof of the guest house. I am asking Zanthius to take his bride to bed and sleep off his current condition. I am asking that the rest of you hold this wedding celebration in abeyance until we have sorted out this new threat.

"Unfortunately, Sam knows our strength in numbers, but he doesn't know our added defense system of allies that are being managed by Clyde and his community. If tomorrow is a clear day and there is no apparent breach of the ranch, I want six people to volunteer to go into town to clear up a local problem with the New York type carpetbaggers." Every hand in the room went in the air.

Carlos said, "Mr. Beckmire, by now they have pictures of you guys and know exactly who you are. They don't know a thing about me and my people. We will shoot first and ask questions later, if Ms. De Lombardo agrees."

Ava advised, "Call me Ava or mi amor, Carlos. That damn horse has already exposed us." Everyone laughed.

Carlos said, "If mi amor will allow us to engage in this event, I think we offer the perfect cover—they don't know us from crap."

Beckmire looked at Mallory who shrugged his shoulders and finally said, "Now, that sounds like a good plan to me. I would like to know how many people got off that plane, Clyde. Can you find out that intel for us?"

Clyde responded, "Got that."

Beckmire announced, "Okay, we have a plan. Tomorrow, Mallory and I will visit the carpetbaggers and give them a deal that will be difficult to refuse. We will be accompanied by Carlos and four of his men. I want Gladstone and McArthur nearby to target threats that we can't see. Carlos, perhaps we only need you and two of your men. I want Jilkes and John Lee to consider our needs for fortifying the ranch. Asiram, do you happen to have a stash of long guns here?"

Asiram answered, "This is west of middle America. You can't survive out here without long guns. I have eight sniper rifles. Why are you looking at me like that? They fell off a truck on their way to a base in Kentucky. I just happened to be driving by and saw them on the side of the road."

#

On the other side of town, Sam was being debriefed by none other than Scottie. Scottie knew that her new opponents were formidable and smart. She thought that the lives of so many men had to be avenged. She was determined to capture the capsule and skin everyone alive just because she could, and without remorse. She felt dauntless.

Meanwhile at the airport, another large private jet landed with at least twenty fierce looking individuals. They exited the plane without any bags. From the cargo hold, a significant number of crates were unloaded as well. Under the cloak of darkness, Jong's pilots witnessed the comings and goings of the individuals. They made a call to Jong and told him that the number of newcomers to the area had increased by at least twenty. They told him they would keep him abreast of all new and potential threats.

Jong thanked them and relayed the information to Beckmire. Before Beckmire could assemble his group, the captain called Jong and reported, 'Sir, there is another large private jet landing, as we speak. I will give you information on the count as soon as we have it."

Beckmire asked Clyde, "Where do those carpetbaggers stay at night?"

Clyde replied, "They are staying at Walthro's place, since it is close to town and they now own it."

"How far is that from here?" Beckmire inquired.

"Thirty minutes once we reach the main road. That there property butts right up to Ms. Asiram's. If we went across the ranch, we could be there in fifteen minutes."

"I don't know what tomorrow is going to bring, but I do know I want to conclude this land issue so that I can focus totally on the impending threat. Mallory, why don't you get me a couple of the guys so that we can go and visit them in their illicitly obtained residence?"

Mallory indicated, "I need volunteers for this one. Anybody interested in helping the locals?"

All hands were raised. Mallory asked, "Can't you guys just say no at least once, and didn't you elect Carlos and his men for backup?"

"Mallory, I have them doing something different." He turned to Asiram and asked her to give him at least $100,000 to offer those carpetbaggers in the name of peace.

# # #

Two hours later, Clyde crisscrossed the property and by chance saw where the fence had been cut. He remarked, "Now, this is interesting. This fence wasn't this way four days ago when I scouted the property. This cut was done by super cutters."

John Lee said, "Looks like about eight to ten people walked onto the property. Let's follow the steps and see where they lead."

Beckmire said, "You and Jilkes take care of that problem. Clyde, I think you should go with them because I don't want those people knowing that you are a part of this visit."

Mallory and Beckmire entered Walthro's old property on foot, along with Bernstein and Brown, who looked for a vantage point to provide backup if necessary. Beckmire and Mallory after walking about a mile, came upon the house where music was blasting inside and seemingly a party was in progress.

They rang the bell for over a minute. A guy who was half dressed answered the door and asked, "What the shit do you farmers want at this hour?"

Mallory placed his pistol to the man's head and retorted, "I want to see your brains splattered against that wall over yonder. How many people are in this place?"

"The half dressed man nervously replied, "There are four of us here."

Mallory said, "We don't have a lot of time, but we need to meet with everyone about some local issues. Call your people down and tell them to meet you in the, ah, kitchen. Remember, any wrong moves and you will catch a .350 Remington round in your head."

The guy backed into the house and yelled for the guys to come down and meet him in the kitchen. Two men came down in their briefs and one didn't respond at all.

Beckmire asked, "Where is the fourth guy?"

The guy responded, "He is probably still busy with his date."

Beckmire said, "Okay. I want you to go up and bang on his door and tell him that you need to speak to him. I am going to be right behind you with this pistol pointed at your freaking head. We have already killed four assholes today and it won't matter if you are number five."

The two men scaled the steps to the second floor. The guy banged on the door. When the door opened, the person on the other side of it had a pistol in his hand.

He asked, "What the hell are you doing?"

The guy doing the banging shifted his head to the left and when the guy looked out of the door, he saw the massive pistol pointing at his private zone. Beckmire told him to lose the weapon and exit the room. As the man walked out of the room, he remarked, "If you are going to rob us then at least let us put on some clothes."

Beckmire responded, "If I wanted to rob you, I would have done it while you had your head buried up that lady's snatch."

As they descended into the kitchen, Mallory took the telephone off the hook and announced, "This won't take long. You guys are from New York and you have stolen, through a bunch of legal bullshit, the properties of our friends. Now, we know the scam. By the time they take you to court, they would have exhausted their remaining funds. You would continue to delay the case until they were out of funds and in debt to some lawyer that is probably in cahoots with you. So, here is the deal. Tomorrow you will reevaluate what you have done, and you will develop the paperwork showing that those people have paid you in full."

The least dressed man said, "We're a legitimate company and we did nothing wrong. Those people defaulted on their loan agreements. We were required to execute their removal. You can't barge in here and demand that we give away valuable property that we earned legitimately, even if you have guns pointed at us."

Beckmire looked at Mallory and said, "They have a point." He touched his handheld radio and said, "Brown, these guys don't think we're serious. Send them a message."

Brown responded, "Roger that."

Two seconds later, a large caliber round entered the refrigerator. The least dressed man yelled, "We're going to report this terroristic act to the police department."

Beckmire said, "Oh, you mean the one with the deputy on your payroll? Okay, listen up, the next round will be in someone's head. Mallory, give them the money and I'll give them the terms. That is exactly $100,000. That is much more than you have invested and a helluva lot more than your life is worth.

In the morning, you will do the paperwork and give those people their properties or you will not live to see the sun rise another day. And you want to know something, I think you're correct. We are terrorists and we have people all over this place. Don't think you can go back East and start some shit. We have your pictures and an active bounty for your asses if this problem doesn't go away tomorrow. Try your luck guys, we don't fail, and we do it for free. Enjoy your sessions with those ladies. Goodnight.

"Oh, and by the way, if I were you guys, I would go back to New York tomorrow and never look back. If we hear that you or any of your carpetbagging friends are in this area, we will send a strike force and you will never be heard from again. Now, be sure you find those people and have that paperwork in their hands for signature before the bank opens. Night now!" After taking individual pictures of the four men, Mallory bid them good night.

Beckmire and Mallory walked out of the door and never looked back. When they reached the point where the fence had been cut, Clyde was patiently waiting and asked, "Well, how did it go?"

Beckmire answered, "We'll know in the morning if they value land over their lives and whether $100,000 makes them whole. By the way, how much were Walthro and the other families in debt to those guys?"

Clyde said, "$35,000 and $45,000, respectively."

Beckmire shrugged his shoulders and remarked, "We usually don't overpay, but this is worth it, if it works out. We shall see in the morning."

As Clyde began to drive, he saw the silhouettes of two people, it was John Lee and Jilkes. He said, "Your boys traveled quite a distance since we let them off."

Beckmire exclaimed, "Those two are probably the best I have ever known: keen, observant, stealthy and deadly, when need be. They have saved our asses more times than I care to remember."

As they entered the truck, Jilkes reported, "They did a recon on us. Ten crossed the property line. Two protected the fence, two went south, two went west, two got within a mile of the ranch house and two must have reached the windows of the house."

Mallory declared, "Guys cut the shit! Give the facts and only the facts."

John Lee emphasized, "Them there be the facts! They must have done a recon on us while we were at my place in Alabama."

Mallory said, "Well, I'll be damned. We have a different kind of beast to deal with this time. They appear to be more strategic and purposeful."

Beckmire uttered, "Now, I am scared."

As the group stopped to pick up Brown and Bernstein, Mallory asked Brown, "What was the distance of that shot into the refrigerator?"

Brown responded by saying, "It was short of a mile."

John Lee quipped, "Hell, boy, you be getting that there sniping shit down to a science, ain't you?"

Brown replied, "Well, you taught me to shoot, didn't you?"

Beckmire asked, "How fresh are the tracks?"

John Lee answered, "No more than a day."

Beckmire said, "I think we need to go on full alert. I kind of had the feeling that Sam was not totally with us. This is what I expected. That is why I let him live and commune with us. He thinks that he knows how we work and who we are. Let's get prepared to show them the real Fab 10 + 2. Let's take a trip back to the Nam and let's blister these people beyond recognition."

John Lee demanded, "Save that wench for me. I want to gut her and have her beating heart in my hand before she goes to hell."

# # #

Back at the house, Zanthius and Asiram had disappeared into her boudoir and the only sounds manifesting from there were slightly decadent. She loved, he loved, she lusted, he lusted and they lusted to completion. It was definitely a win-win conclusive night.

Beckmire walked into the house and announced, "People, in case you haven't noticed, Sam is missing and is probably exposing our hand right now. Not to be concerned. It is kind of what I wanted to happen. They did a recon on us last night and they know the layout. They think we are here on vacation and that is exactly what I want them to think.

"Listen up. We have people who know the land out there looking out for our interest as we speak. I am not going to disturb my son and his new bride because it might be an inopportune time—if you know what I mean. Now, Larry, I know you know how to do close quarter work. I am going to need you to do some really dastardly stuff and I am going to need you, Carlos, to assist him."

Beckmire paused for a few seconds and then blurted out, "As a matter of fact, wake everybody up, except the children, so I can lay this thing out so everyone knows what we are up against and how we can get our lives back. Let's convene back here in thirty minutes."

Carlos said to Ava, "Mi amor, please interrupt your son's wedding night for a moment. Tell him his daddy has an important message to tell him about safe sex." The room fell into stitches.

A few minutes later, a disheveled Zanthius and a sexy looking Asiram descended the steps. Beckmire said, "Nice that you two could join us. We have a situation on our hands. Our man Sam has abandoned ship and has floated to the other side. He's probably telling them about our strengths, weaknesses, and points to attack us.

"More than likely, they are going to try to shoot us while we are in the house. They think we're having a grand old time and that we are not paying attention to details, such as, the breach in the fence that leads to Walthro's house and the footprints that stop about 100 yards from here. Yes, people, we have been slightly compromised, but they don't know about our folks from these parts who have demanded that they help us."

Asiram reported, "It would be useless to shoot at this place. It's like a fortress. The windows are, of course, bulletproof. The walls are 2.5 feet thick and are lined with a Teflon based material, the same thing they use in the manufacturing of bulletproof vests. Now, the guest house is another matter. It is built basically like any other house. As I said, this place is the real deal."

Beckmire asked, "You wouldn't happen to have a tank around here, would you?"

Asiram laughed, and said, "No, but I do have a couple of Laws rocket launchers hanging around."

Beckmire went on to tell the group that at least three large private planes had landed at the airport and together, approximately seventy to ninety bad individuals, got off them. Beckmire warned, "I hadn't heard of any frat parties out here, so he was betting that they were here to attend to them. He informed them that Scottie was probably leading the group." He emphasized, "She has been promised to John Lee, so if you happen to have her in your sights, please just wound her. John Lee has a special course that he wants to teach her."

Beckmire then informed the group that he and Mallory had a face-to-face meeting with the New York types and had offered them money for the return of the land that they swindled from the local people. He said he wasn't sure if they would accept the deal, but he had indicated to them that it was a matter of urgency, as well as, a life or death situation. Jason and Sarah, as well as, Walthro and Mary, lowered their heads and jointly said a silent prayer.

Beckmire said, "We are confident that these guys will make the right decision and appreciate the fact that they are still alive and have made money at that. They knew their scheme was crooked and I think they are happy to get what they got and be gone. We gave them a drop dead time and we will see what happens at that point. Mallory, I think it is time to deploy our people."

Zanthius announced, "Asiram and I are ready to serve." He fell against the wall and almost down the stairs.

Beckmire said, "Asiram, enjoy your wedding night. When this is all over, we are going to have another wedding but the next time it's going to be big and fancy. You can hold me to that."

"Don't worry Daddy-in-Law, I'm going to make you pay really big, especially since you blew up my house."

Beckmire retorted, "No, Mallory pulled the plug."

Asiram said, "Whatever and whoever. It's on you to make it my home again."

Beckmire pulled Clyde and Mallory aside and asked, "Just where exactly are your people on the ranch? I don't want them to get caught up in a crossfire situation and become the casualty of friendly fire. I damn sure don't want them shooting at me or my guys either."

Clyde replied, "Follow me for a second." On the back of a huge painting of a horse was the complete layout of the ranch, as well as, a smaller rendering of the adjoining properties. Mallory asked, "What's up with ranchers and farmers having pictures of horses and talking to them? I mean everywhere we have been people talk to the horses and then tell us what the horse said. Just a wee bit crazy, if you ask me."

Clyde answered, "The horse is the backbone of a farm or a ranch even if you have mechanized assets. The horse is spiritual. You people didn't see that there movie called the *Lone Ranger* with that really weird guy who also played a pirate? Anyway, we have some modern stuff out here such as tree blinds that can be raised or lowered and has thermal heating and all of that solar mess.

Ms. Asiram had four installed so that she could see the sun rise, sun set, and any damn thing else she wants to see.

She is a remarkable young lady and the few folks who know her, or know of her, will sacrifice their lives to keep her property protected. I mentioned to her about the people losing their properties, and we prayed and knew that God would hear us. His message was very clear to us, protect those who live here and any who come with good will in their hearts. God is good, Mr. Beckmire. He sent us Ms. Asiram, you, Mr. Mallory and a few good men to assist. Prayer is powerful and perhaps we should have a prayer before we commit to ending the lives of people who are here to hurt you for the sake of money."

Beckmire said, "Sounds like a plan. Let's do it now before we make our assignments. When we deploy our people, make sure your people don't come up for air until I give them the all clear signal. Make that abundantly clear to your people."

## CHAPTER EIGHTEEN

At approximately 0100 hours, Clyde received a message that ten people, all dressed in black, had entered the property through the breach in the fence. He called Beckmire, who sounded the alarm. Everyone in the house had an assignment, except Zanthius and Asiram, who were still enjoying the bliss of consummating their love under the veil of God. Zanthius was basically useless and comatose.

Courtney, Ava, Marisa, and even Monica had weapons and were securely hidden with the children in the tunnel that led from the main ranch house to the guest house.

At 0200 hours, the intruders had not moved forward an inch. It appeared they were scattered, as if they would be doing long-distance shooting. The nature of their weapons couldn't be discerned in the dark, but strategically they looked like a sniper team.

At 0230 hours, a large contingency of people dressed in black, breached the property. In teams of fives, four parties headed in various directions, but all headed ultimately in the direction of the ranch house and the guest house. Their movements were being directed by the sniper teams. The sniper teams made sure that they had a clear view of the house and any targets moving inside. It was virtually black outside, and the only light was from the house itself.

At exactly 0250 hours, another contingency of intruders breached the property. They were being led by a woman. John Lee said to Jilkes, "That person in the front is a woman. Look at how she walks."

Jilkes asked, "How the hell can you tell a woman's walk in the darkness of night?"

John Lee answered, "She's afraid of stepping in a pile of shit or something that might get them there boots dirty. Look at how she be dodging all that horse shit. That be the witch that hung and killed my woman. I can end this right now with a head shot. Maybe them there other boys will go back home."

Beckmire commanded, "Stay with the plan. Stay with the plan and cut all unnecessary chatter. Focus!"

John Lee told Jilkes, "I can bounce a shot off of her and hit the guy lined up near her to her right."

Jilkes demanded, "Stay with the plan."

At exactly 0315, all power to the house was cut. Thirty yards away from the house and in its own vented compartment, three silent and smoothly operating generators kicked on.

Scottie yelled, "Shit. Didn't they tell you about the standby generator?" No one said a word. Scottie spoke into her communication device and said, "The generators are only illuminating the essentials to the house. Look at it. We are a go at exactly 0330. Don't be late and if you kill the target, do me a favor, shoot yourself in the head. This is about capturing the target. Everyone else is fair game."

One of Clyde's spotters whispered, "I just got this strange transmission that at 0330 it is a go. I'm picking up their talk on my windup radio." Clyde called Beckmire and relayed to him what he was just told. Beckmire radioed his people and said, "Santa will try the chimney at 0330. Jilkes and John Lee, the first two shots are yours. Gladstone and McArthur, the next four shots are yours, then Brown and Bernstein, then Chakes and Montomie, and lastly Whitmore and Jong. Whitmore and Jong continue rapid fire along with Larry and Carlos and his people. After that progression, we will all open fire on their positions. Clyde, I need your people to shoot the snipers. I need those snipers out of action in a hurry. Can you and your people do that?"

Clyde came back on and reported, "At 0330, we gonna shoot that area up really bad. We are done with carpetbaggers and that is just what I told my people they are. I told them that they are now trying to force Ms. Asiram and me out of our places. I asked them, "guess who's next"? I am a man of God, and I am hoping that he will forgive me for this small indiscretion. I felt it was needed."

# # #

Jilkes told John Lee, "I prefer the up close and personal kind of fighting. How about you?"

John Lee responded, "I don't like none of this, but I had to learn to do it to keep me and my bestest friends alive. I wish I could use my bow on these people."

At exactly 0330, John Lee asked Jilkes, "Are you ready?"

Jilkes said, "On, 3—2—1—bang, bang."

Clyde's people opened fire on the snipers and like a well-oiled machine, gunfire erupted from Gladstone and McArthur, then Brown and Bernstein, then Chakes and Montomie, followed by Whitmore and Jong, and Larry, and then Carlos and his people. There was an insane amount of gunfire, and as planned, much of it was delivered by John Lee and Jilkes.

John Lee placed a round through Scottie's arm and into the heart of the person standing next to her. It was an amazing night shot from approximately one mile away. It definitely resembled a war zone because bullets were flying from all four corners of the ranch and at various intervals. The intruders couldn't really focus on a single area since bullets were being fired at them from every direction.

The Sarge said to Mallory, "Now, this is a real firefight and you and I haven't fired a single shot. I can't believe this is the best of the mercs. How on earth are they evaluated? Common sense suggests that you don't breach a person's property with the intent to create havoc without making sure that all possible angles are covered. Their focus was the ranch house and not the outlying areas. This is just crazy. If this is the best that they have, then we don't need a lot of protection. The women can defend against a frontal approach and attack."

Mallory looked at him and asked, "Do you want to move out of this safe zone and go kill someone?"

Beckmire replied, "Seems like the boys and Asiram's neighbors have taken care of the dirty laundry. Why don't we just stay put and take roll call to make sure that all our people are okay? Can you handle that little function? Have all of our people stay in place until first light. Then we can do a recon and see what and who is left alive."

Clyde called Beckmire and told him that Jason and his wife, Walthro and Mary, plus their three sons had cut off the intruders' retreat and had floodlights focused on the breached fence. He also told him that those boys were crack shots and were pissed off at those people who stole their property.

# # #

Zanthius and Asiram woke up, grabbed weapons and descended the steps. Courtney ordered, "Get down and stay down. We are the last line of defense and I don't know who is shooting whom out there. Get down and stay down."

Asiram inquired, "Why didn't someone tell us about this impending action?"

Ava smiled and replied, "Because you were busy banging my son, legitimately. I didn't want to mess with that one." Asiram smiled and attempted to say something but started crying. Ava slid over to where Asiram and Zanthius were hunkered down and whispered, "I hope those are tears of joy, because if the boys aren't successful, they may be the last tears you shed."

Asiram mumbled, "I need a mother. I need you to help me keep my beautiful husband. I don't know shit about being married. I'm lost and afraid."

Ava said, "Oh, my sweet child, you have started off on the right foot. You don't need me. It will all come to you, naturally." Pow! Pow! Pow! Three shots hit the windows and Asiram said, "I told the Sarge that the windows were bulletproof."

By 0400 hours, the sound of gunfire had subsided. At 0430 hours, the sound of a lone wolf could be heard calling his brethren for what would be a few days of feasting on freshly killed meat.

At 0500 hours the sound of wolves bickering over the first or best bite could be discerned from near and far. Mallory asked the Sarge, "Can you hear that shit? Those wolves are fighting over some poor soul's flesh. I am so damn glad that we didn't have to deal with that kind of insult to injury in the Nam. Just think if you are not dead, you can literally watch your ass get eaten alive by a pack of wolves. Damn that has to be the worst."

Beckmire said, "We served our country and performed our jobs in as a humane way as possible. We weren't trying to steal anything. We were just obeying orders as good American soldiers do. These guys came to kill everyone we know and a few people that we just met. They wouldn't hesitate to kill Courtney or Monica or anyone else. I don't feel shit. I hope the animals eat every last piece of their mercenary asses."

At 0525, a shot rang out. Everyone came to attention to discern where it came from. Jilkes got on the radio and announced, "John Lee is keeping the lone woman pinned down until daylight. When she tries to move, he places a shot near her body. He has not taken his eyes off her, and he won't. Sarge, you promised him that woman. Maybe he can do the work that Asiram does and as effectively as she does. I'm mentioning this because if you deviate from what you said, I think you will lose John Lee from our brotherhood, just saying."

The Sarge replied, "And what about you?"

"It goes without saying, if he goes, I go, you know that," Jilkes indicated.

"That strong, eh?" the Sarge stated.

Beckmire looked at Mallory and then advised Jilkes, "I don't make idle promises. We just have to extract information from her first and then when she has given us names and numbers, he can have her."

"Roger that," Jilkes said.

At 0600 hours, the sun began to rise in the East and Scottie attempted to make her move. John Lee blew her weapon out of her hand. She raised both hands in the air. John Lee scoped her head and yelled, "I got you witch!"

Jilkes calmly said, "In order to end this never ending trip, we need her alive. The Sarge said she's yours, and you can play Asiram's role as the extractor. Please, Brother, don't end it like this. We need her for information."

John Lee asked, "What on earth you be going on about over there?"

Jilkes answered, "Never mind. Just don't shoot the woman."

At 0630 hours, Clyde called Beckmire and said, "A few of them fellas are badly wounded. What should we do with them?"

Beckmire responded, "Your choice, just remember, they came to kill us. Since you helped us, they probably would have killed you as well, your choice."

At 0700 hours, a slightly bleeding Scottie emerged with hands held as high as she could manage. She looked around at her team and mumbled, "Bunch of pussies, beaten back by a group of old heads and farmers."

Clyde was the first one to reach Scottie and he warned her, "Keep your hands where I can see them, and turn around." Scottie turned slightly to her left and when Clyde reached for the knife she had sheathed, she kicked him in the head and grabbed his rifle. John Lee yelled, "If you think you can pull that there shit on me, try your luck. Put the gun down like it was your woman."

Jilkes walked over to her and said, "Damn, Old Country, you placed that round right through her. Not that messy and really not that bloody."

John Lee asked, "What be your name?"

The woman responded, "My name is Sergie."

"Sergie what?" John Lee asked.

Scottie said, "My name is Sergie Lenovax."

Jilkes asked, "Do you sometimes go by the name of Scottie?"

She answered, "Scottie is our boss and she is not here." They walked her to a mule and drove her to the shed where all of the tractors were housed. Inside the shed, Beckmire asked Jilkes if he searched her thoroughly and he told him that he had not. He indicated that he just placed wire ties on her ass and that was it.

Beckmire said, "My name is Beckmire. Are you the person they call Scottie?"

"My name is Sergie Lenovax. Scottie is our employer and that is all I am going to tell you."

Jilkes saw an opportunity and inquired, "How was your visit to Alabama?"

This caught Sergie off guard. She smiled and answered, "I have never been to Alabama." It was pretty obvious that she was trying to hide something.

Mallory asked the Sarge if Asiram had ever seen the person named Scottie and he replied, "Great question. Why don't we invite Asiram to the shed to eyeball this person?"

Later, when Asiram, with a still slightly inebriated Zanthius, arrived at the shed, Mallory asked Asiram if she had ever seen the woman sitting in the chair.

"Unfortunately, I have." Asiram replied, "That's Scottie. I want to say hello to her."

Asiram turned the corner and said, "Hey, Scottie. How the hell have you been?"

"My name is Sergie Lenovax."

"You copied my last name as your disguise?"

"Why not. I told you to think on your feet. Yes, people, I am Scottie and I still remain your worst nightmare."

Jong and Whitmore showed up. Jong approached her with his antitracking erasing equipment and scanned her. He found that she had three bugs on her. They were erased and neutralized.

Scottie looked at Jilkes and exclaimed, "Yeah, Negro, I was in Alabama! Too bad you weren't there to join the party. Perhaps my intel got it wrong. Was that maid yours or the farmer's next to you? And Asiram, I know the fricking drill. I taught you everything that your dumb ass knows. So, I'm going to get cut up and lose a finger and perhaps a hand and other shit. Please, country people! This is my game. I invented it. I will pass out at will, and you can kiss my ass between my blacking out."

Asiram said, "Sorry to disappoint you. I no longer do this kind of work. I was married yesterday, and he forbids me to continue in this sordid occupation. However, I do believe we have a new apprentice to fill my little shoes.

As a matter of fact, it is that country bumpkin next to that there Negro. Oh, by the way, she wasn't his maid, bitch. She was his woman, his lady, his love, his everything and most of all, his soul mate. So, I implore you to try to make this easy on yourself. John Lee is the new extractor. I guarantee you he will be the best yet. He is going to learn by doing you and watching your ass cry like the high level managing bitch that you are. Enjoy him, love. I would say some shit like see you later, but I doubt it. Enjoy your last few moments on earth. Oh, and by the way, ask him to show you his knife. He is planning to gut you from your crotch to your brain. That shit is going to hurt. I never really tried that one, but when I see you in hell, let me know how it was."

After a few minutes of silence and private talk between the group, Scottie asked, "Is that the 'idiot spy' that I have heard so much about and who has the key to gaining world power? Is that your new husband? Does he know that you murdered your entire family?"

Asiram turned around and replied, "I'm not wasting any energy responding to your last words in this life."

John Lee approached Scottie and asked, "Did youse have to hang her like she was a caught fish? You stopped my world and created a new me. I ain't going to be merciful or a Christian. Now, my people want to know all that you know. This here blade is my favorite. I smuggled it back from Viet Nam. In the Nam, me and my friends did a lot of killing, but we didn't do none of that crazy shit. We just went out looking for special targets and we just killed them. Jilkes, do me a favor and hand me that there blow torch over there."

Scottie declared, "Take your best shot."

John Lee said, "I ain't going to waste no bullet on you, woman. I be getting the blow torch to close up your wounds after I cut off parts of your body. You can pass out for as long as youse ass wants to, but each time you wake up, something is going to be wolf meat."

Jilkes handed the blow torch to John Lee who said, "I hope this doesn't hurt you." He then took his knife and stabbed it into the wall, lit the blow torch and torqued it. He retrieved the knife from the wall and stabbed Scottie in her foot, penetrating her boot and lodged it in the shed's floor. Her screams could probably be heard in the next state.

He declared, "I ain't going to horse shit you, this here shit is going to hurt!" He removed the knife from her foot and immediately began to cauterize the wound with the blow torch.

He then inquired, "Sarge, do you have any questions you might want to be asking this here lady?"

The Sarge looked at him in disbelief. He was physically and emotionally disturbed by what John Lee had done. Jilkes also gasped and asked, "Can I talk to you for a second?"

John Lee looked at Scottie and taunted, "Don't you go nowhere, now. I'll be back."

Outside of the hearing range of Scottie, Beckmire asked, "John Lee, what was that you just did back there?"

John Lee replied, "Oh, I'm just priming the pump. That there freak is going to give names, numbers, dollars, next of kin, and sexually what she likes and dislikes doing."

Jilkes said, "Brother, that was really out of character. Can we slow this down? We will make sure you get what you need to avenge your mate, but let's not incapacitate the woman and not be able to capitalize on her intel."

John Lee looked at Jilkes, the Sarge, and Mallory and said, "Oh I see. You want me to act normal. Okay, I'll be normal, but I am going to gut that witch from her crotch to her brain. If it be a might too bloody for youse, then disappear. I be putting a hurt on her ass at the end of all of this. As be a matter of fact, why don't youse people just disappear and let me and my man work this one over? Jilkes here knows what needs to be asked. It's gonna be really bloody, but we can fix her to tell the facts." Jilkes looked at the Sarge and shifted his head to the left which meant for him and Mallory to leave.

As John Lee reentered the space where Scottie was, she yelled, "Hey redneck, I cut your woman's inners out. Did you happen to see them in your fucking refrigerator?"

John Lee looked at her and then Jilkes and said, "I be burning the information out of this here witch. I don't think cutting into her feet and chopping off fingers is going to work with this here nut."

Jilkes looked at him and said, "Have fun my brother, but we need information from her."

John Lee studied Scottie and finally exclaimed, "I think youse needs a haircut. Your hair is pretty and all, but I think it might be a little too long. By the way, who sent you here to hurt us country people?"

"Go fuck your dumbass self!" Scottie stated defiantly.

John Lee said, "No need to be yelling at me. I just want to find out some information and then I can put you out of youse misery. I'll ask you again and then I will scalp youse ass like the Indians used to do. Who sent you here?"

Scottie said, "Listen, you dumbass cracker, scratch my ass and lick your redneck ass fingers."

John Lee said, "Okay." He then ran his favorite knife from the base of Scottie's neck to her hairline in the front, removing a significant amount of hair and scalp.

"Kill me, damn it. Just kill me," Scottie demanded.

"Little lady, that won't happen until you give me some information that my boss man can use. Now, you be losing a lot of blood right about now. The only way to stop bleeding is to singe them there wounds," When John Lee finished talking, Scottie had passed out.

Thirty minutes later, Scottie woke up and spoke incoherently. John Lee lit the blow torch and torqued it. He said, "Now, I know this here shit is going to hurt. By the way, I don't care if you never answer any questions. Because all I want to do is gut youse pretty ass from your snatch to your big ass forehead. I have to obey the boss man and pretend that I be trying to get info from you, you know what I mean." He then took the blow torch and quickly ran it up the base of her neck to her front hairline. Her screams were off the chart.

John Lee muttered, "I told you that shit was going to hurt, but I forget to tell how stinky it is too. Now, I am going to ask you again, who sent you here and who does you work for?"

Scottie looking really weary and scared, replied, "Redneck, kiss my shiny white ass."

Jilkes walked in the shed and screamed, "Lady, this is only going to get worse if you keep insulting him. Either you are really fucking stupid or you just like getting a makeover by someone who is really good at developing new ways to inflict pain and suffering. Take time and think about it. Would you like some water?"

Scottie spit her reply at Jilkes, "The only thing I want is to cut him 100 fucking times."

Jilkes said, "That attitude only makes him more devious. Give us something, anything, or he will do this all night long. In the Nam, I literally watched him skin a guy alive with such precision, it made me ill. Give us something, for your sake."

John Lee walked back in and proclaimed, "I call what we just did foreplay. Now, we are going to have consented sex. By the way, I don't like how your head be looking. I might need to do some more work around them fat ass ears of yours to make them match. You know what I mean?" He removed her vest and sliced her sweater down the middle.

John Lee remarked, "This here is a nice vest and it's one of them one size fits all. I think I'll keep this as a souvenir, to remind me of your ass." John Lee sliced her shirt from her midsection to the neck and without warning sliced open her pants.

He said, "Nice bloomers. I like the color." Without breaking flesh, he sliced her panties to the place where she hid what most men sought.

He uttered, "Now, you talk about putting a hurt on your ass, girl. You ain't screamed loud enough. I'm going to heat my blade to make sure it's sterile. Wouldn't want to give your ass no kind of STD down there."

He lit the blow torch, torqued it, and heated the knife until it began to glow. He sat the blowtorch down and Scottie yelled, "Enough you sick bastard. What do you want to know?"

John Lee retorted, "Oh, I don't want to know shit except why you hung my woman and did her like that?" He placed the hot blade at the beginning of her private place, and she screamed for mercy.

Jilkes, in the meantime called the Sarge and said, "I need you down here now, and bring Mallory. John Lee has left the damn planet."

Jilkes said in a loud and commanding voice, "John Lee, I need you to get up and go outside. Wait for the Sarge. Move soldier."

He looked at Scottie and whispered, "They promised me your ass, and I intend to put a real hurt on your butt, girl. Now, don't you go nowhere! I'll be back."

Beckmire and Mallory entered the room in a hurry and asked, "What the hell happened to her?"

John Lee answered, "I just made some cosmetic changes to her looks, that's all. Youse don't like the way I styled her head?"

Beckmire commanded, "John Lee, take a break. Mallory and I will finish interrogating her. Take a break."

As John Lee and Jilkes headed out of the area, John Lee turned and winked at Scottie and said, "Now, don't you go away--ya hear?"

Beckmire looked at Scottie and asked, "Is there anything that I can get to ease your pain?"

"Just a knife so that I can gut that redneck sonofabitch."

"Funny you should ask for a knife. Your sentiments are exactly like his, after all, you did kill his woman."

"I thought she was his maid or something. How was I to know that the redneck had a black ass girlfriend?"

"Okay, help us help you. Who do you report to and how did you pay for those dead people out there? Where does your money come from and how high up in this crooked ass government does this go?"

"You don't have a clue, do you? You rejects, from Vietnam think that because you have won a few victories, you are in control of the action. You don't control shit and after me there will be another and another and another group of people coming to do you harm until you turn over the 'idiot spy' and his double-crossing slut of a girlfriend."

Mallory said, "If you can stay with the answers to the questions then we may figure out how to help you survive our extractor. We don't think we're rejects. If you answer the questions, truthfully, we might be able to help you get out of the mess you are in. Just answer the questions."

"I don't have any answers for you people. I do have a proposition. You give me the 'idiot spy', his dog and ten minutes with the redneck, then I will let you all exist in peace. As a matter of fact, I'll even let you do some wet work for me now and then. The pay is excellent. I must admit, you were methodical in your approach last night and I applaud you."

Beckmire said, "That has to be an agency advertisement that you people use. Each time we manage to capture one of your kind, we are given the same guarantees: a happy life, untaxable revenue and freedom from looking over our shoulders. Do you know Walter?"

Scottie replied, "That boxer short wearing prude. He's on the Government Salary scale. He makes no decisions on his own. He reports to one of my underlings."

"Anyhow, he gave us the same options with a few more perks than you are offering. As a matter of fact, he turned us on to you and your approach. Oh, and Allen, you know Allen? He offered us the same options. Allen was kind enough to throw into the mix the knowledge of you recruiting mercenaries in unlimited quantities. Seems like the only one we trust is Walter and with some reservations, Allen. Wouldn't you agree, Mallory?"

"You nailed that one right in the foot, Sarge--no pun intended. Speaking of which, you must be in a helluva lot of pain. Do you want to continue lecturing us on our inability to right this thing, without giving up the Sarge's son and his wife, or do you want to give us credible information that will help us end this thing without any more bloodshed, including your own?" Mallory replied.

Scottie looked at her foot and said, "We are trained to displace the notion of pain. This is nothing and that is exactly what you are going to get from me: nada, nothing and a go fuck yourself."

Beckmire exclaimed, "Wow. You are one courageous woman. Enjoy the rest of your short life. That redneck, that you like so much, will be back to flirt with you some more."

As Beckmire and Mallory turned to walk away, Mallory asked, "Did you see those keys she had clipped to her belt?"

"No, I didn't. What about them?"

"Those are the exact same keys that T-Rex had on him that led to the money in his SUV."

"Are you shitting me?" Beckmire asked.

Mallory answered, "I think they must be some kind of agency issued keys for carrying large amounts of cash. What are the odds that this crazy woman has a couple of trunks full of cash like that other fellow? Hold on a minute."

Mallory walked back to the area where Scottie was strapped down and said, "I don't think you'll be in need of these keys for anything in this world."

Scottie yelled, "Wait! Let's talk for a minute. Come now, we are all reasonable people. Perhaps I started this row, but maybe we can find a way to settle it to everyone's benefit."

Mallory said, "Go on, but why did these keys spark a newfound sense of dialogue from you. Exactly what will these keys unlock?"

"Listen, I need trustworthy partners. So, Sarge, can I trust you and your friend to do the right thing?   What if I can make all of this go away and leave you with two of those keys, and I'll keep two. We part friends and you never have to look over your shoulder. Can I trust you guys? Now, that is the answer I need before I tell you what those keys open."

Beckmire looked at Mallory and asked, "Can I speak to you for a second?"

Mallory replied, "Of course." The two men walked out of her hearing range but began to speak loud enough so that Scottie could hear what they were discussing. Beckmire and Mallory talked and acted as though they were arguing and trying to decide what to do with Scottie. At one time, Mallory pointed his fingers in the Sarge's face and told him that he needed some extra cash and if she could provide it, then why not trust her. Beckmire argued the opposing side of the equation, saying loudly that he did not trust her or anyone else from those scary agencies.

Mallory returned to the bleeding and desperate Scottie and began the conversation with her by emphasizing, "My colleague does not trust you. If these keys are to a thing that will make my creditors go away then I will learn to trust you, but you have to be very specific with your information when it comes to the Sarge."

Scottie said, "I need a quorum before I expose my hand. Sarge, what are your thoughts? One more thing, I will need at least ten minutes with the redneck. He branded me in a very private place. I can't let that go."

Beckmire said, "Absolutely, no deal! The redneck is my brother. All these guys are my brothers and if you hurt one, then we all will come hunting for your ass until you are no more. The redneck is not in this deal."

Scottie stated, "Hold your horses, just testing the water. Can I get your trust on the other matter?"

Beckmire inquired, "Is everyone in these secret agencies into horses? That's all I hear--horses, horses, and more horses. You know, Mallory, there are things we don't always have to tell our guys about. I guess this is one of those things.

"If we make this deal, rest assured, the extractor John Lee is going to come for you no matter where you end up. I feel compelled to let you know that. He is relentless and thorough and if he has his partner with him, they will travel to Venus to seek their vengeance."

Scottie said, "I hate that redneck and I may have to go after him."

Mallory retorted, "As much as I need some nontaxable money, I would have to join the group in finding you and destroying your essence."

There was a long pause and stillness. Finally, Scottie broke the silence. She said, "I think we have an accord. I will forget about what that redneck has done to me, get you to the right people to turn over the capsule to, I'll share in the bounty that, truthfully, I wasn't going to pay those contractors any way, and disappear into the night."

Beckmire asked, "So those keys are for the payment of the mercs?"

"Dah! Scottie replied, "There are four cases in the cargo hold. Each is rigged to blow anyone other than me to hell. Therefore, you will have to get me to the airport and on the plane. I will release two cases at the end of the runway before we take off."

Mallory said, "Sounds like an excellent plan for you. That sounds pretty stupid for us and not a deal that I would subscribe to. I have a better plan, how about this? We accept your terms, but we place one of our devices on your plane and if the deal is bad, then we detonate your plane with you on it. We weren't born yesterday, and we certainly want to live to see tomorrow."

Beckmire said, "Since we are going to trust each other, why don't we get two cases and bring them back here and you open them? We will then take you to your plane and off you go with the other two cases--sort of a win-win situation."

Scottie said, "I trust you guys because I have heard about your antics in the Nam. I won't try to screw you, and I definitely hope you won't try to screw me. I need to write down the code to the containers first and then to the detonators. There are three different devices activated aboard the plane I rode in on."

Mallory asked, "How much is in each of the cases?"

"There is a total of $40 million on my plane."

"Who exactly owns your plane, the agency or you?" Mallory asked.

Scottie without hesitation boasted, "I own my plane and a friend of mine who is interested in getting his hands on the capsule owns the other planes."

"Does your friend have a name?" Beckmire asked.

Scottie replied, "Not a part of the deal. He is innocuous but is interested in striking a balance in world affairs."

Beckmire asked, "You call that innocuous? An individual wanting to control a game changer. That's your definition of innocuous. Wow, that is some crazy shit. Anyway, back to the cases. Do you want to proceed as discussed?"

"I think we have an accord."

In the interim, Scottie wrote down the numbers and fail-safe systems connected to entry into the container. She advised them not to make a mistake inputting the numbers since that would trigger a clock connected to an alternative system that would have to be reconfigured and programmed within a matter of minutes. It all seemed credible, but something was missing in the rush for newfound wealth. Beckmire agreed with Mallory that she was not a person to be trusted and called upon Jong to listen to the details of entry into the container to discern if he had any issues.

When he arrived, Jong asked, "Why would you travel on a plane with explosives? Many different things could impact them and go wrong at high altitudes. I concur that she is full of shit. No person in their right mind would fly the distance from the East Coast to the West Coast with an active bomb on the plane, especially one they were planning to detonate at the hands of some novice or intruder. Riding in a plane is a scary activity as it is."

Mallory asked, "Would you bet your life on that assumption?"

Jong looked at him and said after a moment of reflection, "Yes, I would. I mean I know she is erratic and left the planet years ago, however, I sincerely doubt she or any sane person would do that. Come on now, bombs all over the plane at altitudes that would make most materials unstable. Naw, she is bluffing and hedging."

Beckmire said, "Call your boys on our jets and have them to seize those two planes and the pilots. Tell them not to hurt them unless they present a clear and obvious threat to them."

Mallory and Beckmire reentered the area where Scottie was. She was barely able to keep her eyes open from the pain. Mallory said, "I trusted you and thought that we could find a way out of this thing for everyone, but you lied about the ordnance on your plane. What else have you lied about? Give me the name of your boss and I will set you free. Keep the money because you are going to need it to hide from the redneck."

"Come on now. You expect me to tell you how to defuse a bomb on my plane while you keep me tied up here like a pig? Let me tell you this, my pilot will leave this area in approximately forty-five minutes, with or without me. I am not going to just lie down and let you rape me and take money that I have plans for."

Beckmire asked, "You sacrificed all of those men so that you could keep $40 million dollars?"

"My plan was to capture the 'idiot spy', slay his whore and reap another $100 million on delivery of the capsule. That is not an amount most people would consider sharing. However, if you give me the 'idiot spy' and he tells me where the information is, I swear to you, I will share half of the $140 million with you, leave the 'idiot spy' in good health and be on my way. It's just a matter of trust. Okay, I lied about the bombs in the containers, but I swear to you that everything else is true."

Mallory said, "We could have an accord if you tell us who you are working for. That would tell us who we have to continue to hide from until we get rid of that damn capsule. He or she may know by now that you have not succeeded in your mission and may be putting together another team. We need to know who the hell he or she is?"

Scottie responded by saying, "If I told you his name, you would not believe me. Therefore, I am going to keep that ace in the hole."

Mallory said, "I don't know if you realize it, but one of my guys has his eyes set on gutting you like a pig. Seemingly, we can take control of the cases on the plane and let him come in here to finish his work. Not many choices for you unless we agree on a partnership that is based upon trust. I mean we want to trust you, but you have lied so many times that we don't know what's fact and what's fiction. You are squandering your bargaining chips with your variations on the themes. Who the hell do you work for and will we have to worry about him coming at us once we let you go? This is a simple question that needs to be answered before we cut the straps off of your arms and feet. You must understand where we are coming from. We have had people trying to kill us for a while. We need to know what to expect going forward.

"Insofar as the money is concerned, you can keep it, if in fact, you plan to go after the so called redneck," Beckmire said. "If you want to cut your liabilities and keep your money, minus two cases, then tell us what we need to know and off you go into the wild blue yonder. Simple as that. You make it complicated by not sharing who Mr. Mystery is, and whether we will have continued threats against us and our people. Give the sonofabitch up and you are free to go. Again, minus two cases. As a bonus, we can also set you up as a hero by letting you handle who we can trust, and when and where we can make the transfer of that damn capsule. It's simple mathematics."

Scottie, leaking blood from her foot and her scalp sighed, and said, "I can't give you a name, but we can discuss other possible threats that you might face from international groups. The main man is off limits."

Beckmire said, "Now, that's loyalty! The kind of thing me and my guys share. I respect you for that. Mallory, can you huddle with me for a moment?"

As the audible conversation of the two men faded into the windy night, footsteps could be heard. The next person to turn the corner was John Lee. His words to Scottie were, "Nice to see you again. Now, let me tell you, my bosses were despondent, or how you say it, disappointed in their meeting with you. You see, we did a lot of bad things over there in the Nam. We were bad boys. We make them there actors, Martin Smith and Will Lawrence look like angels. They don't know nothing about being bad. Now, me and my guys were really bad boys.

"Now, you done killed my favorite pig and hanged my woman and cut her inners out in my house that I can never sleep in again." He slowly picked up the blow torch and kindle it until it lit. He unsheathed his knife and said, "I want you to watch me gut you like a slaughtered pig. I borrowed that television and a cable so you can see me do my work on you. I'm going to cut you from the place I branded you all the way up to your throat. I think at that point you be in shock or something and probably real dead. If not, the sound of me breaking your chest bones with this here knife is really gonna make you sick."

Scottie said, "Okay, I'm scared, now call your bosses in here so that I can give them the intel that they want."

John Lee yelled, "Jilkes, are you out there?"

Jilkes responded, "I'm here at the door."

John Lee said, "She wants to talk, but will you tell her that the Sarge and Corporal have gone to have dinner and they left her ass to me. Can you Roger that?"

Jilkes said, "Roger that, Old Country. This is your time without any intervention. Do your thing brother." As John Lee torqued the blow torch, Mallory and the Sarge walked in and asked Scottie, "You have something you want to say?"

Scottie retorted, "Yes, I do. I work for the head of the CIA and he works for the President of the United States of America."

Beckmire asked, "Does the head of the CIA and the President of the United States of America know that you have $40 million dollars of taxpayers' money that you plan on using for petty cash as you try to hide out? Are you saying that they are a part of this scheme?"

Scottie queried, "What do you think?"

Mallory exclaimed, "Are you saying that they are in cahoots with you and know about your petty cash stash?"

"All I'm saying is, that they want the product, and the next group of people that come for you won't be a bunch of useless mercs. They will be dressed in full battle uniforms sporting the American flag and accompanied by tanks and shit like that. All you have done is escalate your circumstances into a no win campaign that ends with them dropping large amounts of conclusive offensive shit all over this place. Now, I am going to give you one last time to be trustworthy and deliver me from this redneck and enjoy the fruits of our partnership."

Jilkes asked, "What is she talking about?"

Beckmire replied, "She tried to bribe Mallory and me. We discovered some keys attached to her belt that opens the same kind of cases that T-Rex had that led to a boatload of cash. On the plane she rode in on, there are four cases, which according to her, there is $10 million in each. She promised me and Mallory $20 million plus an equal share of the $100 million that she is supposed to receive once she delivers Zanthius and the capsule."

Scottie interjected, "He left out the part where they agreed they didn't have to tell you guys about their sudden wealth. I guess they were planning on keeping it all for themselves. Not very trustworthy people if you ask me."

Jilkes looked at the Sarge and inquired, "Is what she said the truth?"

Beckmire said, "How the hell do I know? She's a spy. I do believe that there is money on that plane, but I don't know how much. As a matter of fact, when John Lee finishes up here, you two go and secure it. Take Jong along because we are going to need some laundering services.

"If you guys remember, we brought a shitload of cash with us and you know we don't do cash. Ms. Scottie, if you think that you can draw straws between us, you are deadly mistaken. That little ploy about Mallory and me making a deal to cut the others out, well let me say this, we are a brotherhood not a dysfunctional government agency. See you in hell. Carry on John Lee."

John Lee proclaimed, "Finally, I get to gut this here pig! Jilkes, you want to watch close up as I show her what a beating heart looks like?"

"Naw. I'll pass on this one, but you clear your head."

Frantic, Scottie yelled, "There must be something I can offer you! Let's just talk for a minute. I bet you we can come up with something and you can forgive me for what happened to your friend. Let's just talk about it for a while." John Lee lit the torch and heated his knife until it began to glow.

Scottie screamed, "I can't believe I'm going to die by the hands of a redneck asshole. Go fuck yourself! I'll see you in hell along with that black wench of yours." She started to cry as did John Lee. He missed his woman and was sad that this evil, bloody heifer killed his love and defiled her as well. John Lee was also sad because this woman killed his favorite pig. He wiped the tears from his eyes and whispered to Scottie, "Goodbye, you evil witch." John Lee took the heated knife and began, as promised, to gut Scottie like a pig.

## CHAPTER NINETEEN

A few hours later, Walter called Beckmire and asked him how they made out against the latest threat. Beckmire told him that there were a lot of fat wolves and bears roaming around, as well as, other animals that were feasting on human carcasses. Walter told him that he had noticed a different posture by the Director. The Director suddenly seemed concerned about what people were doing. He told him that previously, he would just look at you and didn't give a shit about who you were or what might happen to you. Somewhere in her safety deposit box, I think Scottie has something on him.

Beckmire told him that Scottie said she worked for the Director of the CIA and the President of the United States of America, and implicated both in the plot. Walter told him that he heard that Scottie had a sizeable amount of money on her plane. Walter asked, "What happened to the money?"

Beckmire answered, "The money was in a container that was rigged with explosives. The truck carrying it ran off the road, submerged in a lake, and blew up, destroying it. The driver, thankfully, escaped unharmed."

Walter said, "Oh well, I wish you could have increased your coffers with that money. Sorry Buddy."

Beckmire queried, "Did you know she owned a large jet?"

Walter responded, "I did not know she owned a jet. However, her boyfriend has several large jets."

Beckmire asked, "Who is her boyfriend?"

"That rich guy who is running for President and pissing off every living person except those in middle America and the deep south," Walter replied.

Beckmire exclaimed, "You have got to be horseshitting me. That's her boyfriend?"

Walter responded, "The one and only."

"You know what, Walter, I now believe that I know who is calling the shots in this mess--Mr. Mystery is the name. He is going to be really pissed when he finds out that his woman was gutted like a pig," Beckmire indicated.

"What do you mean by 'gutted like a pig'?" Walter inquired.

"You know she murdered John Lee's woman. She disemboweled her, hung her from his top floor landing, and placed her inners in his refrigerator. We in turn agreed that he would be her exterminator. Just last night, she filled the valley with screams of terror and horror. My man gutted her like a pig."

"He's going to be coming after you. Whatever she did for him sexually, he enjoyed, and he fell in love with that crazy ass woman. Beckmire, he is going to come for you and yours. How many planes do you have at your disposal?"

"Including the two that Scottie and her crew rode in on, five totals."

"Do you have an alternative place to set up camp?"

"I hadn't thought about it, but I will bring that to a vote. Do you have someone in the government that is not on the 'take'?"

"I am not on the take and I have two freshmen congressmen and a senior senator from New York, who are squeaky clean. The congressmen are from Pennsylvania and Florida. I trust them as they do me. I will try to make the connection and arrange a meeting. In the meantime, I need you guys to abandon that location and head as far away from it as possible. Don't tell me where you're going. You know how to reach me and when I set it up, I will be in touch. I wouldn't use those other two planes. I'm sure they have tracking devices on them. How are you going to handle the $40 million? Do you need my help, or do you have a broker?"

"What $40 million? It was destroyed."

"If you need my help in cleaning it, I have a great guy who can help. When Mr. Mystery finds out you have destroyed his prize freak, he is going to come after you with every sick son-of-a-bitch that he can find. I would load up and get the hell out of there at first light."

"Thanks for the heads up. If you personally need anything, don't hesitate to call. No matter what it is. Oh, can you help me obtain some passports in a hurry?"

"Go the local post office in the morning and I will have someone there fix you up. How many are we talking about?"

"Not sure? Can I call you back in fifteen?"

"No, don't call. Text me a number and go to the post office first thing in the morning."

Beckmire huddled with Mallory, Zanthius, Asiram, Courtney and Ava and said, "We have to abandon this place. I got intel from a reliable source that a very rich and powerful man will be coming for us because of what we did to his mate. We did what we had to do. I need to send my boys back to their families and our immediate family needs to board one of those jets and fly far, far away.

"My source also has some reliable people that will do due diligence with regards to the capsule. Now, I am tired of running and killing people. I want to go home and visit my ancestors. I do not want my guys to come with us. I feel that my other family can provide us with the protection that we need. I know you are as weary as I am and I'm trying to find a way to stop this madness. Seems like every time we think we can conclude this, at any cost, including our lives, the door opens wider. I need you people to trust my judgment on this, stay focused and follow me to another world."

# # #

John Lee and Jilkes returned from the airport with five massive footlockers. It was estimated that there was a total of $10 million dollars in each case for a total of $50 million. The cases were taken to the shed and were closely examined by Jong. He asked everyone to step outside while he examined the locks, latches and bolts to see if they had been tampered with. He called Beckmire in and stated, "I don't see any potential danger and each case does not look as if it has been tampered with."

"Okay, give me the keys, I'll do this part. Take a hike."

Jong said, "Bad idea. If there are wires and a timer, I'm probably the only one capable of dismantling it."

"Okay, we'll do it together."

There were no explosive devices other than the humongous response that the group had at eyeballing five huge cases with $10 million dollars in each case. One of the cases had a pouch full of uncut diamonds. Beckmire declared, "Now, this is some insane shit! How the hell do people get to play with this kind of money without any checks and balances, and where or how do you come across diamonds like these? I missed a $200 dollar item on my taxes and the sons-of-bitches spent four days going through my records and making me produce all kinds of stuff. Beckmire looked at Asiram and asked, "Any big ideas for handling this kind of cash?"

"We're going to need a significant amount of cash on hand if we are going to go to that place down under, but not this much cash. Okay, considering the cash I had in my safe at the place you destroyed and will have to rebuild, the additional booty that was collected from those amateurs, and now this, my safe here could probably hold half of that amount. Maybe more if we got rid of some of the other stuff in there."

Mallory asked, "What kind of other stuff?" Asiram looked at him and responded, "If you must know, I have more weapons and ammo in it."

Beckmire asked, "Where is it and can we see it?"

"Daddy-in-Law, of course you can see it.   It's impenetrable and totally disguised. Once I set the alarm, if anyone comes within one hundred feet, boom; after that at seventy-five feet, boom, boom; and on and on until the entire tunnel is filled with toxic fumes. If you reach the safe, the final explosion is catastrophic."

On their walk through the tunnel that lead from the main ranch house to the guest house, Asiram said, "Okay, stop here." She proceeded for another two paces and placed her hand on the wall to her left. She then backed up five paces and placed her hand on the wall to her right and told the guys to come forward. After another twenty-five paces, Asiram pushed a strategically placed brick on her left in the middle of the wall. All aspects of the tunnel began to shift hydraulically, and another tunnel revealed itself. In that tunnel was a huge safe that was partially opened and filled with cash and munitions. Beckmire proclaimed, "You're one interesting woman, but I have to say, you are a lifesaver, my dear."

"Thank you, Daddy-in-Law."

Beckmire asked, "In the safe at the farmhouse, how much do you reckon you have in there?"

Asiram replied, "I don't know, maybe $2 million or more."

Beckmire questioned, "How much do you have in this one?"

Asiram answered, "Why don't you count it and let me know. I don't keep an accounting of my assets until they get low. I think there is probably $1.5 million or so in this safe, looking at the stacks."

Beckmire declared, "Okay, lets' say that we owe you an even $5 million! How does that sit with you?"

Asiram looked at her husband and asked, "Honey, do you think that is fair considering your daddy blew up my farm and had my house in Philly shot up? He also caused us a lot stress. Do you think that is fair?"

Zanthius looked at the safe and said, "Sweetheart, we're all family now. Someone is going to pay us big dollars before I turn over that damn capsule. Pops make it seven and you and your guys can increase your foundation donations by $2 million on our behalf. What do you think?"

Beckmire asked Mallory for his input and he responded, "I am thinking like your son. Before this is over, someone is going to have to pay a shitload of money. I think we owe Asiram more than that. Actually, I think we should throw in another $3 million as a wedding gift."

Beckmire said, "There you have it. So, my new and resourceful daughter-in-law, that should replace your house and keep you guys in cash for a while."

Asiram retorted, "Oh, I think we have some other assets that will keep us warm for a very long time. We accept your offer and we want to divide all future revenues generated from this adventure, equally. Is that correct, honey?"

Zanthius replied, "You are an amazing partner and I will use my extraction skills on anyone who looks at you twice. That deal sounds perfect, but at these levels, I would prefer to build housing for poor people rather than squander it on meaningless objects of status. However, I like the deal and its intent. Do we have an accord?" Beckmire and Mallory shook their hands signifying an agreement.

Later that day, Mallory asked the Sarge to walk with him for a moment. When the two men reached the back of the ranch house, the Fab 10 were waiting for them. Jilkes arrogantly asked, "Sarge, have you lost your damn mind? This is how we roll. If you got a problem, then I got a problem. If I got a problem, then you have a problem and if they have a problem, then we all have a problem. Right, Rich Brown?"

"Absolutely! You guys saved me from my own stepfather and believed in me and Bernstein, when we tried to do that deal in the Nam to make you guys rich."

Jilkes said, "I don't know what the hell you're planning, but we ain't going home or nowhere else until this situation is concluded. We go where you go until there is a white flag from the other side. We live, or we die with our brotherhood.

You are our liege. Stop the horseshit. Include us in the deal because we know where we are going next. We have had the damn pilots figure out capacity, distance and weight on our planes and they have assured Jong that we are good to go! Gentlemen, this meeting is over!"

The Sarge looked at Mallory with tears in his eyes.

Mallory mumbled, "You can't let your men see you cry. They might think you're weak."

Beckmire fumbled with his words and finally exclaimed, "Who gives a hoot if they see me cry! My brotherhood is stronger than most families. I just love these guys and I guess they love me as well."

#

Beckmire called the entire group together and laid out his plan. He realized that his guys had their passports, but Larry, Marisa, Rashida, and the children didn't have theirs. Neither did he and Courtney. Beckmire sent Walter a text with the number seven as the only information stated. A text came back with 'done by nine'.

That night, Clyde came over with his neighbors and asked if he could speak with Ms. Asiram, Zanthius, Beckmire, Mallory and the rest of the group. As they walked out the front door of the main house, all the neighbors in the area were standing in front of the house with candles. Asiram walked beside Beckmire and said, "They are thanking you for what you did, and they are sending blessings for us on our next journey and adventure. Zanthius and I set up a fund for them to borrow from. It is interest free and they will never be penalized. That is their way of telling us, they have our backs.

"Clyde has put the entire town on alert, and they have people with weapons watching every move that is made towards my ranch. I just love these people. No lying, cheating or stealing--just honest people trying to make sure their families and friends are protected from evil. That is exactly what you did Daddy-in-Law. I trust you like I trust your son.

"I have never met a more righteous man than you, Mr. Ben Beckmire. I see why these guys leave their families and friends to be with you in your time of need. I love being a part of your team. By the way, don't worry about the house; it had a massive amount of insurance on it. Love you! Oh, and one more thing, I think that money is still in place. That area of the tunnel was reinforced, and it probably survived any explosion or fire. It has no connection to the house."

Clyde invited the group to his ranch for dinner and emphatically said, "You can't refuse this invitation. People from around here want to thank you personally for being good human beings and doing what is right by them. They have all cooked and prepared special meals for you and your guests. Don't worry about security. Our friends from the National Guard will be doing full battle exercises tonight on this property with live ammunition. Ms. Asiram is aware of it, but said that in her house, you and her husband are the masters and the commanders. So, she directed me to you, Sir."

Beckmire exclaimed, "Clyde, it is an honor to join you and a testament to what people can accomplish when they root out evil. We will be there in an hour."

## CHAPTER TWENTY

At 0500 hours, Asiram called Clyde and asked him to come to the ranch. As Clyde was driving down the access road to her place, he saw Asiram walking down the road towards the main highway. When he reached her, he said, "Ms. Asiram, why are you walking out here by yourself?"

"I want to have a private moment with you, so I decided to meet you halfway. Listen, later we will be leaving the ranch and going far, far, away. I might have to change phone numbers, but I want you to always call me and keep me abreast of what is happening on the ranch and in the community, maybe twice a week. I think we have taken care of those carpetbaggers but if there is a problem, I need you to tell me immediately so that I can figure out how to deal with their asses. You have watched my ranch for years and you have never asked me a single question about where I go, when I am coming back, or what I do for a living. I respect that so much. That is why I got my friends and my husband involved in our neighbors' plight. I will need you to care for my ranch as if it were yours, attending to everything possible."

"In case something happens to me or my husband, I will leave this property to you and a key, that is for your eyes only, that will open my personal safe and endow you with a lot of money. The ranch will become yours only if I am certifiably dead and if my husband isn't dead but he doesn't want to live out here and or we have no children to contest this proposition. In any event, if we have children, then they become heirs to the property.

"Several years ago, I had you sign for a box at the bank which contains the formula to enter my safe. As you know, the safe is located between the two houses. If any of our neighbors get into financial trouble beyond the accounts that I have set up for them, then I want you to follow those instructions to the letter for entering my safe. One miscalculation and you will be blown to smithereens. I am going to trust you with everything that I have here. What I need to hear from you is that I can trust you and rely on you to do the right thing by me and our neighbors. Is that a responsibility that you can live up to? More importantly, is the fact if you try to do me the way of the devil, someone will come and punish you, much like that woman who was tortured by John Lee. Can I trust you, Clyde?"

Clyde looked at Asiram with tears in his eyes and answered, "Ms. Asiram, I have been watching and taking care of your property, as if it were my own, for years. I am offended if you believe that my motivations are strictly for personal gain. You helped me when the damn banks wouldn't assist me. You bailed me out when our crops froze and many other times. I don't care if there be billions in that there safe. I know all about it and have been down there many a time. You leave it wide open. You never lock it. I just thought you were testing me in my hour of need. I will never take a penny from you. You and your people have helped me, my friends and neighbors, rid our community of some very bad vermin and I can only thank you and them fellas. No need to ask me about craziness, because I don't do crazy and I certainly don't want to scream all night like that lady did."

Asiram handed Clyde an envelope and said, "I'm trusting you with my life, and I know I can depend upon you."

Clyde responded, "Until the day I die, me and mine got your back."

# # #

Beckmire asked Jilkes, John Lee, Whitmore, and Chakes to make an early run into town with him to scout out any possible problems. The members of his group who did not have passports, arrived at the local post office at exactly 0900 hours. Clyde and four of his people were there, as well, milling around town as usual speaking to their neighbors and friends. One ominous sight that was obviously missing was the sign on the carpetbaggers' office. They made a deal with Beckmire and left town abruptly.

As Clyde and his people made their way through town, there were only two people they were unfamiliar with on Main Street. They appeared harmless but were still reported to Beckmire and his group. Whitmore and Chakes were assigned to monitor or terminate them if need be.

As the van pulled up to the post office, Beckmire noticed a reflection from the rooftop of the building opposite the post office. He broadcasted that he saw a flash from a scope and was concerned. Clyde came back and said, "Not to worry, that would be my Misses. She be a helluva shot. Go on now, go ahead into the building." As the group entered the building, the person behind the window said, "I guess you people are here for passports. Come on in. One at a time."

The entire group was processed, and on their way back to the ranch in twenty minutes. Beckmire muttered to Courtney, "It's good to have friends in high places."

She agreed and laughed. Courtney said, "All of us are going to need some new clothes soon. Should we start shopping now or wait until we are out of here?"

Beckmire replied, "A very rich person with unlimited resources and no common sense, will be after us in a little while. I prefer to get clothes at the end of our journey. If there are pressing items that must be addressed now, then I will make the time. Sweetie, if it can wait, I prefer us to be safe and sound and out of here than worry about what I am missing fashion-wise."

Courtney looked at him and said, "This has been a helluva adventure and I wouldn't have missed a single moment of it. You are a wonderful human being, Ben Beckmire, and I so desperately love you. Oh my God! I haven't had this much excitement and fun since I first met you, when you and Larry were doing your very mysterious projects late at night and into the early mornings. I don't need or have any proof, nor do I want any, but I knew way back then that you and Larry were the 'Vigilantes'."

Beckmire looked at Courtney and said, "You have a wonderful and intense imagination. However, I will not disavow you of any preconceived notions."

On their way back to the van, the young policeman approached the vehicle and asked, "Are you people from around here?"

Clyde walked up and replied, "You might want to take a walk or catch a sniper's bullet in the head. We are sick and tired of you improving your financial status on the backs of common working folks. Rumor has it that since the carpetbaggers got the message, a message was being sent out to you, 'leave now or never be found'. I'm not threatening you but that is the message I heard that was being discussed amongst the locals. If I were you, I would find a new place to play police."

The police officer said, "Why, you little shit. I should arrest you for threatening me."

Clyde said, "I didn't threaten you, but the red dots on your vest should tell you that your time is limited in this town, just saying. If I were you, I would slowly leave my weapon on the ground and drive your squad car to where you parked your personal car and just leave. You apparently have pissed off a lot of locals and they are interested in having you do what your carpetbagger friends did, that is leave in a hurry to avoid an animalistic encounter. Your choice, but I am not threatening you. I am just a messenger who has your interest at heart. Listen, drop your belt and leave your badge on top of it. I don't think that they would shoot an unarmed man."

As the cop looked at the laser dots on various parts of his body, he said, "I don't like this chicken shit town anyway and I hate the stupid people who live here. I quit."

Clyde declared, "You have to go to city hall to resign! I am no official and I certainly won't accept your resignation. You have exactly four hours to get your shit and get out of town. You will be followed for one hundred miles and if you even stop for gas, you will be assassinated. I hope I'm making myself clear to you, piece of shit. Now, get your ass over to city hall and resign your commission. It was nice to know you, asshole. I suggest you go east like your friends did. Maybe they will hire you to pick up their garbage. Get now, just get."

# # #

Walter called Beckmire and advised him that if they were leaving the country, he might need visas for everyone depending on where they were going. Beckmire told Walter if he told him where they were going that could be a problem for all of them. Walter said, "Those are my exact sentiments. However, I know where you are going, Cousin, but I am not the one arranging visas for the group that would be the senator herself. The number I am going to give you is to her personal cell phone and she is expecting a call from you, but only if you are leaving the country. That information would be between you and the senator."

Beckmire said, "I'll give it some consideration. Also, I will be changing phone numbers soon. I will text you the number in the inverse order. Thanks, for your help, and once we figure this thing out, I'm going to give you a call and request a police escort to turn this damn capsule over to you. It is not in our possession and we are being chased further and further away from it. My son feels it is extremely safe and inconspicuous, but you never know about his interpretations."

"Funny you should mention phones, because I am dropping this one in the toilet when I hang up from you. You should do the same, drop yours in the toilet and the new number that I'm giving you, inverse the number and use 1000 for the last four digits; 100 for the next three numbers and ten for the area code. We can't be too careful now, can we?"

Beckmire laughed and said, "You're turning out to be a helluva friend. When this is all said and done, we will have to throw down a few beers and just chill out together. Catch you soon and thanks for connecting me to someone that I believe in and who is doing a great job and soon to be, hopefully, our next President."

## CHAPTER TWENTY-ONE

Beckmire made the call to the number that Walter had given him, and the senator answered by saying, "Hello."

Beckmire went on to say, "Hi there, my name is Ben Beckmire and a friend of mine by the name of Walter gave me your number. He indicated to me that you could help me, and a few other people obtain visas."

The senator said, "Oh, yes. I think that can be arranged but I need you to give me names, birthdates, nationalities, and the country of entry. You can text those to me at this number. I look forward to having a meaningful conversation with you and the one known as the 'idiot spy'. What a clever name for someone who perhaps holds a product that can change the world, quite imaginative and clever. When will you get me the information that I need?"

Beckmire responded, "Within the next two hours and thank you. By the way, I think you are doing a fantastic job and I look forward to casting my vote for you when you decide to run for the Presidency of the United States of America." The senator thanked him and bid him safe travels and firmly stated that as soon as he was settled, she was interested in having a long conversation about her securing the capsule and removing all remaining obstacles.

In parting she said, "I heard a rumor from a reliable friend of ours that you may have to exercise your right to protect yourself in that foreign land that you are heading to. After I get the name of the country, I will make sure that you have enough protective devices to fend off a small army. Let me make one more suggestion to you, do not leave this country with any weapons and I mean not even a pocketknife. You and your people, including the one known as the 'idiot spy', are high valued targets. I pray that you can overcome your next challenge and find yourselves securely in my office. You can run, Sarge, but you can't hide. Have you heard that statement before?"

Beckmire answered, "I am extremely familiar with it and I know the exact meaning of it. Thank you, Senator, and I will be in touch."

Beckmire obtained the information and Jong texted the information to the senator's phone number. He also had Jong make sure that the planes were ready, the course was set, and the flight plan was filed for their long flight. Clyde, in the meantime, had secured the provisions for the flight as dictated by Courtney and Ava, who had become best buddies.

Carlos had two men who had families. He asked them if they were able to make the trip and they responded positively. Everything and everyone was in play and the die was cast. The first stop on the journey would be Los Angeles, California, where the planes would refuel and have a prearranged inspection for the flight over the water and on to Sydney, Australia. From there, places unknown and mysterious to the average urban dweller would be visited.

## CHAPTER TWENTY-TWO

Jong had heard from friends about the Sebel Townhouse Hotel in Elizabeth Bay, Australia. He was surprised to find it available and rented out the entire hotel. It was a small European style hotel in the Kings Cross area. It had been the temporary home for the likes of Michael Jackson and his entourage, as well as, David Bowe, Elton John, Dire Straits and many others, (including the author of this book). He thought it might be a great place for the group to enjoy a few nights of peace and quiet before moving on to the strange and mysterious places that the Sarge had spoken about. It had the distinction of being the world's greatest Rock and Roll Hotel.

Since its heyday, the Sebel Townhouse Hotel, located in Kings Cross, an area that was submerged in drugs, prostitution and any other negative proclivity that one could imagine or request, was a favorite purlieu of musicians and actors. It later became the scourge of Sydney because of the despicable and open use of drugs and the obvious propensity for prostitutes to practice their trades in full view of the local magistrate. Internally, the hotel was immaculate and beautifully furnished with modern conveniences. Each room had a hydro tub large enough to accommodate five large human beings. The bedrooms were huge but intimate with fresh flowers daily. It was a wild shot, but the best shot that Jong could come up with to handle his friends and associates.

CHAPTER TWENTY-THREE

Once in Australia, and in the van that Beckmire rode in, the driver said, "Mate, I have to tell you. In its prime, this place was the bomb. I mean Michael Jackson, Bowie and Elton John and many other celebrities flocked to this place. Mate, I just say that but don't go wandering around at night and do keep these pretty ladies under close scrutiny at all times. They be kidnapping targets or sold into prostitution."

Beckmire asked, "This isn't the best part of town?"

The driver replied, "Mate, you be in the middle of hell down here. This here place, mate, has lost its luster. Everything down here mate, is for sale."

Beckmire looked at Jong and inquired, "How did you find this place, in a girlie magazine?"

"Sarge, you know that I am a big Michael Jackson fan and when I found out that he stayed here, well, I just figured if it was good enough for the King of Pop, then it would be good enough for us. My bad, I should have checked the recent history of the place."

Beckmire said, "Oh great, and all we have as weapons are our fists."

Jong said, "It might be a good thing to practice using them since that may be all we have to protect ourselves with while we're here."

When the Beckmire entourage pulled off the main street and went down the small hill where the hotel was located, there was an obvious knife fight taking place. The driver whispered to Beckmire, "Mate, make your stay short and sweet. By the way, I have a friend in the States who lives in Washington, DC, his name is Walter and he sent a surprise package to your room. It will make you feel warm and fuzzy and provide you with a new level of comfort. I am Walter's first cousin, Mate. I do what he does back there and if you need anything, and I mean anything, ring me up. My card is in the door well. Where you're going, you need to be a holy man and those with you must be those who you love. Mate, this is a journey of faith. Walter's ancestors are related to yours, but you must experience the how, the why, and the when yourself. If you have no faith, then all will be lost and all will be sacrificed. The one known as the 'idiot spy' has been protected by something you don't think exists, and your true faith, as well as those you love, will be tested."

Beckmire looked at the driver and asked, "What did you say?"

The driver looked at him and responded, "I didn't open my mouth."

Jong inquired, "Sarge, are you okay? He didn't say a word."

Beckmire yelled, "Stop the horseshit. You didn't hear this guy tell me about faith?"

Jong looked at Gladstone and then the Sarge and replied, "Perhaps we have to insist that you get a full night's rest. You may be slightly hallucinating."

# # #

Check-in was as smooth as a polished rock. The Beckmire party occupied the entire top levels of the hotel. As Beckmire and Courtney entered their room, they saw three large boxes in the middle of the floor. Courtney asked, "What the hell?" As she circled the boxes, she saw a note on one of them, it read, 'To Sergeant Ben Beckmire, retired, a gift from a true believer, friend and family member--signed Walter'. Beckmire told Courtney to leave the room because he thought this was strange, especially since Walter did not know their destination. As Courtney was about to leave the room, the driver appeared at the door and said, "I'm sorry, but I need to speak with Mr. Beckmire."

The Sarge came to the door and asked, "How do you know my name?"

The driver looked at him and answered, "Your essence is here on this continent. You don't know your roots, Mr. Beckmire? I know more about you than you can imagine and so does every other Aborigine who is from this land and has traveled through Dreamtime and has been on Walkabouts. I just want to say, you will find some hardware for you and your friends.

Ask yourself a question, Mr. Beckmire. Why did you, and why do you trust Walter? Walter is an Abo, sorry, Aborigine just like you are. He may be white with blond hair, but he is from the bush. He is your connection to Walkabout. In this time of cell phones and internet, you will 'ave to trust all that you think you believe in, Mr. Beckmire. If you don't, all will be lost, including your son, the 'idiot spy'. You 'ave come back to a world of mystery and misunderstandings. It will be up to you to decipher the signs and discover your faith or abandon it. All depends on you and how you interact with the 'idiot spy', your son by Ava, another person who has roots here in the Outback.

You will be required to acknowledge Ava, disconnect from Ava and realize that Ava and Courtney are one in the same—the heavenly mothers of your child—Zanthius De Lombardo. Good night, Mr. Beckmire, you 'ave my card. Life has just become a complex set of unbelievable circumstances that will require you to make the perfect decision at each turn or you, your family, and friends will perish. Your faith is all that you will need to complete this task, Mr. Beckmire. Trust your instincts and I will be there to assist, especially on Walkabout."

Beckmire looked at him and then Courtney and asked, "Courtney, did you hear what he said?"

Courtney replied, "Ben, he asked me to speak with you."

Beckmire said, "I need to get some rest. I think my mind is breaking new ground in terms of being fragile. Honey hold me and love me. I fear that I am really losing my mind. I keep hearing this guy say things in the presence of others but no one else hears him but me. I am afraid, I'm losing my mind. I can't have this happen at this point. I need my mind to be clear and focused. Honey, hold me, I am scared."

Jong called Mallory and told him what the Sarge had said during the ride to the hotel. He said, "I guess the boss needs some rest. He kept asking me if I heard what the driver said to him and I told him that the guy didn't open his mouth. Perhaps you need to check on him later. He's probably exhausted like the rest of us and needs to sleep all night without having to look over his shoulders." Mallory told him that he would check on the Sarge later and make sure he was okay.

Mallory and Monica had been in their room for about twenty minutes when Courtney called and asked Mallory to pay her a visit because the Sarge was having some mental issues. Mallory called Jilkes and John Lee and they rushed to her room near the elevator. When Jilkes and John Lee arrived at Beckmire's room, Mallory said, "Courtney called me and said that the Sarge is having some mental issues. The scary thing is Jong told me that the Sarge was hearing things during the ride here."

John Lee said, "He just probably needs to adjust. He be home and his history be calling him for renewal. The Sarge be adjusting to being in a place that is full of strange things and animals and all that history he talked about. It be important that we just let him be. I be going back to bed. Let him be, but it won't be right if we don't go in and calm the Misses down. Trust me, he be good and be finding a way out of this mess. I just be knowing this because it be like my pig telling me how to survive over there in the Nam. Just let the Sarge get his feet wet on this here thing. He'll be good in the morning with a lot of talk that will make no sense to any of us blokes."

Jilkes asked, "Where did you come up with the word 'bloke'?"

"I really think you can't hear shit and you don't know or understand shit, sometimes. I sometimes think my favorite pig is smarter than you be."

"John Lee, kiss my shiny you know what!"

"Naw! I loves you too much to be kissing the nasty part of your body."

Mallory knocked on the door and Courtney whispered, "He is out like a light. I mean he was talking crazy one minute, and the next he was in the bed, undressed and sound asleep. He was really talking crazy for a minute. Asking me did I hear what the driver said when the driver didn't open his mouth."

Mallory said, "He's probably really tired and stressed out like the rest of us, we all need a full night's sleep. Trust me, I will check on him first thing in the morning but if you need me, just call and I'll be here in a flash."

# # #

Zanthius was in the bathroom emptying his stomach. He didn't have time to discuss it with Asiram because the feeling came over him in a hurry. She placed wet towels on the back of his neck after she realized that he had a fever. After fully purging himself of everything that was in his stomach, he began dry heaving which was extremely painful. After getting Zanthius in bed, Asiram called Courtney first and then Ava and told them both that Zanthius was sick. Ava went directly to their room, but Courtney told Asiram that the Sarge was sick, as well, and she didn't want to leave him alone.

As soon as Zanthius got into bed, he fell asleep and didn't move. It would be morning before anyone would hear a sound out of him. Ava called Courtney and told her that Zanthius

had a fever. Courtney suggested that she try to lower his body
temperature without any medication until they could assess
what was going on. Ava asked Asiram if it was okay for her
to hang around for a while and she told her absolutely. The
two women enjoyed a cup of tea while Ava gave Asiram the
4-1-1 on her son.

# # #

Ben Beckmire slept until 11:30 in the morning, a thing
that was extremely uncharacteristic of the Sarge. When he got
out of the bed, he told Courtney that he had some extremely
interesting dreams about places that he has never been before,
all on the continent of Australia. He prefaced his comments
by saying, "I know you didn't hear the driver speak and you
probably thought I was cracking under all the pressure."

"Yes, as a matter of fact, I thought you had left the
reservation and was on a journey way beyond my
comprehension."

"Well, if you thought I was crazy last night, then you're
really going to think I have completely lost my mind when I
tell you that I was visited by relatives from my great-great-
great grandfather's clan--the Beckmire's' including my
father's father who told me to leave this place within two days
and head towards the Northern Territory. They have embraced
Zanthius despite his previous philandering and acknowledge
Asiram as a true warrior who will provide protection and
guidance for him. So, honey, I am not crazy, I am connected
to the earth, air, water, animals and most of all, the Beckmire
clan. I know this sounds incredible, but it's not unlike the
stories I told you many years ago. What is different is the fact

that I know who I am and where and who I come from and their spirits."

Courtney walked over to Beckmire and placed her hand on his forehead and said, "Your fever has subsided, but your ranting continues."

He looked at her and said, "You too will witness things that don't make sense immediately, but in the long run, after processing events, you will know that I am not insane. I must call Jong and make sure the pilots can legally fly by tomorrow. Don't worry, just think of it as another journey that we are taking with the people that we truly love and respect."

Beckmire walked over to the telephone, called Jong and said, "We need the planes and pilots ready to fly tomorrow morning to the Northern Territory. Can you make that happen?"

"How are you feeling, Sarge?" Jong asked.

Beckmire responded, "Rested, enlightened and ready to face the next phase of our journey. I will brief you guys sometime this afternoon, however, I need to make sure that we are out of this place by tomorrow morning. Also, any touring of Sydney will be done in groups. No lone explorers, okay?"

"I will pass the word, Sarge. Glad you're feeling better, but I have one question, why are we heading to the Northern Territory?"

"Do you trust me and my judgment so far?"

"I do, and you know that, so why do you ask?"

"We are going on an adventure that will give us guidance in terms of how to end this matter and get back to our lives as peaceful law-abiding citizens. Catch you later."

At noon, a sleepy Zanthius rolled up out of bed and said to Asiram, "I'm hungry. Can we order in or do you want to go out? I'm famished. Man, I don't know what happened last night, but after that catharsis, I had the most incredible dreams and I never remember my dreams. Asiram, I mean I saw everything so clearly that I felt things were actually happening. My dad was in most of them and it appeared there was a ritual, or something, and you were appointed as my guardian. I mean it seemed so real and every time I tried to wake up, I couldn't. It was some scary shit. I have got to talk to my father. I even met his father, his father's father and his father. It was incredibly real and scary. I even met some guy whose name is Wajickee. He is a spirit and has been charged with keeping me alive. Sweetheart, I'm not losing it, that dream was so compelling that I know there must be some meaning to it.

Asiram in the meantime called Ava and proclaimed, "Julius Cesar is awake and has a lot to tell you."

Ava said, "I'll be right there."

When Ava arrived, Zanthius said, "Mom, give your son a big hug. I'll let Asiram interpret for me since she thinks I have left the planet."

Ava asked, "How do you feel?"

"I feel perfect. I am hungry as can be, but other than that, I feel wonderful. I had some amazing dreams last night that I can't explain, but I am sure my father has a lot of answers. Can you call him and Courtney and see if they are available for brunch? Oh, and by the way, we must

leave this place tomorrow for the Northern Territory, wherever that is. I'm going to take a long shower and then we can all go get something to eat."

# # #

At brunch, Zanthius didn't waste any time discussing his dreams. He started out by saying, "Oh my God! I had the most incredible dreams last night."

Beckmire said, "Why don't we eat before we discuss something that we have in common, like caves and people from long, long ago."

Courtney looked at the Sarge and then Zanthius and asked, "So, Zanthius, one thing before we order, did you have a timetable in your dream?"

"Abso-damn-lutely! We need to be out of here in the next 24 hours and head to the Northern Territory. Why do you ask?"

Courtney answered, "Your father received the same information in his dream."

Beckmire said, "You and I were on something called, 'Dreamtime', where we went through the right of passage that usually happens when one is a teenager. It is a dream state that the Aborigines believe keeps them in contact with their ancestors. We shared a like vision and experienced a whole different world. Courtney, Mallory, and a few of the boys thought that I was losing my mind when I said the driver talked to me and they didn't hear him. I told Courtney the same thing, we have to leave for the Northern Territory in the morning."

Zanthius looked at him and said, "I don't know how you did that, but I am serious about what I just said."

Courtney said, "Zanthius, your father told me the same thing when he finally awakened this morning. Last night, you had a fever. In your case, I can understand how you may have been delirious, but hearing your father this morning scares me into believing that there are things that I don't understand and probably never will, because I don't have any Aborigine blood flowing through my veins. Let's order. This is astounding and I don't practice hocus pocus, I practice medicine based upon facts, but I am not discounting anything in this place."

Beckmire stared at Asiram to the point that everyone at the table noticed it, including Courtney who inquired, "Sarge, why are you looking at Asiram with such intensity?"

"Asiram has been anointed as Zanthius's protector."

Asiram exclaimed, "What the f…! He just told me that I was his protector. How on earth did you know that?"

"I can't explain it, but on Walkabout, many things become crystal clear to you. I am not trying to convince anyone that this place is magical and mysterious, but people get used to the fact that everything is slightly different here and that there are things and forces within this universe that we don't understand but do exist. I am part Aborigine and so is my son. Together we are going to do some incredible things after we finish on Walkabout and in Dreamtime. I know this sounds like a lot of hocus pocus, but you people are our loves for life. Trust me when I say, if he or I are acting out of character, it is because we are sharing some magnificent history as well as ways to undo the evil that has found its way into my son's life and is here on the continent. The capsule must be retrieved in ten days or it might destroy Zanthius. We don't have a lot of time to waste and I beg you, I implore you, to give us the latitude that we need to make sense of all of this and that includes violent sessions of purgation."

Asiram announced, "Zanthius had that last night. I hope he doesn't have another one of those in store. That was horrendous and violently smelly. I got sick watching my man be sick. There was nothing I could do about it but call his Mom to come and sit by me while I tried to make sure I didn't lose my new husband. It was terrible, but I don't discount anything you say. This world is crazy, and I hear in this place, the water runs the opposite way down the toilet."

Beckmire said to Zanthius, "Once we get to the Northern Territory, you and I will disappear for a day or two and find the answers to riddles concerning the capsule, our history and our future."

In the afternoon, Beckmire called the entire group together. First of all, he thanked them for their support and flexibility during this crisis. He indicated to the group that he was part Aborigine and that there are many stories about one of his ancestors who could transform into the Great Saltie. He explained what a Saltie is and begged the group for their indulgence in the next phase of this journey. He responded to the notion of him losing his mind the previous night and told them that he and his son had similar visions of what they needed to do in order for them to survive this craziness.

Beckmire laughed when he used the word craziness and reported, "My son and I will make a journey once we reach the Northern Territory and we will be completely out of touch with all of you for a day or so. Most of you, who know me well, will generally vouch for my sanity and ability to operate under pressure. This is all exciting and mysterious at the same time. I believe in my heritage and it is through my history that I have been able to survive in many different venues. I need you guys and ladies to trust me one more time, and if my dreams and those of my son are correct, we will find the answer to our problems. I just need you people to stay mentally ready and safe. On another note, I am almost commanding that everyone remain on these grounds while we are here."

Brown bumped Bernstein and asked, "Sarge, will the boogie man get us if we wander off?" He and Bernstein began to laugh when John Lee stood up and emphasized, "Don't be messing with shit you don't understand. This here place is for real. You can play with folklore if you want, but it may be the last thing you play with."

Beckmire paused for a full minute and finally said, "I know you guys are weary and want to get back to your lives. I can only thank you for your help and if you like, offer you one of the jets to go home. I agree with John Lee's suggestion, don't play with things that you don't understand. If you want, I will let you two escort us to a certain point and then you can decide for yourselves if there is a boogie man or not. However, in the Northern Territory, there are many kinds of boogie men and women as well as animals that you can't imagine."

Brown stood up and said, "Sarge, that was in bad taste. I will follow you to hell and so will this little Israelite. I apologize, Bernstein and I volunteer to take responsibility for security, if those are your wishes. You know we meant no harm and we love you and will, as I said, follow you to hell and back. Please forgive us for joking about it."

Beckmire inquired, "So, does that mean you're not leaving?"

Bernstein responded, "It was never a consideration. He is simple, I tolerate him and then he gets me in trouble and calls me a little Israelite. I'm Baptist." Laughter erupted.

## CHAPTER TWENTY-FOUR

Jong interrupted the discussion and announced, "Sarge, the planes are ready, fueled and loaded with something extra from Walter's people."

"And what on earth would that be?"

Jong replied, "The finest bows and arrows the government could afford."

"Great. The planes are ready, but are the pilots legal to fly?"

"Absolutely. I need a specific destination for hotel purposes, and they need to file a flight plan. If you can give me those specifics, then we will be good to go in the morning."

Beckmire stated to the group, "We are going to Darwin and from there we will spend the balance of the time in the Outback. I have never done this before, but I think that it's going to be a blast. You won't need reservations once we get there. Everything is prepared and waiting on our arrival. I have some small Berettas in my room for the team and Carlos's people. We now have some wonderful bows from our questionable, government friends and everything else will be provided for us.

"I have one simple request. Please do not offend anyone or attempt to interpret the things that you see once we are in the Northern Territory. Life is strange and remains mysterious and counterfactual, so be ever cognizant about what you express openly. I, like all of you, do not believe in hocus pocus. However, in that place, there be demons and spirits. Choose wisely and please do not shoot the animals."

## CHAPTER TWENTY-FIVE

The following morning and as the group loaded the vehicles to head to the airport, the driver that no one could hear, except Beckmire said, "You and the one called the 'idiot spy' had a wonderful night last night. Your dreams were manifestations of your history and your future. I will greet you when your plane arrives in the Northern Territory and it will be me who will escort some of your people to the outer boundaries of our sanctuaries. They will be tested, and the sum of their faiths will be challenged against all that is seemingly incredible. I feel wonderful knowing what you are about to embark on, and Wajickee that old friend of the family, will be there for you and your son, the 'idiot spy'. The spirit world is in turmoil about your arrival because Ben Beckmire, you ave been away too long and they ave been awaiting your arrival. This is not hocus pocus, this is your connection to a clan that remains royal and in place. Your faith will be your ultimate guide."

After the vehicles were loaded, Bernstein sat across from the driver and saw a young woman being slapped around by a man. He told the driver to stop the vehicle. He got out of the vehicle and yelled, "Hey, what the hell are you doing?"

Brown got out of the vehicle and declared, "Come on, man, this is not your fight!"

Bernstein said, "I am glad I didn't say that when you needed us or the Sarge needed us or any of those guys in those trucks needed us."

Brown paused and said, "I'm sorry, Brother. I didn't read the script. I know that when one of us feels strongly about some injustice, then the rest of us must back his play."

Bernstein yelled, "If you slap her again, I am going to beat you into next year!" The guy slapped the woman again and that is when John Lee, Jilkes, Chakes, Gladstone and Montomie exited their vehicles.

Jilkes said, "Bloke, don't hit her again. I will cut your heart out and place it in your mouth before you die."

John Lee handed him his knife and said, "Oh, yeah, he be good at that shit." As Brown walked over to assist the young woman, the guy pulled out a gun. Jilkes threw the knife and hit him square in the heart. He was dead before he hit the ground. Bernstein asked the woman, "Do you want to start anew?"

Between sniffles she replied, "I was forced into this life and that is why he was beating me."

"Do you do drugs?" Bernstein asked.

"He forced me to do drugs, but I don't like living this life or being with that bastard."

Bernstein stated, "I can give you another life, but you have to trust me and my friends. Do you want to leave this place and go with us to the Northern Territory?"

The young woman replied, "I will go anywhere, I just want out of this life." Bernstein ushered her into the vehicle he was riding in and began to attend to her. Beckmire said to

Mallory, "We have just earned the respect of the spirits. One of ours has taken a complete stranger under his wings to care for."

Courtney entered the van and began to console the young woman who finally said, "My father sold me to that man for drugs and he has beaten me every day for the past two weeks. He drugged me, violated me in every possible manner and forced me to have sex with everyone who came by that corner who was willing to pay. He made me have sex with four men at the same time and they did despicable things to me. I just want to die in peace and away from all of this."

Courtney said to her, "Well, we want you to live, especially the guy who made us stop to rescue you. I am a doctor and when we get to the airport, I will examine you, if you want."

Courtney stated, "Bernstein, we can't take her with us because she doesn't have a passport."

Bernstein replied, "We're only flying in country—no need for a passport." Bernstein turned around in his seat and inquired, "What's your name?"

The young woman answered, "My name is Yvett Beckmire."

A stillness came over the van and Bernstein asked, "Can you spell your last name?"

Yvett spelled Beckmire. Bernstein questioned, "Where are you originally from?"

"I am from Alice Springs in the Northern Territory. My father was purposefully seduced with drugs and when his debt grew so high that he couldn't pay, he sold me to that guy who violated me. I just want to die on my native soil. I don't want any false promises. I just want to die in the outback."

Brown called Beckmire in the lead vehicle and reported, "That young lady that we picked up has an interesting last name."

Beckmire said, "I know. Her name is Yvett Beckmire and we are taking her home. If Bernstein wants to transform and make a commitment to her, she will be traveling with us throughout this journey."

Brown said, "Sarge, I don't know What the hell is going on, but I am beginning to believe in some scary shit. Is she related to you?"

"All Aborigine people are related to me. She is special and perhaps Bernstein is lucky. She is a flower."

The driver said to Beckmire, "Your people 'ave proved worthy. The spirits embrace them as well as you, my friend. The bow and arrow will be all that you will need in the Outback. I will be there to guide you and the 'idiot spy' to your place of reverence."

# # #

As the group pulled into the airport, their jets were surrounded by police cars. Beckmire stressed, "Act normal and drive right up to the planes." Beckmire got out of the vehicle and said, "Good day, Mate. Is there a problem with our planes?"

The lead constable walked over to him and asked, "And who might I 'ave the pleasure of meeting?"

"My name is Ben Beckmire and I am traveling with my family to the Northern Territory."

The constable said, "Beckmire. Are you from around here, sir?"

Beckmire answered, "I am not but my entire history is from this great continent."

The Constable looked at him and inquired, "So, does that mean you believe in folklore?"

"Normally, I do not. However, what are we talking about?"

"Rumor has it, that there was a person named Beckmire who could transform into some kind of thing. If you can answer that question, me and my men will be out of here in a matter of seconds."

Beckmire looked around and moved closer to the constable and said, "I want to whisper something in your ear." Beckmire was almost in the kissing position when he quietly stated, "Andy Beckmire is the Great Saltie".

The constable motioned to his people to disappear. He said, "I wanted to meet a relative, thank you sir. When you return, I will be here to make sure that all is okay." Beckmire thanked him and away they went.

## CHAPTER TWENTY-SIX

In the Northern Territory, the group was met at the airport by a group of people holding signs that read, 'The Great Saltie'. Beckmire said to those in his vehicle, "This is some amazing shit. How the hell did these people know we were coming here?"

Mallory looked at Jong and asked, "Who did you call out here?"

Jong looked at him and replied, "With no disrespect, I don't know a damn soul out here. I am beginning to believe in hocus pocus. Mallory, I swear to you, I didn't make a single call out here. I wouldn't even know who to call."

Later Beckmire said, "You guys remember the faith that we had in each other in the Nam? Start using it here. I certainly didn't make any calls, and believe it or not, that guy, Walter, is a distant relative of mine. I swear to you guys, you will start believing in shit that is against all logic out here. It is crazy, as well as, perplexing. Stay with me."

A tall slender man with a full white beard approached Beckmire and said, "I 'ave the privilege of being your earthly guide while you are here for the next two days. I will see to your guests and will escort you and the one known as the 'idiot spy' to a place that is rich with your history and will give you clarity in terms of what you must do with that damn capsule. It will be destroyed in ten days, but your journey, as long as it may seem, will only last a few moments in this thing called time. I am Wajickee, the one who guided your great-great-grandfather through his transmogrification ritual. There is no need to ask me how I could 'ave done that until you ave had the chance to witness your future. There is great hope for the one called the 'idiot spy', for it is he who will return here and create a new life for the founders of this great continent, the Aborigine."

Beckmire said, "His name is Zanthius De Lombardo. The title of 'idiot spy' has been placed upon him by those he outsmarted."

Wajickee responded, "Indulge us, Mr. Beckmire, we so seldom 'ave the opportunity to relate to spies and people who attempt to assassinate them. The stories of you and your Fab 10 + 2 ave been a comfort for us, and your heroics 'ave been exaggerated and multiplied. I beg your indulgence with simple folk who 'ave the opportunity to view living legends. Our folklore is old and tired and you and the 'idiot spy' bring a revival of faith to our people. Just indulge us if you would, please."

As everyone was loaded into a vintage school bus, Beckmire asked, "Where are we heading?"

Wajickee looked at him and replied, "Don't you know, Mate? We be going to the place where your ancestors bonded to build the Beckmire clan. This place, although changed, is where the Great Saltie and your great-great-grandmother began the birthing process of your ancestors. We will camp along a billabong and if your faith is powerful, you may get to see and/or meet the Great Saltie."

After a one-and-a-half-hour ride, the school bus pulled off onto a track of land that had no visible markings of a road of any kind. Beckmire asked, "Are you sure we are heading in the right direction?"

Wajickee looked at him and answered, "In what direction would you like me to head? Any turns I make will take us to the same place because when we turned off that road, you officially entered the outer banks of the Outback. A place that has seen many a white man leave his bones on land that they thought they could conquer. In forty-five minutes or so, you will be where you need to be and the rest of us will continue on to our campsite. Only you and the 'idiot spy' will disembark there and it is there your faith and ancestors will lead you to Dreamtime and Walkabout. You won't need anything, for all will be provided for you. It might be best if you inform your comrades that you and the 'idiot spy' will be leaving them for a day or two and assure them that you will be completely safe and protected. They too 'ave to believe in you and where you are because it is like one big chain linked circle—all links must stay connected."

Beckmire stumbled back to the midsection of the bus and told Courtney and Mallory that he and Zanthius would be getting off in a few minutes but they would continue on to a campsite. Courtney resisted vehemently but was assured by the Sarge that all would be okay.

He then told Asiram and Ava that he and Zanthius would be leaving the group for a day or two. Asiram announced, "Sorry, Sarge. Where my man goes, I go."

Beckmire looked at her and said, "You have already proven yourself to everyone here and to those who are not here. It is a journey that only he and I can make. I beg you to understand that we are, in essence, in another world and things are rarely what they seem. You must allow him to accompany me or we all will continue to be hunted like animals."

"Is Courtney going with you?"

"Only in spirit."

Thirty minutes later, the bus came to a stop and from out of the bush, a man walked towards the bus. Wajickee spoke to him in his bush tongue and they traded places. Wajickee announced to Beckmire, "It is time. This is the place."

Jilkes rose up and exclaimed, "Ain't no way he is going without us!"

John Lee turned to him and said, "This be the time and place where he gets the answers, we need to survive this thing. Let them go. They will be okay."

In the middle of nowhere Beckmire turned to say something to Wajickee but he was not in sight. He asked Zanthius, "Where did, Wajickee, go?"

"I have no idea."

"Follow me and I am sure he will turn up sooner rather than later, I'm hoping. We have about two hours of daylight left, and I would like to get near some water before nightfall."

The two men walked through the bush. Various kinds of animals appeared in their paths and then disappeared. They saw joeys and jack kangaroos as well as wombats and the very loveable koala bears. Beckmire talked to Zanthius throughout the entire walk and finally reported, "Son, I have a sneaky suspicion that we're being followed."

"Pops, believe it or not, I have been watching our rear for the last half-hour and I really think that someone or something is trailing us. Do you happen to have a weapon?"

"I do not. How about you?"

"Empty as that Fosters beer can over to your left. Perhaps it might be prudent to at least find some sturdy tree limbs or something to offer us a modicum of protection."

"If something wants to have us out here, no little tree trunk is going to keep it from having a healthy meal. Just the same, I think I am going to look for a walking stick that can act as a club. No sense in leaving our urban instincts behind in a place that has so many different predators, right? Still can't figure out where that Wajickee fellow got to."

Zanthius said, "I was looking at him one moment and the next, he was gone like the wind. How much do you know about your ancestors and why do we need to be in this place, of all places, in the Outback? I mean, couldn't you have picked Cairns or Brisbane somewhere that has wonderful beaches and great fishing?"

"Those places are nice, but they were compromised by the European settlers. The settlers tried to settle this area and almost all of them died because they couldn't find water or plant food. They didn't know the land, according to the history of this place. Now, an average Aborigine, can always find water, food and shelter anywhere. They are from the land and know how it works. Those Europeans just saw vast lands and staked out their claims thinking that rain would solve their problems. I hear when it rains out here, billabongs are formed and that is where it is alleged the Great Saltie lives."

"I know I'm supposed to be entering a point in my life where faith is the only thing that matters, along with family. Tell me about the Great Saltie." There was a rustling in the nearby bushes that immediately got their attention and they paused to attempt to discern what it was.

As the sun began to set in the west, Beckmire said, "I hope we didn't do the wrong thing by heading in this direction without telling our guide."

"Pops, where's your faith?" They both laughed and continued to head due south towards the smell of fresh water.

Beckmire said, "I think we need to figure out how we're going to start a fire and set up some defenses against any predators. What scares me the most, is those damn dingoes, they travel strong in numbers and are known to be vicious. I think if we continue to head in this direction, at least there appears to be some high ground that will provide us some protection. Do you know how to start a fire without a match?"

"My mother, God bless her, had the wherewithal to send me to camp every year and it was there that I mastered the art of fire making."

"Great! Let's head for that little mountain over there. That way we can defend ourselves from things trying to get to our position. Gather as much wood as possible."

"Why did you decide to head south? Why not west or north?"

"I have no idea what led me to that decision. Somehow, I felt it was the direction we are supposed to head in. We had the setting sun off to our right and therefore I took this path. Any particular reason why you are asking me that question?"

Zanthius pointed to the sky and responded, "All of the shooting stars are heading in the same direction."

"Oh, you noticed that as well. Now, that's a keen eye Son, way to watch the stars."

As Beckmire and Zanthius approached the small mountain, Zanthius said, "Pops, from here I think I see a small fire flickering near or on that mountain."

Beckmire strained his eyes and admitted, "I can't see a thing."

"Pops, I know I see flames near that mountain. I think there is someone there. We should approach that place cautiously but make enough noise so that we aren't mistaken for some kind of animal or something."

The two men got closer to the origin of the fire. It was apparent that there was no one around. Zanthius yelled, "Hello. We are friendly blokes looking to share a fire. Hello."

There was no response and Beckmire commanded, "When we get to the foot of that hill, I want you to stay at least ten feet behind me and ten feet to the left of me, just in case this is an ambush."

"Okay, Pops, you are scaring the shit out of me. Why don't we go over to that hill about fifty yards away and wait and see who is camping there?"

"You may be right, but I think this looks like a welcoming site for us. I will check it out and you stay out of sight until I call you. Watch my back, Son."

As Beckmire reached the point where there was a huge fire, Wajickee said, "What took you blokes so long? Tell the 'idiot spy' to come out of the cold and join us by the fire. I 'ave taken the liberty to prepare a wonderful meal for you. By the way, your family members and friends are being entertained, fed and enlightened about the ways of the Aborigine. They are enjoying themselves and are under the veil of protection by a strong warrior named, 'Pigeon'. All is good, mate."

When Zanthius reached the top of the small mountain, he inquired, "Why didn't you wait for us and lead us here?"

Wajickee answered, "You are of the most royal blood that exists in this land. If you had not found this place, we would 'ave to check, as you call it, your BNA."

Zanthius said, "It is called DNA."

Wajickee responded sharply, rapidly and asked, "Did you not know what I meant?"

Beckmire intervened and inquired, "How did you get here so fast?"

"Come now, Ben Beckmire. I 'ave been traveling these lands for centuries and yes, I know I look good for my age. First, you must feast on the land and its waters, as well as, its fruits, both good and bad. Then you will begin a journey and you will meet all those who are from the Beckmire clan. Eat. I will return shortly." Beckmire turned to ask Wajickee a question and like magic, he was gone.

## CHAPTER TWENTY-SEVEN

At exactly 9 pm, Wajickee appeared and asked, "How was your meal?"

Zanthius responded, "The chicken was absolutely perfect. What did you season it with?"

Wajickee looked at Zanthius and stated, "When I do a chicken, I will tell you. That was dingo meat; sautéed by the sun, cured by the ants and chewed apart by other dingoes." He smiled and added, 'I really like the 'idiot spy', he has such flare about him. In a moment, I will point you towards a billabong and it is there you will spend the night. No animal or human will disturb your visit and you will 'ave significant dreams and conversations with those who 'ave come before you.

This place is said to 'ave strong magic and I suggest that you stay near the water, but do not enter it, although you will be summoned by a likeness that you know but who is not near here at all. You will see the Great Saltie and he will see you. Be clean of thought and desire and you will live to live your life for the good of the Aborigine people and all the people of the earth.

That damn capsule and its meaning will be explained to you and you will 'ave a chance to talk to Walter-- your kin, a friend and an enemy. Let idle thoughts of pleasure and euphoria leave your mind and focus on the good that man must do for man. I 'ave prepared the drink that transformed your ancestor into the Great Saltie. Experience the world as he has known it; accept his guidance, and trust his absolute confirmation about who, what, when and where. Once those pictures are clear, I will come back for you probably within a day or two. The animals are your friends. Do not hurt them."

CHAPTER TWENTY-EIGHT

Exactly thirty-six hours later, Beckmire and Zanthius were making their way north from the billabong. Zanthius said to his father, "I have never seen a creature that big, nimble and expressive. This journey is magical. We know who and what we have to do to extricate ourselves from any problems because of that kiss. Pops, did you experience all that I did? I mean, I am forever challenged to understand what is almost impossible to comprehend. My dream state and my Walkabout with my forefathers were incredible. I made a promise to spend a significant amount of my time on this continent to right the wrongs against the Aborigine people. Will you join me in my quest to honor my commitment?"

Beckmire stopped in his tracks, wiped away the tears, turned to his son and said, "I have known that you existed, but I didn't know how to find you. Our family and our friends will come back here together, and we will change the way our people are treated, I promise you that. I need a few moments of quiet to make sure that I completely understand our mission and that of our people. Zanthius, I love you and have loved you from the moment that I knew you existed. The magic of this place knew the right time for us to connect. It is here, and we have our work cut out for us. Oh, and by the way, while you were asleep, the Great Saltie slept beside you as Wajickee and I went on Walkabout."

"Pops, no way that thing slept near me."

Beckmire smiled and asked, "Son, have you looked at the back of your leg? You have scales on them that will last for your lifetime. On your next visit here, you and I will meet him head on and you will understand why our clan is so important to our people."

Zanthius looked at the back of his leg and was astounded by what he saw. He said, "What the hell? How the hell did that get there?"

"I told you and you didn't believe me."

"Give me another try, because I didn't have scales on my leg and now, I do. Am I infected with some kind of virus or something?"

As if walking in from a cloud, Wajickee said, "You 'ave been loved by the beast known as the Great Saltie. Your woman, once you are reunited, will bear a smaller version of that on her opposite leg. We are so desperately awaiting your return.

"Mr. Beckmire, your scaling is on your left elbow and your wife has the marking on her right elbow. Ava, too, will show the mark on her ankle. Your people will develop over time, a small indication that they too 'ave been sanctioned and blessed by the Great Saltie. Take time to reflect but share none of your experience because it is truly your experience. Those that you love 'ave had a different kind of experience and will bear similar marks on their bodies.

"You now 'ave seven days to secure that damn capsule and place it into the right hands. Here in the outback, we 'ave a problem that will require your attention and that of your people as soon as you 'ave delivered that damn capsule. You will find that the person named Helga played and plays many roles in this adventure. The capsule, as you well know, is only a part of the formula. The connecting dots are within your hearts and together only you two can manifest that. The time will present itself and you will know when the two of you 'ave to come together as one to choose the right road. Good luck and good day, mates." As if by magic, Wajickee was beyond their scope of realization and was back on Walkabout. He was back on Walkabout with his head held high signifying that he was once again chosen to lead the Beckmire clan down the right road.

CHAPTER TWENTY-NINE

On the bus ride back to the airport, everyone was discussing their varied spiritual encounters while in the outback and sharing their individual perspectives about what they had seen, their interpretations and what it all meant. Every person in the group, including the children saw and witnessed different things about life, family, love and their futures. John Lee had the most prophetic vision and said to Jilkes, "Man, you won't believe this, but my dream was really scary. It showed me and you signing papers that joined us in a partnership that expanded my farm into our farm with an additional 2000 plus acres. Now, when I woke up, I said to myself that there ain't no way in hell that city boy is going to leave the noise of the North and head on down to the South and take up farming and fishing—no way in hell."

Jilkes said, "I think you must be on drugs and they must have given me the same thing because that was the same damn ugly nightmare that I had. It ain't going to happen no matter how much I love you."

John Lee said, "Now, I told them there spirit guys that you don't do farms and stuff like that and they said to me, 'In time he will learn the beauty of the land'."

Jilkes looked at him and said, "I told him that you were crazy as a cracked rock and they said clearly to me, 'that he may be, but he be as local as your heart'. I don't know nothing about none of this except that I thought I was having a really bad dream. What I will say is this, I'm not opposed to trying anything and why not take another adventure with my true friend and soul mate? I'm not promising you anything, other than that I will consider it. By the way, are there two thousand available acres abutting your land?"

"As sure as we be sitting here, and they be prime real estate," John Lee boasted.

"Can I put up a fifteen foot fence?"

John Lee responded, "I was thinking around twenty feet high. That will keep the smell of chitterlings and other soul foods that you be liking away from my farm."

Beckmire hugged Courtney and told her how much he loved her and that he believed that everything was going to be okay. He indicated to her that they still had a few challenges but once they got rid of the capsule, their real work and mission in life would take hold of them in a real hurry. He informed her that a part of their mission was here in Australia and in the outback. She said it didn't matter because where he went, she was going to be hanging somewhere close by.

Zanthius was being questioned by Asiram about his experience and he turned the tables and asked her about hers. She told him that she absolutely loved the people and that she wanted to come back as often as possible to work with them and provide educational services for them. Zanthius told her that he too had a mission here, and that he was hoping that she had a great experience because they all had work to do in Australia.

Everyone had an amazing experience, or an epiphany, and it all centered around helping people and getting rid of that damn capsule. The children absolutely loved the outback and enjoyed listening to and explaining their interpretations of the events of the last few days.

An obvious concern for the group was how could they leave this touchy/feely state of mind and get back to the real world and be done with that damn capsule.

## CHAPTER THIRTY

At the airport the constable welcomed the group, inquired about their experiences and asked when they would be coming back. Beckmire answered, "We have all had an out of body experience and every one of us is committed to coming back. We would like to help with a few small problems that have made the lives of the Aborigine people very difficult, to say the least."

The constable said, "I took the liberty of getting a passport for a young Yvett Beckmire. Will she be traveling with you?"

"Why don't we ask her and her benefactor what they intend to do?" Beckmire replied before he yelled out, "Bernstein, can I see you and Yvett for a minute?" Bernstein and Yvett walked over to where the constable and the Sarge were standing and Bernstein asked, "What's up Sarge?"

"The constable has a passport for Yvett. We want to know if she wants to come with us and what your plans are relative to her future?"

Bernstein looked at Yvett and said, "Listen, I know you don't know me and I really don't know you, but I have a strong feeling that we can be of benefit to each other without abuse or defilement. What say you?"

Yvett looked deep at Bernstein and responded, "I have no money, clothes or anything else. Why are you trying to help me?"

Bernstein looked at her and replied, "Those are earthly issues that you're referring to. I, on the other hand, saw someone that intrigued me and, therefore, I am willing to try to get to know you and see if there is a future somewhere down the line for us. In the outback, I had visions and at each turn you were there. I don't believe in hocus pocus, but I do believe in the name Beckmire and that is your name. I want you to come with us, but I must advise you, there are people who are trying to kill us at every turn. So, I am not sure if I'm helping you by getting you out of the frying pan and into the fire."

Yvett looked at Beckmire and asked, "Uncle, what say you?"

Beckmire reached out his arms and answered, "He will make you whole and proud. Your past will be a forgotten memory and your future will be as bright as the flying stars in the night that we all witnessed in the outback. What say you?"

Yvett grabbed Bernstein's hand and exclaimed, "I am trusting my life in your hands if you will have me!"

Bernstein smiled and said, "You don't have to worry because I never want to tangle with your uncle, my boss and my friend for life." There was laughter and the constable said, "Yvett, here are all the papers that you will need. We took up a collection and we have a few dollars for you as well."

Beckmire thanked the constable and retorted, "She will not need money. I want you to take that money and open up a charity in her name and we will, after a vote, add to it each year to help our people. Thank you for everything. Oh, and by the way, my son and I saw the Great Saltie and he whispered your name. Tell my cousin and your cousin, Walter, that I will call him as soon as we land in America. He has a huge cloud around him that was not discussed, it borders on the wrong side of the road!"

## CHAPTER THIRTY-ONE

After landing in San Diego, Beckmire ordered each plane to undergo a full inspection and maintenance. He huddled with Mallory, Asiram, and Zanthius and placed a call to Walter. Beckmire started the conversation by saying, "Why didn't you tell me that you were from a long line of good people?"

"Would you have believed me, especially looking at my antics with the horse? Really, would you have believed me?"

"Probably not, but I knew that I wasn't going to allow any harm to come to you. Still you could have given me a heads up. My son has randomly executed people and you could have been on his hit list."

"Naw, the 'idiot spy' knows me and knows me well. He, too, felt that there was a relationship when we were in the barn. Why else would he have allowed me to speak to the horse?"

"Anyway, we are back and are having our planes looked at and serviced. Any intel you would like to share with me?"

"I'll call you back in a half hour or so."

Jong had made reservations at a motel that was located five miles from the hospital that would provide services to Yvett. He also rented vans for everyone's transportation. In the confines of secret compartments built on each plane, were pistols which would be the only weapons the group would have.

Approximately three hours after landing in San Diego, Beckmire's phone rang. It was Walter who asked, "Did you have a confrontation with someone in Australia?"

"No, we engaged no one and no one engaged us. Why do you ask?"

"Someone killed a double agent who, I must admit, was pure slime but was currently working on a case for the Agency."

"Oh shit, it may have been the guy who was beating up on a relative of ours he had forced to work the streets and alleys around the Kings Cross area. He pulled a gun on my guys and was dealt with swiftly."

"He was in charge of our interdiction team and had been working on gaining details about a new drug that was being experimented with in Australia but ultimately is destined for America."

"The guy we engaged was an addict and a pimp. One of our nieces had been sold to him by her father and he forced her to use drugs and to sell her body. I also noticed that he had track marks going up and down his left arm. Now, if you are telling me that these are the kind of people you employ, then we need to rethink our potential agreement on doing wet work for you."

"Speaking of wet work, could you and a couple of your people head up to Los Angeles to speak to a person who is waiting on drugs from Australia and is using kids to distribute them at their local high schools? I know that you and Larry are adamant about eliminating drug dealers and you make it impossible for them to exist."

"And just how on earth do you know that, Walter?"

"Come now, Ben, we are from the same clan. I feel and know the deeds that you do for the benefit of mankind, as well as, all of those dastardly endeavors that you have been involved in. You asked me about the horse, so I guess it is time for you to open that brain of yours and realize that we know a lot of stuff that some people would consider hocus pocus. If you can do this for me, I will make sure that Yvett has no problems with visas and stuff, and that the young mate of yours can appreciate her regality and beauty without compromise. It is a small adventure, Ben. It will take you a minimum of three to four hours to have the talk and decide if he will give you all of his contacts and disappear before you make him disappear."

"Walter, I have got to check your DNA. You can't be a true Aborigine because you are asking me to do your dirty work."

"No, Ben, I am trying to save the lives of young people and most of all of a young man who has crossed over to the wrong road. If I get involved, he is dead, dead, dead, and so is anyone else who is benefiting from this disease."

"I will call you back and let you know."

The rooms at the motel were located on the second floor. Mallory made the room assignments placing Jilkes and John Lee at one end of the hall and Chakes and Montomie at the other end.

Beckmire went to Mallory's room and knocked on the door. Mallory opened the door and inquired, "Is there a problem?"

Beckmire looked at him and replied, "You know that deal we considered with the devil; well, he wants me to head up to

LA and have a discussion with a drug dealer. The person who lost his life in Kings Cross, was a double agent for the agency. Now, how the hell were we supposed to know that a low life that beats up on women is a member of our government's covert operations?"

"Well, we can't split up our forces. I know that you and Larry are good at what you do, but we still have a much more significant issue to deal with. My suggestion is that we all head to LA and do business as usual and thus, we guarantee our success. To separate our forces leaves us too vulnerable, especially with the women and the children. Why don't you call Jong and find out when the planes will be ready and then we will all go together and stay in complete protection mode. If you and Larry leave and we develop a problem here, we're screwed. No sir, we all go or we all stay. You came to me for my opinion, right?"

"I came to you for guidance and you have provided that for me. We all go and then plan our trip back to Asiram's place. That reminds me, we haven't talked about our next steps. Okay, you circle around to Jong and get the status of the planes and I will speak with Asiram and make sure we are all welcome."

Later, Mallory called Beckmire and told him that Jong said the planes were ready to go and that the pilots were legal. He also informed him that Bernstein was spending a significant amount of time with Yvett. Beckmire asked, "They aren't in the same room, are they?"

"No, but they do have adjoining rooms. I think he is on the up and up and is just trying to do what we do best, help people help themselves. I doubt very seriously that he is trying to take advantage of her and besides, if I am not mistaken, she is going through what Asiram went through—purgation of her past. He is just attentive and loving in the real sense of the word."

"Wow, if he gets truly interested in Yvett, he will officially be related to me. How about those apples?"

Mallory laughed and said, "Sarge, we are all related and we have the best damn family that money can't buy."

#

Jong called the pilot-in-command and asked if all was ready. He told him that a lot of SUVs had been driving by looking at the planes. He felt that those guys were not friendlies and wanted us to be airborne as soon as possible. He indicated to Jong that it may be his paranoia, but he suddenly felt that they were being watched. He told Jong that when they went to file their flight plan, everyone wanted to know the nature of the trip and who the passengers were on each plane. He felt that they were government types but wasn't sure. Jong told him to keep him informed and immediately called the Sarge to report the irregularities. Beckmire said to Jong, "Let me make a call to find out if our handler is screwing with us."

Beckmire went outside his room, called Walter and asked, "Do you have eyes on us at the airport?"

"Abso-damn-lutely. You have the 'idiot spy' and he is our connection to the product and is the reason over 100 people have lost their lives, not to mention the piece of shit that I had to do. It is routine and it is not only your movements that we are watching but the movements of another group of people who somehow knew that you are in the area. I need you to do me a favor and I am going to make it really easy for you. I want everyone and everything to go through a sensitive object detector when you get to the airport. Someone or something has a universal bug attached to it. Otherwise, how on earth could this group know and be in place when your planes landed in San Diego last night? Something or someone is amiss and we have to figure this thing out."

"We are probably going to head out in the next two hours. Will I recognize anyone when I get to the airport?"

"I would be extremely hurt if you didn't recognize me, Couz. Are you guys carrying any of that money you obtained from T-Rex?"

"I'm not sure. I think 90% of that money was burned up in Virginia when your people blew up the farmhouse."

"I had nothing to do with that one."

"I know and the person who did, paid the ultimate price."

"I, just by coincidence, will be in LA at the same time you are. Perhaps we can meet for a drink. I suggest that you keep your civilian people at the airport with at least half your force staying with them. Bring a minimum of six to LA with you. I will text you the address of the hotel and provide you with a vehicle that will be equipped with some throw away weapons. Once you use them, if you must use them, leave them in the vehicle with the drivers. All of the weapons have a filament that keeps your fingerprints from being captured. Once I have the weapons, I will burn them in a nearby facility and that will be that. I am hoping that violence can be avoided, but if in fact, you have to do your thing, so be it."

"Walter, I am walking into a situation that you and your people scouted, but we haven't. I don't like it at all."

"Ben, you will have a small army of people protecting your back. I will have people on top of the roofs, in distant hallways, in alleys and in cars. I have a total of forty-five people blocking all exists and covering your ass. I can't be a part of this because the dude's father is a powerful person in our government."

"Damn, Walter, is the government where you go for employment when you have larceny in your heart? Each one of the people who are supposed to be protecting us is motivated by money—excluding present company. This is a mess and you know it. When we are done with a few odd jobs for you, I think we might just go to Washington and clean up that clogged drain. I mean exposing and articulating corrupt behavior by getting the press involved will provide pressure and personal oversight to those who are doing wrong."

"You're preaching to the choir. Too often I've had to turn a blind eye to things that I know are wrong but are being done by sanctimonious members of our government who are at a higher pay grade than I am. You might be onto a project that I think we both can have fun with and gracefully find our way into retirement."

## CHAPTER THIRTY-TWO

Two hours later, a caravan of vehicles arrived at the airport and the weary group boarded the planes for a brief stop in Los Angeles. Walter and his people had landed at the LA airport thirty minutes prior to Beckmire's group. His group was on their way to rendezvous with other members of his team and take up surveillance of the target.

After the short flight from San Diego to Los Angeles, Beckmire asked Mallory to make the assignments. Mallory looked at Jilkes and asked, "How are you feeling? Are you 100% or closer to 80?"

"If you're planning on sending John Lee, then I am 100%." Mallory looked at Chakes and Montomie and pointed to them. He then looked at Gladstone and Whitmore and finally at John Lee and Jilkes, and said, "You guys will accompany the Sarge, on hopefully, a small job, but we know what that means. The problem I have with this mission is there will be a lot of those federal types, and they don't know shit about how we work. So, you have to be on the lookout for friendlies, as well as, each other. I want you to look over each other's shoulders and watch each other's backs. Ladies don't come back here with a single scratch. Is that clear?" The response was thunderous.

One hour and a half later, Walter received a call indicating that the plane carrying the illicit drugs had landed and two suitcases had been loaded in a van and were on their way to the drop-off point. The drop-off point just happened to be the Bonaventure Hotel, a circular shaped building rising approximately sixty stories.

When Walter informed Beckmire where the drop off was, Beckmire asked, "Walter, are you crazy? That is a highly visible location and a lot of friendlies are subject to be killed. Do you have an alternative plan?"

"This place was chosen by the target because his father has a high-level meeting there with the Japanese and Chinese governments concerning some beachfront property that they both are claiming."

"How on earth are we going to get weapons into that place?"

"You will enter through the service entrance and my people will authenticate your credentials and direct you to the storage area where you will find a small arsenal. I know the kid handling the drugs does not want to be shot in the head. If we stop him here, we save a soul and capture a shitload of drugs. If the product in each case is ever processed, it turns into 20,000 times the weight of the drugs in each case. That is 40,000 hits of a deadly drug that can be cut as many as five times, equaling 200,000 hits of pure addiction and ultimately, death."

Beckmire asked, "Do you have pictures of the target and his associates?" Walter told him pictures of the delivery men and a photo of the target and his three associates would be with the arsenal in the storage area.

CHAPTER THIRTY-THREE

At the Bonaventure Hotel, Beckmire and his crew entered through the service area and were met by one of Walter's crew. He directed them to a small room that contained a suitcase full of pistols. John Lee stated, "This is going to be some close quarters mess and I don't like doing close quarters. Let me take a look around the lobby and figure out the exit points we can use, if necessary. Sarge, I think we need to keep a set of keys to those trucks. I mean we be taking a lot for granted here and I's personally don't like the feeling I be having right now."

Beckmire paused. He watched the frantic movement of people, bags and food trays and decided that John Lee was absolutely right. This was a no-brainer because they had no exit strategy and didn't even have access to the vehicles. He turned to John Lee and said, "Why don't you and Jilkes take a walk around the place and check out the various emergency exits and where they are located in relationship to where the bad guys will come in. This looks like a recipe for disaster and I don't want to get caught up in this mess.

"Whitmore and Gladstone take up surveillance as well, but focus on who is coming and going, more importantly, who is coming and what they might be carrying. It might be simpler to catch them coming, rather than wait until they get in a room that we have to break into and get the shit shot out of us. I don't like this deal at all. I need to call Walter."

Beckmire called Walter and told him that the entire situation was toxic and that he didn't want to place his men in a situation that they couldn't control. He also stated there were too many variables and that there were a ton of friendlies that could be injured or killed if someone panicked. He advised Walter that he would have to provide security for the visiting dignitaries and the local police. Plus, the bad guys and their group would all be shooting in a place that had a ton of innocent people. He emphasized that he did not want to take part in a slaughter of innocents and felt that he could not commit his people to this kind of nonsense.

Walter asked, "Do you have an alternative suggestion? As I look around this place, I am concerned like you are. Actually, I am going to abort this mission and find another way to intercede in this matter."

Beckmire retorted, "Why not follow the suitcases out of here? I am sure they aren't going to hang around once the deal is done. As a matter of fact, why don't we have this place evacuated? If I start a small fire in the storage room, then everyone will have to get the hell out of here, especially once they smell smoke and see flames."

Walter exclaimed, "Damn, excellent thinking! Do it and we will keep an eye on the suitcases and cover each exit."

"Give me ten minutes and I will gather enough flammable materials to make this thing appear to be a huge fire. It will bring out the fire company as well. There is going to be a lot of movement in a few minutes, so alert your folks. If there is wild driving or a chase, use a helicopter to keep an eye on their vehicle from the sky. This city is too busy with too many people running around to have people driving fast and shooting out of windows and killing innocent bystanders. By the way, the next time you want to plan an event for us, I suggest that you get our buy-in first."

Beckmire huddled with Chakes and Montomie and said, "I need to start a fire in the next ten minutes, but I want the smoke and fumes to rise to the upper floors in a hurry. Any ideas?" Montomie looked around and heard the sound of an air handling unit that sucked the smoke out of the kitchen. He told the Sarge that fires were easy to start.

Montomie said, "Give us five minutes and I can make this place seem like the towering inferno without any real damage and/or the potential loss of life."

Beckmire said, "Once you have started the fire, exit through that door over there to the left. The rest of us will be waiting for the target to exit with the merchandise. Be vigilant because we are in unknown territory."

The team was not sure what Chakes and Montomie concocted, but soon the entire place was filled with smoke and had the appearance of a major threat. Fire alarms began to go off and people began to scramble out of the building. Waiting at the back exit, and strategically placed, were the Sarge, John Lee, and Jilkes. On the rooftop of a building one quarter of a mile away, were two of Walter's sharpshooters, Mike and a guy that Beckmire did not know.

The fire rooted everyone out of the rooms and the elevators shut down automatically once the fire alarm was engaged and they had reached the bottom floor. Beckmire realized this but was taken aback when two women came out of the back of the building with two children in tow and each carried rather cumbersome looking suitcases. John Lee stated, "I smell a rat. I think they be using those kids as shields."

Beckmire saw Chakes and Montomie coming his way and indicated they should detain the two women and search the bags. One of the women attempted to pull a weapon on Chakes but was faced with the barrel of a .9mm weapon held by Montomie. Beckmire never turned away from the door and within a few seconds two armed men came out of the exit coughing with machine pistols in their hands. They were shot by the snipers on the roof. The target, who was halfway out of the door, saw his men laying on the ground with head wounds, and decided to drop the two suitcases he was carrying and throw his hands up in surrender. Whitmore and Gladstone, in the meantime, had driven one of the SUVs to the rear and all of the participants were hustled into the vehicle. The children began to cry which caused a distraction, but John Lee was able to quiet them down. Montomie picked up the suitcases and hustled into the SUV.

Prior to Beckmire entering the vehicle, he told John Lee and Jilkes to make their way to the front of the building and to commandeer one of the vehicles from Walter's people. As fire trucks and other police vehicles appeared on the scene, Beckmire saw Walter and suggested that he enter the vehicle with Jilkes and John Lee. As the two vehicles made their way out of the vicinity of the hotel, Beckmire called Walter and reported, "There were three associates and the target. We are missing someone, be on alert, people."

Mike, who was on the rooftop, said to Walter, "There is a person at your 9 who looks familiar. Do you recognize him?" As Walter turned to look towards his 9, Mike fired a shot and killed the individual who was pulling out a machine pistol.

252 c. benjamin lattimore

Walter said, "Thanks, Mike, you saved my ass."

Chakes in the meantime had placed paper bags over the heads of the occupants of the SUV. Chakes raised a finger to his mouth indicating that the vehicle probably had a listening device in it.

Beckmire called Walter and asked, "Master, what is your wish?"

Walter responded, "Funny man you are, Ben Beckmire, from the Beckmire clan. Follow that blue sedan two cars in front of you and turn off when they do. What I neglected to clear with you, is that we may need Asiram to do her work on the guy. The women are just mules and the kids have to be placed in foster care until we can reach a deal with their mothers."

Beckmire inquired, "Have you ever heard of humility and forgiveness? Can't you at least think of an alternative to placing those kids in some foreign environment? Why not demand rehabilitation for the mothers or anything other than permanently separating those families? It is your boy who is the perpetrator, those women are just being used."

Walter responded by saying, "It is not him that we are after. It is his high ranking and sanctimonious father. He is the real dealer. His son is just a fly by night peddler."

"Walter, we really need to work on our communications skills if we are to remain family and friends. Give me full details or do it yourself." Beckmire hung up the phone and Walter knew that he had pissed off his best asset.

Walter called back and said, "Sorry, Ben, you're right. I must make full disclosure to you from now on. Then you can decide if it is the kind of work you want to do. Please accept my apologies for treating you less than an equal. I will work on keeping those kids out of a foster home and see how I can help the women."

"When you figure that out, get back to me and we can continue our relationship."

Walter yelled, "Please don't hang up on me again. Listen, I will keep the kids out of foster care and I will work personally with the women to try to help them with their addiction, but you must remember, they put those kids in harm's way and for that I cannot forget or forgive."

"I understand what you are saying, but if there is no effort made to change the situation then there will be no change in behavior. You guarantee me that you will work with those women, and me and my boys will help you continue to do botched jobs, such as today."

Walter laughed and said, "Well, at least I saved your ass today."

Beckmire retorted, "Not even in the slightest way. Your people shot them prematurely. My other two guys had them in their sights. You just made a mess by leaving dead bodies. We would have reasoned with them and let our extractor have a go at them. Looks like we are coming up on the turn. The car we're following just made a right turn. Oh, and by the way, Asiram is unavailable to do any work, especially on just a peddler. If you had his father with you then I would attempt to convince my daughter-in-law to do me a favor. From what I can discern about this fellow, he is more worried about 'Bubba' chasing his ass around the cell and trying to nail him."

## CHAPTER THIRTY-FOUR

At the airport everyone was restless and glad to see the team return without any losses. Courtney said to Beckmire, "Ava and Carlos are really an item. I mean, they don't take their eyes off of each other. They converse in Spanish, laugh, hug and now are kissing in public. Zanthius has also recognized the attention that they are giving each other and he is happy for them.

"Despite all of this mayhem and treachery, love has spoken and has spread its wings around several members of our group. For example, Bernstein and Yvett haven't parted ways since they met, and he is as protective of her as he is of you. I mean this guy has jumped the broom and doesn't even know it. Now, Yvett, on the other hand, is cautious but attentive and rightfully so. The poor child has had to endure some difficult situations and is just now beginning to relax around Bernstein. I told him not to make any sudden moves because she's still trying to figure out who she can trust and until she has a conversation with the Sarge, don't push any agenda."

Beckmire looked at Courtney and whispered, "I love you so much and I'm sad that we haven't had any alone time since this mess started. I promise you that we are going to find some soft, salty, blue water and sit our asses in it until they become raw. I am so happy that you are my mate."

Courtney looked at the Sarge and replied, "Ava is beautiful and rich. Are you sure you made the right choice?"

After studying her face and looking at her body, Beckmire answered, "I never second guess my actions. I once loved that woman like no other, until I met the likes of you. I have not looked back, or around, for anyone else because I know that you are my sole reason for existing and those two kids that we adopted are a true testament of my love for you and them. Our own child is blessed to have a mother and a father who are dedicated to the premise to help people help themselves. Blessed are we Courtney, no woman on earth could ever provide me with the comfort and love that you have shown me over the years. So, insofar as making a choice, I guess I did screw up because she is rich."

Courtney punched the Sarge in the chest and he laughed, "I was just messing with you, my love. You know I love you and have loved you from the moment I laid eyes on you in that emergency room. You have filled every possible domain in my life that was empty and sad after Ava's disappearance. Unfortunately for her, she does not measure up to you in any aspect, including wealth, which only buys you more things and toys, and toys I don't need. So yes, my love, I am yours and you are mine, forever! Do you have a problem with that?"

Courtney slid up close to Ben and placed a suggestive kiss on his lips accompanied by a wandering tongue that found its way into the depths of his mouth.

## CHAPTER THIRTY-FIVE

As the planes ascended into the heavens, Montomie saw the suitcases that he had picked up at the hotel and decided to try to open them. They were not locked and when he opened one of them, he yelled, "Holy shit! Look what I picked up at the hotel!"

People began to gather around and Mallory called the Sarge and exclaimed, "You won't believe what Montomie picked up at the hotel!"

The Sarge asked, "What?"

Mallory responded, "Two suitcases full of money. I am guessing there is approximately $3.5 million dollars in cold hard cash in each case."

"Are you shitting me?"

"I am looking at rows and rows of stacked money and as I do a rough count, it is between $6.5 to $7 million in cash."

"OMG! What on earth are we going to do with all of this illicit money?"

Mallory laughed and answered, "I'm sure between the guys and you, we will find some way to help somebody or help ourselves. This so-called wet work is becoming extremely lucrative. Okay, I will see you on the ground once we land."

Chakes positioned himself over Montomie and whispered, "Just between you and me, you could have compromised us all on this one."

Montomie looked at him and said, "You don't have to say a thing. I know I should have checked this out before we got on the damn plane. This suitcase could have been rigged and we all would have died close to heaven. I just wasn't thinking. After bringing them on, I decided to take a look, but I should have taken the look prior to boarding the plane. This could have been disastrous. I would appreciate it if you keep this between us."

Chakes said, "You know I'm a freezer, but you have to do due diligence in the future. We don't make stupid mistakes like that. Let it go but keep your focus because we need each other more than ever in this concrete jungle."

Courtney asked the Sarge, "What was that all about?"

The Sarge responded, "Montomie picked up two cases at the hotel and they have between $6 and $7 million dollars in them."

"Wow, what on earth are you going to do with that money?"

The Sarge looked at her and said, "I am going to do whatever the team deems necessary. I must admit, we have fallen into untold sums of money since this adventure started. Hopefully, we continue to be blessed with means to help others without anyone suffering any major injuries. You know once we get back to Asiram's place, me and the boys, as well as, Asiram and Zanthius, will have to go to the lion's den to retrieve the package and hopefully hand it off without any problems. You and the children will have to stay here to keep an eye on things."

"Now, Sarge, are you stupid? There is no way in hell you are going to go into the District of Columbia, Maryland, or Virginia, without me being close by. We have had a solid run by staying together and you are not about to impose new rules now. This thing started in a restaurant after we were shot at and since then we have gone through all kinds of mayhem and pain. Dear man, get a grip. Where you go, I go and where I go Larry, Rashida and Marisa, Monica, Yvett and every damn body else is going to be just around the corner to provide the ultimate backup, if needed."

The Sarge was about to say something when Ava interjected, "I overheard some of the conversation and I just want you to know that where Carlos goes, I go and where Zanthius goes, I for damn sure am going to be really close by. You need a new plan, Mr. Beckmire."

Beckmire announced, "I need a nap. Maybe I can at least close my eyes in peace for a few minutes."

Courtney said, "Only if you are figuring out a new plan while you are supposed to be sleeping. I can't believe that you think you are going to go off and have all of the fun while we sit back and wait for you to come back. That is so asinine Ben Beckmire, just damn dumb. Take a nap and I'll wake you when the plane begins to descend."

Beckmire said, "I love you, but I need you to reconsider your plans. I can't protect my men and you at the same time. I need to know that you and the others are safe."

"I understand everything that you're saying, Ben Beckmire, but you have gotten me involved in this intrigue and something inside of me is enjoying the danger and the cloak and dagger mess. I did consider it some more and as I said before; where you go, I go. That is the end of this discussion, unless you want to permanently take up residence in our guest bedroom."

CHAPTER THIRTY-SIX

The plane rides, by the grace of God, were uneventful but tiring and long. Those who were lucky enough to be on board understood the true meaning of family, brotherhood, helping other people help themselves, and taking a chance on a stranger. This was extremely obvious to Bernstein with his attention on his new ward, Yvett. Bernstein was ever watchful and attentive to her and her needs. He suggested to Courtney that when they landed, he wanted to take her to the hospital and have her completely checked out and then he wanted to take her shopping to buy her new clothes and personal items. Courtney asked him why he was being so attentive?

He told her that he learned that trait from the Sarge and the rest of the guys. "This is how we roll", he said to her. He then went on to tell Courtney that Yvett was a beautiful woman and he felt drawn to her on so many different emotional and physical levels. Courtney cautioned him about moving too fast on the physical aspect of their relationship because she was just coming out of a traumatic situation where being physical was a requirement of her well-being.

On another part of the plane, Asiram was sketching pictures of what she envisioned as her replacement house in Virginia and was attentively being assisted by her husband.

His focus was on expanding the barn and building a workshop that would allow them to build and replace fence posts as well as other projects that could easily be completed by the two of them. Asiram, out of the blue, asked Zanthius, "Do you want to have children?"

He looked at her and then looked out of the window and replied, "I'm not sure, but if that happens to come along, I will certainly cherish the notion. I mean, I have yet to spend a night with you without the eyes or ears of my family and friends on us. I so want to have you wash my back as I wash yours and just sit in a tub of water drinking champagne, eating caviar with crackers and a little Jamon Serrano on the side. Of course, I want children, but I also want an opportunity to spend some overdue quality time with my new wife, lover, and protector."

She reached over and kissed him on the cheek. He asked, "What's that for?"

Asiram crossed her fingers and whispered, "I missed my monthly."

Zanthius stood up and exclaimed, "Get out of that chair and give me a full body press and kiss! I love you, Asiram Lenovax De Lombardo."

Beckmire woke up and said, "Can you guys keep the noise down," Old people are trying to take a nap."

Zanthius whispered to Asiram, "Can I at least tell my Pops?"

She cautioned him, "Let's be sure first, okay?"

Zanthius agreed with her and said, "I love you and I want to share all your tomorrows. I can still do what I want, but we will have to share and sharing is what this whole family is about. That reminds me, when we get to your place, we are only going to be there a few days before we go to retrieve the package and turn it over to a person that the spirits told us to. I know, you don't believe in hocus pocus, and neither did I until I visited Australia."

Zanthius was about to say something else, when Asiram interjected, "Listen, first, we are going to our place, as well as, everyone else who is here. Secondly, I don't know what happened to me while I was in the outback but for some odd reason, I don't take the notion of hocus pocus lightly anymore. I think we all had some kind of transmogrification out there in that very weird but wonderful place."

"What on earth does transmogrification mean?"

"Look it up. I guess I don't have to concern myself with how you got the name, 'idiot spy'? Anyway, I had all kinds of visions while you and my Daddy-in-Law were on your trip. I sure as hell was on a trip as well. I saw everyone gathering around me and handing me flowers and gifts and congratulating me on the birth of our son. Zanthius, I am not making this shit up. I had all kinds of visions, mostly positive but one that demanded my attention and was about the retrieval of the capsule. So, let me say this, my dear boy, where you go, I go, and I go carrying big guns and I will fire on the President of the United States of America, if he gets between you and me. Now, that's a commitment I mean wholeheartedly. So, don't tell me about leaving me on the farm while you and my Daddy-in-Law go and try to conclude this mess. Where you go, me and the baby goes."

"Is there any room for negotiation in this matter?"

Asiram looked at him and replied, "There is always room for negotiation, however, in this situation, having evaluated the probable outcomes, I would definitely say, naw! Don't even bother considering going without me because I know what I have to do to keep you and the rest of this assorted family alive. That is my task—my challenge and my commitment to you."

Zanthius kissed her and walked to the front of the plane where his father was napping and said, "Pops, wake up. We have to talk."

Beckmire said, "I know what you are going to say, Son. I just got the riot act read to me by my wife. Insofar as I am concerned, minus the children, we stay a few nights at the farm and then we head to the concrete jungle."

Zanthius looked at him and asked, "Will I ever know what you're thinking?"

Beckmire looked up at him and answered, "Well, no! Forget it! I am from the original Beckmire clan, you are from, well, a distant part of the clan so don't hurt yourself trying to overcome your short comings as a Beckmire. As a matter of fact, I do not want you to change your name from Zanthius De Lombardo to Zanthius De Lombardo Beckmire. What I would like and accept, is if you changed your name to Zanthius Beckmire De Lombardo and that would keep your mother forever grateful to me and to you."

"How in the hell did you know I was thinking about changing my name?"

"On Walkabout, you learn a lot of things, Son. You didn't experience it all, but when we go back and set up schools and daycare centers and employment strategies, you will have a chance to venture into the unknown and realize that there are things that science alone cannot explain."

Zanthius said, "I am going to turn around and walk back to my seat and say absolutely nothing else to you for the balance of this plane ride.   This is absolutely crazy and perplexing."

The captain opened the cockpit door and announced, "We are approximately one hour from touch down. Ms. Asiram, do you want me to make that call now?" Asiram indicated that she did.   Zanthius asked Asiram, "When did you ask the captain to call Clyde?"

"When we first got on the plane. I also asked Clyde to form a security party for the planes so that the pilots can get some real rest and relaxation. By the way, Clyde said that he would personally supervise the security detail and indicated that he was also transporting us on their new bus, courtesy of our group's money and bringing personal security items."

"What on earth does personal security items mean?"

"Listen my 'idiot spy', he is bringing us weapons, just in case there are some bad people still trying to hurt us."

The captain called Clyde and told him that the planes would be landing in approximately one hour and requested that he provide transportation. Clyde told the captain that he would be there and that security would be provided for the planes.

Once the planes were on the ground, everyone breathed a sigh of relief. Flying is always a taxing event even when the flights are smooth and without issues. As they disembarked from the planes, a shiny new blue school bus with water and snacks aboard awaited the passengers. In addition to those amenities, the school bus was also equipped with two secret compartments that contained loaded weapons of all sorts, mostly taken from people who would no longer need them. The children waited outside the bus while the adults were outfitted with the additional items.

After everyone was aboard the bus, Clyde said over his new intercom system, "I hope you people had a wonderful and enlightening trip. I would also like to say that you are the first ones to ride in our town's new school bus that is a gift from each and every one of you. I would like to personally thank Ms. Asiram for believing in us and bringing seasoned help (no pun intended) to assist us in matters that we were not familiar with.

"First things first, I have a detail of grateful towns' people at the airport to provide security for the planes. If any of you want to enter any of the planes, I suggest that you contact me first and get permission. The people I have assigned to provide security are on orders to shoot first and ask questions later. I beg of you, please adhere to that basic condition.

"Secondly, since there are so many of you, you will be dropped off at different locations to bathe, shower, wash or whatever. You will then be driven back to Ms. Asiram's place for a spectacular dinner, that is the entire town's contribution and way of saying thank you for saving our farms and keeping our people in place. You guys and gals are the best. People don't realize that on this earthly world that we share, the most important things in it are family and true friends.

"We almost lost a significant number of our local family but are now able to thank you guys for helping us help ourselves. We love you and hope that our little demonstration of our appreciation, no matter how small, enters your hearts and demonstrates our commitment to you and your people. As a matter of fact, it was voted on and approved that if a full battalion of soldiers appeared in our area, we would be your first line of defense. We would proudly die in service to you, as written and approved by our towns' fathers and managers.

"The last thing I want to announce, is that you people don't know how much you mean to this town. I mean, a bunch of strangers show up, under suspicious circumstances, on pretty new jet planes, and apparently, with a lot of people hunting them. You then take time to settle a major issue in our town for our people. You then show us that the good guys, who sometimes look like the bad guys, are really the guys from heaven looking out for everyone that they come in contact with. We love you guys and appreciate all that you have done for us. You gave us back our grit. You gave us back our commitment to each other and most of all you replayed the video with the message that says emphatically; family, friends and communities have to help each other help themselves. Welcome back!"

Courtney kept elbowing Beckmire in the side who finally got the message. He stood up and said, "Clyde, you and your people have become a part of our family and we appreciate all that you have done and will probably do in the future. Our family has one code. We live by the laws but if you attempt to harm one of us, you invoke the wrath of all of us. We thank you and look forward to eating some real homecooked food."

The entire group, including the children, elected to have hot baths. As the group enjoyed the comforts and pleasures provided by the rural folks, it became obvious to everyone that this place was a wonderful and strategically located venue for future gatherings. Asiram mentioned to Zanthius, "We have one other place that I neglected to tell you about. I have a condo in St. Thomas."

"What are you saying?"

"I said exactly what I wanted to say. I have a condo in St. Thomas. What's wrong with you? You act as if I called the devil himself and told him I was coming home." Zanthius appeared to be in a coma and in a stupor. Asiram yelled, "Zanthius, what's going on?"

Zanthius remained silent and comatose until Asiram slapped him on his leg. He finally responded by saying, "I don't know how to tell you this, but I have somewhat of a history on St. Thomas, that you probably won't appreciate."

He attempted to skirt talking about his issues on the island but Asiram interceded and said, "Honey, I was a spy. Your history on that island has nothing to do with me, unless your past transgressions are still a part of your life. You have to tell me. I know about your philandering and your multiple interludes with women. If there is something that we need to discuss, then I suggest that you start the conversation. I can't control what you did in a previous life. I can only have an opinion about what you do in this new life with me."

Zanthius turned to Asiram and said with tears in his eyes, "While on St. Thomas, I lusted after and screwed women, had multiple partners at the same time and thought that I was in love with a woman, who currently is still a part of my life. I mean, I love you and there is no turning back on that but there I was like a wild person: seeking sex, getting sex, joining partners in multiple applications of sex and enjoying it all immensely. It was my downfall and the ultimate reason why my first wife divorced me. She was a good woman, but when

I was there the opportunities that presented themselves to me at an exponentially incredible rate on a physical level were just all consuming. I mean, I met them, I slept with them, I met their friends and slept with them. I slept with everyone on the damn island. I also tried to give back by helping people, but I was all over the place. I was like a 'Chameleon', changing colors, sometimes shapes and having my way with all who looked at me!"

Asiram placed her hand on his leg and said, "The questions you must answer are the following: Do you love me for me and do I make you happy? Do you want to develop a family and life with me until the day we die?"

"I unequivocally love and adore you, but I have to tell you about my previous life, especially on St. Thomas."

"If you were on St. Thomas without me, do you think you would transgress?"

"There are those who I know I would not allow to endanger my marriage. However, there is one who might take me to task and I must admit I might not be able to deny a physical encounter with her."

Asiram emphasized, "I love you, Zanthius. I respect your honesty and only hope that the love I have for you is mutual, thus ending any temptation."

Zanthius said, "I indicated to you that she might take me to task. I never said that I would violate my vows to you. You must believe me. I am in love with you and you are the only woman that I want to touch and have touch me. It's just my past catching up with me. My emotions and my feelings are where they should be, with you my love. No one will ever come between me and my love for you. I am no longer a 'Chameleon'."

Asiram looked at her man and began to cry. She finally said, "I would hate to have to extract your ass for some dumb shit--'idiot spy'." They laughed and kissed and the importance of the honesty of his acknowledgements were recognized, for she knew of his exploits and appreciated his truthfulness and was glad that he came clean. After all, she was a spy!"

## CHAPTER THIRTY-SEVEN

Walter called Beckmire and told him that the transfer of the capsule was on target and that he needed him in DC in two days. Beckmire informed him that they were going to rest up and would be there in three days, in plenty of time to retrieve and turn over the damn capsule.

Walter asked, "Do you ever follow orders or yield to reasonable requests?"

"When I receive a reasonable request from you, as opposed to demands, I will act accordingly."

"Okay, okay. Listen if you can make it in three days, we would greatly appreciate it. I recommend that you and Zanthius come alone."

"That ain't going to happen. My people, including my wife, have told me that where I go, she goes and they follow. We might leave the children, but the rest of the group will be there in full force and will be suspicious of any unknown movements or individuals. I can't place my son at risk by depending solely on your intelligence about who might still be out there and interested in that damn capsule. Now, what I would like from you is some workable weapons. No way in Hades are we going to fly into DC or anywhere else with a planeload of weapons? Can you help us out, Couz?"

"Do I have to outfit everyone or just a few?"

"You wouldn't want my people to start second guessing you, would you? By the way, were you able to place cuffs on the father of that kid?"

"Nope. He left the scene after that false fire and hasn't been heard from or seen since then. His son on the other hand is singing like a canary on crack cocaine. He is implicating people associated with his father, as well as, friends and relatives. By the way, did you guys happen to find two suitcases full of money?"

"Walter, every time you misplace something do you expect us to pick it up or be in a position to find cases full of money?"

"I thought you would say something like that. You never answer questions about money directly. You always attempt to shift the focus."

"How much money are you talking about?"

"I'm talking about approximately, $7.5 million."

"How on earth do you lose $7.5 million? No one had eyes on the suitcases. Was it the government's money or illicitly gained funds from drug peddling?"

"Oh, it was definitely drug money, but with all of that smoke and fire, no one watched the two suitcases. They kept their eyes on the people and I must admit, we didn't do a good job at that because the father got away clean as a whistle."

"Listen, I am going to dump this phone in a few and will text you on my new one. Sorry about your loss. I will catch you later. Oh, and by the way, we will arrange our own transportation. Bye now!"

Beckmire went back into the house and began to load his plate with the fantastic food the neighbors had cooked for the group. Courtney said, "I tried to wait for you, but you seemed to be engaged on the phone, so I didn't bother you. You have got to try this chicken. The ribs are fabulous and wait until you try those filets. Everything is delicious."

After enjoying his meal, Beckmire summoned Mallory, Zanthius and of course Asiram. He indicated to them that Walter had requested they be in DC in two days. He informed them that he told Walter they would be there in three days, a day after they were told to be present in the area by their clan member from over the water. He asked Asiram, "How trustworthy is Clyde? I mean you trust him with your property and he protected us as well but if we were to drop $7.5 million on him to watch until we opened some accounts out here, would we have to kill him and his family?"

Asiram smiled and responded, "Daddy-in-Law, Clyde is a good man. As a matter of fact, the money that we placed in the safe in the tunnel, well, Clyde knows how to access it. I can make a call tomorrow to a couple of the banks and can have that money moved and placed into several accounts if you like. The banks out here are rather accustomed to me making significant deposits and it is all cleared through the channels. Unless this money is going to be missed, I would probably only release $5 million of it. Once in DC, I can easily clear the other $2.5 million without any questions or concerns. I think banking $5 million here is the best way to go on this."

Zanthius asked, "Where on earth did $7.5 million come from?"

His father replied, "One of my boys found it." Everyone laughed.

# # #

Later, Beckmire huddled with Mallory and Jong to discuss finding living quarters in the Metropolitan DC area. Jong asked, "How many people are we talking about?"

Beckmire answered, "The entire crew minus the children and their guardians. Walter is expecting us in three days and I just might take a day off of that and cut it to two days. I somewhat trust Walter as he is cut from the same fabric as I am, but he is a career employee and has to follow certain rules. In our case, we can decide what we want and when we want it and go about our business. Not so with him. Mallory, what's your take on the situation in terms of getting hotel rooms close to DC but not actually in DC?"

Mallory responded, "Sarge, this is exciting, but is beginning to wear on the team. Why don't we go in two days, that will give us all some much needed 'R&R'? We have to be sharp on this last leg of the journey. I think two good nights of rest will have the guys smelling fish from a mile away. They need to rest and those catnaps aren't the answer to their needs.

"On the matter of your cousin, I will yield to you and how you relate to him. Also, I think we need to scout the pickup area and make sure that we have a clear exit strategy. I don't want to study the place on the same day that Zanthius is picking up that damn capsule. Actually, it might be better if Jong, me and a few others left tomorrow to walk the area where the pickup and delivery will happen."

Jong said, "I like that idea because we will not be relying on cover by my cousin's people."

Beckmire stated, "I just don't like splitting our group up and relying on civilians to help, if there is a crisis. I think we all should head there tomorrow, do reconnaissance and try to figure out the logistics and what we are dealing with? How many weapons do we have in the compartments of the planes?"

Jong answered, "On the one plane we have twelve pistols and there are six on each of the other planes."

Mallory said, "That should be enough to do the work. We just have to make sure that we don't encounter any local police persons in DC. Carrying loaded weapons in DC is tantamount to a life sentence in prison. Okay, let's pull the guys in and get their feedback."

CHAPTER THIRTY-EIGHT

Beckmire's ragtag army met in the morning for breakfast. He asked Zanthius, "Where is your wife?"

"She and Clyde went into town with a few other neighbors to open a series of accounts."

"Didn't she know we are leaving today?"

"Pops, we didn't get that email or text. As a matter of fact, we were planning on working on sketches of our new place in Virginia. When was this decision made?"

Beckmire paused and replied, "I guess I neglected to inform you guys of our intentions. I really need to take a break and sit back and have a large glass of rum and just relax. I am so sorry and I apologize to you profusely for my lack of attention to details. What troubles me, is the fact that you let her go into town alone without any of our people looking over her shoulder."

"Pops, the entire town is armed and walking the streets sporting their weapons. She called me and told me they had security on rooftops, in the banks, on every corner and that the town's people are vigilant and dedicated to her security. I'm confident she's in good hands."

"Well, it would have been nice if she had informed us of her movements."

"It would have been nice of you to inform us that we are leaving today, as well." "Touché", the Sarge said.

Ava and Carlos descended the steps and saw that people had packed a few bags and began to wonder what was going on. She asked Courtney, "Are some of the guys leaving?"

"We are all supposed to leave and head into the DC area."

"When was someone going to tell me about this action?"

"Check with Ben Beckmire and while you are at it, give him hell. He thinks that he is going to leave me here while he and his boys go and have some adrenaline pumping adventure. He must be really crazy," Courtney stated.

Ava entered the dining room and said, "Mr. Beckmire, may I have a word with you?" The Sarge got up from the table and heard an earful from Ava and eventually from Carlos who indicated that he felt left out of the equation as well. Beckmire apologized to them and told them that he was so busy trying to end this event that he inadvertently forgot to communicate his intent to the group. Ava exclaimed, "Listen, Ben, where Zanthius goes, I go and where I go, Carlos goes."

Beckmire acquiesced and once again apologized to Ava and Carlos. He told Carlos that he and his men were vital to the security of the entire group and that he really appreciated how he stepped up to the plate and did what was necessary. Carlos thought to himself, 'why is he blowing so much smoke?'

Clyde, Asiram and a few other neighbors pulled up in front of her house and were met by Asiram's husband and Zanthius's father. Zanthius inquired, "Honey, did you know we are leaving today?"

Asiram with her witty self, answered, "I guess the pigeon with that message was eaten by a hawk. Who made the decision?"

Beckmire replied, "I made the decision, but didn't communicate it well. How did it go at the bank?" Asiram pulled out an envelope that contained three checks in various amounts all totaling $9.8 million dollars. Beckmire looked at her and asked, "What on earth is this for?"

"I took the $7.5 million and other cash that we had stored in my safe and turned them into a cashier's check in your name for deposit into your foundation fund."

"Silly girl, you guys keep that money. Me and the boys ran into a shitload of money and we really don't need what you found. By the way, our group will always have your back concerning our funds."

He looked at Mallory and asked, "Do you support that notion?"

Mallory replied, "I am sure everyone will agree, that you should keep that plus probably another $10 million from our other adventures. We just haven't had time to discuss money because we are tired and sleeping with one eye open. Naw, you guys keep that and when we have time to have our meeting, we will figure out additional monies we feel you guys deserve."

Asiram said, "Zanthius and I want to be a part of your fundraising programs that help people. Maybe what you guys decided to give us will allow us to buy into your good works."

Beckmire hugged her and said, "I am proud to have you as a member of my family. Your statement makes me extremely proud of both of you. I do have one request, and that is that we consider setting up a program that keeps the family farm in the hands of family and away from speculators."

Asiram replied, "I think I have already started that. Oh, and by the way, the entire town is armed to the teeth. There were little old ladies sitting out in front of the general store with shotguns, people on rooftops with rifles and the new sheriff and his deputy looked very professional. I mean, I felt secure and protected. I had a caravan of people with guns follow me here. It was amazing and just shows what a little kindness to people can net you. I am proud to be a member of this community."

#

Jong received a call from his Pilot-In-Command (PIC) who said, "I need you to talk to someone who will tell these people to allow us on our planes so that we can do a safety check and make sure that they weren't compromised."

Jong said, "Sarge, the pilots can't get on their planes."

Clyde who was near, asked, "Are you sure they are your pilots?"

Jong answered, "I'm sure. I recognized his voice. I will have your people separate them and ask them for the password." A minute later, the person on the other end of the phone said, "Fab 10 + 2."

Jong said, "They be our boys." Clyde got on the phone and told his people to let them on the planes.

Jong asked Clyde, "How many people do you have at the airport watching our planes?"

"We have twenty people here and there, some obvious and others you couldn't spot with a magnifying glass, all crack shots. You people saved a community, families and farms, we don't plan on letting anything happen to you in our town. Our people have agreed to meet heaven or hell before letting someone injure any of you people. You gave us back our lives, you gave us salvation and freedom. You gave us back each other and we don't plan on ever tripping down that road again, thanks to you, your people and Ms. Asiram."

Beckmire signed the checks over to Asiram, who signed the checks and gave them to Clyde. She told him to take them to the bank after they leave, and deposit them into the four accounts she opened. Clyde was also a signatory on the accounts which made the transactions easy and clean.

Asiram told Clyde that the kids were remaining behind with a few adults and to make sure they remain secure. She also suggested that he take them into town tomorrow and let them live like normal human beings, but that he should keep a watchful eye over them. Clyde told her that they would have the same preparation in town for the children as they had for her, but weapons would not be so obvious. She thanked him and he said, "Me and my kind will forever be indebted to you and that Mr. Beckmire. We live a simple life out here. We don't hurt anyone, but when you come for us from this point forward, you had better be loaded for bear. We got your back, your front and both sides. We can't thank you enough for all that you have done. We are your family and you will never have to worry about a damn thing here because we will be vigilant and conclusive."

CHAPTER THIRTY-NINE

As the group assembled to leave for the airport, Bernstein was having a conversation with Yvett. Yvett had feelings of being abandoned and Bernstein attempted to assure her that he would return. She wondered why she couldn't accompany him and he told her that when he was with this group it was usually very dangerous work and that he didn't want to place her in any danger. His comments clearly didn't convince her but Beckmire walked over to her, and said, "He will return and you will be whole. My wife has planned for you to see a doctor and have a complete physical examination. We need you to get strong mentally and physically. You have been rescued by one of God's gentle human beings. He is interested in you and if you do the right thing, then he will be yours."

Yvett asked, "Uncle, what is the right thing?"

Beckmire assured her, "Be loyal, faithful and loving and you will have a mate for life who will cherish you until the day the Heavens call for you or him. He is a solid human being and I sanction this relationship. So, my love, stay here, get some rest and we will see you in a few days. You have my word on that."

# # #

Beckmire huddled with Mallory and said, "I don't like the idea of all three planes landing at the same airport. It kind of gives us away. What's your take on that?"

Mallory replied, "Great, Sarge. I think you're back and thinking again. You are absolutely correct."

Mallory then summoned Jong and said, "The Sarge doesn't think we all should land at the same airport, and I concur. Can you speak with the pilots and see how they can place us at nearby, but not the same airports, at staggering times?"

Jong looked at both of them in disbelief and asked, "Are you guys trying to be funny? Have you bugged my phone or something? What's going on, Sarge?"

Beckmire looked at Mallory and then at Jong and responded, "I just don't think that all three planes should land at the same airport. What does that have to do with bugging your phone or trying to be funny?"

Jong looked at them long and hard and finally said, "I came to tell you that I asked the PIC to find alternative landing places for the three planes because I didn't want them all landing at the same airport." Beckmire and Mallory started laughing and Jong finally joined in. Mallory announced, "This is how we work. We always know what the other person is about to do and that was what kept us alive and well when we were in the Nam."

"This is absolutely fantastic," Beckmire stated.

Jong said, "I have delayed the departure time as well because I want to get there in the middle of the night and just be able to breathe and not have to look over our shoulders." Beckmire asked Mallory to communicate the approximate departure time to the group.

Two hours later, the group was buckled in their seats. Everyone was pensive and focused. Although it was two full days before they would retrieve the information, everyone knew that the heat was about to be turned up and that they only had each other to rely on.

Ava crawled on her knees to where Courtney and Beckmire were sitting and advised, "Carlos thinks that we should have more of our people just hanging out in the area. He feels that all eyes are going to be on us and it would not hurt to have our guys also playing a role on the street. They know how to rewire cameras that may be filming us and can stake out places. All we need from Zanthius is an address. From there our guys can be online in four hours watching everything that comes and goes. Does that make sense to you?"

Beckmire replied, "When we land, I will huddle with your guys and Mallory and discuss the pros and cons of the situation. However, the suggestion is a good one and one that we will consider thoroughly and strategically. Thanks, Ava."

Courtney inquired, "Do you still feel just a little something for her? I mean she is drop dead gorgeous and sexy as can be. You can tell me the truth. Do you still feel something for her?"

Beckmire retorted, "Forget my feelings. I married you and I am as happy as any man can be. And besides, you are drop dead gorgeous and sexy. I'm good. Are you good?"

Courtney smiled and replied, "You are one smooth operator, Ben Beckmire."

Beckmire watched as Jong exited the cockpit and asked him, "Why don't we fly into Philly, drive to the Maryland area and be done with it. I mean there is Wings Field and the

Northeast Philadelphia airport and they both can handle our planes. Check with the captain and see what he says."

Jong came back and said, "We can do Philly International and won't have any problems. The captain of the third plane is buddies with everyone at the private aircraft terminal. They all flew together in the Gulf War and can slowly turn in our paperwork once we land if you know what I mean. Your call, Sarge."

"Can you get us decent vehicles?" Beckmire asked.

Jong answered, "I can get us five SUVs. That should be plenty and will allow us room to operate if we have to go on offense or defense."

"Okay, see if they can reroute without a problem."

## CHAPTER FORTY

The ride from Philly to the Baltimore area was full of people snoring. John Lee and Jilkes continued to nudge each other while trying to get some sleep. John Lee would be awakened by Jilkes and then Jilkes would fall asleep and begin to snore.

At the selected motel, Beckmire stated, "Well, it ain't the Five Seasons, but it will provide us with plenty of rest and cover. We are backed up to a wooded area and that may give us an opportunity to stretch and run a little bit together. Everyone seems to be in shape, but we still need conditioning."

Mallory said, "I'll be on that first thing in the morning. Right now, all I want to do is get some shuteye."

# # #

At 0600 hours, Mallory began to bang on doors. People knew it was coming and were ready to rock and roll. When he banged on Jilkes and John Lee's door, John Lee said, "I's been waiting a whole hour for you. I mean, I could have slept for another hour. We ready, so let's get going. We scouted the area last night and found that this here property goes about two miles deep and ends at a creek. I think we can make that run and back without a problem."

Mallory inquired, "Do you think Jong can make it as well?"

"He can walk, can't he? There be nothing wrong with him that I be seeing. He just moves a little slower than the rest of us," John Lee stated.

Carlos heard the noise and had his people fall in behind Beckmire's and they all went for a short run and a routine of calisthenics. At 0700, Beckmire who was slightly winded announced, "Hell, I am going to do another run. I think I have sat my fat ass down in front of the television too long and I need to get back in shape. I'll catch you guys later." As he headed out, he heard footsteps behind him. It was Mallory and the boys followed by Carlos's people.

At 0800 hours, a sleepy Zanthius and Asiram could be seen in the lobby stretching. Beckmire stopped the group and said, "Look at those two. I guess they are going to go for a short walk." Everyone laughed.

In a flash, Zanthius and Asiram whisked by them at full speed. Beckmire muttered, "Showoffs!"

Beckmire huddled with Mallory and told him what Ava had suggested on the plane. Mallory said, "I have no idea what we are about to walk into, so the more the merrier. If they can burn into the camera system and give us the positions of possible hostiles, then I say we engage them. If they can provide emergency backup, then I say we engage them. If they are anything like the people that she has here now, then I say engage them."

Beckmire called Ava's room and she answered the phone and reported, "My people are on their way to DC. Once we meet with Zanthius and he gives us the address to the pickup place, we can get to work. Is there anything else you want to say to me?"

"Have a wonderful day, Ava. Hit you later."

Asiram and Zanthius ran a total of five miles. When they returned to the hotel, she said, "Wow, that was a fast run and thrilling. I really feel great after a run, how about you?"

"I'm impressed with your stamina. I didn't think that you would be able to keep up with me, so I really didn't press the run, but you were with me lock, stock and barrel. I am very impressed, Mrs. De Lombardo."

"Well, Mr. Beckmire De Lombardo, I must admit, I was not sure if you would be able to keep up with me at first. It was only about halfway through the run that I decided to hold pace and allow you to attempt to keep up with me. Now, the next time we do this, I am not going to hold back. It will be a grueling five miler and the winner takes all."

Beckmire saw the two in the lobby and asked, "How was your leisurely stroll?"

Asiram replied, "Why don't you come with us tomorrow and let's see who runs and who has to walk? As my new Daddy-in-Law, I will allow you a modest pace of twenty minutes per mile."

Beckmire announced, "If you allow that, you will lose. Anyone of my guys, including Jong, can beat that record. I have an idea, once this mess is over, we should have a marathon. That is the only way we will see who needs consideration. Anyway, on to more important issues.

"Tomorrow, we have to scout out where the package is and what's the easiest way to access the facility. The following day, I want to pick it up and be on our way, like ghosts. From this point forward, neither of you are to leave the compound without my permission. Is that crystal clear?"

Zanthius looked at his father and saw the noticeable transformation of the man before him. Beckmire looked at him and Asiram and asked, "People, do you understand and do I have your word?"

Asiram answered, "Yes, Mr. Beckmire, we understand and you have our word."

Beckmire asked, "Asiram, do you know where the pickup place is?"

"I do not and do not want to know until we are on our way there."

"Son, have you told anyone where the place is?"

"Pops, I have tried to tell you and Asiram and maybe my mother. You all acted as if I were giving you the plague or something."

Beckmire said, "Okay, tomorrow morning we will huddle and you can give us the details. I will have your mother's people scout it out for us and set up surveillance. Until then, please do not wander off the premises without my people or me following you."

Beckmire walked into his room and fell on the bed. Courtney exclaimed, "Perhaps you need to pace yourself, young fellow!"

"Perhaps I need to find an island and just sit in some saltwater and drink Pina Coladas all day. That work out was grueling, but the boys did really well. It was just me and

Mallory that seemed to have a tough go at it. I just want to take a little nap. Wake me if there is any drama."

# # #

Four hours later, Beckmire was awakened by a rap on the door. It was Zanthius who said, "Pops, I really think I need to tell you where the location is now."

A sleepy Beckmire asked, "Why Son? Did you have a bad dream or something?"

"No, Pops, nothing like that. I just feel that I want to share this information with you."

"Son, you will have time to share it with me tomorrow. It's like you said, that thing is like the plague. You keep it for now and like a good father, I will hear all about it tomorrow."

They both laughed. Zanthius asked, "Do you think we can have drinks together? I mean just the two of us. There is still so much I want to tell you and there is so much more I want to hear about you and those over-the-top friends of yours. By the way, those guys are so loyal and dedicated. How on earth did you happen to fall into a lot such as them?"

"Can we talk about that and everything else while we're having drinks or is there something else that is really bothering you that you want to discuss?"

"You are the smartest man I have ever met and I am so sorry you weren't around during my formative years. Yes, there is an issue I need to discuss, but it can wait until we have our drinks. Let's say, in four hours," Zanthius stated.

"I just want to say this. Your child, your wife and you will be okay. Enjoy the idea that you have created life, a very special task that requires follow-up dedication, appreciation and patience. See you in four hours," Beckmire said.

Zanthius looked at his father and asked, "Does anyone else know that she's pregnant? I mean does Courtney know?"

"I'm the only one who knows, Son, and I will not reveal a thing. See you in four."

# # #

Beckmire was drifting off to sleep when the phone rang. It was Walter who said, "When are you people leaving to come this way?"

Beckmire responded, "Walter, we will be in your backyard in the morning. Right now, I really need some sleep."

"Well, we have a problem and I want to hold this action in abeyance until I can find out who leaked some vital intel to some really bad guys. There is a group of people, approximately twenty-two of them, who will be landing in your area in the next two and a half hours. I can have a team there in one hour. Do you want me to intercede?"

"I'll get back to you in twenty."

Beckmire called Zanthius and said, "You and Asiram come to my room immediately, we have a situation." He hung up the phone, called Mallory, and told him to meet him in his room asap.

When Asiram, Zanthius and Mallory showed up to his room, he reported, "We have been compromised and there isn't a damn thing we can do about it from here. Asiram, I need you to get Clyde on the phone for me. Trouble is heading their way."

Mallory exclaimed, "What the hell! Why are they going there when we're here?"

Beckmire replied, "Walter called and told me that trouble is heading my way, but he doesn't know that we're here. My concern is that Yvett, Rashida, Monica, Marisa, Larry and the children might be in danger."

Asiram interrupted the Sarge and said, "Hold on, Clyde, here is Mr. Beckmire."

Beckmire said, "Clyde, I just got a call from a friend who indicated to me that approximately twenty-two bad guys are on their way to the ranch. I still have family out there. Is there any way you can get them out of there and hide them?"

Clyde asked, "Mr. Beckmire, when will they arrive?"

"They will be there in a couple of hours."

Clyde said, "Okay, that gives me time to make a few calls and get things ready."

"Clyde, these people are ruthless, you and your people can't go up against these guys."

"Sir, you done helped a lot of people out here. There ain't no way in hell that even the 1st Battalion can come here without getting an ass whuppin, unless they be bringing tanks and artillery. I just hope they all have paid up insurance. No Sir, Mr. Beckmire, them people won't even get off the plane and if they do, they will meet an armed militia on the runway that will be closed with no return exits. We got this.

"We will move the children into the tunnel where it is safe and full of food stuff and there's even a TV in the vault. We got this. I mean even right now we have ten people out there doing walk arounds and stuff all day and night. They will be safe and probably won't see none of what may happen. I guarantee you this, Sir."

Beckmire asked Clyde to hold on and looked at Asiram and asked, "What do you think, and I need your honest thoughts?"

Asiram shook her head and replied, "I am shaking my head because whoever is on their way will not return. Clyde and his people got our backs. I know it's not like we are there to protect our own, but you got Larry there and he sure as hell ain't going to let nothing happen to anybody there. I think we need to focus on this end and wait for a call from Clyde that the deal is done. If you like, give Walter a call and tell him to have a team on standby. They have offices forty-five minutes away from my ranch."

Beckmire got back on the phone and said, "Clyde, those are my grandbabies and my son and daughter and his wife. If you can't protect them then hide them. Can you do that for me?"

"How about we hide them and protect them? Does that sound better?"

"Now, you're minimizing the risk for everyone. I like that strategy and, by the way, I will have friends from nearby who work for our government do some backup work."

Beckmire called Larry and informed him of the impending threat and the assistance that he could expect from the neighbors, as well as, government types from nearby. He told Larry that he preferred that he let Clyde hide everyone, thereby, avoiding a gunfight. Larry advised the Sarge that he would speak to Clyde about his plan and if it made sense to him, he would agree to it. The Sarge told Larry that he was in charge and if the plan did not make sense, then make the necessary adjustments or go into hiding. The Sarge asked Larry, "Do you remember your street training?"

"It is and will always be a part of my existence," Larry responded.

The Sarge said, "Good, then you will know what to do but just remember this, make sure the ladies know how to use the machine pistols and shotguns and make sure that they always have a .9 on them at all times. Tell them I said, 'never leave home without it'."

Larry said, "Don't worry about us, Sarge. Just take care of that other business so that we can get back to our normal lives."

"Larry, I am depending on you. I need you everywhere and nowhere at the same time. I need you to shoot first and second and if you have a minute, ask a question. Don't hesitate, but you can trust our new neighbors and friends. They are going to attempt to persuade those people not to get off the plane because if they do, they will have to walk home. Promise me you will be vigilant and take care of this mess for me, Larry, and promise me that everyone will be okay?"

"Sarge, I got this! I will keep you abreast of what happens."

"I love all of you and my grandbabies. Don't make me have to kill half of the world. Don't let anything happen to my babies."

As the Sarge considered the possible outcomes, he was not happy with the probabilities of everyone getting out of there in one piece. He summoned Jong and asked, "Can you get me a jet to pick up my family at the ranch in an hour?"

"Let me get back to you." Jong saw the urgency on the Sarge's face and realized that he had to act accordingly. He called the pilot in command and asked him if he knew of any planes for charter in the area of the ranch that could provide an immediate extraction. The pilot asked Jong about his timetable. Jong told him within the hour and the pilot told him that he would call him back in five.

Eight minutes had gone by when Jong received a call from the pilot in command who reported, "I have a buddy filing papers as we speak and could be there in less than fifty minutes. Have your people at the airport. The plane is a brand new G5 that can hold at least sixteen, will that work?"

"Absolutely! Is this someone we can trust?" Jong asked.

The pilot in command replied, "I would hope so, it's my uncle and he flew in the Nam."

"I love you guys and as soon as we get out of this mess, we are going to upgrade the fleet and keep you guys on our payroll."

"Now, that sounds exciting to me and I am sure the rest of the guys are going to jump for joy as well. Mr. Jong, let me just say one thing, we got your back and your front and both of your sides. We know we can do some of the work for you guys, just let us know. We are ready, able and willing."

Jong thanked him and said, "I will be in touch."

When Jong walked into the Sarge's room, he was greeted by a sobbing Courtney and saw the Sarge pacing around the room. He said, "Sarge, call Clyde and tell him to get our family to the airport in thirty-five minutes. I have a new jet on its way to pick them up. It will make an inadvertent stop in Chicago to take on fuel and then bring them to us."

Beckmire walked over to him, gave him a man-sized hug and said, "You're the best." He then yelled to Courtney, "Jong has a plane on its way to pick up our family and will probably be there and gone before the bad people land." Courtney came out of the bedroom, gave Jong a kiss on the cheek and thanked him. The Sarge announced, "I am going to call Clyde and ask him if he can have the air traffic controllers do us a favor by sending the enemy plane into a holding pattern if it gets there before our plane takes off."

Jong declared, "Excellent idea!"

Beckmire called Clyde and asked him to take his people to the airport immediately.

Clyde inquired, "Are you sure, because that is where those people are going to be."

Beckmire replied, "Now, this is where I need you to do me a big favor. If we run out of time, can you call your contacts in the tower and have that plane put into a holding pattern until our plane has taken off?"

"Consider it done. I will make the call as soon as I hang up with you. In the meantime, you call Larry and tell him to get his people in gear because we are going to break some speed laws getting them to the airport."

Beckmire called Larry and said, "Get everybody ready to leave for the airport in ten minutes. Oh, and Larry, reach into the safe and grab four stacks of bills, you keep one and give one to each of the women. Okay, Son, you have ten minutes. Clyde will be in front of the ranch house waiting for you. You and Marisa keep weapons on you until you get to the airport and then give them to Clyde, any questions?"

Larry yelled, "Everybody! Get your stuff together! We are leaving in ten minutes. Don't worry about packing, just get the kids some snacks and water and let's go."

Beckmire said, "Thanks, son. Call me the moment you are at the airport and when that plane takes off. I'll see you in three or so hours."

Jong looked at the Sarge and said, "Sarge, you orchestrated that perfectly. That reminds me of the good ole days over in the Nam when you could figure out the logistics and the points of attack in every conflict that we were involved in. Good to have you back, Sergeant Beckmire."

Beckmire smiled and said, "The deal ain't done yet."

# # #

Clyde had redeployed his people to the fringes of the airport and placed a few of them inside the terminal, but they did not go through the metal detectors. He assumed that the unwise bandits were going to come on a private plane but decided to make sure that he was covered on both sides of the fence. He called ahead to his wife who was on duty and asked, "So, dear, is it safe to bring our family members to the airport?"

She responded by saying, "Roger that. I heard from the tower that all private planes are holding or landing at the airport one hundred miles from here. Is that your work, dear?"

Clyde feeling that he might be able to score a triple double (date, drinks and dinner) with that information responded, "Well, honey, I'm kind of running this show out here. I mean, Ms. Asiram and that Sergeant Beckmire are constantly calling me and asking me for my input. I did tell them that I had a friend in the tower and that we could make private planes circle if necessary."

Gilda stated, "Since all of this started happening, I have noticed a new you and I must tell you I'm liking what I'm seeing and hearing. Maybe tonight we can go out and have a cocktail and dinner. I mean if you want to. I think it would be fun. I like how my man is handling things."

Clyde said, "Let's get our adopted family safely out of town, then we will discuss your proposal in length over, let's say dinner and a few cocktails. Keep your eyes open, honey and stay safe. See you soon."

Clyde yelled out, "Hot Diggity damn! I believe I am going to have some sweet time tonight."

Larry leaned over and asked, "Is everything all right?"

"Larry, between me and you, me and the misses are going to go out and have dinner and drinks and after that, smooth daddy is going to move in for the kill."

Larry laughed and said, "Well, you have been working hard helping us get through this mess, and by the way, I want to personally thank you for paying particular attention to all of us."

"No, Larry, I want to thank all of you guys and girls for being good and decent people, and for helping our neighbors and friends, and as a matter of fact, this whole damn town. We love you guys and will lay our lives on the line to make sure that you are safe. I'm not sure you know this, but when you were asleep, there were at least twenty people watching over you guys every single night.

"See, Larry, a town like ours was ripe for those northern carpetbaggers to find ways to enslave people through debt and then eviction. You people come out here and run the carpetbaggers off, set up funds for us to borrow against without interest, paid off debt and didn't even ask to be listed on the deed. No sir, we thank you and your people and especially that Ms. Asiram and Sergeant Beckmire."

Larry said, "I am going to ask you to do me one more favor while I am here."

Clyde asked, "What might that be?"

Larry said, "I forgot to close the safe because I didn't know how. Will you close it for me?"

"Did you write down on the clipboard how many stacks you took and sign your name?"

"I didn't see a clipboard and I didn't sign my name," Larry stated.

Clyde said, "Okay, I'll sign your name and the number of stacks."

Larry said, "I took four stacks of bills."

Clyde said, "Okay, I'll write that down and close and set the alarm on the safe when I get back."

"Do you think anyone else might go in there and help themselves?"

Clyde took his eyes off the road and replied, "No one here would dare take from a family member. You guys are our family. If I even thought that there was a thief out here, I would handle the sonofabitch myself. No, Larry, when people do good by us, we do good by them. Let me tell you something, Ms. Asiram never locks that damn safe and it stays open sometimes for years. We love who we are and we love our neighbors. When this is all over, you bring the kids back here and we'll show them nature at its best. Okay, we are coming up on the airport

One mile from the airport, two men were tinkering under the hood of a truck. Clyde looked at the men and they gave him the all clear sign. When entering the airport property, two women smoking cigars waved at the bus. Inside the perimeter of the airport two men on cell phones gave the all clear and at the terminal, Clyde's wife came out and winked at him. Clyde said, "I need you guys to stay put until I can find out what's happening with your plane and the status of the plane carrying the unwise people. Larry, keep these pistols near until I return."

Larry handed Marisa a pistol and said, "Watch the back of the bus. If anyone comes too close be ready to fire, and fire to kill. Don't hesitate. Rashida, Yvett, and Monica get on the floor and cover the children."

Larry saw Clyde having words with someone and thought that things were about to go south. Clyde walked the guy back to the bus where the guy boarded and reported, "I'm sorry, your plane will be on the ground in fifteen minutes. Clyde and I didn't communicate very well on this one. I thought he meant all private planes and therefore, I have your plane in a holding pattern and another plane coming into our air space in approximately thirty minutes. I need you guys to sit tight until your plane lands and then I will let Clyde drive you onto the runway so that you can board the aircraft and takeoff. Is that okay with you folks?"

Larry looked at him and answered, "That's perfect."

Approximately ten minutes later, a small jet appeared on the horizon and landed without incident. As the plane was taxiing on the runway, Clyde got a call to proceed on the active runway, stay in the lanes leading to the plane, load your cargo, and return.

The plane came to a stop, turned around and Clyde drove the bus to where the plane was parked on the tarmac. He told Larry and the group, "I will see you guys as soon as this mess is over. We love you here and always know that you got family out here." Larry shook his hand and ushered everyone out of the bus and onto the plane.

The captain welcomed them aboard and announced, "We don't have a lot of time to waste because in twenty minutes another plane will be landing. We don't want it to see us. Okay, everyone buckle up because we are out of here."

In less than ten minutes, the sound of the G5's engines roared down the runway and blasted into the sky like a missile. Larry pulled his phone out, called the Sarge and told him that they were airborne. The Sarge told him that was wonderful news. The Sarge then asked Larry if there was any kind of encounter with the other group and Larry told him no.

The Sarge told Courtney that everyone was on the plane and that they were safe. Bernstein knocked on his door and when the Sarge answered it, he inquired, "Is Yvett on that plane?"

The Sarge looked at him and asked, "What do you think?"

"Thanks, Sarge. I really appreciate this one and I owe you."

The Sarge said, "No, dude, I owe you and the rest of the guys for watching over me and my family. By the way, she is extremely fragile right now, so I suggest that you move slowly and cautiously. I know you fell for her the minute you saw her, but it is up to you to gain her trust and help her transition from that nightmare." They hugged and Bernstein walked away with tears in his eyes.

Courtney smiled at the Sarge and said, "I think it's time for you and me to take a siesta together or at least pretend that we are. I'm going to place the 'Do Not Disturb' sign on the door and take the phone off the hook for an hour. Do you think you can handle that and what I have in mind for you?"

Beckmire smiled and replied, "A wise man never brags about his abilities. He demonstrates them with finesse and grace. The question is, can you handle that my love?"

No additional words were exchanged between the two for fifty-five minutes. One can only imagine what actually happened during that time.

## CHAPTER FORTY-ONE

The private plane carrying the unknown strike force was rerouted to another airport 250 miles away. Clyde thought that this would send a message that the town would not easily be under siege. As the captain of the plane asked for details as to why the flight was being rerouted, the air traffic controller replied, "There is debris on the runway and it will take us a few hours to clean it."

#

In DC, Ava's men arrived at Reagan airport and were met by friends who provided them with video equipment and a few weapons for safety's sake. The only thing they needed was the location of the place where the package would be retrieved.

In Maryland, Mallory asked Beckmire to meet with him prior to him and Zanthius going out for some alcoholic libations. Mallory said, "I think it is time for Zanthius to disclose the location of the product."

Beckmire said, "I will ask him about it. Then we can have a few of our guys go and hang out for a while to see what the terrain has in store for us."

Mallory advised, "I think we only need Jilkes and John Lee attending to that matter, with perhaps Bernstein and Brown watching their backs. What's your take on it?"

"I totally agree with you, but I think Chakes and Montomie will probably blend in a lot better depending upon where the location is."

"So be it."

The Sarge went to Jong's room and asked him if he had considered transportation for his family. Jong told him that he had family members waiting at the airport and doing due diligence to make sure there wouldn't be any problems. The Sarge thanked him and asked, "How are you holding up under this constant stress and strain?"

"The leg bothers me a little sometimes, but other than that, I'm good to go. I think the more I function the less it hurts, so this adventure has been therapy for me in that I'm forcing myself to run and walk long distances without using the cane."

"Well, I know you know, I as well as the others, appreciate all that you have done. By the way, do you think it is time to upgrade our fleet?"

Jong looked at him and asked, "Sarge, are you screwing with me again?"

A perplexed Beckmire inquired, "What are you talking about?"

"I just talked to the pilot in command about upgrading our fleet less than two hours ago. Here you come, once again asking me about something that I have been thinking about."

The Sarge laughed and said, "Australia has made us closer in spirit than we have ever been. We are connected, get over it, and enjoy the feeling."

# # #

Asiram was questioning Zanthius about going out with his father and jokingly said, "I guess you would rather be with your daddy than with me. It's okay, but one day you are going to regret not being with me while I am feeling as amorous as I am now." Zanthius looked at his watch and then moved on the suggestion with urgent speed and with a happy consummation. Eight minutes later, they were both panting harder than they did after their run. Mission accomplished!

Beckmire checked his watch and noticed that Zanthius was at least ten minutes late. He ordered himself a Jack on the rocks and began to think about the adventure with all its excitement and danger. He realized that this was not Vietnam and although his guys were a bit slower, they remained as sharp as ever.

As Zanthius approached him, he said, "I had to do a little homework. Sorry I'm late." He then gave his father a hug. From the back of the small bar, a voice yelled, "This ain't that kind of bar. If you want to hug and kiss, go downtown." Zanthius and Beckmire looked at the three men in the corner and summarily dismissed the comment.

Jong entered the bar and saw his comrades, walked over and said, "I just wanted to give you an update on the other plane." A voice from the back table said, "He's a cripple and from Asia or some damn where. I guess we ain't the only country that has those gay types." Zanthius made a move towards the back of the bar, but his father grabbed his arm and said, "Son, we have enough trouble, no sense in yielding to stupidity. Let it go."

Unfortunately for the people in the back of the bar, Jilkes and John Lee walked in to have a beer and sat at a table without saying a word to the Sarge because they knew he and his boy had scheduled some bonding time. They ordered two Coors Lights and toasted each other's health. The guys at the other table yelled, "How the hell does that cripple do it with them others?"

Laughter broke out at their table and Beckmire declared, "You have insulted some very important people! I suggest that you enjoy your Shirley Temples and stay healthy, and you had better keep your mouths shut."

The biggest mouth and body of the three stood up and screamed, "Fuck you, faggot!"

John Lee stood up and yelled, "That there be my girlfriend and the one you called cripple be my lover. Now, you go on and apologize to them, or I'm afraid I am going to make you my bitch."

Jilkes stood up and shouted, "Enough talking!" The ensuing action lasted two minutes. There were near fatal punches to sensitive areas, slaps to the throats and hooks to the temples. The outcome was statistically significant: one broken jaw and right hand, one broken leg in two places and an eye closed shut, and one broken nose and two eyes closed shut.

The Sarge looked at his boys, then his watch and said, "You guys are slowing down. It took you two minutes to take those guys, I could have taken them in 1.5 minutes. Jong could have done the job in less than a minute. Maybe you two need to do some running or something." He told them to disappear because he knew that the bartender had made a call to local law enforcement. Beckmire placed five $100 bills on the bar and advised, "Don't get in over your head. Let it go and just say that these guys started the dance and a couple of strangers ended the waltz."

The bartender said, "Sounds pretty damn good to me, and thanks."

Zanthius asked, "Pops, are all of your people like that?"

"What do you mean, like that?"

"I mean that good with their fists and their feet? I mean that was like a ballet. Those guys never saw what was about to happen to them until the impacts. That was impressive to say the least."

Jong interjected, "Ah, it was okay for a couple of old guys. They used to be quick. I guess we all used to be quicker." He started to walk away when the Sarge said, "I need you to have a drink with me and my son. I need you to do this for me."

Jong looked at him and then Zanthius and replied, "Another time, Sarge."

The Sarge persisted and said, "Then I will drink with my son another time because I need to have a drink with you now."

Zanthius mumbled, "Pops, I'll catch you another time. See you later, Jong."

Beckmire walked over to the injured individuals and said, "You see this man who you called a cripple, he has killed more enemy soldiers then you can imagine. I was going to let him go at you alone, but he probably would have killed the three of you in less than a minute. Your ass whupping came from his buddies. Listen assholes, I'm glad they didn't have their blades on them, they would have cut you into little pieces. You mess with one of us, then you have earned the wrath of twelve of us. Thank your pagan deity that you only have broken bones and not slashed throats. If I see you again, I will personally send you to hell."

Beckmire and Jong were walking out of the bar when the local law ran into the place. Before they could ask what happened, the bartender reported, "Those three started calling people faggots and cripples and two guys in the corner took exception to their comments and in less than two minutes, they kicked those guys' asses and I mean really kicked their asses. It was magical to watch."

The cop asked, "Where are the people who did this?"

The bartender replied, "They got in a truck and drove off. I have never seen them before, but I did hear one say that they still had a twelve-hour drive to Florida."

As the ambulance pulled in, the paramedic asked, "How many guys did this?" The bartender answered, "Only two."

# # #

Jong looked at the Sarge and said, "You know my skin is thicker than that, don't you? I mean what they said was offensive, but I only become defensive when someone places hands on me or one of our guys."

The Sarge said, "You should have known that Jilkes and John Lee weren't going to take no shit from them or anybody else for that matter."

"Yeah, when I saw them come into the bar, I knew those guys were in for an ass whupping. I'm just glad none of those fools had a weapon on them because then it would have been, call the cleaners."

The Sarge and Jong laughed. Jong said, "Oh, I came in the bar to tell you that the plane has refueled in Chicago and will probably be here in the next hour. My people are already there looking, sniffing and evaluating worse case scenarios."

"Thanks, buddy. Could you have taken them in less than a minute?"

Jong smiled and retorted, "It probably would have taken thirty seconds, but it would have been terminal."

Beckmire shook his head, walked down the hallway and then turned around and said, "I'm glad your ass is on my side. Catch you later."

Beckmire went to the house phone and dialed Zanthius's number. There was no answer. He called Asiram on her cell phone and there was no answer. He called Ava's room, there was no answer. Beckmire then decided to check in with Mallory and there was no answer. He called Courtney, no answer. He asked himself, 'what the hell is going on'?

Zanthius called him back and inquired, "Are you still in the lobby?"

"I am, but I can't find anyone."

"I'll be right down."

As the two men walked into the bar, the bartender said, "Please, no more trouble tonight. What would you gentlemen like to drink?"

Zanthius replied, "I'll have a Cruzan and Coke."

Beckmire responded, "Make it two." The two men began to talk about small but important things, however, Zanthius kept coming back to what his father and his guys did in the Nam. Beckmire really wasn't in the mood for telling war stories and said to Zanthius, "Son, we killed a lot of people. I mean a shit load of souls are roaming around hell looking for us. We were good—no, we were the best at what we did. We were everywhere and nowhere all at the same time. Our bows were our source of success. Every one of those guys could hit a moving head shot at over 100 yards.

That John Lee and Jilkes could sneak up on a sleeping snake and cut its throat before it moved. I mean these guys were absolutely the best. John Lee could smell a fire, hear a copter or a twig break a mile away surpassing any human being that I have ever encountered. I don't know what they fed him, but I mean he is incredible in the field and has adjusted to the concrete jungle as well. The two of them are no better than any of the rest of the guys, as they all have their strengths and a few weaknesses, but those two were always asked to confirm a mission or a direction. Enough of that killing talk, how is Asiram coming along?"

"She's as horny as a rabbit. Every time we are alone, she looks at me and says, 'come on big boy, momma needs some more loving'."

Beckmire declared, "Hell, that's a good thing, ain't it?" The two men continued to talk and discuss their next move. When Zanthius was ready to tell his father where the capsule was, Beckmire mumbled, "I really don't want to know about that damn capsule until the morning. Tonight, I'm going to drink myself into a coma."

"Why on earth would you want to do that?"

"Because sometimes you need to refresh yourself by demolishing yourself."

"Where might that saying come from?"

"I don't know, but it sounded good to me when it was coming out of my mouth," Beckmire stated.

"Do you happen to have any money in your room?"

"I have a few thousand, don't you?"

"Well, I do, but I want to get Asiram a series of little things and I just need a few bills while she is not looking."

"Okay, walk me to my room. I have no idea where Courtney is, I called but she didn't answer her phone."

As they approached his room, Beckmire pulled out his room key and slid it into the slot. It kept giving him an error message. He looked at the room number and announced, "This is my room, but this damn key isn't working."

Zanthius mumbled, "Let me have a go at it, Pops." He too received an error message. "Let's try something novel like knocking on the door. Maybe Courtney is in there." Beckmire knocked on the door and Larry answered it. Everyone screamed at the top of their lungs, "HAPPY BIRTHDAY, SARGE."

Beckmire was thrilled to see his grandbabies, Larry, Rashida, Yvett, Monica and Marisa, and hugged and kissed each one of them. Next, he approached Courtney and said, "I thought you had forgotten. I was feeling a little neglected."

"Never!" she replied.

Prior to the birthday surprise happening, Bernstein welcomed Yvett with open arms and whispered, "I am glad you are here."

Yvett said, "I am happy to be here but more importantly, I am happy to see you again." She placed a small kiss on his lips.

Brown said, "Here we go! Another one bites the dust."

CHAPTER FORTY-TWO

The next morning, the Sarge was feeling upbeat and kind of ready for their morning run. Zanthius and Asiram went with them and boldly announced, "We will set the pace and will beat all of you senior citizens."

Brown retorted, "We only do long distance runs. This is just a warm-up for us. We have run as far as twenty miles with full battle gear and loaded weapons without stopping. You two just have your pretty little Under Armor stuff on that lights up the entire east coast. I guess if we do twenty, you youngsters might not be so cocky in the end."

As expected, the youngsters set a brisk pace, but it was Chakes and Montomie that represented the team with Brown and Bernstein close by. Jilkes and John Lee figured that they weren't in a marathon, and therefore, they weren't in a hurry and had no need to brag. They kept a lively step going and even Jong represented himself well. Zanthius witnessing the obvious dedication of Jong, slowed down and said to him, "You are amazing and man I really appreciate all that you have done for us."

Jong with a surprised look on his face responded, "You are welcome, but this run ain't over yet speedy."

John Lee and Jilkes were last and became distracted by a noise on their left side. John Lee asked Jilkes if he was packing. Jilkes replied, "You know damn well I have a .9 on me. Why do you ask?"

John Lee answered, "We ain't out here by ourselves." He pulled Jilkes to the left and held fast for a full minute. John Lee asked, "Can you smell that?"

"Smell what?"

"You can't smell that damn cologne?"

"I don't smell anything but your stinky ass."

John Lee watched the others head up the road and signaled to Jilkes to follow him closely and quietly. As they stepped through the brush, the smell of cologne became stronger and Jilkes signaled that he caught the scent. As they scurried through the high grass, they caught sight of two men assembling long guns with muzzles on them. John Lee pointed to Jilkes to flank them and he would come up on them from behind.

At the top of the hill, Mallory asked the Sarge, "Where are the two lovers?"

The Sarge stopped, caught his breath and replied, "It's not like them to drop off without a signal. He frantically motioned for everyone to get down!" Zanthius was about to say something when the Sarge pointed to the ground. Beckmire's crew had weapons and he signaled Brown to give the bird call. Brown gave the call, but there was no response. Brown then gave the all clear call and there was still no response.

Beckmire whispered, "I think we have been compromised and those two are on it."

Mallory pointed to Chakes and Montomie and pointed to the right. He next pointed at Whitmore and Gladstone and pointed to the left. He looked at Brown and Bernstein and gave them the point and told Asiram and Zanthius to stay behind him Jong, McArthur and the Sarge. As they moved out, the Sarge looked at his son and whispered, "Step lightly. You are giving our position away." Zanthius acknowledged him and began to watch where he stepped.

Jilkes was in a flanking position as John Lee approached the individuals from the rear. John Lee demanded, "Ease your hands off those weapons or we will blow your heads off!" The guy closest to Jilkes attempted to test fate and was felled by a bullet to the head.

John Lee asked, "Do you think you are faster than your friend? Place your hands on your head or we will cut you down like the snake you be."

Beckmire's team heard the shot. He raised his fist in the air. He looked at Brown and signaled him to give the call again. Brown whistled and received an all clear but be cautious response from John Lee. Beckmire sent everyone full throttle towards the sounds. As they got to where Jilkes and John Lee were, his team positioned themselves on all sides of them and fanned out looking for additional threats.

Beckmire said, "That shot could be heard in DC, was there an alternative?"

Jilkes said, "He tested our resolve and tried to draw quickly on John Lee and I popped him."

Beckmire said, "Good looking out. Okay, we are probably going to have company. I need this one alive and I need this area made sterile."

John Lee reported, "We got this, but I'm wondering how they find us. I mean this place was clean. You'll need to get back to the hotel and get ready to move out. Jilkes and I got this, but we need some eyes to watch our backs. I mean these guys smell like city rats with all that cologne on, but they may be with buddies."

The Sarge looked at Gladstone and Whitmore and gave them the assignment to watch their comrades' backs while they handled the problem. He told them to gag and restrain the other fellow until they had a chance to interrogate him.

# # #

At the hotel, the Sarge separated Brown and Bernstein and told them to enter using opposite doors of the hotel. He motioned for Chakes and Montomie to keep eyes on Zanthius and Asiram. He sent Jong and Mallory through the front door first and followed them cautiously. They looked around the lobby and saw no one suspicious and the Sarge decided to call his room. Courtney answered the phone and asked, "Did I hear a gunshot?"

The Sarge asked, "Is all okay?"

Courtney answered, "All is okay." That was a play on words and a signal that they had devised years ago.

The Sarge announced, "I need you to call the others and tell them we have issues and that we have to leave and for them to take only essentials."

Courtney said, "Gotcha, see you in a few."

In less than an hour, the bills were paid and the group was assembled. The Sarge gave Larry his pistol and said, "You, Marisa, Rashida, and the kids will ride with Gladstone and Whitmore in the third SUV when they finish their work. Shoot first and ask questions later. Monica, Yvett, Ava, Carlos, and

Courtney will be in the second SUV with two of Carlos's guys. Carlos, do you have a weapon?"

Carlos replied, "Si, Senor."

Beckmire said, "Asiram and Zanthius will ride with me, Jilkes, John Lee, Brown and Bernstein, plus, our captive when we pick him up. Mallory you, Jong, Chakes, Montomie and McArthur plus two of Carlos's people, will be in the lead SUV. I haven't figured out where we are heading but once we leave here, we find 95 North and proceed until we can gather and figure this shit out. I am amazed that these people are always one step ahead of us or a half mile behind us. Somehow we are being tracked and I can't figure it out." Zanthius was about to say something when Asiram pulled his sleeve and whispered, "Your dad has this. Don't confuse the issue."

Beckmire asked, "Are there any questions or concerns?" Everyone had learned from previous encounters that when the Sarge is on, he is on! It was about to be on and his plans would be flawless.

When John Lee and Jilkes came back, Jilkes said, "The boys are waiting for a lift about a quarter of a mile from here with a sniper in the bush. Have you made assignments yet?"

The Sarge responded, "You and John Lee are riding with me and that package is going to be introduced to Asiram."

The Sarge turned around, made a head count and said, "I want my people out first and when they give the all clear signal—wait a minute. Everyone stand down." He turned to Jilkes and John Lee and said, "I need a vehicle inspection before we get the hell out of here. What do you need?"

John Lee replied, "We be needing someone to watch our ass while our noses are sniffing up under them there trucks."

The Sarge declared, "Bernstein and Brown, you're up. Mallory and Jong, can you establish a high ground position from one of the rooms to check out the scenery."

Mallory answered, "We got this, Sarge. We'll keep an eye out."

The Sarge said, "I need everyone to stay focused. We are in danger." One of the Sarge's grandbabies walked up to him and proclaimed, "PopPop, I'm focused."

CHAPTER FORTY-THREE

In the vehicle with the captured alleged assassin, Jilkes went through his pockets and found his wallet with several forms of ID, including a particularly interesting picture ID stating that Rumanoff Latimoscovic was a Diplomat. Beckmire turned around in the vehicle and asked, "So, Rumanoff, do you speak English?" There was no comment from him. Beckmire looked at Asiram and said, "We don't have a lot of time to play with this one." He then told John Lee to slide the bottom half of the man's body into one of the industrial trash bags. After John Lee slid the man's body into the trash bag, Asiram reached across the seat and began cutting the man randomly. Jilkes, in the interim, taped his mouth so that his screams weren't heard and he was gagging on his own spit and vomit. Beckmire told Jilkes to remove the tape and again ask Rumanoff if he spoke English?

Once again there was no response. Beckmire signaled Asiram to continue with her sculpturing.

She began to cut him below his stomach and said, "Now, watch what happens when I cut his penis. He is going to bleed out like a pig."

Rumanoff began to make noises and Beckmire instructed Jilkes to remove the tape. Beckmire said, "This is your last chance before you become dickless in America. I want to know do you speak English?"

Rumanoff after gaining his breath stated, "Doesn't everyone?"

Beckmire said, "Now, listen, I want to know how the hell you found us? What was your intent with those weapons and who do you work for?"

Rumanoff asked, "What do I gain by answering your questions?"

Beckmire said, "Wrong answer." He then instructed Jilkes to tape his mouth again. Rumanoff violently attempted to say something. Beckmire said, "This is how this game is played. We ask the questions and you answer them. If not, the little lady will neuter you."

Rumanoff began by telling the occupants of the SUV that everyone knows that there are a lot of people traveling with their group. We checked with rental car agencies and found out that five SUVs had been rented under the same name. We know that each vehicle is equipped with GPS, therefore, we persuaded the manager of the company to locate the vehicles for his own safety.

He then went on to tell the group that they had injured three of his men in a bar fight and the 'idiot spy" was identified by his picture. Rumanoff indicated that he works for a wing of the KGB and they wanted to end all attempts to locate a speculative product that they don't think exists. He then told Beckmire that the intended targets were him and the 'idiot spy'.

Beckmire asked, "Why on earth would I be a target? I don't know shit about any of this mess?"

"You be Sergeant Beckmire and we Russians have a passion for hearing the stories of you and your men when you were in Vietnam. All Russians in training for the military are taught how to adapt to the elements, as well as the environment, like your people were known to do. My superiors understand that the 'idiot spy' is your son and therefore a closing scenario would be to end the legend and his offspring."

Beckmire looked at him and said, "You know I have to kill you or forever look over my shoulder."

Rumanoff mumbled, "It is what I would do if I were in your situation. You will have many more to kill before this saga is over, Sergeant."

Beckmire said, "Give me something that I can use. Tell me a Russian fable but try to save your life."

Rumanoff paused for a brief period and finally said, "These vehicles are your death knell. Ditch them, burn them and go simple. You sit out like the FBI."

Beckmire laughed and asked, "That obvious, eh?"

"That obvious!"

Beckmire inquired, "Asiram, can you patch him up enough so that he can get to a hospital?"

Asiram replied, "Most of the cuts are just scratches, but in strategic places, ergo the appearance of gushing blood, so he is fine to make it to the hospital."

Beckmire looked at Rumanoff and said, "You know you're a dead man either way you cut this thing. You can't go home because all those you know will be at risk. Take this time and figure out a new identity, but don't come looking for me because I will have your family slaughtered like sheep."

Beckmire called Mallory and told him to pull off at the next exit, find a petrol station and wait there for him to return from making a short run to deliver a package. He saw a McDonald's sign and told Jilkes to pull into the lot but to stay far enough away from the cameras. He then looked at Romanoff and said, "I hope this works out for you. My family is consumed by this mess and I want you to understand my resolve. I know about your training because I have friends in high places in your country and we occasionally talk. I will pay a king's ransom to find out about your family and then I will summarily eliminate them from the youngest to the oldest. Don't screw with me or mine and I will not bother yours." He instructed Jilkes to hand him his wallet, minus his official ID. They let him out of the SUV and that would be the last they would hear from or see Romanoff Latimoscovic.

Jilkes drove back to the McDonald's where Beckmire met openly with Mallory and Jong. He told Jong that they were located because of the GPS tracking system that rental car agencies used to find their vehicles. Jong declared, "Damn! I never knew that. We have got to get rid of these SUVs soon. Let me make a call and see if I can find any family members in the area who can help." In the meantime, everyone was ordering food from Mickey D's.

Approximately ten minutes later, Jong rejoined the group and announced, "My cousin told me where the tracking devices are located and how to reconfigure them for misdirection. He suggested that we call Uber and order five vehicles for twenty people. Once they arrive, we give them $200 each and tell them to go to this address and pick up the twenty people. While they are counting the money, we magnetically attach the tracking devices to their vehicles thus misdirecting the signals for the SUVs that we have. I don't know if it's a solid suggestion, but it sounds pretty damn good to me."

Beckmire reported, "John Lee and Jilkes checked under each vehicle and saw nothing."

Jong said, "The devices are not under the vehicles but inside them and under the passenger's seat."

Beckmire said, "I'll be damn, but how do we disengage the devices long enough to affix them to the Uber cars?"

Jong explained, "They go dormant after the vehicles are cut off, leaving the last set of latitudes and longitudes readings in the system."

Mallory asked, "Are there any other options available?"

Jong answered, "I don't have any, do you?"

After locating and removing the devices, Jilkes and John Lee prepared to attach them to the Uber cars that showed up. Jilkes told the group they needed five vehicles. There were only four available and until the fifth vehicle showed up, he just wanted them to wait.

After the fifth vehicle showed up, he invited the drivers into McDonald's and gave them the address to St. Vincent Pallotti's High School. He figured everyone knew about the big basketball giant. While he was assigning random names to the vehicles for pickup, John Lee was installing the GPS tracking devices underneath the vehicles. Each driver was given $200 + another $100 as tips for their services and was promised an additional $100 once they picked up the individuals and brought them to the McDonald's.

Once the Uber drivers had left the area, the group boarded their SUVs and proceeded to the lion's den, DC.

Zanthius and Asiram were in the SUV with the Sarge, Jilkes and John Lee. When Zanthius said, "Asiram, when we are apart, I only have one 'H' going on. Now, I have all three 'Hs' in place."

She looked at him and asked, "What on earth are you talking about?"

Zanthius replied, "I only have one 'H' for healthy when we are apart. Now, when we are together, I have all three 'Hs'—Healthy, Happy and Horny." Asiram blushed with embarrassment and Beckmire mumbled, "That is a little too much information for the rest of us. The real question is where is the package that we're supposed to deliver tomorrow."

The 'idiot spy', being ever so aware of his surroundings, stated, "Finally, I am important again. The package is at my old girlfriend's apartment in La Plata, Maryland." He then gently banged on the seat and got everyone's attention. He placed his finger over his mouth and pointed to the dashboard. "I know where she hides the key. She is out of town until next week." Everyone noticed that the light would blink whenever there was conversation. Beckmire called Mallory and said, "I need to speak with you." After he and Mallory got out of the trucks, Beckmire said, "The truck we are in has a recording device in it and it's working overtime. Check your dashboard. Have a random conversation and just mention La Plata. After you see what I am talking about, let's check all the vehicles, find the sources and terminate them."

After forty-five minutes, it was determined that all the vehicles had listening and recording devices in them. The Sarge thought they needed to figure the problem out before deactivating the devices. When Jong looked at the wiring, he realized that there were multiple wires leading to multiple listening devices. He informed Beckmire that the entire SUV was rigged not only with listening devices but with 'C-4'. Beckmire immediately ordered everyone out of the vehicles and directed Jong, Chakes, John Lee and Jilkes to disconnect the explosives.

Beckmire said, "It seems we're all expendable. Therefore, each person that is against us shall be shown no quarters. If they are wounded, we terminate. If they offer us useful intel, we terminate. This is now war, people. We kill first and wonder why later. Are there any questions?"

Everyone realized that the 900-pound voracious beast was pissed off and knew that when he was angry, the savage animal in the man controlled his actions, and mayhem and destruction would soon follow. It was wartime!

## CHAPTER FORTY-FOUR

Five sticks of C-4 were removed from the vehicles. As Beckmire looked at them he muttered, 'When I find the place that you came from, I will gladly set you on your course of destruction'. Beckmire then called Walter and informed him about the GPS tracking, listening devices and the C-4 that were discovered in all of the vehicles. He told Walter that he would like to know who to return the C-4 to. Walter indicated that he would research the issue and get back to him within the hour.

Beckmire walked over to Larry and asked, "How are my grandbabies holding up?"

"They're focused and understand that bad people are trying to hurt us. Do you see an end to this madness?"

Beckmire looked at Larry and responded, "Son, I hope so. I pray to God that this ends tomorrow, but until then we need to stay focused, shoot first and ask why later."

#

Walter called back and reported, "I have some important information for you, but I need to call you back after I attend to some personal business." Beckmire, noticing the urgency in Walter's voice said, "Whenever you get a chance, hit me back."

Beckmire's phone started to ring and he noticed that it was a west coast area code. He hesitantly answered the phone and discovered that it was Walter who said he had picked up a few throwaway phones while on the coast. He then said, "That package was a gift from the father of the man you captured in LA. It turns out that the meeting the father had with the Japanese and Chinese authorities was not about an island but was about a joint effort by the two countries to seize your son.

"The two Russians you encountered while on your run were working for this guy and their intent was to target you and your people. So, while the father was assisting the competitors, the son was selling his product. What a family. The C-4 was placed to kill everyone including your grandbabies. These people are ruthless. I am trying to get a fix on our runaway government official so that you can deliver those bars of C-4 to him. I have only one suggestion for you, shoot first and ask why later. Until tomorrow. Oh, and by the way, there seems to be a frenzy of activity in La Plata, Maryland. Pictures of the 'idiot spy' are being circulated and people are being stopped and asked if they know him or the woman that he is dating. I think that was brilliant to direct them there. It buys you some time and peace. Is there any way you can separate the children and women as you approach the pickup time?"

"In the name of God, I wish I could. These women can't be persuaded to seek shelter and wait for the news that all is well or that they are widows. Also, we can't protect them while they are away from us, and it seems like no matter how hard we try to evade the bad guys, they find us."

Walter said, "Well, hopefully, this will all be a bad dream and it will be over tomorrow. By the way, are you going to give me a heads up about the pickup place?"

"My son was about to tell us when he noticed that the dashboard was flashing as he was talking. When I find out, I will let you know."

"I will call you soon if I hear anything," Walter stated.

"One more thing, it is important to me that I have an opportunity to return those five bars to their rightful owner. Please attend to that with diligence and you will always be appreciated by me and the Beckmire clan. I may even put in a good word for you back home," Beckmire declared.

Walter mumbled, "Whatever."

Prior to entering the truck, Asiram gave Beckmire a pen and pieces of paper. He asked, "What's this for?"

Asiram replied, "This is what your son will write the address on. We don't trust these trucks and, therefore, this is a recommendation as to how we interact while in them."

"Great thinking. I hope we got all the C-4 out of these things. As a matter of fact, have everyone disengage the Bluetooth in the vehicles. I think that may be the way the culprits intended to detonate the explosives."

Beckmire and Asiram walked over to Zanthius and he said, "As long as we are in these trucks, this is how we will communicate, by writing down the information. Oh, and by the way, that was some real spy shit that you pulled in the truck. I never noticed the blinking light nor did anyone else. Maybe there is some truth to your title, the 'idiot spy'."

"Pops, now you're calling me the 'idiot spy'?"

"No, Son, I know they have underestimated your survival skills as well as your awareness of things that are out of place, like the blinking lights on the dashboard. Now, that was incredibly astute of you, if you ask me. I need you to write down the address where you posted the capsule, the box number as well as your pseudonym and password."

Prior to entering the SUV, Zanthius wrote down the address and then his pseudonym.

Beckmire looked at the note and asked, "Really? Is that the best you could come up with?" Zanthius had written down the name Richard Noggin as the user identification, and the log in was Dick Head. Beckmire said, "I must admit, that is pretty clever, I mean how many people would be able to guess that you would use those interchangeably? Not bad, not bad at all, 'idiot spy'."

Asiram said, "I want to see what he wrote."

Zanthius said, "Honey, it's nothing, really! Let it go."

Asiram declared, "Okay, if it's nothing then nothing is what I am going to look at." She reached over and retrieved the paper from Beckmire. She paused for a moment and then smiled and then she broke out into hysterics. Jilkes said, "Okay, I have got to see that."   After reviewing the information, he said, "Now, that's some funny shit."

Jilkes passed the piece of paper to John Lee who said, "This here be some real spy shit. Ain't nobody in the world going to believe this." The car erupted into laughter. Zanthius looked out of the window realizing that once again, he was the butt of the laughter and that it wasn't over yet.

As the occupants of the SUV calmed down, Zanthius wrote, 'those two only get you into the secure room'. He then wrote—while Asiram was trying to look over his shoulder, the password. He scribbled, 'it's from one of my favorite James Bond movies'. As everyone looked at what he had written, they raised their hands as if they were clueless. Zanthius looked out the window and muttered to himself, 'now this is really going to be embarrassing'. Beckmire looked at him and inquired, "So, Son, are we done here or is there more?"

Zanthius looked at his father and replied, "Prepare to get a real laugh at my expense."

He wrote the password to the box is 'Pussy Galore'.

Beckmire looked at the note and said, "That was one of my favorites as well." He then began to laugh out of control.

Asiram demanded, "Pass it to me."

Beckmire responded, "I can't. You might divorce your new husband." He continued to laugh out of control.

Asiram exclaimed, "Daddy-in-Law, if you don't pass me that note, I am really going to be mad at you for a long time!"

Beckmire, still laughing, passed the note to her. Asiram flinched at first and then whispered, "You have that stuff on your brain. You are one funny human being." She then passed the note to Jilkes who mumbled, "Damn son, was it that hard meeting women?" Jilkes started laughing and passed the note to the philosopher, John Lee who said, "Wow, you must have been one horny toad to come up with shit like this. I like it and I think you be the best damn 'idiot spy' in the world. You be a real funny guy."

As the group continued laughing, Beckmire got a call from Mallory who asked, "What the hell is going on?"

Beckmire answered, "We are just playing a sex game with my son. I'll fill you in later. You're not going to believe the shit he comes up with." Zanthius, in the meantime, is looking out the window and thinking to himself, 'hell, they needed to laugh so why not at my expense.'

# # #

Jong had secured rooms at the One Seasons, a place that was definitely a joint where people came for a few hours, did their business and ventured off into the night. He rationalized that this was the kind of place that no one would suspect they would be at, and no one would come asking about them. Beckmire said, "Seedy, but great cover."

Beckmire walked over to Carlos and asked, "Can I have your boys do rotations on the vehicles. People have a way of finding us and planting explosives. I, at this point, am very paranoid."

Carlos looked at Beckmire and responded, "They're not my people, Mr. Beckmire. They are your people to deploy as you see fit."

Beckmire thanked him and said, "I respect the lines of authority, therefore, insofar as I am concerned, I come to you for deployment and ratification of assignments for your men. This way it works best for us all. You are their leader and therefore, I should make my requests through you, which cuts down on any misunderstandings."

Carlos inquired, "Will you walk with me for a minute?"

A few feet away from listening ears, Carlos announced, "I have loved Ava since she was a teenager. I hope I have your blessings in terms of what she and I have begun."

Beckmire hugged him and said, "Dude, just between you and me, she is a wonderful, beautiful and sexy woman. I will always love Ava De Lombardo, but I am in love with my wife. I only have one suggestion for you, and that is, don't let her out of your sight. She might disappear." The two men laughed and shook hands. As they were walking back to the motel,

Beckmire turned to Carlos and said, "I haven't had the opportunity to thank you and your men for covering my family and my friends. Please accept my apologies for the oversight and recognize that you are a part of the Beckmire clan and we are forever indebted to you."

"No Sir, had it not been for this adventure, I would still be watching over Ava as opposed to loving her openly. No, Sarge, I thank you."

When the two men returned, Ava asked, "What was that all about?"

"That was two men talking about a wonderful woman and that's all you're going to get. Let it go."

Ava smiled at Carlos and whispered, "Am I giving too much control to you too quickly? I am at a point in my life that you are the only person that matters to me and what you say and think means a lot to me. Carlos, keep me near and dear and I will keep you dear and near." They smiled, kissed and laughed.

# # #

As Asiram and Zanthius were walking to their room, Mallory heard her say, "Zanthius, really, Richard Noggin, Dick Head and Pussy Galore? That is absolutely brilliant, I must tell you, I am surprised at each venue that I witness you in. I love you and hope to hell we come out of this thing alright."

When Mallory entered his room, he smelled stale cigarette smoke. He called the Sarge and told him that he overheard Asiram talking about a Richard Noggin, Dick Head and a Pussy Galore with Zanthius. He asked the Sarge, "What's up with that?" Beckmire responded by telling him that those are Zanthius's pseudonyms for his lockbox and his password. Mallory replied by saying, "He didn't fall too far from the apple tree, did he? That's fricking brilliant. I love it."

# # #

Later that night, Carlos got a call from his team that had entered the DC area. He told his lead man that he would call him back. Carlos called Beckmire and said, "I have additional eyes on the ground, but I need to know where they should be looking."

"Meet me in the hallway in five and I will give you the information."

In the interim, Beckmire called Mallory and asked him to join him in the hallway in five minutes. As Carlos approached the two men, he said, "We have several sets of eyes on the ground in DC, however, I want to specifically have them look at a distinct target and not the entire Metropolitan DC area."

Beckmire smiled at him and asked, "Would you believe it if I told you that it is at the MMHF?"

"What the hell is the MMHF?" Mallory inquired.

"MMHF stands for the Main Mail Handling Facility—the main Post Office that is next to Union Station," Beckmire replied.

"I don't know if that is pure genius or damn dumb luck, because wow, people come and go from there by the thousands. That presents a bit of a problem because we have no clue as to who we should be looking for, but on the other hand, neither does the other side. I don't like our chances of survival in this situation because it is the government, and it is the total wrath of the government that will come after us if we stage a fight in the post office. I don't like it. Maybe this is not such a good idea," Mallory confessed.

"It's a perfect place because anyone of us can go in and access the box. They have Zanthius's picture and probably mine and yours, Mallory, but one of Carlos's people could do it since they don't have pictures of them. Wait, I have the right guy for this job," Beckmire stated.

Mallory asked, "Who do you have in mind?"

Beckmire smiled and replied, "My son, Larry the Wanderer."

Mallory declared, "Great thinking! Larry is smooth and articulate and when need be, he can be rough, depending upon the situation, not to mention suave. Damn, Sarge, he has been silent throughout this entire adventure. He's a ghost. No one knows him." The Sarge pondered the idea for a moment and paused to think about what he and Larry used to do many years back.

## CHAPTER FORTY-FIVE

As a sergeant on the Philadelphia Police force, Beckmire was always interested in giving people who had strayed on the wrong side of the law, a break. Larry Holland was one of the individuals who the Sarge saved from the streets. He also engaged Larry in an extremely nefarious scheme that ended the lives of drug dealers. Larry the Wanderer, as he was known, changed the complexion of the landscape for those who engaged in the drug trade. He and the Sarge were methodical in their application of justice on those who afflicted communities with the scourge of drugs. The Sarge knew that if anyone could pull this post office thing off and be absolute in resolve if confronted, it would be Larry the Wanderer.

The Sarge approached Larry and said, "Son, I know you have a wife and kids, but I want to request your participation in an event that might leave your children fatherless, your wife a widow and me without the son, who I love so much."

Larry looked at the Sarge and said, "You know we don't roll like that. What is it you need and what is it you want me to do?"

"Everyone is focusing on Zanthius and they probably have photos of him circulating all over the area. No one knows you. Zanthius gave me his passwords and his entry code word to the box that contains the item that a lot of people have died trying to capture. What I want is for you to enter the main post office in DC, go to his secured box and retrieve the capsule. I will have people placed all over the place to watch your back. But in life, there is the unexpected that catches you by surprise. I need you to go into the closet and bring out Larry the Wanderer. Can you do that for me?"

Larry looked around as if he was searching for something or someone and finally replied, "Sarge, I would go to the ends of the world for you. If you need me to be that other person that we placed in that dormant space, then I can make that happen. I just need time to transition my focus less on my family and more on the mission. I need you to give me time to open the vault that has that other person suspended in cryotherapy. You know once that other person is out, it may be almost impossible to reverse his mindset."

"That other person doesn't have a set of twins and a wonderful wife. Therefore, I don't believe we are facing that issue with cryogenics. It's more like allowing that encapsulated being to come out for a minute, stretch and do something good. You know what I mean? Larry, can you, and will you, bring me Larry the Wanderer?"

Larry hesitated for a moment and answered, "He never left our mission. If they want to see the boogie man then so be it."

"Thanks, son. I know I can count on you to pull this thing off and to find your way out of there if all hell breaks loose." The Sarge once again thanked Larry and told him that he would get back to him with specific details.

CHAPTER FORTY-SIX

The Sarge sought out Zanthius and Asiram and told them about his plan to retrieve the capsule. Zanthius asked, "Pops, are you sure about this? I mean Larry seems to be a bit of a homebody. Suppose things go awry. Can you count on Larry to improvise on the move?"

The Sarge looked at Zanthius and wanted to say, "if you had the metal that kid has, we probably wouldn't be in this shit'. Being diplomatic, the Sarge responded by saying, "You ever hear the old saying, 'Never judge a book by its cover'?"

Zanthius looked at his father and wanted to inquire, "what the hell does that have to do with anything'? Instead Zanthius said, "Last I looked, people are trying to kill us. Do you think Larry can pull the trigger without hesitation?"

"Oh, hell yeah! That seemingly quiet individual has a body count that you wouldn't believe. I am not going to put his business out there, but Mr. Homebody and Mr. Quiet can be extremely explosive and deadly. Not the kind of person you want to piss off because he looks soft. Trust me on this one. I know what I'm talking about. Besides, every damn place in the world has a picture of your handsome ass plastered on the wall. No, I need you on the periphery with your eyes on your brother's back to make sure that he is not blindsided."

Asiram asked, "What will you have me do? By the way, I think Larry is a perfect selection."

"You, like your husband, are wanted by any number of people. Your picture as well is probably posted all over the world. So, what I need you two to focus on is working with Carlos and his new people that are in town and try to break into the post office's security system. All your work from now on will be from remote locations. I may use you two as decoys to show your faces in some random place around the city at least an hour prior to the rest of us retrieving the package. My only problem with that idea is that I leave you guys without back up and that ain't good at all. Otherwise, I would have to split our forces and that for damn sure ain't good. I must work that out with Mallory and get his feedback on that one. After that, you two will stay in the SUV and be loaded for bear."

Zanthius said, "Yes Sir, General."

Beckmire retorted, "Son, this is not the time to be funny."

"I am not being funny, Dad! You sound like you have done this a thousand times and I have just raised your rank because I am impressed with how you handle the minutia, as well as, the monumental details. Not funny at all, Pops. And since we are at this point, I have to say that I would probably be dead by now if it weren't for you, your good friends, as well as you, Asiram, my new and wonderful wife. I love you people and I owe you both and everyone else in my life because the people who want me dead would have found my dumb ass by now and Lord knows what they would have done to me until they got what they wanted."

Asiram hugged her husband and the Sarge joined in. He said, "Months ago I only knew you existed in the spirit world.

Today my love for you is as strong as my love for everyone else involved in our lives."

# # #

Ava's people were perplexed when Carlos told them that they would be hacking into the United States of America's, main post office systems. His lead guy Benito asked Carlos, "Do you know how much time we will spend in jail if caught?"

"A lifetime! Therefore, you had better do your best work so that you don't get caught. At least your families will be cared for."

Both men laughed. Carlos asked, "Can you cover the surrounding streets and all of the exits?"

"Now, that we can do. We have already borrowed a few trucks and have placed the cable company's logo on them, which will lower suspicion. I think we can have the hacking done in a few hours, and you will be able to monitor the comings and goings of people in HD. What shall we do once we have the system set up? Are we hurting or killing anyone?"

"Beneto, I'm not sure how this is going to play out. I think you should access the system but keep it dormant until I give you the thumbs up. I don't want to be detected until after we have accomplished our tasks. So, set it up and I will tell you when I need it to be live," Carlos responded.

Carlos met with Mallory and Beckmire and reported, "I told my people that they have to hack the US Post Office system and they turned in their resignations."

Beckmire declared, "I don't blame them!"

Carlos said, "We are going to have coverage on all of the entrances and exits and movement from all directions. What we won't have coverage on is inside of that building. Is that a problem for you?"

Beckmire answered, "Not a problem, but a concern because I am going to have my son go in and retrieve that package."

Carlos jumped up and exclaimed, "You can't use Zanthius on this because surely his picture is all over the place!"

Mallory said, "Calm down, Carlos. The Sarge is one prolific individual. He has more than one son."

Carlos racked his brain and said, "Oh, I see, Larry, the unassuming person. He's going to get the capsule. Well played, Mr. Beckmire, well played. Okay, I told my people that I would get back to them when I want coverage. I also told them that I did not want to be a resident in the security system and that we wanted in and out—no lingering."

Beckmire said, "You are really focusing on this one. How did Ava miss your presence all of these years?"

Carlos smiled and replied, "I often wondered that as well, but what matters is that she now recognizes and appreciates me on a whole new level."

When Beckmire and Mallory were alone, Mallory asked, "How on earth did you let her get away? I know Courtney is stunning and everything a man could want, but so is Ava."

Beckmire analyzed the question and answered, "She abandoned me and I almost got you and everyone else killed in one of our skirmishes. I lost all of who I was, for a moment, but returned to reality when the bullets started hitting around us. I truly loved that woman from the moment I laid eyes on her, when I was in a restaurant. Just between the two of us, I still love that woman but there is no other woman on earth like

Courtney. My heart aches for her every moment that we are apart."

Mallory said, "I know the feeling. My Monica has been through a lot. You know the story. But when I first saw her, man, I was lost in the jungle trying to figure out how to talk to her and show her how much I loved her. It took a while, but hey, I got it going and I think she is as happy as can be."

After reminiscing about their past, the two men decided that they needed to scout the area and make some determinations. Beckmire summoned Jilkes and John Lee and asked them to take a ride with him. In the meantime, Mallory summoned Chakes and Montomie. He left Brown and Bernstein in charge of the group.

Brown and Bernstein began to argue about who was in charge when the Sarge interrupted their little marital dispute and advised, "Guys, do like Mallory and I do. Throw out your ideas and choose the best option. Now, I know you both can handle this and protect our people, right?"

Bernstein looked at Brown, threw his hand out and said, "Come on, Bro, give me a hug, and I will forgive you for challenging my authority." Everyone laughed and the scouting team mounted up to do some surveillance work.

Everyone in the two vehicles were wired and could hear the full extent of all conversations. As they approached the circle leading towards Union Station, Beckmire requested, "Mallory, you guys hold tight here for five minutes and then find your way around the building from your own vantage point. Have one of your guys record the street names and discern the one-way streets from the two-way streets. We just want to know in case we got to get the hell out of here before the entire government comes down on us. We have to figure our best options for escaping this scene, if it all goes wrong."

Mallory suggested, "Perhaps the other thing we need is a second and third set of vehicles, just in case these things are identified."

Beckmire said, "I am going to call Jong and get his input on that. Make your run but do it only once and gather as much intel as you can. Look at all of the damn cameras placed around this area. Get back to you in a few."

## CHAPTER FORTY-SEVEN

Later, Beckmire called Jong and said, "I think we're going to need some new escape vehicles in case this thing goes south. Can you handle that?"

"Give me ten minutes and let me check with some of my cousins. I know they are extremely resourceful and can probably hook us up with some clean wheels."

As Jong walked down the hallway towards his room, a woman ran out of another room screaming "You freak! You like beating on women!" Jong sidestepped her and a humongous individual ran out behind her and screamed at Jong, "What's your problem?"

Jong answered, "I don't have a problem, but you will have one if you continue this approach with me."

Brown entered the hallway with Bernstein and asked Jong, "Do you need our help?"

Jong responded, "Naw, I got this." Brown and Bernstein assumed a relaxed position against the wall and decided to watch their little brother kick the guy's ass. As the guy started towards Jong, Bernstein yelled, "You might want to reconsider what you're about to do, Sir."

The rest of the members of the group opened their doors to see what the commotion was about and saw Jong go to work on this gargantuan of a human being. He round kicked the guy to his head, threw three lightning fast and thunderous punches to his solar plexus and concluded with a smack to the throat. The aftermath was both humbling and humiliating.

Brown and Bernstein grabbed the guy's arms and pulled him back into his room, shut the door and placed the 'Do Not Disturb' sign on the door. Brown said to Jong, "I really want you to teach me that new shit that you used on that guy."

Jong said, "I just made that up."

# # #

Meanwhile, Beckmire and his crew and Mallory and his, made their videos of the streets and plotted the best options for getting away from the center of government if need be. Mallory searched for high points where long guns could be deployed and realized that the train station was ideal and secure but was under heavy surveillance. He recognized that there were people coming and going all day and that the level of security around the MMHF was minimal and its direct connection to the train station was ideal. He made a mental note that if the action was scheduled in accordance with a departing train, they had an additional escape route.

Beckmire, on the other hand, was waiting for a call from Jong. When the call came through, Jong announced, "My cousins have some throw away equipment that can be used and they will drive, if need be. They have two suggested transfer points with two sets of vehicles that are untraceable to anyone other than the owners who will miss them in the morning."

Beckmire declared, "Great! We are just finishing our rounds here and will be back at the joint in thirty."

From the motel, Carlos had coordinated the viewing screens with his people. They had essentially tapped into the camera system and sent a ping to make sure they were into the system. Beneto informed Carlos, "In addition to the cameras' eyes, we can have people in the place who are willing to provide backup to the backup."

Carlos said, "I will get back to you once we have decided on the action plan. Are you guys going to hang out around the place?"

Beneto responded, "Absolutely not. We can do this from anywhere."

Carlos said, "Good work. I will get back to you when we have a complete strategy. By the way, if there is action by our people, is there anyway of blocking or killing the camera in a particular area?"

"Once we go live, we can delete all events until they run a virus scan and detect an unauthorized unit."

Later that night as the group reconvened, those with reports to make, made them. Yet, everyone acted as if there was something not being said and no one knew how to broach the subject. The Sarge, perceiving there was tension in the air, said, "You all have met my son Larry who will do the actual retrieving of the capsule. What you don't know about my son is that he is calculating, thorough, precise, and focused. Without revealing too much about Larry, I will just say this, in an urban war, there is no one I would rather have beside and or backing me than Larry. He has proven skills and understands this kind of mission better than anyone here, in my estimation. Do not let that quiet demeanor of his fool you, for he can be as ruthless or as gentle as any man that I know. I totally trust him with carrying out this mission. I can guarantee you that if anyone can pull this thing off and confront and escape potential enemies and or circumstances, it is Larry. Are there any questions about what we have to do?"

Larry raised his hand and said, "I need to transmogrify myself and take a walk through the place prior to doing any work. Is there anyone who can get me close to the place so that I can walk through?"

Zanthius raised his hand and the Sarge adamantly said, "No way in hell!" Jilkes and John Lee indicated that they were low on the radar and could drop him off.

Larry said, "I will need to do a little shopping first, and then we can head over there."

Chakes asked, "What the hell does transmogrify mean?"

The Sarge looked at him and replied, "After he goes shopping and after you see him again, then you tell me what it means."

# # #

Jilkes and John Lee escorted Larry to a Super Walmart that was open all night. Larry proceeded to purchase things that most men wouldn't consider buying. Larry had studied the art of make-up and disguises with a friend of the Sarge's on the West Coast and had become good at dramatically changing his looks.

When the three men returned to the motel, Larry said, "I need to use your room to change. I can't let my kids see me when I make myself over," Jilkes told him to help himself.

Forty minutes later, Larry came out of the room dressed in women's clothing and seemed almost a foot taller. John Lee said, "What the f…?"

Jilkes said, "Now, that's some crazy shit. Larry, is that you under that stuff?"

The person replied, "No, Larry is still in your room." As the group descended the steps, Larry passed Mallory who smiled and kept walking. John Lee inquired, "So, Corporal, you like that lady you just saw?"

Mallory answered, "She had a nice look about her, but I am married."

Jilkes said, "Thank goodness for that one."

Mallory looked at them and said, "No f…..n way? Is that who I think it is?"

John Lee responded, "That be that baby making dude with the twins."

Mallory exclaimed, "No f……n way."

# # #

Later, as Larry entered the post office, he searched for the nearest public restroom with his GoPro like camera filming his surroundings. Once inside the restroom, he noticed that there were lookout galleries in the ceiling. He thought to himself that he had read somewhere that they were deemed invasive, unethical, an invasion of privacy, and therefore, illegal and consequently, not in use. Taking no chances, he filmed the two locations and used the restroom. Once he washed his hands, he began to look at the two-panel window that was on his left.

As he entered the main area, he noticed that there were two guard stations at both exits, one leading to Massachusetts Avenue and the other leading to North Capitol Street. As he scanned the ceiling, he noticed a series of cameras that captured the movement of everyone coming and going. He walked to the area where patrons purchased stamps and other items and noticed a series of P.O. boxes behind him. He wondered to himself whether this was where Zanthius sent his package. Larry got in line and asked the person behind the counter, in a feigned voice, "Are any of those boxes for rent and do you have bigger ones anywhere?"

The clerk replied, "Those are our only boxes and most of them are rented, at this point in time, but I can call a supervisor over and have her check it out for you."

Larry stated, "I will check with my husband and see if this location is the most convenient and accessible for receiving packages from our daughter. Thank you very much."

As Larry walked down the street, he noticed cameras that were practically on every light pole. He tried to get a shot of each one as best he could but realized that if he left from the Massachusetts Avenue exit, depending upon the time of day, traffic would probably be an issue. He also realized that the North Capitol Street exit was a gateway to several alleys, tunnels, and small streets where he could disappear without a trace.

Once in the vehicle with Jilkes and John Lee, Larry reported, "There are cameras everywhere in that place and lookout galleries in the restrooms."

John Lee asked, "What on earth be lookout galleries?"

Larry looked out of the window at a small street that dead-ended and replied, "Back in the day, people used to send money through the mail and your good old government workers would take the envelopes to the restrooms, snap them open, retrieve the cash and flush the evidence down the toilet."

John Lee retorted, "That's bullshit. Ain't nobody that stupid to steal from the mail."

Larry said, "Google it. People would literally send thousands of dollars through the mail. These guys and girls would spot the package, kick it aside or motion to their comrades that 'she was coming through'—an indication that pure cash was on its way to the next stop. It was not until the advent of the letter sorting machine, that was developed by Colt Manufacturers, that the government got a handle on the theft problem and then, strategically, started sending marked bills through the system to capture those who thought that they were too slick to be caught and above detection."

John Lee declared, "Now, that's some crazy story and I kind of believe you."

Larry yelled, "Stop, stop, stop! Slow down and pull over until this traffic passes."

Jilkes asked, "Do we need to have our weapons ready?"

Larry answered, "Naw, I noticed another way of getting out of that place if shit happens, and you guys can't cover my ass. Look up that hill to the right. You see those guys throwing bags into the trucks? I might have to hitch a ride with them if all else fails."

John Lee asked, "Exactly what did you and the Sarge do?"

"If I told you that, I would have to kill you and your boy would kill me. So, let's just say we did a lot of garbage work and leave it at that."

Back at the motel, it seemed as if everyone was waiting in the lobby. As the trio walked in, Brown asked, "Who's your lady friend, guys?"

John Lee replied, "Too much of a woman for you, so let it go."

Larry entered Jilkes and John Lee's room and made his transformation. The three men headed for the lounge and when they arrived, Brown inquired, "Where is your lady friend?"

Jilkes responded, "Oh, she's waiting for us in our room."

"Can I at least watch or join in?"

Jilkes said, "I assure you. You won't want to deal with that one. Let it go."

"I thought we were brothers. I guess that only applies to certain nefarious things that we do!"

Jilkes said, "We are brothers but this one will be made clear to you real soon and you will feel a bit embarrassed, to say the least."

Mallory exclaimed, "Enough with the 'BS', can we get down to business!"

Brown, who was scouting the place, announced, "Corporal, I don't like this venue. We have eyes on us, as well as, ears. Why don't we move this outside on a staggered basis?"

Beckmire said, "Yeah, I see what you mean. Jilkes, buy us all a beer and let's take a walk outside for a minute or two."

Outside Larry began to show the group the video from his camera and discussed all of the security issues that were in play and stated that it might be best not to have a lot of friendly eyes walking, watching, and communicating. He said, "I have discovered several options that would get me in and out of there without a hitch, but once you enter that place you are definitely on candid camera with facial recognition capabilities. They also have outdated lookout galleries in the restrooms but who knows whether they are a ploy or are active surveillance apparatus. I suggest that someone drop me off a couple of miles from the place and I catch a cab to the post office. You can set up whatever surveillance you feel necessary but if the deal goes south, then I am out of there without any notion of looking behind me to help anyone. It's a quagmire with just two entrances and exits. However, there is a lot of loading and mail handling shit going on at the same time. It would help me if I could get my hands on one of their uniforms prior to entering the place and then layer that with my other outfits."

Brown interrupted and asked, "Who the hell is that woman in the video and where are you filming all of this?"

Larry replied, "I am that so-called woman, and I am the one recording the video on my iPhone."

Jilkes asked, "You still want to go to my room and watch or join in?"

Brown said, "Go poke yourself, that was just pure mean and uncalled for."

The group laughed and the Sarge said, "I need you guys to stay focused. Carlos, none of us know your men who came up to assist. Do you think they can play inside security for us and if they're pinched, are they subject to let the cat out of the bag?"

Carlos assured him, "My people would rather die than betray Ava, I mean Ms. De Lombardo. They are as solid and committed to Ava as your people are to you. Trust me on this one." The Sarge was about to say something when his cell phone rang. He excused himself and answered, "What's up?"

It was Walter who said, "My people have agreed to be at the front door of the Hart Senate Office Building to welcome you at exactly 5:00 pm. Can you and your team make it happen by then?"

"We are in the final stages of planning as we speak. Let me get back to you in thirty."

The Sarge walked over to where his people were and announced, "They want to meet us at the front door of the senate office building at 5 pm."

He looked at Larry and asked, "If everything goes wrong, how long do you think it will take you to get out of there?"

Larry laughed and reported, "I have approximately three options--I can leave by one of the two main doors; or find my way around the floor and blend in like an employee; or get on the 3:30 train that leaves for New York which makes a stop in New Carrolton. Those are the options I see available to me at this time. If others pop up, I'm on them."

McArthur said, "Sarge, I'm not challenging any of this, however, are you sure that this young guy can get this done without our direct intervention?"

The Sarge asked, "Larry, why don't you answer that one?"

Larry looked directly at McArthur and answered, "I'm up for considering other options if you have any. I am doing this because my father asked me to do this. If he has faith in me, then I suggest that you display a little as well. I've seen you guys work and I must say I am totally in awe of you. However, in this jungle, I'm the king of deception, the master at circumventing capture, and the czar at cutting and running."

McArthur said, "Listen, I'm not doubting any of your skills. I and the rest of the guys are not that comfortable with working with civilians."

Larry said, "I understand, and those are my sentiments exactly. I'm not used to working with a group of ex-military types."

Everyone laughed, and McArthur declared, "Touché'!

The Sarge said, "Mallory, make the deployments and remember that they probably have pictures of all of us by now. Carlos and his men are the enigmas in this scenario, so use them well. Let's be ready to roll out of here by 1 pm. Good work, Larry. Can you take a walk with me?"

Zanthius inquired, "Is it possible for me to go as well?"

Larry replied, "Sure, Bro." The three men walked towards the rear of the motel and the Sarge said, "Larry, are you sure you're up to this?"

"I don't think anyone else can do this because probably, they all have been made. So, what are your options? As I consider them, there aren't too many. You can't use Zanthius because he is the most wanted person on the entire planet. Your, guys, well let's say, they are probably used to shooting their way out of things rather than finessing through obstacles."

The Sarge said, "Well stated, Larry."

Zanthius chimed in, "Larry, we have a lot of catching up to do when this is over so I'm demanding that you keep your ass safe and if you have to abort, don't hesitate."

Larry announced, "If I smell or see a rat then the deal is over and we start with a new strategy. By the way, Sarge, wouldn't it be easier if the people we are delivering the package to, met us there? That way we cut down on the drama."

"That's a good question, Larry, but the people who are after this thing are probably ready to eliminate anyone who gets in their way, without prejudice. We have stacked up a lot of dead bodies and the majority of their families will never know what happened to them. This is a messy business and I wish I could make this thing go away, but lover boy over there likes kissing beautiful women who demand that he swallows." They laughed and walked back to the lobby of the hotel.

Larry said, "Sarge, I'm going to need your boys to help me get a uniform tonight, legally or otherwise."

The Sarge replied, "I'll have one of Carlos's men go to that uniform store that does schools, police and all other kinds of outfits."

As Zanthius walked into his room, he found Asiram sitting in the corner crying. He walked towards her and thought to himself, "she must be having her cycle and I need to be extremely sympathetic with this one". Zanthius gave her a hug and kissed her on her cheek and said, "Honey, if not this time, then next time. I love you with or without children and always will."

Asiram looked at him and asked, "What the hell are you talking about?"

"I saw you crying and I just figured that you had bad news about, well you know, our pregnancy."

"Oh my, 'idiot spy', I am crying because of all of this destruction and death that you and I are a part of. I was wondering if it were not for that damn capsule would you be with me and would I be with you? More importantly, I am happy about the fact that I am truly pregnant according to that

$2.89 kit. My tears, excuse the cliché, are of joy and happiness and my love for you." Zanthius kissed her eyes and then her mouth and then guided her to the bed for a confirmation session.

CHAPTER FORTY-EIGHT

At 0600 hours, Larry was up and walking out of the door to go running. He stretched by the steps and descended them to find a group of former military types stretching and getting ready for a long walk, or so he thought. The Sarge exclaimed, "Good morning, Son, fancy seeing you up at this hour."

Larry sarcastically asked, "Are you ladies about to go for a slow walk?"

The guys started yelling, "No, he didn't just call us ladies and assumed we're going for a walk. Bring his young ass along and let's see who ends up walking." As the group prepared to exit the lobby, Asiram and Zanthius descended the steps and exclaimed, "Oh I see, you guys are going for your morning walks! Come, dear, let us not disturb the yoga class members."

John Lee inquired, "What's with these here youngins? They be sassy as my favorite pig. I guess we be having to show them again who be making the long journey."

Beckmire had also received an early call from Walter who had asked, "Is the game time still in play?"

Beckmire replied, "We jump ball at three pm at the main post office by the train station. Have your people near, but not obvious so as to spook our retriever."

"Are you using the 'idiot spy'?"

"Now, why on earth would I use someone whose picture is posted in too many places for the wrong thing? No, I am using my other son, Larry."

"The quiet guy?"

"Yes, that would be Larry."

"Don't you think that's a risky decision given the fact that he hasn't played this game before?"

Beckmire emphatically stated, "Larry is as good as they come! I have faith in his abilities to blend in and out, and get in and out, without any real complications. Just don't have one of your trigger-happy people shoot a black man running down the street, if they see him."

Asiram and Zanthius started out the door, followed by Larry, who passed them immediately; next came the Fab 10 + 2 and finally Carlos and his group. Beckmire yelled at Mallory, "Damn, we even got the civilians up and at them today. You know when this is over, we must have a party on some island and just have the group enjoy themselves. No more looking over our shoulders. What say you?"

Mallory replied, "That be an excellent idea. Let's plan it in thirty days after today."

As the group began to run, Asiram and Zanthius slowly began to lose their focus. Beckmire shouted, "Zanthius, stand down!" Zanthius and Asiram came to a stop and wondered if there was imminent danger about. As Beckmire caught up to him and Asiram he asked, "Are you carrying?"

Zanthius answered, "No."

"Are you, Asiram?" Beckmire inquired.

Asiram replied, "No, I'm not." Beckmire commanded, "Fall your dumb asses into the middle since me and my boys are always packing!"

Zanthius asked, "What about Larry?"

The Sarge responded, "What about Larry? I bet you my right hand that he has a weapon or two on him." Zanthius whistled, which caught Larry's attention, who immediately stopped and began to scour the area. As the group caught up with him, the Sarge asked, "Larry are you carrying?"

Larry looked at the Sarge and asked, "Really, Sarge?"

Zanthius demanded of his father, "Hold out your hand so that I can cut it off!"

Larry looked at him and asked, "Why on earth would you do that?"

Zanthius replied, "He bet me his hand that you had a weapon."

"I have two on me, a .9 and a .38. Are you serious or what? I have to get my run in to calm my nerves so there is no problem when I have to transcend into that other guy who is good at what is needed. Catch you people later."

Zanthius asked, "Why don't you have him watched and followed?"

The Sarge responded, "You have to know him to love him. Once you see him work, you will understand that he's as good as they get. Larry is like John Lee and Jilkes. He senses shit that most of us wouldn't even consider or understand. He would have been a wonderful asset in the Nam."

After a grueling five-mile run, Larry entered the motel thirty-two minutes ahead of the group and was planning his wardrobe. By the graciousness of Carlos's people, a well pressed post office department uniform was waiting in his room. As he entered, Marisa asked, "What is that uniform for?"

Larry walked over to her and explained, "The Sarge has asked me to help him out at this event and I have to be that person I was years ago. I know, I promised you that I would never go back to that life, but my father, the only man that has ever cared about me, asked me for help. What am I supposed to do?"

Marisa's eyes teared up and she grabbed her man and whispered, "He has been there for you and he will always be there for us. I love him because he is so genuine and reassuring to me and the kids. I know this is dangerous. All I want you to do, is promise me that if all goes bad, you will find your way out of hell and back to me in one piece. I will never ask or demand that you go against his request because he is who we are. I mean all that we have, and we don't even realize it, is a function of his generosity and love. Courtney will kill him if anything happens to you. I don't have to worry about that. If I know him, he has checked and rechecked the options, otherwise he wouldn't have asked you to do whatever it is he has asked you to do. I just want my man back and not that stranger. Can you promise me that at least?"

Larry kissed his wife and responded, "I love you so much! I'm not suicidal and I don't love the Sarge enough that I would jump off the Brooklyn Bridge, so, I am going to be on my toes. What I need you to know is that I will return and if this feels wrong, I won't go through with it."

# # #

Later, Larry began to imagine his outfits and in the midst of his soliloquy, he yelled, "Oh shit! I don't have a basic black outfit!"

He called Beckmire and said, "Sarge, as I was preparing my look, I realized that I don't have a basic black outfit. I need someone to get me a black jogging outfit and a pair of size 9 black running shoes. I wouldn't bother you if I didn't think this was important. The outfit that I wore yesterday is the one that I want the cameras in the place to capture. From there I have two options, the postal uniform that I will fix as a snap on and off outfit, and the jogging suit that I need."

Beckmire said, "I understand, and I will have Carlos's people pick up the items."

At 1300 hours, Larry turned to Marisa and said, "I will see you soon. Don't worry about me because I know what I'm doing. It's not like I'm going to rob the place. I'm just going to pick up a package that can shift the balance of power in the entire world. Now, that's some scary and crazy shit. Don't you agree?"

Marisa kissed her man and demanded, "Stay focused, Larry the Wanderer--stay focused. We will see you as soon as this is over."

At 1330 hours, Larry knocked on the Sarge's door and reported, "I'm about to go wandering around the center of government. Any last-minute suggestions or changes to our plans?"

The Sarge looked at his headphones and said, "You can't wear those things because you won't be able to hear us communicate with you."

"Sarge, come into the 21st Century. These are attached to your communications system. Do you want to do a radio check once I get downstairs?"

"Good idea. Now, Son, when you walk into that place, I want you to focus on your surroundings first before you head in the direction of the boxes. If you suspect or get that feeling that things aren't right, walk the hell up out of there and don't look back. I want you to post, or act as if you are posting, a letter to OIC in Philly, you know the address and zip code, don't you?"

"I do. Sarge, I got this! If it smells bad, then I am out of there in a flash."

"You look fat."

"Thanks, I hope it's the three layers of clothing that I have on and not much more."

"Jilkes, John Lee along with Jong will be waiting for you outside at 1400 hours. Don't be late and watch your back at all times. We'll have eyes on you that you and I don't know about. You know enemy aggression and you know when people are on our side of the equation, so just be mindful not to shoot the friendlies if it comes to that."

# # #

At 1400 hours, Larry the Wanderer entered the black SUV driven by Jong with John Lee and Jilkes as passengers. John Lee said, "You sure look pretty. I like your dress."

Larry mumbled, "Here we go with the girly jokes shit."

Jilkes told John Lee to focus and let Larry cogitate about what he has to do.

"Do you have an English word for that there cogitate?" John Lee asked.

Jilkes replied, "John Lee, don't worry about it because you have to have a brain to understand how it works."

At 1440 hours, Larry got out of the SUV at North Capitol and K Street. He checked himself in his compact mirror and began the short walk up North Capitol Street to the post office. Larry walked slowly, taking in all of the sights and trying to ascertain if there were hostiles in the area. As he passed an obviously unmarked black Marquise, he knew it was a police car, he took notice of the occupants and continued his walk. He called the Sarge and reported, "I have identified only one suspicious vehicle. Hold on a minute." Larry noticed a truck on the same side of the street that had a sign on it stating it was a plumbing supply company. It had an antenna on the top and a revolving dome that was a camera. The next vehicle he passed was a large ten-wheeler with signage indicating it was from a moving company. Both vehicles had their motors running. After passing the moving van, he called the Sarge and said, "Their calvary is here in two trucks on the west side of North Capitol and are parked approximately one and a half blocks from the destination. An easy way to disable them is to lock them in their boxes."

The Sarge asked, "Are we still a go?"

"Roger that. So far so good."

Larry entered the post office on North Capitol Street, wandered through the place to the Massachusetts Avenue entrance/exit and then turned around frantically, as if he had dropped something. He retraced his steps while watching the habits of both guards, as well as, people who seemingly were just hanging out. Larry noticed two men at different counters with bulges in their coats and surmised that they were carrying guns. On his way out of the North Capitol Street exit, he dropped a quarter slyly and bent down to pick it up. He then went directly to the boxes and mumbled to himself, "Oh shit, these things require keys." Larry immediately called the Sarge and announced, "The boxes require keys."

Beckmire looked at Zanthius and scornfully stated, "Larry said that the boxes require keys."

Zanthius retorted, "He's in the wrong section. Tell him to walk maybe fifty feet down the hall and he will see another set of boxes that are computer operated."

Larry hearing the conversation said, "Roger that, but what is the number on the box?" Beckmire repeated the question to Zanthius who said, "Oops!"

Larry responded, "Tell my brother that 'Oops' shit ain't working right now. I need a number and in a hurry."

Zanthius answered, "234 is the box and you have to put in the password, just like I stated. Richard Noggin, Dick Head, and then Pussy Galore."

Larry reported, "I'm attracting some attention, but I can handle it. By the way, are Carlos's men inside and are they big and Russian looking?"

Beckmire said, "They are in and are watching those two Russians, as we speak. Is the mission still a go?"

"Roger that. Are you in communication with Carlos's people?" Larry asked.

Beckmire responded, "Yes, why? What do you need?"

"I need them to draw attention to those two big guys with guns and cause a distraction. I am at the box and if they do it now, I can be out of here and on my way without any issues."

Carlos called Beneto and commanded, "Walk up to one of those big Russian looking fellows and ask him, 'why are you carrying a gun in the post office' or some shit like that?"

Beneto asked, "Are you serious?"

Carlos yelled, "Do it now and keep your volume up so I can hear what is going on." Beneto started fumbling with forms, acted as if he was not watching where he was walking and bumped into the guy who turned and pushed him down and reached for his weapon. Beneto screamed, "He has a gun!" Someone hit the alarm and armed guards came running from all parts of the post office and circled the man and told him to drop his weapon. He complied and announced, "I have diplomatic immunity." His comrade eased toward the North Capitol Street exit and left the facility.

Meanwhile, at box # 234, Larry began the tedious task of punching in the letters to Zanthius's box. He got all the characters correct in the first two sets of passwords but misspelled Pussy Galore. This negated the attempt and required a new effort to open the box. Larry methodically and slowly spelled each word and after what seemed like an eternity, the box opened. He reached in and retrieved the package. No one was watching him because everyone was concerned about the man with the gun in the post office due to the recent rash of disgruntled and mentally challenged postal workers who had gone ballistic and murdered their co-workers. Larry considered keeping his current outfit on but saw a sign for restrooms. He entered the one titled female but came out as a man in a postal uniform. Luckily for him there were no ladies present and his snap-off dress disappeared in less than ten seconds. His postal uniform was his next disguise.

As Larry got to the Massachusetts Avenue entrance/exit he noticed a plethora of unmarked cars and people in suits rushing into the building with guns drawn and flashing ID badges. Larry the Wanderer began to walk slowly down First Street North East. Larry called Jilkes and asked, "Where are you guys? I'm walking south on First Street."

Jilkes responded, "That is a one-way street."

Beckmire chimed in and said, "I'm on First Street heading south."

Jilkes said, "Stand down. Its blocked off at the top of the hill where the post office and the train station are. Lots of police action. You have no exit."

Larry interrupted the chatter and reported, "I have the package, but I also have three bogies approaching me rapidly."

The Sarge said, "Turn right on F Street and I will meet you two blocks down. Can you outrun them?"

Larry answered, "I probably could but they're too close. Hold on, I got this, but get here as soon as possible." Larry began to cross the street and noticed that all three men had converged on the same side of the street. That was exactly what he wanted them to do. Larry turned on a dime and yelled, "Move, and I will drop you. Let that iron hit the ground."

One of the men said, "We are with the FBI and we need to talk to you."

Larry responded, "I'm with the fucking CIA and I don't talk to you people. Drop your guns or you will see how better trained we are than you. One at a time, starting with you in the back. One false move and your kids or boyfriends will be crying in the morning." As the person in the rear began to slowly maneuver his weapon for a clean shot, they all started to reach for their weapons and that is when Larry began to fire crippling shots to their legs. He screamed, "I told you people not to move and you thought that because of your numbers you were faster than my aim. Lose the weapons for good or I will end your lives here on this nasty street."

The three men complied. Larry circled them and removed each man's wallet and kicked their guns away from them. Larry looked at the first man's credentials and said, "FBI my ass, who do you work for?" The guy smiled and Larry blew his head off. The next guy said in broken English, "You can't get away with this." Those were his last words as Larry fired two rounds into him. Larry said, "If you want to live, you had better give me a straight answer. Who do you work for?" The guy lowered his head and told Larry, "Go fuck yourself." Larry summarily shot him in the head and made off with their wallets. As he turned the corner on F Street, he saw a black SUV heading his way and surmised that it was the Sarge. John Lee who had abandoned Jilkes, ran down the street and saw the three men lying on the ground. He called the Sarge and announced, "We all had better disappear because there be three bodies lying on the ground out here and ain't none of them Larry."

The Sarge said, "I got him and the package. Get your ass out of there and if you have time, get rid of any weapons and make sure that no kid can get his hands on them." John Lee saw the weapons and noticed a sewer grate. He kicked the weapons into it and ran down the street.

At 1600 hours, all were accounted for except John Lee who was in sight. Beckmire asked, "What did we do wrong and how did those people know to follow Larry?"

Mallory replied, "We must have a mole in this party and I can't imagine who it could be."

The Sarge then asked, "Larry, are you okay?"

Larry looked at him, shrugged his shoulders and said, "I guess. I'm not bleeding or anything, am I?"

The Sarge inquired, "What happened back there?"

"They came up on me, told me that they worked for the FBI and that they needed to talk to me. I told them to drop their guns. They tried to pull some bullshit maneuver where the last guy would distract me and the first two would shoot me. Initially I shot them in the legs and asked them who they worked for and their answers were insufficient, so, I shot them in the head. I asked the last guy standing who did he work for and he told me to go fuck myself."

When John Lee entered the SUV, he said, "We need to move and dump these trucks. There be three dead men back there and I don't know who did the work."

The Sarge said, "Run this thing down to the tunnel so that we can dump it and burn it."

John Lee said, "I be missing something. What be going on?"

Mallory answered, "I think we have a mole in this group because at every turn, these guys are ahead of us or only minutes behind us."

John Lee said, "Well, it don't take a genius to know that when these here vehicles are parked outside at night even a rat could place a chip in them. What I be saying is that they be showing us some of the devices, but others be hidden beyond where's we can see." He placed his finger over his mouth and popped open the cover to the stereo speaker. Lo and behold there it was, another listening device. John Lee announced, "We need to take these here SUVs over to Anacostia and leave them there and get new rides." Everyone began to talk in gibberish, much like John Lee does all the time.

Larry handed the package to Zanthius and whispered for his ears only, "Brother, I hope this has some kind of redemptive ethereal value to all of those who have lost their lives seeking this unknown product and hopefully, we can conclude this not-so-fabulous fable. It has been quietly disturbing, exciting, deadly, treacherous and bonding. I will always be here for you if you need me."

Zanthius looked at Larry and said, "The Sarge did right by you and let it be known that I will always be there for you." Beckmire hearing this from his genetically produced child and his protégé said, "I love the fact that you two have naturally bonded and have committed your lives to each other."

## CHAPTER FORTY-NINE

At exactly 1700 hours, a caravan of different SUVs and a few stolen vehicles pulled up in front of the Hart Senate Office Building. Standing patiently was the senator who would dare to become the President of the United States of America. Standing beside her was Walter who smiled and whispered in her ear, "That's my cousin, a great American patriot."

She smiled and said, "Sergeant Beckmire, on behalf of the Government of the United States of America, I welcome you and accept this package that has been alleged to contain power shifting capabilities. Would you like to come in and discuss anything?"

"I think we're good. I just want to get back to us being simple voting people who you can count on to vote for you for President. We just want to disappear and return to being simple folk."

Walter said, "Leave your vehicles and leave your tools in them and walk with me through this magnificent place, just for a few minutes."

The Sarge asked Walter to wait a minute and returned to his vehicle and requested over the over the radio that the team wipe down their weapons and leave them in the cars.

John Lee announced, "I don't know if that be a good idea because if you look over to your left, there be some people who don't look like they be friendly." The Sarge turned his head and believed they were Walter's people. He radioed his team and stated, "I'm hoping the group across the street is a part of my cousin's team."

As the group walked through the majestic hallways, the Senator turned to Beckmire and asked, "Are you sure there is nothing I can do for you?"

Beckmire smiled and answered, "I think we are okay for now. However, we do have a farmhouse in Virginia to rebuild that the other side destroyed. If you have access to an agency that could help us qualify for some Federal funds, now that would be appreciated."

The senator whispered to Beckmire, "Walter is taking care of that as we speak, including those special windows. All will be okay in a few months."

"Thank you very much."

"Which member of your group is considered the 'idiot spy'?"

"That would be my son, Zanthius Beckmire De Lombardo. Zanthius, come and meet the Senator."

Zanthius shook her hand and declared, "I'm so happy to get rid of that package!"

The Senator said, "You have been through a great deal and I express the gratitude of an entire nation for your ability to weather those storms. You can tell your wife that I have taken the liberty of retiring her from official service and her record is as clean as possible." The Senator looked at Asiram, who was trying to hide in the back of the group and winked at her. She then asked Zanthius, "Do you know what's in this package?"

"A capsule with some data on the Carbon Factor."

The Senator handed the package to a Colonel who was escorted out of sight.

After a half of an hour of chatting, Beckmire and the group thanked the Senator for her hospitality and indicated they would be voting for her if and when she decided to run for the Presidency. They turned and left her office and were being escorted out by Walter, when the senator asked, "Walter, please come back after you have escorted our guests out of the building."

At the edge of the massive doors, Walter said, "You and your team did good and that stunt at the post office was just amazing. I will have a package dropped off to you to repair Asiram's place in Virginia. When are you going home again?"

"I'm thinking that I need to go there sooner than later because there are some things going on there that need attending to. I have to talk it over with my crew and see if they're up to it."

"I must end this little chat, but I want you and your crew to remember that you people owe me some time. You depleted the government of wet workers, and seemingly, your people are the only ones still standing. I hate to put it to you this way, but I have two jobs that will require the skill set of you and your people. Also, as a condition of getting the new bride off the hook, I volunteered her and her husband as well; quid pro quo."

Beckmire looked at him and said, "You're family, but you're a snake. When I go on Walkabout, I will be sure to tell the elders about your one-sided coins. Catch you later."

Walter started to walk away, turned and yelled, "Hey, I need to see Zanthius for a minute! I have something that belongs to him."

"What might that be?"

"I have his wallet. My people cleaned up after him in St. Moritz looking for any clues and they found his wallet with the $300 he had in it."

Beckmire turned around, started up the steps and said, "Give it to me I will make sure that he gets it. Thanks, and don't call me, I'll call you."

As the Sarge entered the vehicle, Zanthius exclaimed, "I am so happy that this is over and done with! I just want to stand by some warm blue water and scream until I pass out."

The Sarge smiled at his words and handed Zanthius his wallet. Zanthius asked, "Where on earth did you get this?"

"Walter said his people found it after cleaning up issues in St. Moritz." Zanthius looked inside of it and saw that there was money in it as well as a strange card and what looked like an unopened condom.

Asiram inquired, "You carry condoms in your wallet?"

"Hell, no. I have no idea how that got in there or how this card that looks like it's from a Russian strip joint got there, either."

"Likely story and one that I don't believe."

"Asiram, I have never been to Russia, therefore, I have never been to a strip joint in Russia. I have never purchased a condom made in Russia and I don't speak Russian. These were put here by someone else."

Asiram grabbed the card and quickly looked at it and said, "Yeah, right, Mr. De Lombardo. As she continued to look at the card, she noticed that when the sunlight hit it, the card produced a hologram effect. As she continued to rotate it, she saw the image of a woman and a series of numbers. Asiram announced, "Oh shit! I can't believe how cunning that wench is. This card is from Helga and it has her picture and a series of numbers on it. I know the outfit because I purchased it for her on her birthday.

This card is a part of a message. Zanthius, give me that condom."

As she opened the condom, she saw there was writing on the inside of the package. She looked at Zanthius and reported, "Your ex-girlfriend left you the directions to the actual transcript. I'll bet you anything that this is the key to understanding the package. Look, on each side of the package there are coordinates, latitude and longitude or some kind of markers."

The Sarge said, "Take a photo of it, quickly."

Asiram said, "Ask Siri to tell you the location of those coordinates."

Zanthius paused for a moment and then cautioned, "I don't think we should communicate this information until we have a game plan and are sure that we are the only ones listening. It is obvious to me that this mess may not be over. I wonder if Walter is aware of this matter?"

The Sarge said, "Once we get out of here, we'll contact him and see what he knows."

Asiram looked at Zanthius and whispered, "I'm sorry, but a condom and a card from a strip joint in your wallet, that would make any bride mad."

"We weren't married at that time. Therefore, I think my past, as well as yours, should be handled with a little more understanding rather than immediate accusations."

"Please, forgive me. It will not happen again, my love."
She kissed her man and all seemed okay.

# # #

Jilkes looked deep at the Sarge and said, "You know we
need to take a break and go our separate ways until something
comes up again. Perhaps we should bury this stuff in a hole
somewhere and revisit it after we have had time to attend to
personal issues at home."

The Sarge said, "I was thinking the same thing but this
Carbon Factor mess may be one of those matters that can't
wait until we settle back into our individual personal lives. I
don't know what it means but I will bring it up at the airport.
By the way, where on earth, are we going?"

Asiram stated, "Let's get to the airport and then we all can
decide. I want to go to my ranch and take a long bath with my
husband and if you guys want to join us, not in the tub, but at
the ranch, you are more than welcome. I'm sure some of your
guys have to make some trips on their own."

## CHAPTER FIFTY

Later at the airport, Beckmire huddled with everyone outside of the airplanes and reported, "I probably can make a deal on those two jets that were left in Wyoming by those mercs. What say you?" There seemed to be agreement if they were available, then why not.

Beckmire pulled out his cellphone, called Walter and said, "Hey, here's the deal. You transfer those jets that were used by those mercs over to us and you refurbish them under our watchful eye then we will do limited wet work for you, subject to our approval. We will try to keep you and this corrupt government out of trouble. You can call me back later to discuss the particulars."

Walter reported, "They have been confiscated and are up for sale. Stay close to your phone, I will call you back."

## CHAPTER FIFTY-ONE

As the Sarge was boarding the plane, he asked Jong, "Where are Zanthius and Asiram?"

Jong replied, "Sarge, they're on the plane that you, your wife, Larry and his family and Rashida and her child are on. Enjoy your flight. I will see you once we're on the ground."

As the planes ascended into the heavens, Beckmire breathed a sigh of relief and said to Mallory, Zanthius, and Asiram, "I think it is time to call Walter and tell him what we have discovered. He, hopefully, has no idea that we have left the area and, therefore, can't demand a face-to-face meeting about the new information that we have."

Everyone thought it was a good idea. Beckmire pulled out his phone and dialed Walter's number. When Walter answered the phone, Beckmire said, "I hate to be the bearer of bad news, but I'm of the belief that the capsule is only part of the answer. Did you or your people examine my son's wallet?"

"Yeah, we saw his cash, credit cards, a condom and a solicitation card from a strip club. Why?"

"That card is a hologram and features numbers that are probably only illuminated by sunlight. The condom has strategic information written on both sides of the package. By the time we get to where we are heading, I expect you will have made the necessary arrangements for those planes and we can begin the next chapter of this adventure, if you're so willing, cousin. I have the actual coordinates but will need a month or two of absolute rest and recuperation, as will all of the other members of my family and friends. Couz, talk to you real soon, I'm sure.   I can't believe you had strategic information in your hands and you just passed it on. Thanking you in advance for the aircrafts."

Walter turned to Mike and vehemently asked, "That wallet that belonged to the 'idiot spy', who examined it?"

Mike replied, "It sure as hell wasn't me. My first knowledge of it was today. I assume the cleanup people in Europe did their due diligence on it. Why are you asking me about his wallet?"

Walter looked at him with eyes that could kill and said, "The wallet has the true information about the damn product--not the capsule. The capsule is minor in my opinion. I want to know who examined that fucking wallet and I want to literally see his head on a platter."

# # #

The next thing the Sarge did after making the call to Walter was to give his grandbabies big hugs and kisses. One of them said, "I'm still focused." The Sarge smiled and gave her an additional kiss and hug and told them all that he loved them so much. He sat down next to Courtney who inquired, "I have a feeling this matter isn't close to being over, is it?"

Beckmire looked at her and asked, "Honey, can you please kiss me and tell me you love me? I need that more than anything else right now. I'm literally traumatized by the fact that this thing may not be over. The capsule, I believe, was a ruse. The real information is on a card from a strip club in Russia and on a Russian made condom. Can you believe that?

"Walter had it in his possession and gave it to me. I subsequently gave it to Zanthius. Asiram who was next to Zanthius as he opened it, and to his surprise, saw the card and the condom. She grabbed it from her husband and began to ridicule him. As she looked intently at the card in the sunlight, she saw that it was a hologram with a picture of a woman named Helga Spengatsenburg, and a series of numbers. When she examined the condom, she saw more numbers, as well as, latitude and longitude bearings written on it. I'm afraid, my love, that you're correct. This mess is not over and I think it may have just turned nuclear."

the end

also in the 'idiot spy' series

book 1: *hell, hell, the gang's all here!*

Zanthius De Lombardo is a womanizing, home-wrecking, self-absorbed, inconsiderate screwup. But all that is about to change. After the failure of his marriage and a suicidal bout with alcoholism, he lands a job as the HR director for a government-run energy company, where he expects nothing more than watercooler gossip and maybe a casual office romance.

Instead, Zanthius discovers the business trip he has been sent on is a one-way journey with no return ticket needed, and that the energy company he works for is a front for a consortium of off-book government assassins and spies. When Zanthius doesn't die after swallowing a capsule containing a world-changing formula—as was expected of the 'idiot spy'— he finds himself caught up in a game of international espionage as world governments race to get their hands on the secret formula for the Carbon Factor, a powerful, cheap dirty bomb that fits in a half-gallon milk carton.

While attempting to keep the Carbon Factor formula from falling into the wrong hands, Zanthius's once lackluster life is suddenly filled with spies, crooked politicians, terrorist groups, a secret government society, mercenaries, and the threat of death at every turn. He has a passionate romance with a spy who later becomes his wife, and he discovers from his mother shocking revelations about his father, Ben Beckmire, who, along with eleven of his friends, comes to his rescue. Little by little, the 'idiot spy' becomes the man he is meant to be. But is it enough to save the world?

Available at Amazon and BarnesandNoble.com

www.ingramcontent.com/pod-product-compliance
Lightning Source LLC
Chambersburg PA
CBHW021431240626
47153CB00001B/108